George Davis

Recollections of a Sea Wanderer's Life

An autobiography of an old-time seaman who has sailed in almost every capacity

before and abaft the mast, in nearly every quarter of the globe, and under the flags

of four of the principal maritime nations

George Davis

Recollections of a Sea Wanderer's Life
An autobiography of an old-time seaman who has sailed in almost every capacity before and abaft the mast, in nearly every quarter of the globe, and under the flags of four of the principal maritime nations

ISBN/EAN: 9783337083502

Printed in Europe, USA, Canada, Australia, Japan

Cover: Foto ©Raphael Reischuk / pixelio.de

More available books at **www.hansebooks.com**

RECOLLECTIONS

OF A

SEA WANDERER'S LIFE

AN AUTOBIOGRAPHY OF AN OLD-TIME SEAMAN WHO HAS SAILED
IN ALMOST EVERY CAPACITY BEFORE AND ABAFT THE
MAST, IN NEARLY EVERY QUARTER OF THE GLOBE,
AND UNDER THE FLAGS OF FOUR OF THE
PRINCIPAL MARITIME NATIONS

BY

GEORGE DAVIS

ILLUSTRATED

BY PORTRAITS OF THE AUTHOR IN YOUTH AND IN AGE, AND A
HUNDRED OTHER ENGRAVINGS

NEW YORK
A. H. KELLOGG, PRINTER
100 AND 102 READE STREET
1887

CHAPTER OF CONTENTS.

ILLUSTRATIONS.

IN THE FORETOP

PREFACE.

"Cease, rude Boreas, blustering sailor,
    List, ye landsmen, all to me ;
Messmates, hear a brother sailor
    Tell the dangers of the sea."

When, to the intense astonishment of my acquaintances, it was noised abroad that I had determined to write the history of my life at sea, I was overwhelmed with advices and suggestions, not only widely differing from one another, but utterly conflicting and irreconcilable.

On one point, however, all my friends agreed : that a preface was *de rigueur*, and that to write a book without a preface would be as absurd as to play "Hamlet" without Ophelia.

Slowly and sadly I yielded a reluctant assent, and hence these few lines. Should my patrons pass them over unread, I shall be the last to blame them, for I believe that in most instances (I know it to be so in the present one) a preface is as superfluous and as useless as a "Sergeant of Marines."

Of course, it is quite natural that writers of the calibre of Mr. Dickens should not deign to put pen to paper without claiming for their labors a higher motive than the design to gain wealth and reputation, or to furnish amusement for an idle hour.

Like the mythical heroes of old, "Jack the Giant Killer" and "Don Quixote," their lance is ever poised to hurl the giant oppressor to earth, and right the wrongs of the afflicted and the fair.

In such cases a preface may be useful, in order that the sedate and scrupulous reader may satisfy his conscience that he is not reading a mere novel, but a book replete with highly moral instruction and destined to effect a radical reformation of some real or fancied abuse.

Now, in one respect, I am very much in the same predicament as the Knife Grinder immortalized by Canning ; "he had no story to tell, sir ; and I have no mission to pretend to."

As now in the decline of life I sit, on this wintry night, in my comfortable arm-chair, in a cozy corner near the cheerful fire, and see my children and my grandchildren grouped around me, and listen to the pelting rain or hail, and the furious winds as they strive to force an

entrance within the hallowed precincts of our home, memory carries me
back to the days of yore—days of hardships, privations, and peril, as
well as of pleasant excitement, wild frolic, and heartfelt enjoyment.

I am once more young, active, and daring, and am walking up and
down the top-gallant forecastle, spinning yarns with Jack Mason or Bill
Nye, or some other tried and trusty friend, whose bones, long ere this,
lie bleaching in the depths of ocean or mouldering into dust afar from
their childhood's home.

The seas roll heavier and the gale comes down in sudden fury. "All
hands reef topsails" is the word, and, springing from their hammocks,
the crew lay aloft to their perilous post of duty ; methinks I still hear
their voices amid the howling of the winds, "Light over, light over,
light over, to windward," "Haul out to leeward."

Far away from home, at anchor at the mouth of some African or Asiatic river, or amid the Chinese junks at Whampoa, Shanghae, or Amoy,
the flute and violin are brought into requisition, and the eye moistens
and the bosom heaves as the seamen join in the plaintive lines :

> " The home we loved near the bounding deep,
>   Where the hills in glory stood ;
> And the moss-grown graves where our fathers sleep,
>   'Neath the shade of the waving wood.
> I remember yet with a fond regret
>   The hills and the flowing lea,
> Amid the greenwood shades, where the wild birds made
>   Their nests 'neath the old mountain tree."

To invite the attention of the present generation to the hardships and
perils inseparable from a life at sea, in days when seamanship was not a
lost art ; to give landmen a faint idea of the dangers of those who go
down to the sea in ships ; to recall to the surviving seamen of my own
time the memories of former days ; and last, but not least, to afford
myself the gratification, pardonable in an old man, of recounting the
adventures of my youth :—such, and no other, is the object of these
pages.

GEORGE DAVIS,
Paterson, N. J.

INTRODUCTION.

It is a strange fact that a love of the sea and proficiency in seamanship should have become a distinguished attribute of the people of the North.

True it is that the Phœnicians, the Romans, and the Carthagenians, in ancient times, and the Genoese, the Venetians, the Spaniards, and the Portuguese in more recent days, have been noted for their exploits, and their zeal in pushing their discoveries to the ends of the then known world.

Yet all this was done, not through a love of the sea, nor by seamen —properly so called—but rather through a greed for gold or thirst for conquest, and by means of expeditions composed rather of soldiers than of seamen.

The vessels of those days were rude in construction, unwieldy in bulk, and intended rather for fighting than for sailing ; their crews were soldiers, or rather a sort of hybrid mariners, entirely innocent of the first rudiments of seamanship, and whom any ordinary seaman of our days would contemptuously style a set of ignorant swabs and cowardly land-lubbers.

Feeling their way from headland to headland along the shores of the Mediterranean Sea, or creeping with trembling fear and superstitious awe a few leagues beyond the Pillars of Hercules, they trusted more to a white ash breeze during the day than to the spread of their canvas, and the skill of their officers and crews. Toward dusk they hastened to shelter themselves under the lee of some headland or in some land-locked bay, and all hands turned in to wait for broad daylight, and a soft and favoring breeze. Even when the inventions of the mariner's compass emboldened a few of the more daring of their pompous admirals to venture out of sight of land, it was with fear and trembling on the part of the commanders, and ill-concealed terror on the part of the crews, that they saw fading in the gloom the headlands of the land to which they bade, as they thought, an eternal adieu.

Many and many a time did this superstitious fear culminate in frantic fright and open mutiny, frustrating many a bold design ; and whenever a resolute commander succeeded in allaying their fears and suppressing their mutinous designs, it was rather by good luck than by good seaman-ship that they finally stumbled across some unknown land and made discoveries which they neither expected nor appreciated.

Vasco de Gama never realized the vast empire discovered in India, and even the great Genoese died without being cognizant of the fact that his was the fame of having trodden the shores of a new world.

But, long before the magnetic needle guided and encouraged the navi-gators of the South to plough the briny deep, long before they consented to lose sight of their beloved terra firma, the Vikings of the North, in their long ships of war, launched boldly forth upon the stormy waters of the North Sea, and carried fire and sword along its coasts from the north-eastern coast of Britain to the shores of Normandy in France, founding principalities, conquering kingdoms ; then, like Alexander, panting for other worlds to conquer, they steered forth into the wild Atlantic, and with stout hearts and strong arms propelled their deeply-laden galleys discovering Iceland, colonizing Greenland, and beaching their adventur-ous prows upon the shores of Narragansett Bay. They were true seaman, more at home upon the ocean than in their homes ; never so happy as when the tempest roared, the lightning flashed the arrowy hail, and the din of battle combined in dreadful unison.

No wonder then, that, as the world went whirling down the circling grooves of change, the descendants of those famous sea-rovers should have developed that love of the stormy waters and that proficiency in seamanship born of affection and long practice. Such, in fact, has been the result. True it is that France, Spain, and Italy have good mercantile fleets ; they are not ignorant of the art of ship-building, and they are painfully awake to every advance made in torpedoes, rams and Krupp guns ; but constant experience has shown, as in the naval engage-ments with the Armada, as well as at Trafalgar, at Cape Vincent, at La Hague, at Navarino, as well as at the Nile and Aboukir, and in scores of other engagements, that the seamen of Great Britain, and Holland, and of those countries adjacent and contiguous to the North and Baltic Seas, were an overmatch for the chosen tars of France and Spain.

And now, in our own day, the noble clippers that breast the wild seas as they surge around the world at the " Horn," and the gigantic waves around the "Cape of Good Hope," are manned and officered almost exclusively by those whose native tongue bears witness that they are the descendants of the stormy Vikings of the days of Rollo, 'and Canute, or of Eric the Red.

And when on the uneasy bosom of the Western Ocean the seaman spies a superb creature, that walks the water like a thing of life, her magnificent hull looming high above the seas, her delicate spars gleaming through the upper air, and her spotless canvas yielding to the wooing of the amorous breeze, while her black funnels pour forth a torrent of smoke, and her great screws churn the water into spray, he fully expects, as he pauses in his work to see her pass by, that in answer to his captain's signal the meteor flag of England, or the ever glorious Stars and Stripes, shall be flung to the breeze.

The reader having patiently gone this far, may take breath and very reasonably say : Why this glorification of Northern nations?

Well, I shall answer as a sailor should, very candidly. It is because I am one of them by birth, training, long service, and affection; have witnessed their skill, their courage in danger, and their uncomplaining fortitude amid the most trying hardships, and have in their company visited many a land, and sailed on almost every sea.

Having said so much, I think it time to reveal my own identity and give my readers an idea of the trials and pleasures of a life on the boundless Ocean.

GEORGE DAVIS.

AT THE WHEEL

GOOD BYE, MR. CRAPSER.

A SEA-WANDERER'S LIFE.

Chapter I.

'A gallant bark got under weigh,
And with her sails my story."
TOM HOOD.

" A life on the ocean wave,
A home on the rolling deep,
Where the scattered waters rave
And the winds their revels keep."

When Daniel DeFoe wrote that very pleasant story of
"Robinson Crusoe," it is supposed that he intended to give
young boys such a salutary warning of the hardships of a
life at sea that they would be contented to stay on shore;
but it is now well known that the book had a contrary effect,
and that its perusal has sent many men aboard ship, fired
with the desire of adventure upon the wide ocean. It was
not that book that stirred my fancy, but the much finer,
more soul-stirring one written by Charles Dibdin, from
which I cull these lines, which exactly describe my boyish
notion of the first ship I sailed in :

" I sailed from the Downs in the *Nancy*.
My jib! how she smacked through the breeze.
She's a vessel as light to my fancy
As ever sailed o'er the salt seas."

Dibdin wrote many a fine song which was sung both on
shore and on board ship, and he is responsible for turning
the head and heart of many a young lad towards the sea
who, but for his rollicking songs, might have remained at
home and passed a quiet life as a grocer, draper, tallow-
chandler, or other occupation as useful, if not so full of
romance and reality, as that of the jolly jack tar. Moreover,

he who stays on land has the additional chance of ripening off into a staid and respectable member of society, who may perhaps secure a sort of immortality by founding a hospital or a school; and, dying at a venerable age, leave an inconsolable widow and a numerous offspring to bewail his loss and divide his estate—or at least so much of it as the lawyers cannot agree to share among themselves.

How very different is the sailor's lot. He deserts home, loved ones, friends and neighbors, ventures on the treacherous deep, is stowed away at night in a dingy hammock in a damp and moldy fo'castle, fed on "salt horse," drinks water thick with living things, and odorous but not pleasant, and is driven like a galley-slave day and night by men whose very nature, in many cases, is brutal in the extreme; and after a life-time of the severest trials and suffering his resting-place is in the salt, salt sea. Or if he escapes, he may be favored by a berth in some "Sailor's Snug Harbor," where everybody is favored and petted except Jack Tar.

The history of my life, which is here given in veritable extracts from the log book of my memory, will show how and why I have not brought up alongside of any "Snug Harbor," so called, as yet, although my actual harbor is snug and well secured against evil winds, as sung by the English poet Alaric A. Watts.

> " What care I for the sullen roar
>   Of winds without, that ravage earth;
> It doth but bid me prize the more
>   The shelter of my hallowed hearth:—
> To thoughts of quiet bliss give birth.
>   Then let the churlish tempest chide,
> It cannot check the blameless mirth
>   That glads my own fireside!"

Loving the delights of home on shore, I naturally feel a strong aversion to those ballad writers who, sitting at home in their easy-chairs, encourage others to dare the dangers of the deep, luring thousands of young men away from home and all its joys and educational advantages, and plunging them helpless into a life of hardship and peril. I am

convinced that the most of those writers of sea-songs and
sea-stories do the work for money merely—it is their occupation ; that is, they trade in youthful credulity, and love
of romance and adventure, without any regard to human
sympathy, or even respect for the ties of humanity.

Now, since I have rattled off a few lines by way of clearing the decks, or freeing my mind, we might as well lay to
and spin a yarn. As this is to be my autobiography—whatever that big word is—written by myself, I shall naturally be
excused for speaking of myself on all proper occasions,
which I shall proceed to do without further apology. So
here goes :—

My father—of course you will expect to hear something
about him. He had no long pedigree to bother about, nor a
fortune to keep him awake nights, so he was apprenticed
early to a furrier in London, England. He was a native of
Silesia, formerly a part of Poland, before that country was
divided between the Cossack and the German, and his father
was also a furrier. So he inherited a fitness for the business
which pushed him along rapidly—so fast that, like the " star
of empire," he took his way westward and touched shore in
Philadelphia, in 1796.

The fame of John Jacob Astor dazzled him, and he sought
the presence of that shrewd merchant, who applied to him
all the tests that were usual in such cases, and then engaged
my father to teach him the secret of dying sealskins in the
English manner, paying him a thousand guineas for that
information.

With this capital in cash he went to Montreal, Canada,
where he began business in furs for himself. As might be
expected, and as my readers must suppose, a young man
with a thousand guineas and a prospect of a good business,
being a fine prize for some young maid, my father was
captured. I never knew exactly how it happened, but have
every reason to believe that it was an old-fashioned match,

such as Giles Fletcher sang about two hundred and fifty
years ago:

" Love the strong and weak doth yoke,
And makes the ivy climb the oak ;
Under whose shadows lions wild,
Softened by love, grow tame and mild."

Captured and married in 1818.

There is not much more to say about my father, and what
there is, as you will see, is not very consoling to me as his
son and heir. I was honored with a first appearance as his
son in the morning of June 17, 1821; but the honor of

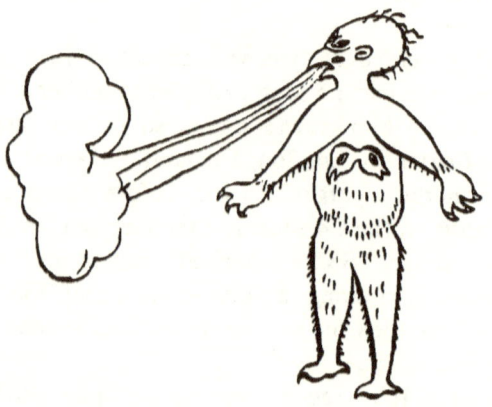

CHINESE CARICATURE OF A SAILOR "SPINNING YARNS."

inheriting any of his wealth was denied me, perhaps for the
best of reasons—so that I might make headway for myself on
the sea of life.

Just exactly why the 17th of June was selected for my
first appearance on deck is not so clear. I have consulted all sorts of almanacs, farmer's and nautical; inquired
of "the only reliable and highly gifted astrologers," had my
horoscope constructed several times by the most learned
adepts in occult knowledge, but all in vain. Nor does
history afford any light on the question. There is no record

of earthquakes, meteors, comets, tidal waves, or even a decent-sized epidemic of that time, which might have heralded the advent of a stranger in the house of Davis, who was soon named George.

There, the craft is launched, but not yet rigged and provisioned for a voyage. We will now attend to that part of the log.

My father felt the anxiety of a fond parent for the welfare of his son and therefore extended his business connections until he virtually monopolized the fur trade of Canada, when he began, in 1828, to invest in real estate and in building houses. The disturbances caused by the rebellion in 1837–38 in Canada so upset all sorts of business that the fur trade was totally used up and a dead loss, and real estate ventures sunk clean out of sight. It was a total wreck so far as my father was concerned. He left Canada for the States, came to New York in 1830, and found employment at his trade as a finisher of fine furs, and I went into a grocery store as a clerk.

The fascinating game of billiards drew me away from cheese and sugar, and I was employed in the saloon at 28 Park Row, next to the old Park Theatre. It was there that I met Mr. Crapser, who was the cause, indirectly, of my first venture on the briny deep. He was a large land-owner in St. Lawrence County, this State, and had been a neighbor of my father's in Montreal. He was also a shipper of large quantities of square timber to England, and in the course of trade knew many ship-masters. With my father's consent I returned to Quebec in the employ of Mr. Crapser, and through his kindness had many hours to myself, which were spent in lounging about the lower town, among the quays and the ships, occasionally taking a trip to the Falls of Montmorency, the Isle of Orleans, or other ones among the many pleasant resorts about Quebec. All this time my mind was absorbing ideas, notions, and fancies about the sea,

the glorious life of a sailor, the rosy side of which was all
that I could see then.   The thorny side appeared to me in
sad reality as the years wore on. ·Carroll Ryan, a Canadian
poet, has written much that touches my feelings, and con-
vinces me that he has had experience away from home and
friends as well as I.   He writes :—

> "Come, I will tell a tale to thee
> Of one—a lovely youth,
> Who sought o'er land and over sea
> For peace, and love, and truth;
> But never could the seeker find
> Aught like the form that filled his mind."

But as traveling is beneficial to the traveler, in addition
to former preparations I studied geography earnestly, early
and late, as I could find time, and became familiar with the
maps of many countries, wondering at and trying to master
the queer-looking names.   The office globe was nearly worn
out by my frequent turnings.   I often wondered, if the earth
itself was really round like the office globe, how was it possible for ships to sail safely around on the opposite side.
Many years passed before I was able to feel and know that
I was on the surface of the great globe of the earth, and
that it appeared of the same level in all places, except only
when on or near high mountain-tops.

Many times have I spied with great interest the white canvas of some vessel while rounding the point of the Isle of
Orleans, and watched it until it should "come to" and furl
sails abreast of the citadel on Cape Diamond, lower its gig,
manned by bronzed seamen, who made the spray fly from
their oar blades as they brought their captain ashore.   How
I gazed with awe at all—captain and sailors—who had
brought from remote lands spices, silks, perfumes, and
strange-looking fruits.

I am quite sure that my senses were captivated one by
one by the various belongings of the vessels that I visited.
The smell of tarred rigging, the tropical fruits; the noises
made by the huge chains, hawsers, creaking yards ; the

QUEBEC FROM POINT LEVIS.

shouting and singing of the sailors ; even the swearing of
the ruffianly mates and master stevedores did not seem very
awful, but on the whole somewhat fascinating.   To be sure,
some of the more violent swearers actually made the cold
chills run down my back, and caused me to wonder why
such terrible words were needed; but time wore off such
sensitiveness, and I grew familiar with a vast catalogue of
oaths in many languages, which were poured out from habit
rather than in rage.   Oaths in a sailor's mouth are simply
salt, spice, seasoning, or, as the writers say, italics, small
caps, and exclamation points, necessary to give piquancy and
force to the discourse.

I usually embraced every opportunity to talk with any
grizzled veteran of the sea whose kindly nature bore with
my inquisitive habits, for I was hungry and thirsty after
knowledge of the sea and its surroundings.   How delightful
those days were !   In some respects the happiest of my life.
All was fairy-land to me in the future, and I was to be the
prince, the favorite of the powers of good, and even the
stories of Sindbad the Sailor, which I read with infinite enjoyment, seemed merely prophetic of what I should enjoy when
once I should become a sailor.   The most attractive of all
the old salts were those who were grizzled with age, bronzed
with tropical suns, and strengthened by battling with the
storm-kings of the Bay of Biscay, Cape Horn, and a hundred
other regions.   I was often invited to come aboard and see
all the sailors eat out of one kid without biting one another.

On such occasions the coarse repast would be seasoned
with broad jokes, keen witticisms, jolly songs, and sometimes
by a hornpipe, and the hours would glide unnoticed by until
the watch sounded eight bells.   Then I reluctantly went
home to dream of top-sails and reef-tackle, bowlines and
clew-lines, with a faint flavor of the reported beauties of
Fayal and the girls of Spain.

So my readers will see that I naturally became entranced

with the bright side of a sailor's life as it appeared to me, in the persons of certain seamen, officers, and men who went and came at regular intervals, as the duties of the service required. The other side, including the hardships and trials,

LOAFING.

sufferings and dangers, if they were mentioned at all, took such a romantic shape in my mind that they seemed unreal and so lost their proper effect. The pleasures of a sailor's life were my hopes and aspirations, the rest I did not fear—

how could I fear what I knew not ? Personal experience alone can teach those lessons which are, after all, the essential elements in character, and of that I had my share, as will appear before my line is run out.

But as I intend to present as complete a picture, in as few words as possible, of the influences that induced me to go to sea, I must again refer to the log of my early life while with Mr. Crapser at Quebec. His business was chiefly shipping square timber to Europe, and while the vessels were discharging cargoes and loading timber, the sailors would have many an hour ashore, when they would make the streets echo with their merriment, boisterous but harmless, and the saloons charming resorts for those who loved, as I did, to hear their stories of adventures in far-off lands. I remember many times in which I followed such frolicking parties through the streets on moonlight nights to the vessel's side, sometimes going on board and continuing the fun in the fo'castle, or on deck, near the fore-rigging, until reminded by the watch that it was time for land-lubbers to make scarce. Parting from such pleasant companions was often painful when duty called them seaward, and at such times I watched their ships move away as if reluctant to leave me behind; for I longed to go, and I looked and looked until the last spar and sail disappeared beyond Cape Diamond, or Point Levis, or were lost behind the groves of the woody Isle of Orleans.

My fancy followed them far away into the tropics, where the air is heavy with perfumes, and the shores peopled with dark-skinned and almond-eyed beauties, who welcome the sailor with smiles through which white teeth like set pearls gleam and bewilder the visitor. The poet aptly voices my feelings at that time :

> " Like an eagle caged I pine
>   On this dull unchanging shore ;
> Oh, give me the flashing brine,
>   The storm and the tempest s roar ! "

I was then in the most important years of my youth, when a father's counsel and example would have been of the greatest value to me; but my father was far away, and Mr. Crapser was too much absorbed in his business to pay much heed to me. So I drifted out to sea because there was no anchor or other strong attractions at home. As the poet Longfellow says :—

> " Something the heart must have to cherish,
> Must love, and joy, and sorrow learn ;
> Something with passion clasp, or perish
> And in itself to ashes burn.''

In short, my heart was set on a ship instead of a maid at that time, although it is a popular notion that every sailor boy has his sweetheart and every sailor man his maid in every port. That saying is merely a popular scandal. The true sailor, boy or man, is as true to his sweetheart or wife as the needle to the pole ; and both are noticed to vary a few points, as evidence of which may be seen on all good maps, marked as variations of the compass.

So I resolved to " see the world." What an ecstatic moment that was ! I thought of nothing else but the joy of being a sailor boy among jovial companions, skimming the blue wave from port to port, seeing the famous countries that I had heard of, and a thousand other thoughts, rushing in wild confusion through my brain, made me in reality drunk with youthful spirits.

The arrival of the first craft from England, after the breaking up of the ice in the spring, was to be my signal for the first effort at shipping myself in any line for any service. If no place was open for me in the cabin or before the mast, I resolved to go as a " stowaway." You see I felt desperate.

One fine afternoon in the latter part of the month of April, 1831, as I sat musing on the wharf, and as the poet Cowper sings :—

> *   *   *   *   *   *   with eager eye
> Exploring far and wide the watery waste,
> For sight of ship from England,   *   *''

I was roused from my reverie by a deep voice beside me saying, "There she comes! Ain't she a beauty! I tell you old
Knight is the skipper to make her walk. He's kept his word
too, for I heard her consignees say that Knight swore that
his ship should be the first of the spring fleet to round to
under the guns of Cape Diamond." Then I was alive all
over with pleasurable excitement. There was my ideal of a
vessel clearing the icy waters of the St. Lawrence, her jet
black hull finely contrasted with the white ports, every yard
of canvas stretched in the bright morning sunlight.

The speaker was my ideal of a British seaman—stout,
athletic, well-rounded in form and feature, and with a
healthy glow in his countenance. His dress indicated his
prosperity, for it was of deep blue pilot cloth, cut in the
style so loved by sailors, pants close-fitting at the hips, and
wide and flowing at the ankles, with a short sack coat close-
fitting also. His cap was blue, and shoes well made and
polished up brightly. His beard was a deep chestnut brown,
close trimmed. His general look was of self-reliance and
well-to-do officer in power. It was with some diffidence that
I ventured to inquire of him the name of the incoming
ship.

"Why, my lad," said he, "that is the *General Hewitt*,
of and from London to Quebec for orders. How do you
know she is a ship ? She may be a bark, mayn't she ?"

"Oh no, sir," said I, proud of showing my knowledge.
"A bark would not be square-rigged on the mizzen mast.
That vessel has yards crossed fore and aft."

"What yards, my boy ?" asked he, turning his keen eyes
on me with a look of kindly amusement.

"Why, sir, the lower top sail, top-gallant, and royal yards.
—Ah, there they go," shouted I, forgetting myself for a
moment. "They are hauling down the head sails, and hauling up the courses, and clewing up the royals, to'-gallant
sails, and top sails. Now see how quickly the men go up

aloft ! What a splendid ship, and what a fine crew she must have !"

" Why, my boy, you are quite a tarry old salt," said my nautical friend. " Where did you learn so much about ships ?"

" Right here on the wharf, in this harbor, sir," said I. " I have been aboard many vessels and know some of the men."

" What do you do when you are not studying sea-craft?"

' I am in the employ of Mr. Crapser in the Upper Town."

" Crapser," said he, as he nodded knowingly to his companion. " Well, my boy, you seem to know something about ships, and have quite a fancy for the *General Hewitt.* Would you like to go aboard of her ?"

Would a duck swim, thought I, but I said, " Oh yes, sir, I shall try it with the first boat that comes ashore."

" You won't have long to wait for that, youngster, for the ship is coming to, and they are dropping the captain's gig. But mind you, young man—by the way, what's your name ?"

" George Davis, sir."

" Well, Davis, don't try to take French leave of Mr. Crapser and stow away on board of the *General Hewitt,* for she sails again in a week or two, and you might be sorry for leaving home. Good day." And he walked away with his friend, he wearing a quizzical smile, and both laughing heartily.

Their merriment did not affect me, although I have learned since that it was at my expense, for I was too full of the ship and a desire to get on board to notice anything else, and just then the captain's gig came gliding up to the dock, with the captain, in his best suit, in the stern sheets. I expected to see the boat crash into the planks of the dock, but the crew knew their work too well, and the sharp imperative tones of the order " in bow" and "way enough" gave them directions when they checked the headway by backing the oars and bringing the boat gracefully up to the dock.

The oars were tossed together in the centre of the boat, and the bowman stood ready with his boat-hook to fend off and leap ashore with the painter.   The next moment the craft was alongside with stern close in and the captain stepped ashore.

YOUNG DAVIS.

As he stood beside me I took in his rig.   He was fault-lessly dressed in a new civilian's attire of black cloth, tall beaver hat, calfskin boots, standing collar, diamond shirt studs, and massive gold fob chain—a contrast in dress to my nautical friend who left a few moments before, but like him in clear cut, bronzed features, and bright piercing eye.

   "Here, Mason," he called to the stroke oarsman, "treat

QUEBEC FROM THE RAMPARTS.

the boat's crew," and he tossed him a half sovereign to do it with. "See that they don't drink too deep. Wait here for the fresh meat and vegetables, and then pull aboard and report to Mr. Murray. Tell him to send a boat for me in the morning, and make ready for heaving up."

"Aye, aye, sir," said Mason, as the captain strode away with immense mien and dignity.

I knew Mason, and as soon as the captain was away I leaped down the landing stairs, and was immediately recognized by him. "Hello, youngster! So you have not yet gone to sea, eh?'

"No, Mr. Mason, but I expect to go very soon."

"Well, lad, we are going up Champlain street to splice the main brace. You stay here as boat-keeper till we heave in sight again, will you?"

"Certainly," said I, delighted with the honor conferred on me. Never was boat better tended. How carefully I kept her bow from chafing the string-piece, how neatly I arranged the oars, bailed and sponged her dry, wiping the gunwale and thwarts; and, although the crew were away a long time, I was not weary, for my heart was in the work. I felt that it was my first lesson in actual work as a sailor, for I was a sailor already in spirit.

The crew returned in a hilarious condition, and Mason seemed to read my thoughts, for he said, "Hello, George, you've been swabbing down. Jump in and stow yourself away under the meat and vegetables under the bow grating, and we'll show you a ship as is no 'Drogher,' and can show as clean a pair of heels as any square-rigger out of London, any how, if she is a wet B——e. What do you say, mates?"

"Aye, aye, that's so, Bill," they all agreed, and added, "and a bully crew aboard, with a rousing captain, even if he does look more like a chaplain than the jolly sea-dog that he is."

There was some delay in getting ready to cast off, when one of the crew said:

"Bill, is this the youngster you used to talk about when we were outward bound in the brig *Triton* ?"

"The very same young man."

"Werry well, young lad," said the seaman, whose name was Bill Nye, "if ye feel sick a hankerin' for seein' the world, as ye call it, ye will never have sich a chance as aboard the *General Hewitt*, for as ye know the old song says :—

'A British ship and a British crew,
Tally-hi-ho, you know.
A British mate and captain too,
Tally-hi-ho, you know.' "

This he roared out lustily, and the others joined in the refrain. So pulling and singing, and I crouching among the provisions, we were soon close alongside the ship and made fast by the painter. The crew shinned up the fore-chains like monkeys, but I could not follow them. My arms were not toughened and corded as theirs were then, and mine were afterwards, so I had to wait until the boat was made fast at the foot of the gangway, when I climbed up by aid of the man-ropes. I thought my appearance was not observed by the officer on deck, but probably he was prompted by Mason or Bill Nye to turn his blind eye towards me, and so give me a chance. Anyhow, I hurried to the forecastle and was heartily welcomed by the crew, who had been informed of my coming by Mason. As it was towards sunset, I was invited to stay all night, which was accepted; for I thought I could go ashore in Mr. Murray's boat in the morning, if I wished.

That first night aboard ship was destined to be the beginning of many a long year's sojourn on the bosom of " Old Father Neptune." My eyes and ears were open, and taking in information on every occurrence. Every sound told me something, and I soon became so absorbed in the new surroundings that all thoughts of Mr. Crapser and the shore were laid aside. Instead of them my mind was filled with snatches of poetry in praise of a life on the sea, such as that in Eliza Cook's "Song of the Mariners."

> " Choose ye who will earth's dazzling bowers,
> But the great and glorious sea be ours ;
> Give us, give us the dolphin's home,
> With the speeding keel and splashing foam.
>
> Right merry are we as the sound bark springs
> On her lonely track like a creature of wings.
> Oh, the mariner's life is blithe and gay,
> When the sky is fair and the ship on her way."

And that other verse of hers which hit my case exactly:—

> " And many a time the sturdy boy
> Longed for the hour to come
> Which gave the hammock for his couch,
> The ocean for his home !"

I was afloat at last. The several and many incidents that occurred in rapid succession that first evening on board made a deep impression on my memory, and I have often recalled them since then, and will now repeat a few of them for the benefit of my readers, who may, in imagination, suppose themselves on board as I was, happy in a new place, with glorious anticipations, youth, health, and friends, all conspiring for my happiness.

When night came on the anchor watch was set and the lights were swung from the fore-stay and both fore-swifters, and the spanker-gaff end. Then all hands except the watch were free to spend the night as they might wish. Mason, a half dozen others, and myself lounged on the top-gallant forecastle, near the heel of the bowsprit. That was a glorious night, with a bright moon, thin clouds, gentle breezes, and calm waters, reflecting the shores with their many lights, the moon and stars, and bearing many a craft, not one of which could compare, as I felt, with the *General Hewitt*. Across the water was Wolfe's Cove, and the river could be seen dimly far beyond Point Levis and the Upper Town; the Lower Town and its confused noises were nearer, but only dimly visible. The sounds of merriment at inter-vals came across the water from some other vessel, lying

near ours, where other crews were enjoying themselves.
This doubled our pleasure, and added to this was the feeling
of security which came to us with the hourly cry of the
sentinel on the fort at the Cape, "All's well."

Soon after four bells (ten o'clock) we went below, and
Mason showed me to my hammock. In a moment I was
undressed and into the swinging bed, but not to sleep. The
strange appearance of the fo'castle in the dim light of a

AFLOAT.

single oil lamp, swinging amidships, and the all-pervading
odor of tar and bilge-water, with many other strange sights
and sounds, and above all my lively fancy, kept me awake
until five, six, and seven bells struck. Soon after I saw a
burly figure enter the fo'castle, and going to one of the hammocks say in a gruff whisper, "Eight bells, Mason; turn out."

"Aye, aye," was the answer, and in a moment Mason fully
dressed came to my hammock and said, "Hello, my lad; not
asleep yet? Well, if you can't sleep you might as well turn
out and stand your first watch with me. Come, bear a
hand." And he climbed the narrow steep stairs to the deck.

I hurried on my clothes and followed, just as the sailor
who had been relieved and turned into his hammock began
to snore as if it was a part of his duty.

On deck all was still.   The moon had not yet set, and its white light illuminated the deck with its silvery radiance. My friend Mason, pacing the top-gallant fo'castle, seemed like a ghostly keeper of an enchanted ship.   I approached him with hesitation, when he called out :

" Well, youngster, how do you like turning out at midnight? Better staid ashore and have your sleep, and all night in. How are you going to work to-morrow without rest ? "

" I don't intend to work to-morrow," said I.

" Eh, what, what's that you say ?" said he.

" Just that.   I am going to sea with you if I can manage it."

" Whew," said he, and he blew a long whistle; " here's a rum go!   How do you know that the old man will ship you, for we are full-handed now.   But hold on, you may perhaps ship as cabin-boy.   How would you like that berth?"

" I had rather ship before the mast," said I, "and you must help me to do so, even if you have to help me to stow away."

" Well, well, well.   We'll see, my lad, what can be done. I'll talk with my shipmates and may be you'll have a chance to see blue water before long.   So belay that and spin me a yarn all about yourself and how you came to want to go a sailorizing."

My brief story was soon told; he listened most attentively to it until finished, when he told his own.

Left an orphan in London at the age of ten years, he picked up a precarious existence in the streets until good fortune shipped him on a north country collier.   Several years were passed in the coasting trade, in which he visited nearly every port of England and Scotland, with occasional visits to Holland and France, and then on long voyages around the Cape of Good Hope and the Horn in the China trade.   When married he settled down into the Canada lumber trade in summer and the Mediterranean in winter, because they afforded him an opportunity of seeing his family in London frequently. After warning me of the hardships and dangers of a life at sea, he promised that, if I was determined to go, he would try and get the consent of his shipmates to stow me away until the ship was off soundings on her course for London.

At four bells Mason called his relief from the fo'castle and told me to turn in for a nap. The watch, roused from a sound sleep, turned out growling and muttering, and came on deck sullenly.

Mason did not turn in, but I heard his voice in earnest tones advocating my cause in the fo'castle. He was often interrupted by grunts of disapproval, and seemed to have a hard task in bringing them around to his way of thinking. When he did succeed they all three indulged in loud laughter, and probably I was the subject of their merriment. I felt so, but was content to be laughed at, or to bear anything, rather than be put ashore. Very soon Mason came close to my hammock and said, "All's right, my lad. Bell and Steve are agreed. Go to sleep now and I will arrange things in the morning watch. Don't you stir out of your hammock unless one of us calls you. I'll tell the rest of the men, and I'll be bound not one of 'em will split the gaff on a friend of mine. But you must look out for the after guard."

If I had been told that I had fallen heir to ten thousand a year I could not have felt happier. Sleep stole over me in a few moments and I dreamed of sun-lit skies, and seas, and tropic islands, where I was the monarch of the quarter-deck of a noble ship of the line, whose gallant crew had been victors in many a hard-fought conflict, and who stood ready to brave every danger at the word of their young commander. Relieved as I was from all anxiety, my sleep was sound, and broad daylight found me still slumbering. The clatter of breakfast among the sailors in the fo'castle waked me, but remembering Mason's injunction, I lay quiet, resisting the craving of a sharp appetite. When the simple meal was over and the inevitable pipe lighted, Mason began by saying:

"Now then, my mates, we're going to have a new hand aboard."

"What's that you say?" inquired a grizzly sea-dog of about fifty years, whose name I learned afterwards to be Dick Stuart. "A new hand aboard, man? The ship's company is full already."

"Well" said Mason, laughing, "I don't know as how the new hand will make it much fuller. He's only a kid about ten or twelve years old."

"Only a kid of ten or twelve years," growled Stuart; "what the h—l is he going to do aboard of us?"

"Going to stow away," said Mason. "Now, mates," continued he, "this here boy has been a wanting to go to sea for a long time. He's got no father nor mother here in Canada, and he's working for Crapser, and he doesn't want to work for him any more, and wants to ship in the *General Hewitt* and see a little of the world."

"He's more likely to see the inside of a jail, the young cub," growled Stuart, "as I take it, for he wants to run away from his master. What's he going to do here? The old man won't ship him."

"Right you are, old shipmate," said Bob Inglis; "old Knight will send him back kiting to Crapser and make him acquainted with a rope's end before he goes over the side."

"Captain Knight shan't see him till long enough after the anchor's catted, topsails sheeted home, and mast headed," answered Mason. "I'll stow him away, and once down the river will bring him aft and show him to the captain. He'll make a smart cabin boy. Now, mates, I want you to stand by me and give the lad a chance."

"Nevaire, nevaire, Jack Mason," said the French cook, "we vant no boy, no sare; ze boys is von trouble aboard ze sheep."

DICK STUART.

" Who the h—l asked you to shove your oar in, Doctor,"
roared Bill Nye; "wait till your betters have spoken. If the
boy wants to go to sea, who's agoing to stop him. If he
wants to run away in this here ship he's only adoing like
most of us have done, and I'll stand by him." Here Bill
pounded the lid of his chest with his enormous fist, and
continued, " I'll stand by him, and the man that plays the
'white mouse' on him will have to square yards with Bill
Nye."

"Aye, and with us too," chimed in the deep voices of Jim
Brown and Steve Allen, " Hallo there," shouted Mason,
" turn out here and show yourself, you young rascal."

I was before them, dressed in a moment, timidly waiting
for a word from my judges. Something in my demeanor
appealed for me, and I found favor with them, but still had
to listen meekly to a good-natured scolding from Stuart, and
a long lecture on the dreadful consequences which would
probably follow such a headstrong course as mine. Then
the crew resolved itself into a committee of the whole, to
decide what steps were necessary to secrete me until it was
safe for me to make my appearance.

It was agreed that for the present I should remain in the
forecastle during the day; that all hands would keep a
lookout for breakers, in case any of the inmates of the cabin
should show a desire to visit my hiding-place; but that at
night I might go on deck, but must keep well out of sight.

Having so settled it, all the crew from that time showed
me every kindness. Dick Stuart considered me a special
subject for his fatherly advice, and even the cook Frenchy
(nautice, the doctor) took special pains to bring me some
tid-bits from the galley.

" You von grand idiot, von gros fou. Mon gars, den
you vant make you von sailare. Ah! mille tonneres, if vas not
for dat big pig, ze Bill Nye, and dose beasts, Steve Allen
et Jim Brown, I would ver soon see you on de shore, a

terre. Mais, mange donc, mange donc, gamin que tu es."
His kindly nature led him, although he thought me an
idiot, to invite me to eat, and he supplied me with the best
the galley afforded, which he urged me to swallow in quantity enough to spoil the digestion of a rhinoceros.

Ten long days in that forecastle were the longest I ever
saw before or since. The labor of discharging cargo kept
the men busy all day, and they were too tired at night to
pay much attention to me, but were more inclined to bad
humor than saying anything to smooth the way for a young
aspirant for nautical honors.

As all mortal things must have an end, the cargo was discharged, the ship cleaned up and made ready for a new
cargo, which then appeared in large rafts from the Ottawa
river, the St. Lawrence, or the "Sault au Recollet." They
were soon moored alongside and rapidly hoisted and stowed
aboard. When all this was over, and the vess.1 ready for
sailing orders, the crew assumed a more genial aspect; their
brows unbent and mouths once more wreathed in smiles,
looking more like the jolly tars of my youthful fancy. This
change was favorable to me, and those who had most loudly
opposed my going to sea now were most ready to sing the
glories of a seaman's life.

The orders came in due course of time to get under way
for London, and soon the clank, clank, of the cable told of
the capstan's work in lifting the heavy anchor from its oozy
bed. I felt thankful that I would soon be at sea and all
fears of being set ashore gone. Come what will, I should
soon see what a sailor's life is, and be able on my return to
tell the other boys about the strange things to be seen in
the "old country." I had been specially cautioned to keep
shady, and while the great excitement caused by those who
were busy in weighing anchor was going on I remained close
below. Of pilots and officers there seemed to be no end, so
many were to be seen and heard in every part of the ship.

The singing of the men as they pulled altogether was music
to my ears, for it meant freedom for me, and the hurry and
confusion on deck seemed especially designed for my
benefit. But it was a fearful din at times. The dropping
of a heavy coil of rope, the falling of the great iron cable
from the capstan, the rushing feet of the many sailors, altogether suggested an awful expression that I had often heard,
" that hell was let loose." So I lay snug in my hammock,
not daring to put my nose out of the forecastle—terrified lest
at any moment one of the officers should happen, for some
reason or another, to look into my hammock and find what
he would consider one of the watch on deck asleep or
" skulking."

We were soon under way, and in an hour or two I felt
a new sensation, which was anything but pleasant. I became
conscious that *terra firma* had slipped out from under me,
and that the ship was not the most steady article I knew of.
One moment my head bumped this side, then that, then the
hammock swung endwise, and I felt that something must
soon give way, and that my ribs, of course, would go first,
when suddenly I tumbled out of the hammock upon a chest
and fell to the deck. About that time my stomach began
to rebel, and joined the ship in rising and falling in unison
not at all comforting to me. It seemed as if the St. Lawrence had been turned into my interior and my sole object
in life was to eject it, and I proceeded to do what I could
in that line of duty. My performance was very energetic
if it was not heroic, and it was increased by the rolling,
pitching and tossing of the vessel, and intensified by the
horrible stench from the ship's hold. And then the ordering, shouting, stamping, and, I am ashamed to admit it, the
cursing and swearing on deck increased, as it seemed to me,
out of all proportion to the cause. The rough waters of
the St. Lawrence have a worse effect on a youngster than
the waves of the ocean, and besides it was my first voyage.

I am not able even now to describe my sensations at that time, although my memory holds fast to every item in the disagreeable catalogue. I was utterly used up, sick, limp, helpless, hopeless, despairing, and even thought death would be a relief. In this mood I began to wonder if it was a

UNDER WAY.

mistake in going to sea, and doubted the wisdom of the choice; but while thinking it over tired nature yielded and sleep, although uneasy, was welcome.

Only a short time was allowed for my rest when I was aroused by smothered laughter, and on looking over the side of my hammock saw Frenchy the doctor and Dick Stuart   fairly doubled up with merriment on one of the chests.   Frenchy caught my eye and nudged Dick to call his attention to the fact that I was wide awake.

"Vell, mon gars, have you enough sleep? You vant go aboard sheep, to noting do, is it not? Nom d'un nom, I go right avay on deck and de capitaine come vith one cat and tails." And Stuart shouted, "Come, rouse out, you young rascal, and pay for your lodging. You were anxious to go to sea, and now you're there. We're abreast of Grosse Isle, and it's your watch; so turn to, rouse out, or by the man of the mast I will light you along with a rope lantern." Thus abjured, and alarmed by the fierce expressions and ferocious countenances of the two whom my previous experience had led me to consider as not my friends, I made a desperate effort to rise, and succeeded in suddenly plunging out of the hammock and landing on all fours, which seemed to amuse the two sailors immensely, for they roared with laughter.

"Now then, you lubber, get into your duds and stand by to go on deck," and he looked as ferocious as his suppressed merriment would permit. My toilet was brief and I staggered out on deck just in time to meet my first heavy sea. I was dazed for a moment with the bright light of the May morning after the long confinement in the darksome forecastle, and was astonished to see an enormous wall of water rising over the side of the ship and tumbling down on the deck. Howling with terror, I was swept off my feet and completely drowned in a salt-water bath, which rolled me to and fro on the deck like a log. When the water had run out through the scuppers I found myself once more on dry land, or rather on a very wet deck. At that moment my stomach, perhaps from the shaking up it had got from my rolling over on the deck, began to operate on its own account, and it did itself great credit, judging from appearances and the remarks of the sailors.

If the reader wishes my opinion on what can produce the most misery, wretchedness, heart-breaking, soul-rending, stomach-demoralizing suffering—worse than any hunger

BILL NYE.

and thirst, or any fever, coast or yellow, and a general summing up of all the ills that flesh—that is, sailor's flesh, is heir to—I can cordially recommend a regular old-fashioned bout of sea-sickness. If you will only take one dose of it you'll be convinced that I speak from experience.

Well, I crouched, wet to the skin, unable to hold on to anything, leaning against the lee bulwarks, and looked with glazed eyes at the foamy white waters raging beneath. Often I felt that I was swinging overboard, when a sea heavier than usual made the ship lay over more deeply; but my only care was to rid my stomach of its intolerable load.

"For'ard there."

"Aye, aye, sir."

"Who the h—l is that on the lee fore-chains?"

"Don't know, sir. He's just showed his-self, sir. 'Pears to have stowed his-self away aboard of us."

"Thunder and guns! A stowaway, eh?" roared the deep voice of the officer. "Clap on to him, a couple of you, and lug him aft here, while I get a rope's end, and teach the son of a sea-cook to stow himself away aboard of the *General Hewitt*." In a second Jack Mason and Bill Nye had grabbed me, and were dragging me off with a great show of zeal, but, however, with great gentleness, to the quarter-deck. On the way Frenchy the doctor whispered as I passed him, "Du courage, mon petit; les amis sont, sont jours pres. Du courage, nom d'un nom."

As soon as I was brought before the officer he roared out: "Now then, you d—d young scoundrel, who are you, and what are you doing aboard of us?" Mason and Nye held me up and gave me a grip on the sly, as much as to say, now then, my lad, out with it. Spin your yarn, and we'll stand by you.

Many is the time that I have listened to the plausible promises of landsmen, and been beguiled by their flattering words and oily tongues; but when man speaks to man, and we look for a guarantee of good faith in preference to promissory notes or bonds and mortgages, give me the honest word and the sterling grip of the true-hearted sailor. This reflection recalls the words of the great poet Shakspeare:

> "This above all : to thine own self be true,
> And it must follow, as the night the day,
> Thou canst not then be false to any man."

Mason's grip nerved me to meet the trying ordeal, and I

spoke up: My name is George Davis, sir. I am or was apprenticed to Mr. Crapser of Quebec. I wanted to go to sea and so stowed myself away aboard of this ship.

"Hallo!" said the second mate, "you were an apprentice of Mr. Crapser's, were you ? and you have been stowed away since that evening I saw you scramble into the gangway. Is that so ?"

To that I very discreetly answered by silence.

"Where did you get your rations these last ten days?" inquired he, and there was more silence, when he turned to my friends and said, "Now, look you here, Jack Mason and Bill Nye, none of your innocent airs with me. You were in the boat that brought this youngster aboard. You've been stowing him away and giving him his rations since he's been aboard, and I have a d—d good mind to serve you as I intended to serve him." So saying, the infuriated officer swung a rope's end over his head, which rope seemed thick enough to serve as towline to a frigate.

Just then a deep voice called, "Mr. Samuels, please to come here a minute." Mr. Samuels started at the call, grew very red, furtively dropped the rope's end and hastened aft. Looking after him, I saw the friend whom I had met on the wharf on the arrival of the *General Hewitt*. When Mr. Samuels joined him they had some conversation and together went down into the cabin, and a subordinate came towards me with an air of great severity (probably assumed), saying, "Well, youngster, you have made a mess of it. You may thank your stars that Captain Sellers came on deck in time, or I'd have warmed your hide for you; but never mind, my lad; you're like a young cub, your troubles are all to come yet, so lay aft with me to the cabin. Captain Sellers wants to see his stowaway."

So speaking, he led me aft to the cabin like a felon to the gallows. As I approached the sound of glasses clinking and merry laughing somewhat reassured me, for I felt that if my

judges were so good-humored they would not in all proba-
bility become my executioners.

Mr. Samuels, my jailer, halted at the companion-way and
seemed to be afflicted with a very peculiar cough, which
was not exactly like bronchitis or any other pulmonary
trouble; but it was significant, for it hushed the merriment
in the cabin, and caused such a calm there that I was frightened more than ever.   Mr. Samuels gave me a shake and
said: "Here he is, Captain; here's the stowaway. Look up,
youngster, this is Captain Sellers."

I looked up as I was ordered, and there sat, to my amaze-
ment, in the place of honor at the table, my quondam
acquaintance of the wharf; at his left sat Captain Knight,
and on the other side a grizzly specimen of the French
Canadian, whom I immediately recognized as a pilot of the
Lower St. Lawrence, or, as they are generally called, a "Gulf
Pilot."

I noticed a fourth chair half drawn back, and a wine glass
in its place not quite empty; the napkin dropped as in haste,
as if the guest had suddenly left the cabin.

"Well, young man, I see that you have disregarded my
advice and have run away from home to become a stowaway. You have deserted your kind employer, Mr. Crapser,
and have endeavored to steal a passage on board of my ship.
What ought we do with him, Captain Knight?" he inquired,
turning to him.   Now, Captain Knight had been as utterly
indifferent to my presence as if I had never existed, and he
went on sipping his wine with the utmost composure, and
when the glass was empty he held it out to be refilled. When
that was done, he tasted it and made a horrible grimace
towards Captain Sellers, saying:

"This wine is really detestable, Sellers.   'Pon my honor,
when I go up to Montreal I shall let Victor Hudon know
my opinion of it. Just imagine, he sold it to me as the very
finest Chateau Margaux, and as you see it is no better than

HOME THOUGHTS.

common Saint Estephe. Oh—ah—yes, the lad—well, trice him up in the main rigging and give him a cool three dozen. Young rascal deserves twice as much. Allow me to suggest that all hands be called to witness punishment, and that it take place immediately; for really the presence of this young man in his present condition is not at all desirable. Since you have had the courtesy to ask my opinion, I suggest that he get a sound flogging and be returned in the pilot-boat to his master, or to the common jail."

I am ashamed to confess that the prospect of being flogged and then ignominiously sent back among my associates, and to the custody of Mr. Crapser, or, still worse, to the jail, completely unnerved me, and, sobbing violently, I was on the point of being led away, when a state-room door opened and a kind voice said

"One moment, George; just let him go, Mr. Samuels."

That was the well-known voice of Mr. Crapser. In a moment I was at his feet and crying bitterly

"Oh, Mr. Crapser, do, please, let me go home with you ; I will never run away again. These gentlemen say that I shall be flogged and then put into jail for running away.

"Not quite so bad as that, George," said he kindly ; "I do not believe that either Captain Sellers or Captain Knight will insist on flogging you or sending you back to jail. I have long since noticed your desire to go to sea, and knew of you being stowed away on board of the *General Hewitt*. Now, since you desire it so much, I give you my permission. You will find a good chest on board with a sailor's outfit, and I trust that you will never regret your choice. So now, George, good bye. We must part soon. Captain Sellers, allow me to introduce to you my quondam apprentice, George Davis. Will you accept him as one of your ship's company ?"

"Right heartily," answered Captain Sellers, "and especially as he has been one of my hands for the last ten or more

days. The lad thought that he had all snug, but Mr.
Samuels had his eye on him all the time."

'Yes, sir," said the second officer; " I saw the youngster
come aboard, and Frenchy told me where he was stowed
away. Frenchy took good care of the boy, Mr. Crapser;
and for that matter so did Jack Mason, Bill Nye, old Dick
Stuart and all hands."

" Back the maintop sail," was shouted from the quarter-
deck, and the chief officer, coming to the skylight, said :

" Pilot-boat alongside, Captain."

" Well, gentlemen," said Captain Knight, " we must part.
Captain Sellers, permit me to wish you a prosperous voyage."

" Good bye, Sellers," said Mr. Crapser, " and take good
care of my stowaway."

" Aye, aye, he'll be lulled into shape," was the reassuring
reply of Captain Sellers.

Then Mr. Crapser, with a hearty shake of my hand,
slipped a few sovereigns into my palm, and we all went on
deck. The pilot-boat's skiff came up to the lee gangway,
and in a few moments Mr. Crapser, Captain Knight, and the
pilot had bidden us adieu. We filled away and the *General
Hewitt* was fairly under way homeward bound.

Captain Sellers turned toward me and said, "Are you
wet, my lad ?"

" Yes, sir, to the skin."

" Here, steward, take this boy into the cabin and give him
a good tot of grog. Then you go for'ard, George, change
yourself, and have a comfortable snooze. We shall want
you by-and-bye."

After swallowing a wine-glass full of Jamaica rum I went
forward and was received with a hearty welcome by the
whole crew, who were elated by my having passed so successfully through a very trying ordeal. I would have remained on deck had not the chief mate sung out in stento-
rian tones:

"For'ard there; let that boy turn in, and two of you lay aft for his dunnage. Here, you, Stuart and Mason."

"Aye, aye, sir." In a few minutes I had changed clothing and was comfortably stowed away in my hammock, and my head, heart and stomach being at ease—for the fright at the dreaded trial had cured my sea-sickness—I soon fell asleep. All through that afternoon and night I slept soundly, perfectly oblivious of the roaring of the wind, the thumping of the seas, or the shouting and stamping on deck. At eight bells next morning I was wakened by the watch being called, and, hastily dressing, enjoyed a hearty breakfast with the men below. I then went on deck, and for the first time in my life enjoyed the proud pleasure of being part and parcel of a noble ship's crew, and repeated mentally, "She walks the water like a thing of life and seems to dare the elements to strife," which I had read many times, longing to realize the sensation of being actually on board for a voyage, as I then was. Then also I remembered and felt the force and beauty of Eliza Cook's stirring poem, entitled "Through the Waters," of which this is the closing verse:

> "All sail away ; ah! who would stay to pace the dusty land
> If once they trod a gallant ship, steered by a gallant band
> Through the waters, through the waters? Oh! there's not a joy for me
> Like racing with the gull upon a broad and dashing sea."

And surely even the most critical and fastidious eye could find no fault with the *General Hewitt*, as it seemed to me. She was a Bombay teak-built ship of 2000 tons measurement, and belonged to the Honorable East India Company's service, whence she was temporarily detached to ship a cargo of square pine timber at Quebec for the company's use. She was armed *en flute*, and was manned in proportion, as were most merchantmen at that period, because pirates and freebooters were not then things of the past, but rather often inconveniently present, especially in the tropics.

As I was ruminating in this poetical vein and on the point of constructing a glowing future full of "castles in Spain," the steward came forward and said very simply, but with an air of indisputable authority:

"The Captain has appointed you cabin-boy; bring your chest aft and I will show you a berth. Come, be lively." I was delighted at the promotion, but sighed at parting from the fo'castle, where I anticipated so much "good time" among the jolly tars, so many of whom were already friendly. But as there was nothing else to do I obeyed the order instantly. "Frenchy, the doctor," from that moment considered that I was his special subordinate, and was delighted intensely.

So now, dear reader, behold me duly installed, inducted, and invested in and with all the dignities of my new and honorable though humble position, as part of the crew of the *General Hewitt*, of the Honorable East India Company's service. The first chapter of the " Recollections of a Sea Wanderer's Life " ends here.

> " Lads of the land, ye shrink and hide
> As the tempest-cloud spreads black and wide,
> But the sailor boy leads the gayest life
> While the storm-fiends wage their fiercest strife."

Chapter II.

— — —

" There's lightning in yon horned moon,
 And tempest in yon cloud,
And hark the music, mariners,
 The wind is piping loud;
The wind is piping loud, my boys,
 And the lightning flashing free,
The hollow oak our palace is,
 Our heritage the sea."

A spanking breeze sent us flying down the St. Lawrence, safely past the threatening " Brandy Pots," a very dangerous reef of rocks, about which many tales of disaster are told by the old sailors. Near the mouth of the river is the most desolate, forlorn, gloomy and wretched coast out of the latitude of the Okhotsk Sea or Cape Horn, called Anticosti Island. It is well named " anti," for it is against all nature as a dwelling-place for anything beside the howling winds and pelting sleet, and possibly the region to which the gods have banished some of the evil spirits that are supposed to be hostile to sailors. It was a veritable " Cave of the Winds " to us, some of which got loose and came booming down on us from the nor'west, and obliged us to shorten sail until we were staggering along under a close-reefed maintop sail, reefed fore-sail, and foretop-mast-stay sail. Then I felt for the first time the cold, dark seas striking the ship like so many trip-hammers, and deluging the decks as if a river had been let loose. It was delightful to cling to the mizzen rigging and view from the high weather side of the ship the huge waves, inky black below and light green above, crested with foam, as if in rage at our intrusion on their domain. But the ship outrode the gale and, as if shaking the baffled foes off her sides, rode resolutely on her course.

"'The Lord only knows what " day dreams I was indulging in when the warning cry was shouted, " Look out,

George!" when that instant I saw the whole Gulf of St. Lawrence towering above me, and I was smothered for a moment in its waters, which dashed me from the rigging, threw me against the spars lashed to leeward, where I lay dazed, bruised, and helpless through terror, and in danger of drowning, although the water escaped through the lee scuppers and over the planksheer.

"Go below, my lad, and shift yourself, and then lend the steward a hand to get the cabin ship-shape and 'Bristol fashion.' Next time you come on deck you must keep your weather eye open, and be ready to dodge the seas."

I obeyed the captain's orders with alacrity—no delay was possible under the circumstances, and as I changed my clothing, and got dry and warm again, the thought occurred that, although the deck was a more romantic place, yet the cosy cabin was far more dry and desirable in rough weather. If the celebrated opera of "Pinafore" had then been written, I should have heartily appreciated the lines:

> "And when the breezes blow
> We generally go below."

The heavy pounding of the seas continued for several hours, and when the pitching and tossing of the ship decreased a little, concluding that the storm was over, I ventured on deck, and timidly approaching the man at the wheel ("Old Dick Stuart," as he was called), said: "Is the storm really over, Mr. Stuart?"

"What the blazes do you mean by talking to the man at the wheel, you young lubber? Go ax the cook; he's a seafaring man. Tell him I sent you. Do you hear? Always ax the cook when you want to learn anything about sailorizing."

Very much dismayed at this rebuff, and fearing to disobey the rough order so bluntly given, I went to the galley door, where "Frenchy" was swearing furiously over his pots and kettles, and sweating like a bull, as he dodged the frequent splashes of hot water that flew about at every lurch of the ship, yelling " Mille diablés! " and repeating, when a liberal dose of hot soup lit on his breeches, '' Quel temps infernal ! "

CONSULTATION.

"Vell, vat you look?" yelled he at me; "vat you vant? You come see burn me vit du sacré soup, eh?"

"Oh, no, Mr. Cook," said I; "but Mr. Stuart told me that you could tell me if the storm was over, and if the wind had gone down.   And he said "——

That sentence was never finished; for with a wild yell the cook seized a rolling-pin, and with blazing eyes made a dash at me.   I did not stand on the order of going, but tearing across the deck gained the cabin door; the ship giving a fearful lurch at the moment, tumbled me down the companion-way, and frightened the steward nearly out of his wits.

There was a tremendous racket on deck.   Dick Stuart's laugh was mingled with the frantic curses of "Frenchy" and the clatter of pots and pans, followed by an altercation between them.   "Frenchy" was profuse in words and shrieks; but Stuart answered only by peals of merriment; so, of course, the cook's ire increased, like his own galley fires, until the Captain's voice, like oil on the waters, stilled the tempest by ordering the cook to his galley, and rebuking Stuart for talking at the wheel, and causing the ship to yaw in her course.   The old seaman answered in a low and apologetic tone, and the Captain's steps were soon heard descending the companion-way.   Once in the cabin, he threw himself into a seat and chuckled with suppressed merriment. However, he did not forget me, for he soon said:

"Look here, George, don't go asking any more sea questions of the cook.   You see what you have done.   The ship came by the lee; the cook is badly scalded; our soup and coffee are lost; and he will be no friend of yours or of Dick Stuart for many a day to come.   And now, my lad, what on earth was the wonderful problem that the 'doctor' was to answer?"

"Why sir," said I, "after I had changed my clothes and helped the steward set the cabin to rights, I noticed a queer

change in the ship's motion, and the wind seemed to have
abated; so I thought I would ask if the storm was over, and
Mr. Stuart told me to ask the cook. When I did so the
cook got mad."

"Aye, aye," laughed the Captain; "Stuart is always
ready for horse play, and he would give up his grog rather
than lose a chance of plaguing any one. Now, if you will
look at this chart, I will try to do as well as the 'doctor'
could in explaining the cause of the sudden change in the
weather. Here is Anticosti, now on our weather-beam, or,
rather, quarter; and here is Cape Rozier, at present on our
lee quarter. With the wind nor'west, we had to give Rozier
a wide berth, and stand about east-north-east to get an offing. As soon as we had stood long enough on that course,
we let her fall off two points, bringing the wind further aft,
easing the ship considerably. This made you think the wind
had abated, and caused all the trouble. If you go on deck
now, you will notice that the seas are running as heavily and
the breeze is as stiff as when you were rolling about in the
lee scuppers. Wait, though, until Stuart is relieved; for he
will be sure to get you into more trouble, old salt that he is.
Just tell the cook that it was not your fault, and ask his par-
don. He's not a bad fellow. The boys give him no peace
because, poor soul, he is a 'Johnny Crapeau,' as they
call it."

At four bells Bill Nye relieved the wheel, and I went on
deck and easily succeeded in mollifying the "doctor."

Although, as Captain Sellers said, the seas were still running very high and the wind blowing half a gale, the crew
had set the foretop sail close reefed, shaking reefs out of the
maintop sail, and got a pull of the weather braces, and we
were reeling off twelve knots an hour by the log. The wind
still continuing, we soon cleared the Gulf and the Banks,
when we got into blue water and reached the nor'western
edge of the Gulf Stream. Then the wind began to mode-

rate into a whole-sail breeze, and the weather to grow sensibly warmer. Then we made sail in good earnest; shook out all the reefs, set the mizzen-top sail and all to'-gallant sails, jib, mainsail, and spanker, flying jib and royals. Soon after we rigged out larboard stun'-sail booms, and set fore and maintop-mast and to'-gallant-stun' sails, with lower stun' sail. We ran along under this canvas at a lively rate for the next three days and nights without starting tack or sheet.

During this resting spell the sailors gathered in groups on deck or in the fo'castle, and "spun yarns" about their adventures at sea, which were delightful to my fresh ears. Among many I remember one distinctly, because it gave me a lesson, or rather several lessons in one. Through some carelessness or other, one of the sailors cut his foot with the carpenter's adze, and an ugly wound it was. The foot was bound up, Jack was put to bed in one of the officers' berths, and every care was taken of him. I was allowed to attend him when not on other duty, and spent some hours a day reading to him. One day, when the wound began to heal— or, rather, had closed up all across, except at one spot where it was still obstinate—one of the old sailors came in to his messmate, and Jack complained of the pain the foot gave him. The old salt said that it would never be better until the ax that made the wound had been baked in the cook's oven until it was very hot. So he volunteered to ask the "doctor's" permission to bake the ax, and it was done. Jack said that the moment the ax was put into the oven the pain left, and only returned to plague him when it was taken out and allowed to cool off. So "Frenchy" was kind enough to sling it with a stout ratline above the coppers, and Jack was relieved of his pain altogether. I doubted very much the supposed value of the ax in curing the wound, but said nothing, preferring to be a silent listener when there was anything in the superstitious line going on. I have never knowingly given way to any silly notions of that kind, although when I have noticed a lot of sharks following close in our wake, the notion that they knew that some one of us would soon be thrown over as "food for fishes" would make my flesh creep just a little, resist it ever so much; but creep it would.

After the spell of steady wind we had a change, with the wind to the northeast, when it began to blow big guns, with a fine, warm rain so characteristic of the Gulf Stream. This wind was dead against the current of the Stream; there was an ugly sea, and the ship labored accordingly. The bows rising high above the water and then plunging down, sometimes shipping a heavy swell that washed the decks from stem to stern, was a new experience to my young eyes, and I wondered if the ship would not go down altogether. But as it seemed I was the only one on board who felt any uneasiness, I concluded there was no real danger, and took in the situation as a matter of course. Many times since, when there was real danger from a genuine storm, I have felt less anxious than on that first voyage, because my confidence in the staunchness of the ship was so great that it could not be shaken—at least not until the decks sank below the waters; and even then, unless loaded with railroad iron, or salt and sugar, there is always faith that she can be floated.

As I lay in my berth, thinking over the case, and tossing from side to side uneasily, the sound of "eight bells" came down the hatch-way, and following it in the same breath: "All hands shorten sail!" When the watch were on deck the orders came rapidly succeeding each other: "Haul the main sail up; haul down the jib; brail up the spanker; lay out, some of you, and furl the jib; some of you stop the foot of the spanker; lower away the top-sail halyards; haul out the reef tackles; up buntlines; steady the weather braces;" and "lay aloft."

These orders, shouted so nearly in a breath, only confused

me; but the men acted as if by instinct, and, reckless of the howling winds, blinding rain, and drenching seas, felt their way with their hands and feet; for they could scarcely keep their eyes open, and it was pitchy dark besides; and, surprising as it seemed to me, each one singled out the particular rope among the many grouped in the running rigging, and hauled away with a hearty will, many joining in a chorus as they tugged at some very heavy pull.

Suddenly the cry arose, "Man overboard!" The shouts of the men, rushing aft, heaving over coils of rope, and cutting loose life-buoys, in the forlorn hope that the poor fellow might catch on to one or another of them. No earthly power could avail, and both officers and crew were sorrowful and dumb as the ship rode on, and left the sailor to drown and sink, perhaps food for fishes. The seamen peered into each other's faces inquiringly when some one shrieked, "It is Bill Collier!" And several called out loudly, "Bill Collier! Bill Collier!" as if to make sure that he was not among them nor anywhere on the ship. He was not. Poor Bill was far behind the ship, out of the reach of their call. Their voices were drowned a thousand times by the howling winds and swash of the blinding spray. Bill had been out on the foot-ropes of the jib-boom, clinging to the life-lines, holding up the folds of the heavy wet sail, slatting wildly about him, when some pitch of the ship threw his feet off, and he was plunged into the sea. Lost in the line of his duty, we honored his memory with many kindly words, while we strove to imagine what his feelings were as he slipped away into the furious waves. How he must have hoped against hope, if he heard the cry of alarm and the orders to heave the life-buoys; and what bitter agony he must have felt as the great ship swept by him, and her stern-lights faded in the storm and distance. How memories of home and loved ones must have crowded upon him. It is said that the drowning see beautiful visions of their early

days. Even if so, such visions are paid for at far too dear
a price—life itself. Poor Bill! Of all the ways of taking
us off, it seems to me that the loss of a seaman in a stormy
night by falling overboard is the most terrible. I can
heartily join in repeating the prayer: "From such a fate,
good Lord, deliver us."

Bill Collier was a favorite with all his shipmates, and even
with the officers; for he was a true type of a British seaman—willing, kind, able, fearless of danger, resolute, and,
withal, simple as a child. Of him it might well be said:

> "His form was of the manliest beauty,
>   His heart was kind and soft;
> While here below he did his duty;
>   But now he's gone aloft.
>
> "Still shall poor Jack find pleasant weather
>   When He who all commands
> Shall give, to call life's crew together,
>   The word to pipe all hands."

"Well, shipmates," said Captain Sellers in a deep voice,
that showed his kindly emotions, "poor Bill is gone from
among us forever. Let us all do our duty, as he did, so that
when the call comes we may be ready to answer, and show
an honorable discharge from the Ship of Life. Now, boys,
turn to again," he said more firmly; "turn to again, and
hoist the top sails."

Silently and sadly the men went to their work, which was
soon done, when the watch went below and turned in.
While we were below during the last dog-watch, from six to
eight in the evening, a sound like that of a hundred-pounder
made us rush on deck, when we saw that the close-reefed
foretop sail had blown clean out of the bolt-ropes. We were
then under storm canvas, close-reefed maintop sail, reefed
fore sail, and foretop-mast-stay sail; and so we flew over
the waves, with favoring, although brisk, winds, making ten
or eleven knots, and, counting two of the Gulf Stream with
us, even thirteen knots an hour, for days at a stretch. After
a few days of this sort of racing with the dolphins, early

one morning the welcome cry of "Land ho!" brought all hands on deck. Sure enough, there it was, broad on our port bow-way, the dim outline of the Lizard Point, which lies to the east'ard of Land's End. This welcome sight cheered us all, and some of the men broke out into snatches of song, others into exclamations of delight and joy, at the prospect of seeing home again. As for me, the romantic vein was touched, and I recalled the lines that were once so popular:

> " Like slaves in the galleys
> We'll plough the salt seas ; "

and also other lines:

> " We'll rant and we'll rove
> All o'er the salt seas,
> We'll rant and we'll rove,
> Like true British heroes,
> Until we strike soundings
> In the Channel of Old England.
> From Ushant to Scilly 'tis forty-five leagues."

The next day proved rainy, but with a fresh sou'west wind towards night we made the Start on the Devonshire coast, when we took in all the stun' sails, rigged in the booms, and unrove the gear. Next morning we sighted the Portland Bill; at midnight we had reached Beachy Head, and by morning were off Dungeness, where we spoke a sea (or King's) pilot. The manner in which one of those pilots boards a ship is to be commended, if not for comfort, at least for its simplicity, which is extreme. A heaving line is hove aboard of the pilot-boat, which line the pilot makes fast about his body, under his arms, in a bowline knot, and he then jumps into the sea, and is hauled aboard the ship as if he were a porpoise.

As we were sailing up the Channel, Captain Sellers caught sight of an American packet, at that time painted in the style called bright-sided, and he growled out: "Blank blank the blank Yankee ship! I would like to sink her." Perhaps he would have done it if he could have done the job on the sly, but he may have been no better than many another who has proved more noisy, braggy and beery in the ale-house than on the sea.

Being then at the entrance of the Straits of Dover, we could see the shores of both France and England at the same time. By three in the afternoon we were off the South Foreland Light, and, hauling our wind to the nor'ard, came to an anchor in the Downs. The Downs is the noted anchorage of the "Wooden Walls of England." I had read about the famous fleet, and expected to see something grand; but, like the boy who first visited a city, and said he could not see the place very well because there were so many houses, so I was also somewhat confused by the great number and variety of vessels visible far and near, and found it difficult to make out the fleet of war vessels; so I repeated to myself the fine old song written by John Gay two centuries ago:

> " All in the Downs the fleet lay moor'd,
> The streamers waving in the wind,
> When black-eyed Susan came aboard.
> ' Oh ! where shall I my true love find ?
> Tell me, ye jovial sailors ! tell me true,
> If my sweet William sails among the crew.'"

The sentiment was fine, but did not quite hit my case, for I had no lassie to meet me, and had not even left a sweetheart in Canada. In my eyes it was a glorious sight, and it was in England, where I so much wished to be. We were still about one hundred miles from London when we furled sails for the night, cast anchor, set the anchor watch, and could enjoy the reflection so well put in these words:

> " The dangers and the perils of the voyage were past,
> And our ship at anchor's moored at last ;
> The sails are all furled, and the anchor is cast,
> The happiest of the crew, Jack Robinson."

The "Jack Robinson" in that case was your humble servant, George Davis, and he enjoyed the liberty of that anchor watch with the best of them. While the rest of the crew went below to smoke a pipe, play at cards or spin yarns, I remained on deck gazing at the lights on shore, and won-

dering what manner of people there might be, or listening
to the various sounds which arose from the numberless vessels near us.

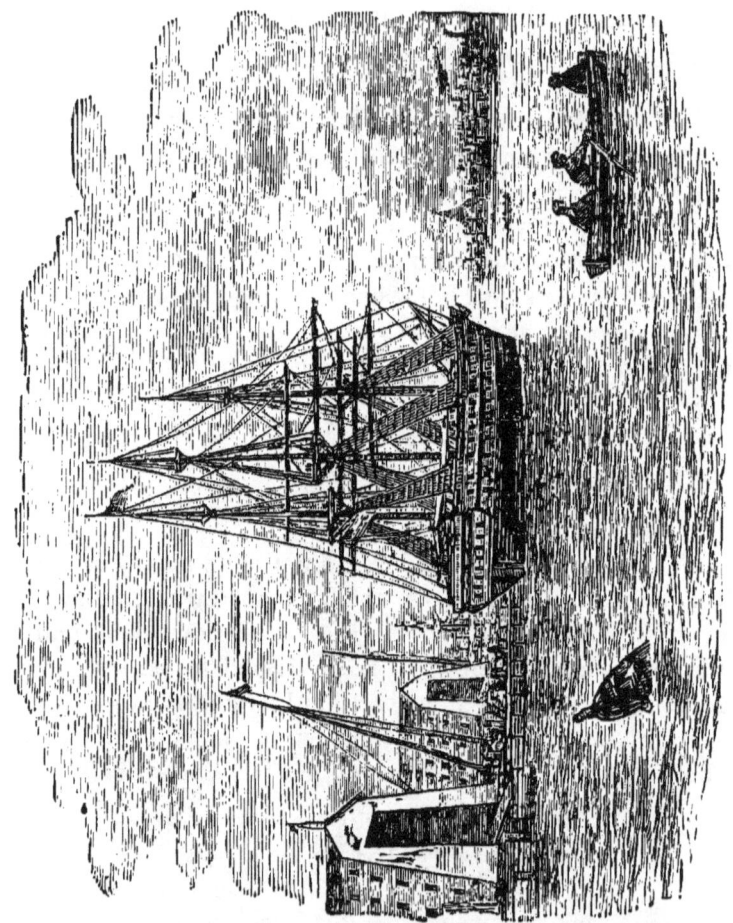

SHIPYARD, SHEERNESS.

Early next morning two powerful black tugs made fast to
the ship, one on each side, and having weighed anchor, we
were soon making way towards London with great speed.

On the way up the river Thames Dick Stuart acted as cicerone, and pointed out to us the various objects of interest as they passed in review. The first place was Sheerness, with its naval dockyards. This port is protected by extensive fortifications on both banks of the river. The Isle of Thanet near was the landing place of Hengist and Horsa, the Jutes, who came across the sea from Jutland in the year 440 A.D., and established the power which afterwards became the English nation, with the addition of the Saxons fifty years and the Angles a century after, and the Normans five centuries later. The Welsh should be included, but then they are a people by themselves. We passed Gravesend on the left, and were told that on a clear day, from the mast-head, we could see Chatham and the spire of Rochester cathedral to the sou'east. Tilbury Fort is opposite Gravesend, and would be a wicked customer to wake up in case of an enemy attempting to sail up the river. Soon after passing the fort Woolwich hove in sight. This is the most ancient royal dockyard in England, established in 1512, only two and a half miles from Greenwich—the home of the English sailors who have worn out their health and strength in the navy. The hospital building was built by King Charles II for a palace, and was assigned to its present use by King William III about 1700. The income, chiefly from confiscated estates, is enormous. The Sailor's Snug Harbor, on Staten Island, New York, is a similar institution, with an enormous income, said to be more than any one knows. Well, it is a source of comfort to poor Jack to feel and know that there are good berths ready for him when his hulk is disabled, and he can no longer brave the Storm King. Tom Hood says: "A Greenwich pensioner is a sort of stranded marine animal, that the receding tide of life has left high and dry on the shore. He pines for his element like a sea bear, and misses his briny washings and wettings. What the ocean could not do the land does, for it makes him sick; he cannot digest properly unless his body is rolled and tumbled about like a barrel-churn. *Terra firma* is good enough to touch at for wood and water, but for nothing more."

While we were passing the Nore, off Sheerness, Stuart gave us an account of the famous mutiny of the British fleet in 1798, and pointed out the place where "Queen Bess" stood on an eminence while the Dutch fleet, under Van

IN DOCK.   LONDON.

Tromp, was destroying the English fleet, and she cried, "Oh, my poor fleet!" And there were many other notable objects in view. Late in the afternoon we were laid alongside of the *Bashemere*, an old Dutch man-of-war that was abandoned by a squadron under the Dutch Admiral De Ruyter, who, after ravaging a part of London, and destroying an immense amount of shipping, retreated down the river, leaving his mark as he went. The *General Hewitt* was warped into Blackwall Basin, which lies between the East and West India docks, where she was securely moored. Thus ended my first voyage. Many years have passed since then, and nearly all of my old shipmates have long since stood their last watch, and have departed for the land of the hereafter. Peace be to their gallant souls, one and all. They showed naught but uniform kindness and tender solicitude for a friendless boy, so unexpectedly cast among them. Kindly Jack Mason, gruff Bill Nye, and fatherly Dick Stuart, fare ye well, wherever ye may be. Your memories are ever green in the inmost heart of your former shipmate, George Davis. Only this last fall there died in San Francisco one who was in the crew of the *Ewing* with me. So they go—some after short trips, others after a long voyage. There also died, aged 75, in San Francisco, "Joe Winrow," the leader in the mutiny on board the *Columbus*, Captain Depeyster, from Liverpool.

SEEING LONDON.

CHINESE BRIDGE.

Chapter III.

" Loud roars the dreadful thunder,
   The rain in torrents pours;
The clouds are rent asunder
   By the lightning's vivid powers.
That night, both chill and dark,
Our poor devoted bark,
       There she lay,
      'Til next day,
In the Bay of Biscay, oh."

The crew were paid off next day, and after many kindly leave-takings dispersed, some to hunt up relatives, friends, or sweethearts, and others, less fortunate, to hunt up quarters in a sailor's boarding-house. This last was not a difficult task as to quantity, for there was an " embarrassment of riches" as to number, but as to quality—well, one land-shark is very much like another, that's all I have to say at present, except that they were in those days, without exception, excessively anxious to serve poor Jack, and assist him in getting rid of his hard-earned money. Clamorous as a pack of wolves eager for their prey, the runners for the boarding-houses came at you, a dozen at a time, and tackled on to poor Jack and his box, or sea-chest, and hauled him this way and that, amidst a war of words and ear-splitting shouts and curses, which often led to bloody fights. Jack must at such times keep his weather-eye on his dunnage, or it would disappear without hope of recovery. However, that was not the most serious danger; when in the boarding-house the kind host supplied him with liquor in abundance that was almost more strong than pure. The result was too often that Jack remained moored head and stern in the grog-shop until his money was spent or stolen, when he was shipped for another voyage, the first notice of which would be a kick and a curse from the mate, who ordered him to go on board at once.

Dazed and stupefied, he looks for his chest, and feels in
his pockets for his money, and both have vanished, and he
learns that he is outward bound for "God knows where"—
around the Horn it may be, without a second shirt to his
back or a "sous marquee" in his pocket. Such an experience was too common in those days. It is to be hoped that
the customs of the shippers and the greed of the "sharks"
have improved and moderated since then. But if we are to
judge from certain reports about the United States Shipping
Commissioners, in South street, New York, of a few years
since, the world moves very slowly in some matters. Poor
Jack! The insurance companies keep patrol wagons and
complete sets of fire apparatus to protect property on shore;
I ask, would it be unreasonable to do a little something to
protect the property afloat that they insure? The safety of
a ship may depend at a critical moment on a sailor. It is
important that all sailors should be trustworthy, for the sake
of safety to all. And besides safety to property, there might
be a slight effort made for humanity's sake. The Bethel is
all right, and it may be that many of the prayers offered
there by preachers and others, who never slept in a sailor's
berth, are answered. Let us hope they are. But still the
true way to benefit the sailor is to protect him from the posi-
tive evils and dangers that so often wreck him on shore.

With Captain Sellers' permission I was allowed to remain
on board until I could find another ship, in exchange for
some light duties. Young as I was, I saw many interesting
things in the great city, beginning with the docks, of which
I remembered most particulars of the East India and the
West India, because the *General Hewitt* lay between them
and I saw them often. The London and St. Catherine were
not far away. I was greatly surprised at the enormous
storage capacity on the docks, and walked through miles of
huge casks in rows, and tier on tier, filled with wine or other
liquors from foreign countries. I had read about the Tower,

and hurried there as soon as the docks had been looked over. There were too many things to see in the Tower, and I soon tired of the monotonous drawl of the guide who showed us around, for I knew so little of the history of the times to which the relics stored there related that they had little interest to me. I determined to remedy that omission in my education, and from that day asked questions of those who were supposed to know, and read the best books that could be had where I was, and by so doing was better prepared to profit by and enjoy seeing the sights. My recollections of the wonderful things in that ancient fortress and palace combined are rather confused. I now think the fat and wheezy guide said that in one of the towers (for there were towers and towers in the great Tower) King Richard the Third murdered his nephews; in another the Duke of Clarence was purposely drowned in a butt of Malmsey wine; in a third Lady Jane Grey was beheaded; in a fourth the famous Anna Boleyn was imprisoned; and there was something said about Sir Walter Raleigh and Sir Thomas Moore, the noble William Wallace, and other historical personages of one or two or more centuries ago; but all I remember is the name, and I am not quite sure of that. I am certain of one thing, and that is that a gentleman of our sight-seeing party gave the puffy guide a sovereign, while I could hardly afford a shilling; but I noticed that he seemed as pleased with my small gift as with the other. I stayed behind to ask him a question or two, when he kindly told me to come next day and call for 'Arry 'Unt, and he would show me "hall hover the 'ole business for nothink." I went and was delighted, but it was like rain on a ship's deck—the torrent of information was wasted on me, and ran out of my noddle as fast as it was poured in.

I stumbled into St. Paul's, and there were a great number of workmen busy doing something to the inside, working on scaffolding that was built up all around against the walls. I was surprised at seeing so many tombs inside a church. Why,

it seemed more like a cemetery.   There were Lord Nelson's,
Sir John Moore's, and a great many other famous English-
men of whom I have since read, but am not even now sure
that they are buried in St. Paul's or in that other cemetery
called Westminster Abbey.   The greatest curiosity at St.
Paul's was the big bell.   I paid a shilling for the privilege of
seeing it; and while I was near it the hour of three was
struck, and it made my ears ring again.   I could not hear
ordinary conversation after that for an hour or two.

Stuart had told me about the Zoo.   I hastened there
early one day and spent most of the time watching the
antics of the bears, and feeding apples to the elephant by
allowing him to pick them out of my pockets.   I was cautioned not to give him tobacco, but as I did not use the
weed I was in no danger.   It is said that an elephant never
forgives an offense of that kind, and sometimes inflicts
serious injury in retaliation.

London Bridge (I mean the great one, for there are many
of them) was one of the objects that drew me often to see

OLD LONDON BRIDGE.

the large stream of humanity pouring both ways at the same time over its broad roadway. The route to the bridge led by several of those famous gin-palaces for which London is famed, and I often stepped inside to see what were the attractions; but as I had not then acquired an appetite for the ardent, my visits did not tax my pocket nor fuddle my brain.

When I had tired of seeing so many new things I hunted from dock to dock until a vessel was found bound for the United States, which was then the great goal of my ambition. But I could only find a brig, the *Paget* of Bermuda, bound for St. Vincents, one of the Windward Islands in the West Indies, which was near enough, for I could hope to find another vessel there bound for the States. The *Paget* was loaded with an assorted cargo of British goods.

On the morning of our departure from London, as Captain Brophy was coming up the gangway ladder, "as we lay in the City Canal," one of the man-rope stanchions broke, and he tumbled back upon the dock, fracturing his left ankle bone, which was attended to and set in splints as soon as possible, and he was carried, groaning with pain, into the cabin.

In spite of the suffering he endured, he would not listen to the surgeon's advice, but roughly telling him to go ashore and be d—d, he ordered the mate to cast off and haul out into the river and make sail.

This was done; we dropped down the river Thames and reached the Downs, where, as the wind was blowing up channel from the west'ard, we came to an anchor, windbound.

In the morning I commenced washing the table and other linen of the cabin, and, having finished, hung the articles to dry in various places.

One large table-cloth I fastened to the main try-sail-boom topping-lift, where it got the full swing of the breeze, and then rested, well content with my work.

In a few moments I noticed a whole fleet of small boats set out from the shore of Deal and come toward us, where we lay at a considerable distance from other wind-bound vessels.

At first I thought it was a regatta, and, shouting to the

SWIPES IN A GIN-PALACE, LONDON.

mate, I called his attention to the now rapidly-approaching boats, and said:

"Look! Mr. Williams, look at the boat-race."

"Boat-race be d—d," said he gruffly; "just like a b—y Kanuck to think that 'Deal luggers' have no more savey than to risk their skins boat-racing in a breeze like this. But what the blazes are they up to, anyhow?" said he.

At this moment three or four of the boats came within hail, and, luffing up under our stern, began shouting in chorus:

"Brig, ahoy! Brig, ahoy!"

"What do you want?"

"What's the matter with you?"

"What the h—l is the matter with yourselves? Are you all drunk or crazy?"

"Who sent for you to come? Who said anything was the matter with us, eh?"

"What are you flying that bunting on your main try-sail-boom topping-lift for, then?" roared the infuriated boatmen.

"What bunting?" roared the mate in reply; but just then his eye caught the unfortunate table-cloth. In a moment the truth flashed upon him.

"Oh! you infernal son of a sea-cook," yelled he, and, snatching up a piece of rattling stuff, he made for me with uplifted arm. I had just time to slip into the galley and bolt the door when he began to batter against it with all his might, and throwing his body against it, tried to burst it open. Fearing the worst, I took a saucepan full of hot water from the coppers and threatened to heave it in his face if he dared to put foot inside of the galley.

This threat produced a salutary effect, and he walked slowly away, vowing all sorts of dire vengeance against that Kanuck cook. He then went to the gangway and, laying all the blame on my poor shoulders, sent the boatmen away growling at the time and labor they had lost.

There the matter ended. The mate regained his usual good temper, and I never afterwards hung table-cloths on the topping-lifts while in a roadstead at anchor. I afterwards learned that any large object in the rigging of a vessel was a signal that we needed something from shore.

After we had been at anchor for two days a fine breeze sprung up from the east'ard, and, weighing anchor under easy sail, we rounded the south foreland and stood "down channel" past Dungeness and Beachy Head, and got down to the Isle of Wight.

There the wind died away and we were becalmed, our brig losing steerage-way.

Looking lazily over the rail I noticed a spar, which, though floating on the surface of the water, seemed fixed in one spot.

Hastening aft, I called the mate's attention to it.

At first he was disinclined to believe me, but finally sauntered to the rail and looked carefully at the floating spar.

"Why, by heavens, that's a spar-buoy," said he. "Lay aft, some of you, and lower the dingy. Be lively, lads."

The boat was soon lowered and two men jumped in her and soon reported that it was a spar-buoy, and had a long rope attached to it. We fished it up, and soon had the pleasure of hauling on board about 150 ankers of the finest French brandy, a most welcome flotsam and jetsam.

This valuable prize had, without doubt, been dropped and buoyed by some French smuggler that was being chased by an English revenue cutter.

I strongly suspected that there were more than the 150 ankers reported by the mate; from his appearance and that of the crew, and the seemingly causeless hilarity which prevailed forward, I concluded that the brandy had paid very heavy duty on its way aft.

Of course, I kept my own counsel and looked very innocent indeed, and from that day forward the mate, Mr. Williams, was my fast friend, and grudged no time or trouble to teach me all sorts of knots, hitches and splices, and to post me upon many useful and intricate points of seamanship.

The wind meantime had come west of the same quarter and freshened until it blew a whole-sail breeze, which continued for about three days, when we found ourselves tumbling about upon the boisterous waters of the Bay of Biscay. Here dirty, disagreeable weather is the almost invariable rule, and we were not to have the benefit of an exception.

All night long "Old Stormy" kept us busy; but not contented with that much, he woke us early in the morning, put a fresh hand to the bellows, and out it came, howling, from the sou'west. The canvas was greatly reduced, and we felt like singing out, "Blow, winds, and crack your cheeks." If we did not say it we thought it, and old Boreas, or some other windy god, seemed to divine our hidden thoughts and to resent them by an extra supply of what we had enough and to spare already.

Out it came from the west'ard, and we shipped tremendous seas.

I was standing near the lee main rigging, when the sea to wind'ard seemed to rise bodily, and a moving wall of water, like a tidal wave of the Pacific, came sweeping down upon us. Shouting a warning cry to the men busy at their work about decks, I sprang into the rigging, and climbed half way up to the top.

Well for me that I did so; in an instant it struck the brig; she quivered with the shock as if she had struck on a rock; the next moment she was almost hidden from sight by the watery avalanche. The galley was torn from its lashings, also the water-casks; and, plunging wildly across the decks, carried away about ten feet of the bulwarks. Through this opening the deluge of water rushed, carrying with it the greater part of our water-casks and the wreck of my galley, with an assortment of pots, pans, kettles, meats, and vegetables.

The long-boat would have shared the same fate but for the fact of being stowed on very high chocks, so that the force of the water flowed under it.

Talk about Marius amid the ruins of Carthage! What were his feelings compared with mine amid the ruins of my galley! That galley, so neat and trim, with everything in its place, and as bright as rotten-stone and elbow-grease could make it. The once well-polished caboose alone remained, and it was now a dirty, water-stained, dismantled thing, tumbled over on its side, with half its covers gone.

Well, "What's done can't be undone." We moved the caboose into the cabin, and I did the cooking there for the remainder of the passage.

We had now received our full allowance of the weather in the "Bay of Biscay, oh!" and the gale began to moderate and work round to the nor'ard sufficiently to allow us to lay our course free with the wind abaft the beam, with whole topsails, mainsail, and jib, main trysail, and reef out of the foresail.

The wind finally settling in the nor'west, with a strong but steady breeze, and good weather, we set to'-gallant sails, royals, flying jib and stun' sails, not stirring tack nor sheet for near two weeks.

Then the sailors' tongues were let loose again; for they had been somewhat restrained by rough weather and our losses, which affected our provender, and that was a serious matter. And when a sailor has had a spell of rest for his "chin-music," prepare for breakers! We had many stories of adventure and shipwreck in the Bay of Biscay, of which I remember one in particular about a sailor named 'Arry Moss—who was the hero, or rather the victim—among many others. 'Arry had sailed many times between London or Southampton or Portsmouth and the Madeira Islands in a fruit vessel, and experienced all sorts of mishaps, including shipwreck; but the end came when he, with the whole crew, were thrown on a rocky shore on a stormy night, and only one or two were so fortunate as to escape alive. This Harry, or Henry, Moss was a brother of the celebrated actress, Laura Keene, whose maiden name was Mary Moss. They reported to the owners after a long journey on foot to Boulogne, and by ship across the channel, and that was the only word that 'Arry's friends in London ever had of his fate. I afterwards saw some of his relations, and had to repeat the story of the shipwreck as I heard it from one of the surviving sailors; for tidings, even at second-hand, was news in the absence of any other. I called on 'Arry's sweetheart in Camberwell, London, and found her a quiet, middle-aged spinster, who had waited patiently for many years for her 'Arry to quit the seas, and settle down at 'ome. And that was to be his last voyage—and so it proved; but with an undesirable ending. Poor Susan! She was not black-eyed; for hers were blue. I can fancy now that I see her sitting, as she did on that cool autumn day, close to her cannel-coal fire, making a cup of tea from a sixpence-worth I had brought her. She had rooms over a second-hand dealer's store, and I have often thought of what a bewildering variety of iron things that old sinner had in his shop. What a world of work and contrivance and uses they represented! Well, Susan was only one more item added to the nearly worn-out things that once had a place in the world; but, on becoming second-hand, only desirable as curiosities, or make-shift for some service that better material cannot be spared for. This is a strange, practical, busy world, anyhow.

We put into Funchal, the capital of Madeira, for water, the Bay of Biscay having appropriated our first supply. The casks were rafted ashore, filled, and towed off to the ship, when we hoisted them on board. The Madeiras belong to Portugal, and are about 800 miles distant from that country. The language is Portuguese. The islands rise straight out of the sea, and are covered with sharp peaks, with very narrow, deep ravines between. The soil is said to be very fertile. Nearly 200,000 boxes of oranges and 20,000 pipes of wine, beside other goods, are exported yearly.

Funchal and other parts of the Madeiras are said to be a favorite resort of invalids in search of relief from one disease or another. The great change in scenery from my home in Canada, or from England, was noticed at first glance. Instead of oaks and pines, there are oranges, bananas, coffee plantations, immense palm trees, and many others, whose names I do not now recall, which make the scenery very charming.

After rafting off and hoisting our water-casks aboard, we got under way and stood on our course, passing the Canaries and Cape de Verde Islands, soon after which we fell in with the "Doldrums," or "horse latitudes."

Why this delectable part of the world rejoices in the name of "horse latitudes" is a matter which I deferentially leave to be settled by those who delight in solving abstruse problems. My humble idea is because seamen had to work like horses until, after days and nights of unceasing labor, they bade a heartfelt adieu to the "Doldrums," and at last realized the blessings of a steady breeze.

Torrents of rain—"Paddy's hurricanes," straight up and down the masts—followed each other with exasperating regularity, excepting an occasional "cat's-paw," as vain and delusive as the mirage of Sahara, holding out to us the promise of a breeze, and sending us flying to the braces, hauling to port, then to starboard, then squaring away in a manner which outrivaled the "Ancient Mariner" and surpassed the "Flying Dutchman." All on board were greatly morose and despondent, and seemed to have served

IN THE MADEIRAS.

in the army of Flanders, and to have merited honorable mention for proficiency in the catalogue of oaths.

The men ripped out imprecations upon the brig, grumbled at the wind and their own organs of vision; the mate fumed and swore, and the captain from his berth below roared more lustily than ever, "Steward, bring me a glass of brandy."

Infected by the sulphurous atmosphere which pervaded the brig, and, as the lawyers say, impelled thereto by the devil, I out of sheer malice determined to make Captain Brophy as miserable as the rest of us. I knew that he was unable to leave his berth to punish me for my capers, and I was also fully aware that the mate would chuckle at any little annoyances I might cause the captain; for Mr. Williams was very much discontented at the way in which the captain was "sogering" below, putting upon his officer's shoulders double duty and the entire responsibility of the voyage.

When, therefore, a dozen times a day the captain would roar out for his glass of brandy, I always responded cheerfully, and, taking a bottle out of the locker where it was kept, would fill out a glassful and hand it to him; but just as he would be on the point of seizing it in his eager grasp, I would sometimes make a profound obeisance, and saying, very gravely, "Here's your good health, sir, Captain Brophy; I hope your ankle will soon be well; we're all dying to see you on the quarter-deck again," I would then drain the glass, smack my lips, and, making another bow, retire amid a perfect tempest of imprecations.

Well, we did get out of the "Doldrums" at last, and falling in with the regular nor'east trades, squared away, with all stun' sails alow and aloft.

In vessels of our class it was customary for the cook to steer in the last dog-watch, from six to eight in the evening,

VIEW OF BRIDGETOWN, BARBADOES.

and in daytime to set and haul in the mainto'-gallant stun' sails from the maintop, and work the main-royal.

These duties I performed with the greatest pleasure, and endeavored, by assiduous questioning and careful observation, to learn the duties of the vocation to which I intended to devote my life.

The trade winds continued steady, and in eleven days more we made Barbadoes, and hove too off Bridgetown, the chief port, where we received orders to proceed to St. Vincent, to leeward, and the next morning dropped anchor in Kingston Roads, off Kingston, the chief town of the island.

Captain Brophy now seemed to be rapidly convalescing; as his ankle knit together, my apprehensions increased. Conscience makes cowards of us all, and I feared that he would commemorate his recovery by inscribing on my back tablets of certain hieroglyphics which would be neither agreeable nor ornamental. I therefore concluded that discretion would be the better part of valor, and determined to flee from the wrath to come. As my chief reason for preferring to ship in the *Paget* had been to get as near as possible to the "States," I now eagerly sought for an opportunity to carry out my project, and at the same time escape any undesirable acquaintance with a rope's end.

In my capacity as steward it was my duty to scull the dingy ashore every morning, and do the marketing.

On every trip made for this purpose, I paid particular attention to the names of the various craft in the roadstead, and of the ports from whence they hailed.

About a cable's length in shore of us lay a top-sail schooner, on whose stern read, *Greenville*, Washington, N. C. She had just discharged a cargo of staves, and was now preparing for sea. Here, then, was the very chance I wanted! Afraid of being seen from our own decks, and my intentions suspected, I did not dare to go on board, but waited for an opportunity to see her captain. The occasion soon presented itself.

I had sculled passed her one morning, and was close in shore, when I saw her boat, in which were two men, hauled up to the gangway, and the captain stepping in. I stepped

THE PLANTAIN.

ashore at the same moment, and going up to the captain, asked him for a passage to the "States." Without asking any questions, he said, yes; that he was very glad, as he had lost two men overboard on the outward passage, and was short-handed.

As Captain Darden was anxious to catch the land breeze, he had given orders to weigh anchor between two and three o'clock next morning, at which time we weighed anchor, made sail, and stood out to sea on our passage homeward, heading for Washington, on Tar River, North Carolina, where we arrived after a tedious passage of nearly eight days of calm and variable winds, interspersed with a mild hurricane or two, having touched at the Bermudas to repair damages such as a split mainsail, foretop sail, and so on; and where we sold a lot of plantains and cocoanuts.

We crossed Acracoke bar, Pamlico Sound, and up Tar River to the port, where, as soon as the vessel was made fast to the dock, I went on shore, and inspected the town. Washington at that time consisted of the immense number of two houses, both filled with negroes. These negroes were stevedores—slaves then—who loaded the vessels with tar and turpentine.

The soil, where it was cleared, was rich, but the negroes had no time for agriculture; for they worked often from four in the morning till eleven at night, loading vessels. So it was the custom—and it may be said, also, the local law— for their female associates to lazily till, or rather scratch, the fertile soil, and raise vegetables enough to supply the inhabitants of the "city."

The main reliance of both town and country was placed, and very justly, too, in the poultry, which, left to their own devices, thrived and multiplied amazingly, in spite of the constant depletions of their ranks by their black and white foes, and, with a praiseworthy spirit of forgiveness, filled every nook and corner with real fresh, new-laid eggs.

The pleasures of this Arcadia of the New World soon palling upon my rather fastidious taste, I shipped as second hand on board of the fore-and-aft schooner *Valiant*, seventy-two tons measurement, Captain Farrow.

This vessel was engaged in carrying freight between

BERMUDAS, OR SUMMER ISLANDS.

Washington, Philadelphia, and New York, and carried
600 barrels of tar or turpentine, 300 below hatches, and
300 on deck. Philadelphia was then but a small city
in comparison to its present vast extent. At that time there
were no houses above Fourth street. Camden, where we
discharged, had about a dozen houses.

I remained in the *Valiant* about a year and a half, receiving good wages and better food, perfecting myself in
knotting, splicing, setting up, reefing, furling, and steering,
so that at the time I parted company with Captain Farrow
at Philadelphia, and my shipmates of the *Valiant*, I felt
justified in calling myself an ordinary seaman.

On board of the *Valiant* we lived on salt makerel, corn
dodger, poultry and eggs, with Yupon tea, sweetened with
molasses, which I preferred to the China tea of commerce.
It grows on the sea islands of the Carolinas, and sells at
from ten to eighteen cents a bushel, and I think there is
money in it if cured for market.

Full of the idea of my own importance, I set out for New
York, and, finding a boarding-house, spent several days in
hunting up a ship of size sufficient to satisfy my ambition.
I was unsuccessful in all my efforts; for, although several
magnificent vessels were ready for sea, their officers seemed
to have nothing to say about shipping the crew. Speaking
of this to my boarding-master, he burst into a scornful
laugh at my verdancy, and asked me what ships I had visited.
I named several, among them the *Columbus*, Captain Depey
ster, of the famous " Black Ball Line" of Liverpool packets.

"Why, you greeny," said the boarding-master, "the
Columbus will haul out into the stream in a day or two; if
you want to ship in her, I can fix it for you in half an hour,
if you will agree to pay me ten dollars."

To this exorbitant demand I assented, and was soon in a
dingy office in South street, where, being introduced by my
boarding-master, I was accepted without demur, and signed

articles as ordinary seaman for the voyage to Liverpool and back. The *Columbus* hauled into the stream next morning, and saying good-bye to my friends at the boarding-house, I went alongside, and made the best of my way to the fo'castle, and was delighted to find it well lighted, roomy, and comfortable.

Late in the afternoon I saw two large boats, which appeared to be very heavily laden, judging from the slow progress they were making, while if the erratic course they were steering and the confused Babel of voices, shouting, cursing, swearing, yelling, and singing, were any criterion, their crews must have been drummed up in some inebriate asylum or some retreat for dangerous lunatics.

"Come on deck, Huntington," said Mr. Cornish, our chief mate, to the second officer, who was down in the cabin. "Come on deck, and see the blankety blanked lubbers coming alongside. The drunken swabs are not fit to scrape the decks of a blubber-hunter. Stand by to wake 'em up with a little belaying-pin soup, Now, then, G—d d——n your drunken souls, get on deck, and lay for'ard, will you? Lay for'ard, do you hear? What are you growling about, you blanked scoundrels? Do you know where you are, eh? I'll show you!" and, leaping down from the poop, he seized a belaying pin, and Huntington, second mate, doing the same, they began to belabor the heads and shoulders of the men, and hunted them for'ard like a flock of sheep, or rather like a drove of hogs, to the door of the fo'castle, heaving their bags in after them.

Scarcely were the men in the fo'castle when they scrambled into the first bunks they came to, and were soon sunk in a drunken sleep.

And so, thought I, this is our crew, and this is life in the fo'castle; these are to be my messmates and Cornish and Huntington are to be my superior officers, whose every command is to be obeyed, and (in appearance at least) cheerfully.

Think as much as you please, but don t think too loud, is
a very wise rule of conduct for a foremast hand.

Sooth—to say, I was horrified and disgusted, and bitterly
regretted leaving the homelike little *Greenville* and *Valiant*.
But the die was cast and retreat impossible.   There was
nothing to do except to "grin and bear it."

"Perhaps, after all, thought I, these disagreeable scenes
may not occur again, and when Captain Depeyster comes
aboard the mates will not dare to illtreat the men as they
have done."

With this faint attempt at consolation I fell asleep, only
to be roused in a few moments by the gruff voice of Mr.
Huntington calling me to stand "anchor watch."

"You'll have to stay on deck pretty nearly all night, Davis,"
said he, "for every one of those scoundrels is dead drunk.
Never mind, you can have a spell below during the forenoon to-morrow, while we're rigging out the jib-boom and
getting under way."

With these words he left me utterly dumbfounded at
the kindness of his tone, and the consideration which
prompted his promise of a "spell below."

After all, sailors are a queer compound of good and evil ;
rough diamonds, whose best qualities lie hidden beneath a
most unattractive exterior.

At times I have felt shocked and indignant at the brutality with which officers have treated their crews; at others
I have marvelled at their forbearance with the filthy, drunken
and withal notorious ruffians, who, picked up in the slums
of large seaport towns, are "shanghaied" aboard by the infernal scoundrels that infest "sailor towns" and gain a detestable living by first pandering to the follies and vices of
seamen, and then, having appropriated their advance and
stolen their outfits, kidnap them on board ship and abandon
them to the ill-treatment of their officers and the inclem-
ency of the stormy Atlantic.

Strictly speaking, there should have been four of us on duty during the anchor watch, one for each gangway, one for the to'-gallant fo'castle, and another for the afterpart of the poop. As things were, Mr. Huntington stood watch aft for two hours, and was then relieved by the chief mate. The latter came forward, and, seeing me alone, was on the point of asking me some question when he suddenly turned on his heel, looked into the fo'castle, from which, even at my post, I could hear the heavy snoring of the men. The mate stood there a moment and then muttered some imprecation on the unconscious sleepers, coupled with a very audible reference to "hazing them." He strode fiercely to the quarter-deck, and spent his whole watch in walking up and down. He then went below and the second officer reappeared but did not come for'ard.

At last, just as the stars were paling, and a faint gray streak appeared in the eastern sky, the chief mate came for'ard once more, and, seeing me still there, said abruptly:

"Look here. What's your name? Do you drink?"

"No, sir."

"How long have you been to sea?"

"About two years and three months, sir."

"In what sort of craft, and whose?"

I told him briefly.

"Hum!" said he, thoughtfully, and then raising his forefinger and holding it within an inch of my nose, he added:

"Now, youngster, you just log down what I say. You're rather young to ship before the mast in as heavy a ship as this is, and you'll find that you have a rough lot of shipmates in the fo'castle. Now, you just do your duty shipshape and Bristol fashion, as well as you can. I'll choose you in my watch to-morrow and keep a weather eye on you. If you want to know how anything is to be done I'll tell you. And now, mind you, if any of those drunken swabs try to haze you, just let me know, and I'll give them a dose to make them remember Jim Cornish and the old *Columbus*. Where are your father and mother ? "

I told him my history in a few words.

" All right.   Go below, now, and turn in ; I'll rouse you when I want you."

Well, well! thought I, wonders will never cease, and I went below with a light heart and soon was in the land of dreams.

Chapter IV.

Get up, get up, for shame, the blooming morn
Upon her wings presents the god unshorn.
See how Aurora throws her fair
Fresh-quilted colors through the air.

"All hands up anchor. D'ye hear the news? Come, turn out and pay for your lodging." Those words, shouted in a deep, gruff voice, awakened me, and I was on the point of obeying the order when I remembered that I had been told by my officers to stay below until called.

Besides the fact that I was not at all eager to participate in the hurly-burly inseparable from heaving up anchor and making sail, I thought it good policy to show that I appreciated the favor granted me.

The rest of the crew, aroused from their stupor by the repeated summons of the mate, turned out cursing and swearing, eyeing one another in anything but a pleasant manner.

Those who were most befuddled by their previous potations were unceremoniously shaken into consciousness by their shipmates, and went on deck shivering and shaking like dogs in a wet sack.

Soon after I heard the clank of the windlass and the voice of the mate. "Start him up there. Make a noise some of you. Let's have something."

But the men had a dim remembrance of their treatment the day before, and they wouldn't sing. Besides their pipes were out of tune. Their advance was gone, their clothes gone, their voices gone, and they couldn't sing; so the anchor was hove up in silence.

The tug now took our hawser and we were towed down the bay until we had got outside of the bar.

I now determined to go on deck and do my share of the

work, and was in time to witness a scene which made my
blood run cold.

"Lee main braces," shouted the mate. The men who, in
their demoralized state, had no more spirit than so many
hares, ran aft to the braces; one seaman, however, a fine-
looking fellow, a native of Chili, as he afterwards told me,
was somewhat behind the others. In a moment Cornish
was upon him with an iron belaying-pin raised. "You black
— — —, I'll teach you to 'soger' aboard this ship." Down
came the belaying-pin with a sickening thud upon the man's
head, and he fell senseless to the deck, whence he had to be
carried still insensible into the fo'castle.

This dreadful scene still further demoralized the crew,
and those who were naturally timid, realizing their disad-
vantageous position on account of their prolonged spree,
were painfully precipitate in their hurry to obey; those who
were used to the life in the Liverpool packets, and who were
case-hardened, scowled darkly and seemed to be registering
a vow that "they'd square yards with Jim Cornish before
reaching Tuskar light." The evil effects of this feeling were
soon made manifest.

All sail had been made, the tug had bidden us adieu, and
we remained with the maintopsail aback, waiting for the
steamboat which was to bring the captain and cabin passengers.

"Furl the royals. Lay aloft there, lively, some of you
youngsters." Nimble as a cat and eager to distinguish
myself, I was in the maintop-mast rigging before the others
were half way to the futtock shrouds.

Young as I was I was healthier, stronger, more active, and,
above all, more willing than my friends on the fore and
mizzen, so that I had the bunt of the sail up on the yard,
and was reaching for the gasket before either of them had
reached their yards.

I was making the bunt gasket fast to the yard rope when

I heard a crash, a fearful shriek, and the next moment saw
the poor fellow who had been in the fore-royal yard, pre-
cipitated from that dreadful height, his head striking the
cross-trees and toprim, and his body coming in contact with
the lower sternsail boom, thence falling overboard it was
lost to sight. Clots of dark blood were on the cross-trees,
toprim top of the boom, and the deck was bespattered with
his brains. Poor fellow! his fearful death was due to his
drunken shipmates, who, full of rum, hauled too taut on the
braces in laying the yard, and carried it away. This was,
indeed, a most inauspicious beginning. How I managed to
finish furling the sail and lay down from aloft I know not;
but I do know that on reaching the comparative *terra firma*
of the deck I was taken most violently sick, and had to pay
tribute to Daddy Neptune, like the veriest landsman.

At this moment the steamboat came alongside with the
captain and the cabin passengers. The captain, after shaking
hands with the mates was on the point of escorting the passengers aft to the quarter-deck, when his quick eye caught
the absence of the fore-royal yard from its accustomed
perch, and, walking a few steps forward, saw the signs of
blood on the deck. Hurriedly excusing himself he confided
the passengers to the care of the steward, and when the last
of them had disappeared he returned quickly to the mate,
and, in stern, imperious tone, said:

"What's the meaning of this, Mr. Cornish?"

"Why, sir, these drunken fellows hauled so taut on the
fore-royal braces that they carried away the yard, and one
of the light hands fell and knocked his brains out."

"My God! this is awful. Have you recovered the body?"

"No, sir!" said the mate; "it sank immediately."

"Poor fellow! poor fellow!" said the captain. "Well, Mr.
Cornish, fill away and let the ship stand on her course. By
the way, you may as well choose watches and give the men

a watch below; some of them look as if they wanted it pretty badly."

" Aye, aye, sir," said Cornish, and the captain went aft.

The crew had been attentive listeners to this conversation, and their first impressions of Captain Depeyster was extremely favorable. He was unanimously voted a real gentleman; no " raw-head-and-bloody-bones" about him.

I am glad to say that he improved on further acquaintance, and was as able an officer as he was a thorough gentleman.

He was a native of Guernsey, of the Channel Islands, and was at that time somewhat past forty years of age. His olive complexion, clean-cut features, raven black hair and piercing eyes bore testimony to his French lineage.

Mr. Cornish, the chief mate, was a tall, wiry Englishman, born in the vicinity of Liverpool, and his florid complexion and red hair and beard were true indexes to the irascible and tyrannical nature within. He was a born bully, and, like all bullies, a despicable coward. He was, at the time I had the misfortune of knowing him, about thirty-two years of age, and, to give the devil his due, an active, vigilant and efficient officer. He afterwards became captain of the *Sheridan*, a packet of the " Dramatic Line."

Mr. Huntington, the second mate, although the senior of Mr. Cornish by several years (he was over forty) was by no means as good an officer. He was thoroughly under Cornish's thumb, and seemed to pride in vieing with him in ill-treatment of the crew. He was from Rhode Island.

Now came the time to choose watches, and, as some of my readers may not understand this technical expression, I beg leave to explain it.

On board merchant ships the crew is divided into two parts, one called the starboard and the other the larboard or port watch. The port watch is commanded by the chief mate, the starboard watch by the second mate, who acts as the captain's representative.

These watches are on duty alternately, four hours on and four off, with an exception to be noted hereafter. The time is marked not by the hourly striking of a clock, but by the tolling of a bell every half hour.

Eight bells, that is, eight strokes of the bell, announce four, eight, or twelve o'clock; at every half hour after any one of those hours the bell is struck once, twice, thrice, and so on, denoting the half hours as they pass, until eight bells is struck, and the watch is changed.

This arrangement, if not modified, would divide the twenty-four hours into six parts of four hours each, and the same watch would be on duty during the same hours day and night for the whole voyage. This would be very unfair to the watch, which would have to be on deck in all sorts of weather, from four to eight in the evening, and from midnight until four in the morning. To avoid this, the evening watch from four to eight is divided into two parts, called the first and second dog (*i. e.*, dodge) watches, the first being from four to six, and the second from six to eight; the twenty-four hours are thus divided into seven parts, and by this device the required alternation of watches is attained.

"Lay aft, here, all of you," said the mate, and we all walked aft to the waist, and stood in single file along the deck, the officers standing on the main hatch.

The second mate, as the captain's representative, chose first, and then the chief mate did me the honor of being his first choice for the port watch. This was continued until all were chosen, and the chief mate sang out, "Port watch, go below," setting the example himself by turning on his heel, and going aft into the cabin, leaving Mr. Huntington and the starboard watch on duty.

We were now well clear of the land, bowling along with all stun' sails set.

I had now to make the acquaintance of my mates of the port watch, and acquire my first experience of life in the fo'castle of a Liverpool packet.

Even at the period of which I write, although emigration from the Old World was as yet in its infancy when compared with the gigantic proportions it afterwards assumed, the sailors who manned the passenger vessels between the ports of Great Britain, Northern Europe, and New York formed a class by themselves. Rarely, if ever, extending their voyages beyond the North Atlantic (nautical, the Western Ocean), and shipping, whenever it was possible, in some of the numberless packets, which then afforded the only means by which emigrants could reach the promised land of America, they were looked down upon by their brother tars of the merchant-service, who styled themselves "deep sea sailors," disclaimed all kinship with "packet rats," and "Western Ocean laborers," ranking themselves in the same category as "blubber hunters" (whalemen). These latter being, for the most part, quiet, sedate fellows, recruited principally from the country districts of New England, had no great love for either sea or seamen. They regarded the sea, the ship, and the rudiments of seamanship as they would the implements and the elementary knowledge of any other trade—namely, as means to attain the end proposed, which was nothing higher or more romantic than to get as much oil as possible, and retire upon their earnings to the seclusion of their native villages, and buy a few acres of ground, or start a country inn. To them the swaggering, roystering packet sailor was an enigma, an object of apprehension and disgust. It is needless to add that the gentlemen in "blue coats and brass buttons," viewing with the disdain born of conscious superiority all classes of seamen except their own, had a special contempt for the *mariners* of the "Black Ball," "Black Star," "Tapscott," "Swallow-Tail," and numerous other lines.

JACK ASHORE.

Whatever may have been the origin of this aversion, it certainly existed, and the packet sailors, actuated, perhaps, by sheer bravado, or by a determination to have the game as well as the name, drew deeper and broader the line which separated them from other seamen.

Ashore they were to be found in the haunts of vice and drunkenness moored head and stern in the grog-shop, inseparable from the lower class of sailor boarding-houses,

JACK TARS ON LAND.

until their money gave out, when they would be very bluntly ordered to look for a ship. In the street, dirty, drunk, and blasphemous, they were the "b——y sailor" all out. Rolling down Waterloo Road, perpetually making short tacks across the sidewalk, with a battered sou'wester, red or blue flannel shirt, belt, and huge sheath or enormous clasp-knife, tarry trousers tucked into his sea-boots, his cheek bulging out with a "chaw," and his mouth, lips and chin soiled with tobacco juice, he reflected but little credit upon the noble calling which he claimed to represent.

And yet, despite their swagger and bravado, they have little of the jaunty independence of the fine seaman; their rollicking, boisterous, roystering ways too often are the unavailing mask of hearts soured and discontented.

The lamentable truth is that they are not free agents, but are bound hand and foot by the chains forged by their own follies and vices. Their wages, small or large, are squandered in riotous profusion; they are then dependent upon rapacious boarding-masters for every morsel they eat until they succeed in getting a ship; their advance is rarely more than sufficient to meet the exhorbitant charges made for food and drink; and, unable to purchase even the most necessary articles of a sailor's outfit, they are too often compelled to face the terrible hardships of a mid-winter passage across the Atlantic without a pea-jacket, a pair of sea-boots, a suit of oil-skins, or a sou'wester.

Unfortunately, rum of the vilest quality is never wanting, and their last night on shore is spent in drunken revelry, encouraged by the watchful boarding-master, who, having drawn their advance at his favorite shipping-office, is held responsible for the appearance of his men on board at the specified time. It was his cue to egg on the men to drink themselves into a state of insensibility, in which condition they were carried down to the landing-stage, hustled into a boat, and huddled aboard the ship like so many bales of rags. What reception awaited them on deck, and what their treatment was next morning, I have endeavored to describe. For humanity's sake, let us hope that the Cornish style of officer has ceased to exist.

Besides, the weather in the North Atlantic, is, as a rule, boisterous, and permits few opportunities for real seaman-like work. Hence it follows that although in quickness in making sail, reefing or furling, they have few equals, yet the more scientific part of a seaman's avocation is never learned, or if learned, very soon forgotton through want of practise.

Roaming from ship to ship, seldom remaining in any one more than a voyage at a time, and remembering of each only the amount of hardships endured, and the cruel tyranny of such a mate or such a captain, it inevitably follows that they have no affection for any ship, nor pride in her reputation.

Let not my readers imagine that this description of the packet sailor is intended to apply to all. There are many, very many exceptions; men who lead sober, chaste, industrious lives; married men with helpless little families, who have been compelled to adopt this life on account of the shortness of the voyage and the high rate of wages; men who, worthy of all praise as faithful husbands and loving, self-sacrificing parents, are, at the same time, models of endurance, having in privation and hardship, and in the hour of danger, the education, skill, and all that constitutes true seamanship.

But while in the fo'castle the follies and vices of the many are redeemed by the virtues of the few, the tyranny and cruelty of the inmates of the cabin are almost without exception. Numberless are the Cornishes and Huntingtons, few indeed the Depeysters.

And here, let me say to my friends on shore who have never sailed the ocean blue, do not imagine that the acts of tyranny and brutality described in these pages are invented and exaggerated, or painted in too lively colors. I solemnly aver that they are strictly true. In describing them I have "naught extenuated, nor aught set down in malice." In proof of this I refer you to the records of our courts and the files of our own daily papers. It was only a few days ago, December 16–22, 1884, that I read in one of our New York papers of the trial of the captain of the *I. M. Chapman*, an American vessel, for murder. That worthy had, for some trifling offence, seized up by the thumbs a Russian sailor, and kept him in torture until the man died

The newspapers report all such cases in our day, but " such shames are common."

But revénous á nos moutons, or rather let us go down into the fo'castle of the *Columbus.*

Let our kind reader imagine himself opposite a low and narrow doorway, from which dirty and greasy steps descend almost perpendicularly into the obscurity below. Dark and dismal is the pit most certainly, and it is the source of as many separate and distinct varieties of noisome odors as the far-famed City of Cologne; strange noises, too, in the shape of indistinct mutterings and deep-drawn growls and unmusical snores issue from the cavern, and uncouth figures flit to and fro in the obscurity.

This, my cabin friend, is the fo'castle, the home of the sailor. Be not afraid; pluck up courage and let us descend. I can promise neither edification nor amusement, but can most certainly guarantee that your adventure shall be free from peril and replete with novelty.

These steps are rather slippery, and, as the ship is beginning to roll somewhat, you had better descend with your face to the ladder and your hands on the sides. Unless you adopt that precaution your descent may be undesirably rapid, and your introduction to the sailors' quarters unaccompanied by that easy grace and languid interest which betokens those of the ship's company who inhabit that part of the ship which lies abaft the main-mast.

There, that was well done! Here you are, then. Now, keep a good hold of that stanchion and look around you. Take care not to let your feet slip on the deck, as she rolls to leeward.

You must excuse the disorder in which you find us; we have just moved in, and everything is at the bottom and nothing on top; the servants have not scrubbed the floor yet, and may forget to do so, and our new carpet has not been unpacked; but in a few days we shall have our chandeliers up and the curtains hung in front of our berths, and then we shall set our table and bring out our china, and plates, and knives and forks.

Yes, it does look rather odd. The triangular shape of our apartments, and the constant thundering of the seas at our very ears are not conducive to slumber. In fact, we were on the point of remonstrating with the captain, and requesting him either to alter the course of the ship so as to avoid the annoyance, or to assign us quarters in another part of the vessel. The cabin itself would not be too good for us.

Much more valuable and correct information would I have imparted to my inquisitive friend had not a terrific explosion of laughter burst from the recesses of the fo'castle, in which I was forced to join; whereupon my friend, in a state of thorough mystification and no small alarm, beat a precipitate and very undignified retreat up the steps, and stopped not until he had gained the poop, where, to judge from Captain Depeyster's merriment, he was relating to that officer the strange and exciting experience of his first, and, no doubt, last visit to the quarters of the "common sailors."

Well, the fo'castle was, like other fo'castles, triangular in shape, because inside the bow of the ship; two rows of bunks extended on each side of the bulkhead which separated the fo'castle from the between decks. The bottom of the lower bunks was about two feet from the fo'castle deck, the bottom of the upper bunk about three feet from the deck, and three feet between both bottoms, making the height in the fo'castle eight feet.

The sea-chests of the crew were securely lashed at the foot of the owners' bunks, and served a double purpose, namely, as receptacles for clothes and tobacco, with mending gear, and as seats on which their owners sat to enjoy their frugal meals.

Sooth to say, the crew of the good ship *Columbus* were, for the most part, in no very great need of sea-chests. Like

Paddy, who, when asked why he did not get a chest to put his clothes in, very naively and inquiringly answered, "And me go naked?"

My shipmates, thanks to the attentions of the pawn-broker, the rum-seller, and the boarding-master, were comparatively unimpeded with baggage, and not a few veterans faced the winds and waves of the North Atlantic in a suit of dungaree.

To describe at length the attire of the crew, their food, drink, and bedding, the routine of their life at sea, and the hardships inseparable therefrom, would be, in my humble opinion, a waste of words, because there was, and is, in such cases a never-ending variety of dress. The jolly-sad poet, Thomas Hood, has touched off many a point in Jack's rig, one of which I quote here:

> " His hat was new, or, newly glazed,
>   Shone brightly in the sun;
> His jacket, like a mariner's,
>   True blue as e'er was spun;
> His ample trousers, like St. Paul,
>   Bore forty stripes in one."

Many, very many, of my readers have had ample opportunity for seeing for themselves what my pen could by no means describe to my satisfaction; and those who have never ploughed the briny deep have, if they indulge in maritime literature, read and re-read graphic descriptions of life in the fo'castle. To surpass, or even to rival, those pen-pictures would necessitate a more facile pen, and an imagination more fertile and more vivid than I possess.

In sober truth, Jack's life in the fo'castle is very dull, and intolerably prosaic.

His clothing, something like Joseph's coat, is of many colors, and of many patches.

His menu is tough salt beef, very lean or very fat; mouldy and measly pork; biscuits remarkable for age and toughness, and for the weevils which therein do live and thrive. Milk is known to him by name; sugar is represented by molasses, and the tea and coffee so sweetened are fearful and wonderful decoctions of some herb or bean unknown to the denizens of Araby the blest, or the almond-eyed dwellers in far Cathay. The use of canned milk and vegetables has come into vogue since I left the salt sea, but I presume Jack has heard very little of it.

The crew of the *Columbus* was the usual mixture of good, bad and indifferent. Passable seaman, but unpleasant ship-mates. Few days passed without a wordy wrangle, which not unfrequently ended in blows. Thrown together for a few weeks, they did not form, nor did they care to form, those friendships so usual among seamen accustomed to long voyages.

For the ship they had no affection; for their officers, with the exception of Captain Depeyster, they felt the most bitter dislike, and longed for a quick run, which would enable them to desert before their month was up, and afford them an opportunity to square yards with " Jimmy Cornish, and that slab-sided, lantern-jawed sneak of a Huntington.'

As the winds continued favorable, and as Captain Depeyster was famous for carrying on a press of sail, we made a splendid run across, and in sixteen days sighted Tuskar Light. Next day, being abreast of Holyhead, we took a pilot, and soon afterwards a powerful tug took our hawser, and before night we were in Prince's Dock.

Scarcely had the ship's bow touched the pier-head, when half the crew leaped ashore, and went scurrying like mad-men towards the gates. Foremost among them was the Chilian whom the chief mate had knocked down off Sandy Hook. Pursuit was useless, and Cornish had to content himself with a volley of imprecations against the delinquents.

As the dock regulations forbid the use of fires or lights, the crews of all vessels have to board on shore. Our men boarded with a Mrs. Hughes, in Union street, near the dock, but long before the *Columbus* was ready for her voyage home, her ship's company was reduced to five, myself included.

Even the four who remained with me would have followed the example of their shipmates were it not that they were married men, and thus mutually desirous to revisit their families in New York.

SAILOR BOARDING HOUSE.

Of Liverpool, I saw very little, and that little was "Sailor Town."

At last the *Columbus* was ready for sea; we hauled out of the dock, and made fast to the pier-head outside the dock-gates, where we received about 700 steerage and ninety cabin passengers, and where we were to lay until our crew should be recruited up to its complement.

We were now destined to experience some more of the consequences of Cornish's and Huntington's brutality. The men who had made the passage with us from New York had not failed to describe, in the most vivid language, the tyrannical conduct of that worthy pair, and the Chilian, well known in more than one boarding-house and shipping-office, and universally respected as a quiet, sober, and most thorough seaman, was questioned again and again, and forced to repeat all the circumstances of his ill-treatment by Cornish, until the *Columbus* achieved a most unenviable notoriety, and was not unfrequently spoken of as the "hell afloat."

Now, reckless as that class of seamen are usually, they do not fancy insults, curses, blows, and kicks as a steady diet more than other men; and they know that to submit to such treatment is worse than negro slavery, and to resent it, mutiny or death.

It is, "kill or be killed;" and the alternative is not pleasant to contemplate.

Hence the shipping articles of the *Columbus* remained unsigned for eight days, with our passengers aboard, pilot engaged, and tug waiting all that time, with a fine spell of easterly winds blowing, while we were endeavoring to ship our crew.

At last, urged on by their boarding-house keepers, taunted with cowardice, and, above all, forced by their own necessities, a gang of men walked down to the shipping-office, and signed articles.

Having thus bound themselves, they met the inquisitive questions of their friends and the rough bantering of their acquaintances with resolute silence, and, refusing all invitations to drink, they marched off to one of the boarding-houses, and had a long conversation, the results of which became apparent during the course of the voyage home.

Meanwhile, Cornish and Huntington were in a frenzy of passion. Captain Depeyster was out of temper at the delay, and fumed at seeing ship after ship leave the docks, get its crew aboard, and proceed to sea, with rousing songs, saluting our ship in passing with derisive groans as "Old hell afloat." Perfectly aware of the causes which led to this disgrace, he summoned Cornish and Huntington to him, and gave them both a sound rating, which added fresh fuel to their wrath.

Well, one fine morning while the captain and both mates were moodily pacing the quarter-deck their attention was suddenly riveted towards a gang of men marching from the direction of the boarding houses on Gibraltar row, and coming toward the pier-head to which we were fast.

They were our long-expected crew. They halted at our gangway, and, springing lightly on deck, they assisted one another to get their dunnage on board, and carried forward, whither they followed it. They were evidently acquainted with one another for some time, for it was Joe, Bill, Tom, Dick and Charlie, whenever anything was needed.

The captain and officers looked on in silence, and the former beckoning to the clerk from the shipping-office, had an earnest conversation with him near the taffrail.

We who had made the voyage out in the *Columbus* were delighted at the stalwart appearance of our new shipmates, and gave them a right hearty welcome to the fo'castle. Every man of them was perfectly sober, and they seemed to know all about the ship, as if they had been apprenticed aboard of her.

To our stories about Cornish and Huntington their stereotyped reply was but a muttered oath, and a dark and meaning glance under their eyebrows at one another.

Finally, as the summons: "All hands on deck!" broke up our conference, one of them, who had hitherto listened in silence, "Joe Winrow" by name, brought his fist down on

his sea-chest with a blow like that of a pile-driver, and, in a
voice husky with suppressed passion, said: "The man that
lays a finger on any one of us shall have to tackle me, or my
name's not Winrow!" "That's so, Joe! So say we all. Aye,
aye," rose in loud chorus from all hands.

"Well, then, belay that; haul in the slack of your jaw-
tackle and lay on deck. Here comes some one of the after-
guard."

"Fo'castle, there. Bear a hand."

"Aye, aye, sir!" and, after a gesture of caution from Winrow, we hurried on deck.

Then, indeed, we of the old crew realized the value of our
new shipmates. The tug was ahead and a pilot on board.
A heaving-line was hove on board of us for the hawser,
which was payed out and double-bitted, at the same time
the pier-head fasts were hauled on board, the tug started,
and we were homeward bound.

Then came the order: "Set the topsails, jib spanker and
courses." The men sprang aloft like squirrels, and after
letting the topsails fall, and, sliding down the backstays,
hauled home the sheets, and, with a rousing chorus, mast-
headed the yards, which were braced to a firm breeze from
east sou'east. Meanwhile the jib, spanker and courses had
been loosed, tacks boarded and sheets trimmed down. By
this time the tug had let go of our hawser; hands now sprang
aloft to loose to'-gallant sails while the hawser was being
hauled on board and coiled away on the fore-hatch. Top-
gallant sails were now set and decks cleared, and running
rigging coiled up, and every movable about deck lashed.

All orders were anticipated, the men were on the spot ere
the words were spoken.

Evidently, we had a picked crew, for they resembled one
another not only in bodily proportions, but also in ability
as seamen.

"Got a fine crew, there, Captain," said the pilot, a veteran whose grizzly beard well nigh covered a face on which many a year of hardship had left its imprint. "Fine crew, sir. Many of them fellows has sailed out of Liverpool for nigh onto twenty years. They're no or'narys, I can tell ye."

The captain nodded assent. He had been intently watching every movement of the men from the moment they came on board. His face had lighted up with pleasure when he saw the rapidity with which sail had been made on the ship, and the intelligent alacrity that proved their proficiency in seamanship; yet now, as the pilot spoke, a cloud came over the captain's face and he glanced uneasily towards the spot where Cornish was standing.

"Yes; they seem to be fine active fellows, pilot. I hope we shall have a pleasant passage, and sight the Highland lights three weeks from to-day. We've lost too much time already waiting for our crew; now that we have them I trust our trouble is over."

"Yes, I heard about that," said the pilot; "that boy that was lost from the fore-royal yard left a widowed mother in Union street, and that other fellow, a sort of dog, or some sort of a foreigner, has been telling queer stories about the mates. Mr. Cornish didn't go ashore much, eh? 'Twouldn't have been healthy for him to cruise around Gibralter Row after dark. 'Twould be good-bye, Cornish, I tell you."

"That's what troubles me," said Captain Depeyster; "I fear some altercation between the mates and the men."

"And a haltercation they'll have, I'll be bound, with a halter in it for somebody, if Cornish or Huntington tries any of their didoes with them fellows."

Good for you, old surly, thought I, as I passed around the poop, eagerly drinking in every word uttered. At this rate belaying pins won't be flying around quite so lively as they were off the Hook.

In a few hours we were abreast of Holyhead, when, after discharging our pilot, we set all royals and flying-jib with all our larboard stern-sails, and stood down channel with the wind a little abaft the beam.

The watches were now chosen, and the old hands of the *Columbus* seemed to have the preference, a significant fact which caused looks of covert meaning to pass among the new-comers.

I found myself again in the chief mate's watch with two of my old shipmates and ten others.

"Joe Winrow" was in the starboard watch, being the very last man chosen, a slight which he met with the most perfect indifference, correctly attributing it to its true source.

All hands were kept on deck during the first day, and the wind continuing to blow from the east sou'east the men were not disturbed during the night.

Next day, being now abreast of Tuskar Rock, and the wind hauling more aft, all hands were kept busy getting everything shipshape.

About two in the afternoon (the wind having hauled round to our starboard quarter, we were shifting our stun' sails over to starboard), one of the new hands, Cornelius Emery, "a Boston boy," was aloft on the starboard foretop sail yard-arm, rigging out the fo'to'-gallant-stun' sail boom, when the second mate, Huntington, wishing, no doubt, to assert his authority, sung out: "Bear a hand, you son of a b——h!" The new comers, scattered all over the deck, cast a glance aloft to see who was thus addressed, and an ominous tightening of belts ensued. Cornelius Emery instantly laid in from the yard-arm, and, shaking himself well together, came rapidly down the fore-rigging, and, jumping on deck, made a rush for the astounded Huntington, knocking him down and kicking him. Huntington shouted for assistance, and Cornish, hearing the uproar, first shouted for Captain Depeyster, and then, armed with his favorite weapon, an iron belaying-pin, came rushing forward, frothing with rage.

"I'll teach you, you mutinous scoundrel. I'll let you know that "——

His didactics were cut short. Starting from his work in the fore-rigging, "Joe Winrow" thrust his athletic form between Emery and the chief mate, wrenched the belaying-pin out of his grasp, and then with one terrific blow split his cheek from his eye to his mouth, and tumbled him in a heap upon the deck, the blood spouting in torrents from the wound.

"You wanted first blood, did you? Now you've got it! I've writ 'Joe Winrow, his mark,' on your figure-head, any how. Let the beggars up, Corneil; here comes the after-guard."

Sure enough, Captain Depeyster, hurrying on deck upon Cornish's call, was just in time to see Huntington lying helpless, Cornish felled like a log by "Joe Winrow," and the whole crew rushing to take part in the fray. Fearing the worst, he hurried into the cabin, and opening the arm-chest, distributed pistols to the more resolute of the cabin passengers, and, hastily explaining to them the dangerous turn things had taken, bade them follow him and returned on deck.

"Joe Winrow," who was now tacitly acknowledged as leader, saw the captain come on deck and return to the cabin. Divining his purpose he determined to prepare for defense.

"See here, lads, them two fellows aren't so badly hurt but what they can point a pistol. The old man will muster the cabin gang. Any of you got pistols better get them lively. Jump for them capstan bars and handspikes; get them heavers, some of you."

We were pretty well armed, and had thrown up a sort of breastwork across decks, when the captain appeared with the officers and about ten of the cabin passengers.

Cornish and Huntington had had their wounds dressed,

and now advanced flourishing their pistols, Cornish breath
ing death and destruction.   The captain, when he saw the
barricade and the whole ship's company ranged, armed, silent
and resolute behind it, grew pale, and, turning aft, began a
hurried consultation with the passengers.

This hesitation did not satisfy the officers, and they
vehemently insisted upon crushing out the mutiny and
making an example of the ringleaders.   They were exaspe-
rated beyond endurance by the indifference with which Depeyster treated their alleged injuries and wrongs, and continued to demand that measures should be adopted which
would strike terror into the hearts of the crew.

The captain now came forward to within a few feet of
our barricade, motioning to the others to remain at the
main hatch.

"Now, men," began he—— "Put the scoundrels in
irons," shouted Huntington.   "No parleying with mutineers, Captain Depeyster.   Come on; let's shoot them like
dogs," roared Cornish.

"Mr. Huntington, you may retire to the quarter-deck.
Mr. Cornish, go to your state-room; you are relieved from
duty until further orders."

At these words Cornish and Huntington slunk away like
whipped curs, and the men raised a hearty shout, "Hurrah
for Captain Depeyster," and, throwing down their weapons,
removed the barricade and came to meet him.

"Now, men; now, men; what's all this?   What's the use of
all this?   Come, now, turn to and let's hear no more of it."

"Captain Depeyster, sir, we all know you, a gentleman
and a seaman; and we know Cornish and Huntington, and
they're a pair of d—d tyrants.   Now, if this thing is to be
called square we're satisfied, always providing that you let
them gents understand that they're not going to kill anyone
on this passage if we can help it."

"Well, so be it, my men, and now turn to and do your duty like men."

"Aye, aye, captain," and so the "mutiny" ended.

"Joe Winrow," the ringleader in this, died last winter in San Francisco at the age of 75 years.—1884.

"A true and ardent vindicator of human rights."—DAVIS.

Huntington reappeared sulky and crest-fallen. Cornish remained below for two or three days, and whether from loss of blood or from fear of losing his position in the "line" and imperiling his prospects for promotion, he was very quiet and dejected during the rest of the passage.

Thus did a few resolute men establish their right to decent treatment before we were clear of St. George's Channel. But how seldom is there courage and resolution enough on board a vessel to resist cruel officers. The majesty of the law is ever at the back of the officers but is so slow to defend poor Jack. As this proof-sheet was passing under my eye I noticed, in the New York Daily *Sun* of June 25th, that the New York Society for the Prevention of Cruelty to Sailors has been incorporated by Hamilton Fish, August Belmont, Cyrus W. Field, Elbridge T. Gerry, Elihu Root, Cornelius N. Bliss, Chester A. Arthur, John T. Agnew, William B. Dinsmore, Henry Bergh, Richard A. Elmer, Edward Schell, and John E. Develin. It proposes to help the law look after poor Jack and those who ill treat and rob him, and to promote his physical and moral welfare. I feel sure that these men intend to carry out their declaration to benefit poor Jack, and sincerely hope that no wolf in sheep's clothing, or shark in disguise, will succeed in thwarting their endeavors. There has been a great change since Cornish's day. Cruelty to a seaman, if it results seriously, is sometimes brought into court, as the newspapers report. But why not establish the rule that ruffianly conduct on shipboard, as well as on land, is all the same? No employer on land drives his men around with a marlinspike or crowbar, or if he does, to the serious injury of a man, the courts can be appealed to at once. On sea the laborer is more precious than on land, because if killed or lost overboard, he cannot be replaced so readily as on land, and the protection of the law should be the more certain against all wrongs. Until that is true, and known to be so by seamen, every sailor is a possible mutineer in self-defense, when officered by Huntingtons and Cornishes. And while we are overhauling this part of our ship's log, it may be well to reel off one of the many yarns that were spun in the fo'castle, and which was suggested by our recent experience. We had only the premonitory symptoms of a mutiny, and they were allayed by a kind-hearted and sensible captain; but mutinies do occur from brutal treatment and bad grub, as the tale I am about to repeat shows.

When you come to speak of dreadful things, you may set it down that a mutiny at sea can be classed first. It is in most cases the turning of the worm. Men who have had it drilled into them for years that they must put up with such food as hogs would refuse, obey every order without question, peril their lives at the word, cringe and tremble before one of their own species because he is in authority, are not to be driven into mutiny on the high seas without extreme provocation.

When the worm turns, then look out!

Your cringing foremast hand, who only the day before thanked the mate for knocking him down, may be a tyrant in turn.

The ship becomes a floating hell. The slaves of yesterday are the masters to-day. If once they take the step which renders them mutineers, they will not hesitate to go further, and add murder to the crime.

This is how Jack Allen, of Providence, R. I., spun his yarn:

In the year 1845, after having served on coasting vessels for several years, and made one voyage from New York to Liverpool, I shipped as second mate on the bark *Medway*, bound from San Francisco to the Sandwich Islands, and thence on a trading voyage to the islands of the southwest. The bark was a small one, but a good sailer, and a dry ship, and I believed I was in luck in securing my berth. The captain, whose name was Burrows, seemed a very pleasant man, making use of no profane language, and appearing to be as mild-tempered as a parson. Mind you, I am giving my first impressions as I sized him up while we yet lay at the wharf. I shipped at Honolulu, the bark having already completed the first part of her voyage. I heard rumors to the effect that her whole crew deserted her on her arrival at the islands, but rumors among sailors are not to be depended on, and I gave the matter no investigation, though I saw that she was shipping a fresh crew. We left Honolulu with twelve men before the mast, and we were not yet off soundings when trouble began. The meat which had been boiling away in the cook's coppers during the forenoon gave out strange odors. From the whiffs I had caught now and then I knew something was wrong, and when the meat was carried forward in the kids at noon the stench was enough to turn one's stomach. The mate, whose name was Berry, saw that I was surprised such meat should be placed before the men on a voyage just begun, and he growled:

"Ah, d——n 'em; it's too good for such as they. Just let me catch 'em making a fuss over it, and I'll work up their old iron in a way to open their eyes!"

I was astounded. Mr. Berry had seemed a quiet, even-tempered man, and I had said to myself that there would be no bullying aboard of the *Medway*. The watches had not yet been set, but the bark was on her course before a light breeze, and things were being made ship-shape. The captain was already at dinner, and soon after uttering the

remarks quoted above, the mate went down to join him.   I
was thus left in charge of the deck, but the crew, with the
exception of the man at the wheel, went forward with their
kids.   As the beef made its appearance, there was a movement of surprise, and I heard several of them utter expressions of disgust.   The meat was picked up and closely
examined, and then all faces were turned in my direction.
Then, after a brief consultation, an old sailor, whose every
look and action proved the genuine tar, picked up the
meat-tub, and came aft with it.   He was going to make a
complaint, which he had a perfect right to do, and I, as
officer of the deck, had no right to refuse to listen.   He put
down the tub, doffed his hat, and very respectfully said:

"Mr. Allen, the meat isn't hardly fit to bait a shark.   It
is probably the fault of the cook.   Will you kindly forward
our complaint to the captain?"

At that moment Captain Burrows appeared on deck.
Taking in the situation at a glance, he walked straight up
to the sailor and thundered :

"What in hell's name does this mean, you dog?   Finding
fault with your provisions before the first meal is begun !
Get forward, you infernal whelp !"

The man retreated without a word in reply, but left the
tub behind him.   I'm telling you the solemn truth when I
say that the odor of it was enough to turn my stomach
seven or eight feet away.

"It's just like 'em, the hounds !" roared the captain.
"It's the beef they find fault with, eh ?   Here, every mother's
son, come aft ! "

The men slowly obeyed, knowing that a storm was at
hand.   The captain picked up the tub, held it out toward
them, and said : "Is there anything wrong with this meat ?
Who says this isn't as sweet beef as was ever placed before
sailors ?   Who is the man ? "

For a minute not one of them answered him.   Then the

man who had brought the tub aft stepped out, made a respectful salute, and replied : "Captain Burrows, we didn't find fault with you, but with the cook. The meat is so far gone that no man aboard can eat it."

"Oh, it's bad, is it?" sneered the captain, as he placed the tub in my hands. 'No one can eat it, eh? Let's see about that."

With his naked fingers he lifted up a piece and bit off a mouthful and swallowed it. At that moment the mate appeared on deck, and the captain called : "Mr. Berry, the men declare this meat unfit to eat. Come and taste it, and give me your opinion."

The mate came forward and tasted it. I saw him wince as he chewed at the stuff, but he bravely swallowed it down, and exclaimed : "The best beef I ever saw aboard a ship!"

"You whelps ! You hounds ! You gang of lazy sojers, but I'll teach you to find fault !" screamed the captain, as he threw the tub at the nearest sailor ; and then he dashed among them, followed by the mate, and four or five men were knocked down and kicked about in the most brutal manner. Not one of them made any attempt at resistance, and they were not followed beyond the foremast.

"There ! I guess they've had an introduction to me, and will hereafter know how to brace their yards," chuckled the captain as he came aft. "I run this craft, Mr. Allen and I want every man aboard to know it. I want no man in the cabin who coddles the fo'castle. Why didn't you knock the dog down when he came aft with the beef?"

"Captain Burrows," I replied, "I was never aboard of a vessel yet where the master would not listen to a complaint when respectfully and regularly set forth."

"Oh, you weren't ! And so I've got a second mate who can teach me something. How very fortunate I am ! Let me say to you, sir, that you had better go slow. I can break you and send you forward among the men, and I'll do it if you give me the slightest excuse."

With that he turned and went below. In a little time the watches were named and set, and as I was ready to turn in the mate took occasion to observe :

" The old man is a little headstrong, but it needs a strong hand over these fellows.   If once you begin to palaver with 'em they'd demand cabin stores within a week."

" But the meat was horrible."

" Well, I've seen better; but they had no business to kick up a row over it.   They're lucky to get meat of any sort."

I went below realizing that I had shipped aboard a floating hell, and that my position was a precarious one.   As for following the example of captain and mate I would not, and if I was degraded and sent forward—a matter which lay entirely with the captain—I had better go overboard at once.   Had the captain been a just and mild-tempered man the mate would have been under restraint.   As the captain had taken the lead and shown that he intended to govern by kicks and blows, the mate felt free to exercise his brutal nature.   Within half an hour after I had left the deck he forced an excuse for knocking one of the men down, and an hour later he reported to the captain that he had never sailed with such a gang of mutinous dogs.

During my night watch I saw and heard enough to realize that a feeling of deep indignation had taken hold of the crew, and that it needed only another act of brutality to incite rebellion.   The man at the wheel invented an excuse to speak to me, and presently observed:

" Some of the men feel pretty sore, Mr. Allen, and I hope they won't be driven to——"

He did not finish the sentence, and I said:

" Let them take their grievances before the first American consul.   There are laws to protect the sailor as well as the officer."

"But who of us ever saw those laws enforced, sir ? Jack is a dog at sea, and a nobody ashore. The captain tells his story to the Consul, and if Jack follows after he's more likely to be sent to prison than to receive justice."

I could not gainsay it, and I, as an officer of the ship, had no right to encourage a spirit of complaint. Sailor men will stand poor rations and the most brutal abuse so long as they are without a leader. What had happened during the day might have been passed over and forgotten had not the scenes been renewed. The mate came on deck in bad temper, and as my watch turned in he was abusing his for their tardiness in answering the call, though I never saw a quicker change on any craft. It happened that the man who had acted as spokesman in regard to the beef was the last one out of the fo'castle. It was no wonder, for several of his teeth had been loosened and one of his eyes closed by the blows, and he was probably stiff and sore. As I went down the companion I heard the mate shouting:

"Ah! you infernal skulker, but I'll cure you of this! If you've come aboard this bark to sojer and live on sweet cake, you want to look out for me!"

I turned in sick at heart, now realizing that there would be no let up on the part of captain or mate to the end of the voyage. It did not seem as if 1 had been asleep half an hour, though in reality three hours had passed, when some one pulled at my arm, and a voice said:

"Mr. Allen, you are wanted on deck, sir."

"Who is it ?" I asked.

"It's me, sir—James Martin. Will you come on deck at once ?"

I knew that the man was a common sailor, though I did not know any of them by name as yet. I reached the deck a minute behind him. The bark was on her course, but the breeze was very light. To my astonishment I found most

of the men aft, and I was no sooner on deck than I saw that
something was very wrong.

"Mr. Allen" said the man who had complained of the
beef, and whose name was Johnson, "the *Medway* is in our
possession. We have been driven to mutiny."

"It can't be!" I exclaimed, as I looked about.

"But it is true, sir, and now we want to know whether
you are going to stand by us or side with the captain?"

"Where is the captain?"

"Lying over there in the lee scuppers, bound hand and
foot. The mate went overboard half an hour ago."

I walked over to where the captain was lying. He was
securely bound, but no harm had come to him as yet. He
was, however, in mortal terror, and as soon as he set eyes
on me he called out in broken tones:

"Mr. Allen, for God's sake, save my life! Don't let them
murder me in cold blood!"

As I looked from captain to mutineer, Johnson said:

"The mate was among us with a belaying-pin, seeming
bent on murder, and we had to do for him. Then we rea-
soned that we might as well be hung for a sheep as a lamb,
and we secured the captain."

"Men, you have done a terrible thing! Don't you know
every one of you will swing for this?"

"We want no preaching, Mr. Allen," replied Johnson.
"What we want to know is, how you stand? The mate has
gone, and the captain must follow. If you will navigate the
bark for us, no harm shall come to you. If you refuse, then
we shall set you adrift. We've gone too far to back water."

"Talk to 'em, Mr. Allen," gasped the captain, who was
greatly broken down. "Tell 'em that if they will spare our
lives they shall not be punished for what they have done. I
give my word they shan't."

"What will you do with him?" I asked.

"Set him adrift in the yawl at daybreak."

"And if I refuse to navigate the bark ?"

"You go with him, though we'd be sorry for it, for you've used the men right."

"What point do you wish to make?"

"The coast of Brazil."

"Will you all sign a paper to the effect that I had nothing to do with bringing about this mutiny, and that I navigated the bark under duress ?"

"We will that!" they shouted in chorus.

"Very well, I will remain; but why not keep the captain a prisoner instead of sending him adrift?"

"He must be punished, sir," replied Johnson.

I argued with 'em together and separately, but it was no use. They had decided on a course, and could not be swerved from it. Captain Burrows was a cringing coward. He begged, entreated, and sought to bribe, and when day fully broke he hadn't the heart of a woman. A man was sent aloft with a glass to survey the sea, and when he came down and reported the waters clear of sail the yawl was lowered, a keg of water, some of the spoiled meat, and a lot of wormy biscuits were placed in it, and they were ready to send the captain adrift. His cowardice was so great that one could not pity him. He had to be lowered over the side like a bail of rags, and as his boat floated away he cowered down on the bottom, and seemed to fall into a stupor. When he was half a mile astern Johnson called every man aft and said :

"Now, men, Mr. Allen is to be our captain, and he is to be promptly obeyed. I shall be first mate, Peterson second, and, though we berth in the cabin, you shall have just as good food as we do. We will now name the watches, and things will go on as if there had been no trouble."

His word was not questioned. There was no exultation, no lawlessness, no boasting. Every man was quiet and thoughtful. They had been wronged. They had righted that wrong in their own way, and were now simply seeking to make a safe escape. In twenty minutes after the captain was set afloat you could not have told that anything out of the routine had happened. The decks were washed down, breakfast prepared, and when things had been cleared away Johnson came down into the cabin and said :

"Mr. Allen, how far are we out from the Sandwich Islands ?"

"Not to exceed seventy miles."

"Very well; you will please give us the course for the Paumotu Islands."

I got out the charts, gave him the course, and followed him on deck. Everything was ship-shape, the men as respectful as you please, and it was hard to realize that anything like mutiny and murder had occurred. It seemed as if the very winds looked upon the revolution with favor, for the breeze hauled to our best sailing point and sent us along hour after hour and day after day until we were far to the south of the Sandwich Islands.

I am telling you now what I afterward swore to, that a better crew never trod a deck. There was no wrangling, no drinking, and not the least indication of insubordination. When we came to overhaul the ship's stores we found four-fifths of them as fresh and sound as any sailor could ask for. The other portion must have been put in by the captain on some speculation.

Near the line of the equator we had light winds and calms for several days, but finally got a slant which carried us to the south until we got a holding breeze, and one afternoon we sighted the islands for which we had long been headed. The group comprises fifty or more islands, with those of the Society, Cook, and Tabna lying just to the south. At this day most of the islands are inhabited. At that date only a few of them were, and there were not above three or four ports of call, mainly for the convenience of whalers in want of vegetables and water. The bark had planned to visit the Marshall, Gilbert, and Phœnix Islands, lying near the equator, and much nearer Honolulu. The Paumotu Islands had been selected by the mutineers because two of them had once been wrecked among them, and spent a year or more in leading a half-civilized life.

Before dark we had made a safe anchorage, and, though the voyage was now ended, discipline still remained as strict as ever. That evening Johnson came down to me and said:

"Mr. Allen, the voyage is ended. You have done as you agreed, and you must admit that the men have been well behaved. Will you go with us to-morrow or stick by the bark?"

"I must stand by the craft."

"Just as you say, sir. This is a sheltered spot, and we will leave you in good shape. We shall take the long boat, some spare sails, a few stores and other things, but nothing to cripple the bark. Good-night, Mr. Allen."

The next day the longboat was hoisted out, and the men took some muskets, a few hatchets, kettles to cook in, fishing tackle, tobacco, pipes, and a keg of rum, and finished off with shipstores enough to last 'em for a couple of weeks. There was over $2,000 in gold in the cabin, and as Johnson knew it the others must have known it as well, but not a man asked for a dollar. It was 3 o'clock in the afternoon before they were ready to go, and the last two hours were spent in making everything snug. All the light sails were sent down and put into the sail room, and the others were carefully stowed. The second anchor was dropped, and the captain's dingey was hoisted out and made fast alongside for my use if I wanted to go ashore. Then every man signed the paper I had drawn up, and as they went over the side each one took my hand and bade me good-by. I never saw one of them again.

Six weeks later a Massachusetts whaler discovered the

Medway in her snug berth, and, as she happened to have the crew of a wrecked vessel aboard, I had no trouble in securing a complement of men to return the bark to San Francisco. The captain, as was afterward learned, had drifted two days before he was picked up by a trading steamer, but he died several days after his rescue. So far as I know no steps were ever taken to overhaul the mutineers, as after my statement in the courts public sympathy was altogether in their favor.

———

We stowed anchors abreast of the Old Head of Kinsale, and after lashing the spare spars, and securing the water-casks, were fairly on our voyage.

When in about thirty degrees west longitude, the wind blowing very fresh from the northeast, and the ship staggering along under a heavy press of canvas, we had the misfortune to carry away our main-yard.

Unbending the mainsail, we got the pieces of the yard on deck, fished it, and swayed it aloft and slung it.

During the first dog-watch, while all hands were on deck, we bent the mainsail and set it, as well as the maintop sail.

As the wind increased towards night, all hands single-reefed the topsails, with to'gallant sail set over them, the log showing thirteen knots an hour.

Under this sail we passed a comfortable night, and early in the morning shook out the reefs, and set the foretop-mast stun'sail.

We had an unusually good crew, and the fo'castle was a delightful resort all that voyage until we reached the Banks of Newfoundland. There were men who had been in the Indian Ocean, others round the Horn, in the Pacific, to Australia, and China, and their tongues were ever ready to reel off the yarn of their adventures. To me this was new and exciting. I often lay awhile awake wondering when I should be favored with a sight of those strange places.

On the "Banks" near Newfoundland, it is necessary to keep up unceasing vigilance, especially at night, on account of the numerous fishing craft at anchor or under canvas.

These fishing-vessels are the source of infinite annoyance to the captains of vessels which ply between the United States and the ports of Northern Europe.

A large ship from one of the Northern European ports will come booming along under all sail with a strong breeze a couple of points free, reeling of twelve or thirteen knots an hour in a fog so dense that the look-out on the forecastle can barely discern the outline of the flying jibboom end, and every eye is strained peering into the gray mass of vapor into which the ship is rushing, when a startling "sail, ho!" rings out, and before a "where away" can be uttered, a mere speck has appeared, darted across the bows and disappeared in the gloom, having succeeded in creating intense excitement on board of the huge three-master. Again, when to the misty curtain of the fog is added the intense darkness of night, the danger is increased tenfold; yet, while all is watchfulness and anxiety on board of the leviathan, and captain and officers, crew and passengers are on the alert, the fisherman, whose motto seems to be—

"Fear not, but trust in Providence,
Wherever thou may'st be,"

drops his anchor, graciously condescends to show a light on the fore-stay, and sometimes, but not always, sets a hand on the look-out.

Having thus satisfied themselves that they are not likely to run down the *Great Eastern*, or one of H. B. M. line of battle ships, the bold fishermen of Gloucester or Martha's Vineyard will turn in for an all-night's snooze, and snore as musically as if they were safe in bed at home.

Fearful indeed have been the consequences of their foolhardiness; many and many a time as the weary eyes of the lookout peered into the darkness ahead has he been horror-

stricken to see a dark spot in the gloom—too late ! Ere the
words can be uttered the ponderous bow crushes the frail
pinkey or dory into lumber.   For an instant, a glimpse of
half-dressed men rushing from their couches, one agonizing
shriek, and many a home in New England is filled with the
orphan's sob and the widow's wail, while the great ship
shears her way through the fog, the night and the tempest,
insensible, remorseless, reckless of the brave hearts stilled
forever beneath her flying keel.

> " But little do we bold mariners car
> What hour we fall, or what risk we oare,
> For the groan on the strugging sailor's lip
> Is less for himself than his dying ship.
> Oh ! our's is the life for the free and the brave ;
> We dance o'er the planks that may yawn as a grave,
> We laugh 'mid the foam of our perilous home,
> And are ready for death whene'er it may come."

Boarded by a pilot off Montauk Point, we cleared away
our anchors, overhauled ranges of cable, singled our shank
painters and ring stoppers, and next morning a tug took
hold of us and put us alongside a wharf in the East River,
at the foot of Beekman Street.

We were but partially fast before the entire crew whom
we had shipped in Liverpool leaped ashore, with their
dunnage hove on to the wharf before, and betaking themselves to their haunts, began to spend like asses the money
they had earned like horses.

Thus ended my first voyage in a "Blackballer" after a
passage home of twenty-two days, and although personally
I had been subjected to no ill-treatment by either officers
or crew, I felt perfectly disgusted with that phase of a seaman's life, and I determined that no ordinary circumstances
should induce me to ship again as foremast hand on the
Black Ball line of packet-ships.

Chapter V.

" Welcome the seas where the southern breeze
  Is laden with odors rare,
Where the tropic isles and the meadows smile,
  Are comely, kind, and fair.
And now bright eyes are looking forth,
  In hopes that they may see
Our snow-white sails before the gales,
  Rolling down to " Old Mani."

Bill Chapman, a seaman of about forty-five years old, had, notwithstanding the disparity in our ages, been my constant companion and chum on board the *Columbus*. He had ran away from school at the age of fifteen and shipped as a cabin-boy on board the bark *Midas* of New Bedford, bound for a five years' cruise in the South Pacific. During his long apprenticeship on board of the old blubber hunter, he, like Ulysses, saw the cities and learned the customs of many men; for the *Midas*, not being overburdened with success in filling her casks with oil, had ample leisure to poke her nose into all sorts of out-of-the-way places, where, on pretence of rafting aboard water or getting a fresh supply of potatoes and onions, the officers and men would enjoy the luxury of a run ashore.

In fact the good-natured skipper of the whaler seemed to be convinced that pleasure and adventure were the chief objects for which his owners had fitted out the ship.

In accordance with this idea, he carried out their supposed intentions with most praiseworthy assiduity.

Beginning with the Cape De Verdes, where all hands experienced the pains and pleasures attendant upon too liberal potations of "aguardiente," he visited Tristan D'Acunha to lay in a supply of potatoes and yams, and to have a long "game" with an old chum of his, who, preferring a hermit's life ashore to the quarter-deck of a blubber-hunter, had become quite domesticated among the dwellers in this remote island of the South Atlantic.

Leaving Tristan D'Acunha, our worthy spent a month or so cruising, in a perfunctory way, off Gough's Island; but the right whales which there abound were too wild and too full of fight to be captured by the boats of this easy-going sperm-whaler, so that our captain made sail for Table Bay "to recruit." Zanzibar and Madagascar were next visited, and after a flying visit to Mauritius, St. Paul's, and Desolation, the *Midas* came to an anchorage in the harbor of Melbourne, and the captain went ashore with a letter for his owners, reporting all hands in good health and the ship "clean."

After a short cruise on the New Zealand whaling grounds, he pointed the good *Midas* to the northward and eastward, visiting Whytatekee, Roratonga, Otaheite, Nukahiva, and in short every island of note in the South Pacific.

Continuing his exploration to the north of the "line," he made a conscientious survey of the Hawaian group, and the "boys of the *Midas*" were considered well posted in all that a sailor would care to know about Hawaii, Molokai, Maui or Oahu.

As far as I could judge from many a long conversation with Bill Chapman, the crew of the *Midas* had not extended their inquiries or their observations to matters of geology, politics or religion. His ignorance on all such points was truly phenomenal, and I would have hesitated to give credence as to the truth of his never-ending yarns, had he not shown himself a complete master of the details which make up the social life of the dwellers in those far-off lands.

At last, wearied of the intolerable sameness of an unsuccessful whaling voyage, young Chapman deserted the old bark in the roads of Honolulu and shipped on board the *Trident*, an English ship, bound to the coast of China.

After a delay of several months at Whampoa, the *Trident*

received her cargo of tea and silk and sailed for London. Satisfied with his new life, Chapman entered as apprentice, and passed several years in voyages to Bombay, Calcutta, Singapore and Canton, realizing quite a handsome sum of money from his wages and a few private speculations in crape shawls and other silk goods, which he disposed of to good advantage without the aid of the Custom House. This money must, as a matter of course, be spent somehow, and my brave Chapman determined to revisit his native city of New York in grand style.

In pursuance of this sapient resolve, he sailed on board of the *Adirondack* from Liverpool to New York, but not in the fo'castle, oh no! that was beneath his dignity—the cabin, and the best state-room in it, were not half good enough for my aristocratic friend. Well, he arrived in New York and had a grand "blow out." Ostentatious of his newly-acquired wealth, he, like the man going from Jerusalem to Jericho, fell among thieves, who stripped him not only of his money but of his clothes. In this predicament, a Cherry street boarding-house keeper seemed to him a veritable Good Samaritan, and, one fine morning, my friend Chapman made his appearance on the deck of the *Columbus*, in a suit of old dungaree, to face the Western Ocean and the tender mercies of Huntington and Cornish.

Here I made his acquaintance, and, attracted by his splendid seamanship and quiet manners, I rendered him some little services which he seemed to think deserving of unending gratitude.

Like all old whalemen he was an adept in the arts of cutting, sewing, making, repairing and altering clothing.

He would patch and repatch a shirt until the original material was entirely hidden; then he would take another shirt reduced to the same state of decreptitude, and, sewing the two together, get a few months more service out of them. This he called "patch upon patch and patch overall." By these means he succeeded in making the few articles of clothing which I forced him to accept do excellent service during the passage out to Liverpool, and he took great pride in making me proficient in using thread and needles. In teaching me this useful knowledge, and in explaining to me the more difficult problems of seamanship, he spent the day watch below. Our night watches on deck were spent in long stories about his adventures in the Indian or the South Pacific oceans, or in some one of the Chinese ports. Ah! George, he would frequently say, that is sailorizing; no bobbing in and out of port, loading and discharging cargo every two or three weeks, and making and shortening sail, and reefing, furling, bracing and hauling every time the watch is relieved, day and night, with a lot of half-licked cubs in the fo'castle and blood-sucking hyenas abaft the main-mast. If ever we haul alongside of a New York wharf again, you and I will ship for a voyage to China and back, and then you'll see something like comfort and you'll feel as if you were a sailor."

Well, we agreed to make the voyage together, and, on arriving in New York, we went to the same boarding-house, and began to look out for a ship bound to Canton.

On mentioning our project, we found that several of the seamen who boarded with us had signed articles for a voyage to Canton in the ship *Niantic*, Captain Griswold.

They were fine jovial fellows, and gave us every encouragement to join the crew, being quite enthusiastic in praise of the ship and her officers.

After conferring together, we went down to the shipping office and signed articles.

The few days which remained before the *Niantic* would be ready to haul out in the East River were spent by us in visiting some of Chapman's friends in the city.

New York has changed in its upper parts, beyond Canal street, and around the Central Park, since the times of which I write, "before the war," but the docks remain very much as they were, except that the various kinds and sizes of craft have improved in size and quality since I was a sailor boy.   Then steam was the exception in sea-going vessels, now it is the rule for long voyages, although sailing-ships are still known, and very fine in model and construction are they.   It is a delight to go over their fine lines and note the improvements since " my day."

SIGNING ARTICLES.

Changes in New York within the past three decades have been slow in some places, rapid in others, enduring in all ; and the river fronts mark the transition with unerring certainty.   The North River, formerly denominated "the Seamboat District," maintains its prestige.   The big boats round the Battery on their way up the Sound, and the high-way of the Hudson claims its quota of steamboats and barges, which even the railroads cannot crowd out of a profitable existence. The East Side, with some steamboat lines left, has changed its front materially. Whitehall and Coenties Slip still harbor their canal boats, and the "Flour District" maintains its pasty identity on wet days. Toward Wall street, however, things have changed, and beyond this the big bridge stretches its cabled spans over the old buildings near the Roosevelt street ferry. Thence to the sectional and balance-dock vicinity, and further on toward the "Hook" the old identity has been successfully merged into a present, which, according to an old "sea-dog's" ideas of how things ought to be, would be unsatisfactory. Some of the larger buildings are still warehouses, with their importance on the wane and a struggle for existence. The marble yards exist at the bend, where the big bulkheads are, but there are fewer vessels at the wharf and there is less marble in the yards.

In the palmy days of South street, twenty-five or thirty years ago, every pier was a scene of busy life and money-making. Square-riggers from every port pointed their jib-booms far over the pavements, and the forest of tall masts extended from below Wall street away up beyond Market and Pike streets. The only break in the line was just at the balance-docks, where half a hundred sloops "snuggled" themselves into place, and made things generally lively with their trade in merchandise and market stuff from the big and little places on the Sound. Palmy days those were for the harbor masters, the shipping agents, the stevedores, 'longshoremen, and the ship-owners. The monthly fees from registered vessels and the perquisites from coasters made the harbor masterships the plum worth struggling for in the distribution of executive patronage. Politicians sought them for their friends and secured them for themselves. When there were seven harbor masters the wire-pulling was energetic. Then there were nine, and the wires were still taut. Then there were eleven hungry officials to bite at the cherry, and yet the wire-pulling continued, and the skilled talent in requisition at the old Capitol chambers, the Delavan House and Stanwix Hall, successfully engineered non-confirmation by the Senate, and the stubborn harbor masters held over for more than one term. And this, too, while stubborn old Commodore Vanderbilt was fighting against paying the fees. The fight amused the commodore, who was as much of an autocrat, in his way, as the harbor masters. But the old commodore failed to win, and finally paid for his amusement, when such active political magnates as Owen W. Brennan, Alexander H. Schultz, James Bevins, Mathew D. Green, "Lew" Brainard, S. S. Benedict, David Herrick, A. D. Barbour, W. H. Burleigh, Abram Pierce and James W. Husted found the harbor masterships profitable, convenient, consoling and computable.

In those busy days "before the war" there was much to be seen along the docks, and the rural visitor had reason to wonder where all the big ships came from. The Southern coasting trade was an important factor in the revenues to the merchants of New York from inter-State commerce. From Beekman Street to James Slip the "two dollar fellows" (for the schooners, as a rule, paid this amount for the berths provided by the harbor masters, and the schooner district was the pet one on the East River) had their regular places. Such firms as Dollner, Potter & Co., Jonas Smith & Co., R. M. Demill and others, had the cream of the naval store trade. The North Carolina and Virginia ports did their heaviest business with these houses. The "Down Easters" had a trade of their own. The lumbermen from Maine and the traders from New England east of Boston made their headquarters among the Wall street offices near the river. Among them J. W. Elwell & Co. and the circle of merchants who originated and supported the Marine Bank were the leading spirits.

The immigrant trade with the Old Country was represented in the vessels belonging to the Tapscott, Black Ball
(C. H. Marshall's), Spofford and Tileston's and Morgan's
lines, while Howland & Aspinwall, Dunham & Dimon,
Snow & Burgess, Grinnell, Minturn & Co., N. L. & G.

BLACKBALL LINER IN DOCK, NEW YORK.

Griswold and other old-time houses had regular vessels
plying between New York and English ports.

The discovery of gold in California in '48 begat the excitement in '49, when golden visions of the riches of the
Pacific Coast enticed the adventurous spirits from the Atlantic States. The hard-handed farmers built air-castles and

followed their fancies across the plains, many of them to be lost in the cañons of the Rockies. It was a long way round the Horn, but the Pacific Coast beckoned with its golden hand, and the American shipbuilders were to meet the emergency by craft which should shorten the voyage by speed and bring the golden shores closer. New York had its half dozen shipyards, and the contest for superiority began with the New Englanders. Webb, Westervelt, Steers —such men were ready to begin work, and the blows of the axe and mallet resounded unceasingly. Strong-ribbed ships grew steadily under the practised hands of enthusiastic workmen, and the careful eyes of the master, who owned the yards and took the risk of failure or reputation in success. New England's competition was earnest and generous. East Boston, Rockport, Kennebunk, Portland, Bath— all deep-water ports—were busy. The California trade must be supplied with swift-winged racers. Abundant capital and stimulated labor produced with marvelous rapidity the sharp-bowed, long-hulled, rakish clippers, modeled with as much care as yachts, and much like the fleet of fast-sailing vessels peculiar to Baltimore and trading in and out from Chesapeake Bay. "There's another new ship," was an expression to be punctuated with a period instead of an exclamation point, and the big ships were moored three and four abreast in the East river docks awaiting turns at the wharves. Freight awaiting shipment was piled up taffrail high, and at the 'longshoremen's nooning an army of sunburnt men lounged along the river front. Such firms as W. T. Coleman & Co., Sutton & Co., Snow & Burgess, the Austins and the Griswolds made money fast in the California trade.

There were big records for the big ships in those days, and a "slice in a clipper" paid roundly, while the builders were proud of their work. The *Challenge*, a 2,000-ton ship owned by the Griswolds, was a racer. So was the *Red*

Jacket. The *Flying Cloud* in 1851 cast the foam from her bows in a run from Sandy Hook to San Francisco in eighty-nine days, making 433 miles in one day. The *Comet* made the run from San Francisco to New York in eighty-three days, and the *Sovereign of the Seas* came home from the Sandwich Islands in eighty-three days in the spring of 1852. All the ships were fast, and the records of so many are notable that comparison would be unfair, but the voyage of the *Dreadnaught* in 1853, when she made steamer's time of thirteen days from Liverpool to New York, was one of the noted.

The ship-building industry which began so lustily in 1850 had lost no strength in 1853. There was no less demand from California, and European business had been turned into the clipper service, while the carrying trade between China and New York called for the best attainable speed. A. A. Low & Brothers, then the leaders in the tea trade, numbered in their fleet the ships *N. B. Palmer* and *Samuel Russell*, and the noted barks *Benefactor* and *Benefactress*. In 1853 the *Great Republic* touched the water from the stocks of Donald McKay, at East Boston, built for the Lows, and having a tonnage of 3,356. She was a four-master and a four-decker, designed for the China trade, and to be the largest possible "box of tea" afloat. All New York was anxious for the coming of the big vessel, and for several days, while berthed at Pier No. 28, East river, she was on exhibition. Then when loaded and ready for sea, with crew all shipped, the ship was held at her berth, because the rule of the owners was to send no vessels to sea on Sundays or on holidays. But the *Great Republic* was destined to destruction. At midnight the cry of "fire" sounded in the silent streets of the old Fourth Ward, and the lumbering engines, drawn by the willing hands of the old volunteer fire department, were hurried to Goodwin's cracker bakery in Front street. It was burning like tinder, the shower of

THE OLD BREWERY.

sparks carried toward the river falling upon the shipping. The tall masts and partly unbent canvas of the *Great Republic* were a shining mark, and an hour later, despite all efforts, the ship was afire aloft, and the fiery fragments of rigging and sails were falling upon the resinous and varnished decks.

The *Great Republic* was doomed. So was the *Joseph Walker*, grain-laden, lying on the lower side of Pier No. 29, near the end of the wharf. The *Constellation*, lying ahead of her, was barely saved, and a new clipper lying at the end of Pier No. 28, astern of the *Great Republic*, was cut loose and sent adrift, all afire, to speed away up the river on the strength of the flood tide, ground near Blackwell's Island, and there to burn to the water's edge. The interest in the *Great Republic* was national, and such was the regard in which the big clipper was held that every effort was made to confine the fire to the spars and the upper deck. But while anxious crowds watched the burning vessel and while Donald McKay, her builder, stood with tearful eyes upon the steps of the ship-chandler's store at South and Dover streets, the orders were given by the chief engineer of the fire department to scuttle the vessel, and she sunk in her berth, there to lie for some months. Then she was taken back to her birthplace at East Boston to be rebuilt. She did service in the Pacific, and was used as a troop-ship in the Black Sea by the allies during the Crimean war.

The ascendancy of the clippers was maintained for several years. Gradually they crowded out the square-sterned, clumsy-bowed packets plying across the Atlantic, and the shipping interests of the port of New York were counted in big figures, notwithstanding the impending monopolization of the steamship lines by English capitalists.

A fleet of stout-built, sea-going, side-wheel tow boats was constantly employed in the Sandy Hook service, and many found paying jobs in cruising off-shore under constant orders to pick up incoming ships and hurry with all speed in order to secure berths; for wharf room was inadequate. The race for berths was lively, and under the rule of " first come first served " a contest between rival stevedores of the ships *Emerald Isle* and *E. C. Scranton* created much excitement and threatened a conflict between the State and the municipal authorities while Fernando Wood was mayor.

The outbreak of the civil war changed all this, and suddenly. That change, inevitable then, has been lasting until now, when there seems to be a well-grounded revival in shipbuilding in the eastern yards, and the Sewell free ship bill is setting the door ajar to the rehabilitation of an American merchant navy. When the war became a certainty the wharves of New York were worth seeing. There were busy expectation and more haste than discretion, especially in the dispatching of South-bound vessels. The schooners which were regular as clockwork in their appearance on the East river were hurried away to their home ports, not to return. They were wanted in the Confederacy, and their captains were generally willing to take chances on the "other side." Bermuda, Cuba and foreign ports were havens of safety and profit, when the light craft, laden with cotton or naval stores, could be run out through the narrowing lines of the blockading squadron. Many vessels which were owned jointly by Northern and Southern owners were chartered for use in the quartermaster's department, or sold at an appraised value to the government. The tug-boats were taken up under charters, with the accruing clause, and when there was little to do in New York harbor found ready employment elsewhere, from Washington and Baltimore, down to Virginia and North Carolina waters.

After the war everything had changed. Reconstruction elsewhere led to reconstruction of the shipping. The fast-sailing clippers had been wearing themselves out by hard-pressed voyages ; many had fallen prey to the Confederate cruisers, and were destined to be the basis of claims growing out of the Geneva award, and many had for safety changed ownership while in foreign countries, and found a living in far-off waters under another flag. Steamers which had survived the arduous requirements of the government service were to be had cheap. Vessel-owners who were early on hand when the war broke out had grown rich by the sale or charter of their craft, and were willing to take second-hand boats at auction prices when the government offered bargains. Many of the Southern trade houses were extinct ; others were crippled financially beyond resuscitation. The trade at home ports for Southern productions had fallen into new hands. The schooners gave way to small, moderately fast steamers. Fernandina, Charleston, Savannah, Galveston, Wilmington, Newbern, Norfolk found these steamers entering their waters instead of the "fore-and-afters," and the schooner became the exception, not the rule. Nearly ten years of inattention gave American shipping a chance to die out. The war and the legislation which followed it had given such enterprise hard blows. There was little encouragement, and certainty was dimmed by constant additions to the fleet of ocean wanderers from foreign ports. Intended blockade runners became "tramps" here and everywhere, and until 1874, when the clipper *Ocean King* was launched at Kennebunk, Me., there was nothing notable in the ship-building way. Ten years later Maine gave another American ship to the foreign trade, and, with the *Henry B. Hyde*, of 2,453 tons, asserted the claims of American owners to recognition for speed and beauty. Her first voyage to San Francisco was made last year in 123 days; thence, grain-laden, she reached Liverpool in 95 days, and has just reached home in 22 days from the latter port.

The status of American shipping, taking New York's wharves as a criterion, is peculiar. We are creeping back in a measure to the familiar outlook of years ago—but only creeping, while the features to be restored will be but partial restoration at best. The fleets of steamers, which are ocean ferry boats, sail under the English, French or German flag, and the stranger vessels, loading "for a market," are foreign-built and foreign-owned. The coasting trade is by steamers, of a better class than at first, doing the work more quickly, and leaving nothing for the trim schooners to do in their wonted channels. The brigs and barks which were identified with the North of Europe trade, still come here, looking just as they used to do, and their characteristics are pleasant as permanent remembrancers of old times. The light work vessels which cruise "Down East," over beyond the Maine coast, are more trimly built and larger; the schooners are nearly all three-masters, and have double the tonnage of twenty years ago. The square-rigged vessels, few and far between, are, except the German-built ones, neither an improvement upon nor a decline from the models of twenty years ago, although some of the foreigners riding at anchor in the North river, or lying well up toward the bulkheads on the East river, are faster-looking and more rakish. The return of the clippers, which is again to be hoped for, will be a repetition of history aptly illustrated. The clippers will hold their own with any chance at honest competition to Pacific ports. The petroleum trade gave the new ship *Frederick Billings*, a Rockport clipper of 2,500 tons, a full cargo to Yokohama, and the ship will return with a paying cargo, already insured. The California lines have held on tenaciously, not withstanding the immense business of the Pacific Mail Company, and in view of the encouragement of last year's ventures the ship-builders at East Boston and Bath are about setting up clippers of equal size with the *Hyde*, the *Ropes* and the *Billings*, to be off and away at sea before the season closes.

It may seem strange that I keep the run of these things, but the truth is I have lived so long on or about the "briny" that it is a second nature, if not my very first desire and pleasure, to keep abreast of the news in the shipping line. Every new improvement interests me.

One item of news seems worthy a place here. The good ship *Niantic* was beached at San Francisco, and left there where the sands blew about her hull, and the docks were built out beyond her moorings, as the city and its commerce grew, and now the Niantic block, a fine group of buildings in the center of the business part of the city, marks the site of the wreck of thirty years ago. But I must take up the log of my narrative, lest I lose my reckoning altogether and be swamped in the quicksand of memories of bygone days

But just now, when thinking of the fate of the *Niantic*, it occurs to me that she was not such a large vessel after all. The ships of those early days of my sailoring were moderate in size compared with the large steamers and sailers of the present. If you will look over the advertising columns of the newspapers of say 1836 to 1838 you will frequently read some such notice as this: "Now ready for Bombay and Calcutta, the swift-sailing, but teak-built ship Marietta of 400 tons;" or, as another reads: "We will dispatch as soon as cargo is complete the copper-bottomed packet brig of 142 tons register for Madeira, with excellent accommodations for passengers." Could you persuade a consumptive to risk a passage now in such a small vessel?

In the "Annual Register" for 1838 you may read of the launch of the *British Queen*, with this remark : This immense steamship is intended to carry passengers between London and New York. Her length exceeds any vessel in the British navy by 35 feet, and that was 275 feet ! Her engines were of 500 horse-power, she carried 600 tons of coal and 500 tons of cargo ! You could stow away three or four such cargoes, ship and all, in the "immense" steamships that now carry passengers from London to New York. Longer, larger, swifter is the aim now-a-days, always excepting the *Great Eastern*.

Having succeeded with almost infinite trouble in getting a decent suit of clothes to present himself in, he invited me to go with him to call on his sisters, who, having married two industrious young men, were living in Hudson street, near Vandam. Arriving at the house at about eight o'clock in the evening, it was agreed that I should go in first, while Chapman should remain behind and enjoy the pleasure of surprising his sisters.

In answer to my rap, a young lady came to the door, and after a momentary glance of astonishment at the appearance of my rig, inquired whom I wished to see.

" Does Mrs. Perry live here ?"

" She does."

" Tell her, please, that a friend of her brother, William Chapman, wants to see her for a few minutes."

" O, yes, sir; walk in if you please"—and the young lady ran or rather flew into the next room, leaving both doors open so that Bill and myself could hear her say excitedly " young sailor "—" Uncle Bill—perhaps he has good news."

In a few moments Mrs. Perry came in, and inviting me to be seated, sat down with her back to the door, her daughter sitting opposite to her and gazing intently at me. " Oh, sir, have you any news about my brother William ? Have you seen him ? Is he alive or dead?"

" Yes, ma'am, I have seen him, and I am glad to say that he is in very good health."

" Oh, thank God, we were dreadfully afraid that he was lost at sea ; he had written to say that he was about to pay a visit to New York, and would come to see us. We were all delighted to think that he was coming, for he had been away for nearly ten years, but he never came. My husband and my brother-in-law went down to South street to the office of the owners of the ship he was to come in, but there was no such person among the crew."

"Very true, thought I, but there he was in the cabin, and the Lord only knows what name he sailed under."

"And where did you see him?" continued the lady.

"In Liverpool, ma'am," said I, "he was about to sail in the ship *Columbus* for this port, and she cannot be far behind the ship I arrived in, so you may——"

At this critical moment, I caught sight of Bill edging cautiously into the room behind his sister, and, I could not continue, for I was ready to burst with laughter.

The young lady caught my glance, and, following it, spied a fierce-looking sailor man on the point of bending down to kiss her mother's cheek.

"Mother! mother!" she shrieked, and her mother, startled beyond measure, tried to rise, but found herself held fast in her chair by a pair of sturdy arms, while a gruff voice, mellowed by affection, said: "Don't be frightened, Sarah, it's only brother Bill."

Then followed the inevitable crying spell, in which both sister and niece spent an unconscionable length of time—all the while holding the wanderer's hands and gazing into his weatherbeaten face; then round they went on the other tack, and, drying their tears, began to banter the life out of my shipmate with allusions to the splendid presents he had promised and the immense riches which he claimed to be the owner of at the time he had last written to them.

The entrance of Mr. Perry, and of Bill's sister Ella and her husband, afforded my friend a brief respite; but it was very brief indeed; in a few moments the attack was renewed with threefold fury, and the men entered with great gusto into the spirit of the joke.

"Oh, dear Bill," said Sarah, "I had nearly forgotten to thank you for the beautiful crape shawl you sent me. Just

BILL CHAPMAN IN HUDSON STREET.

to think how kind and thoughtful you were to bring it all
the way from China."

"And my silk dress, Will; why, when I took it to the dress-
makers, she said she had never seen anything so rich even
in France, and she's a Parisian, ain't she, Sarah?"

"I tell you that camphor wood-box is just the thing to keep
one's Sunday clothes in, Will; I'll never part with it," said
one of the men.

"And oh, Uncle William," chimed in the niece, "how delighted I was with that beautiful little box of toys and the
queer little Chinese dolls you sent me. I gave them to the
baby and she plays with them all day long."

"All right, all hands of you," said Bill, good humoredly.
"I say, George," said he, turning to me, "did you ever see a
poor devil get such a rating? It beats Cornish all hollow."

"Better tell about how you had to disappoint them," I
suggested.

"Yes, I suppose I shall have to spin the whole yarn,
George," and thereupon he told of his success in the China
traders, his passage to New York and the loss of his money,
not forgetting to speak of what he called my kindness to
him when he came on board of the *Columbus*.

After a pleasant visit we bade farewell, and, returning to
our boarding-house, learned that all hands had been notified
to be on board of the *Niantic* early the next morning.

The next morning broke clear with the wind at nor-west,
and, after bidding a hasty adieu to our friends ashore, we all
went aboard in a "Whitehall boat."

Clearly borne over the waters of the river came the boom
of the morning gun from the receiving ship in the navy-
yard, and, an instant later, a jet of flame and a puff of
smoke from one of the embrasures of Fort Columbus was
followed by a dull reverberation echoing up the river, and
the shrill notes of the fife and the roll of the drum beating

the "reveille" saluted our ears as we stepped on board of the *Niantic*.

Some of the crew needed breakfast, and others seemed more in need of sleep. The pilot and captain determined not to get under way until the afternoon, at which time the men would be in a fit state for duty.

After dinner, when all were sober and refreshed by sleep, the chief mate, Mr. Capie, came forward to the forescuttle, and, stamping with his foot, sang out, "Turn to, men. Man the windlass."

By this time the tug was alongside and made fast. The men began to heave in the slack of the cable as the tug forged ahead, until the anchor was under foot. "A hand lay out and loose the jib," sung out the mate ; "heave up, boys, and break her out." When the anchor was in sight the jib was hoisted, which canted her head down stream.

While some hands were overhauling the catfall, hooking on and catting the anchor and passing the stoppers, others were aloft loosing sails. "Man at the wheel," shouted the captain. "Mr. Capie, set the top-sails and to'gallant-sails." Our voyage was now fairly begun.

As we swept down the lake-like expanse which lies between the Battery and the north shore of Staten Island, and extends from Gowanus to the Jersey shore, the afternoon air was laden with the long-drawn chorus of many a crew as they sung out at the windlass. Quarantine and Fort Hamilton were soon well on our quarter, and we began to feel the swell of the mighty Atlantic as we curtsied to the surges of the lower bay.

On they came rearing their foaming crests aloft in the bright sunshine of the summer afternoon. The northeastern horizon began to assume a leaden hue, and a few ominous clouds appeared in that direction.

The gallant little tug, which up to this time had steadily headed to the southward and eastward, midway between

Coney Island and Sandy Hook, now changed its course
more to the southward in obedience to the orders of our
pilot, and in a short time towed us into the placid waters
inside Sandy Hook.

The wind was now blowing a living gale from the northeast, the lower bay was a wilderness of white water, and the
breakers dashed furiously upon the outer beach of the
Hook, with a roar which made our hearts beat faster as we
thought of the danger so narrowly escaped.

Darker, darker grew the sky as the storm swept onward,
increasing in violence as it approached us. With the tug
astern, in case of necessity, our anchors down and sails
securely furled, and the "Horse Shoe" acting as a breakwater, we felt no uneasiness, and spent our time in watching
the small craft which, caught outside by the sudden approach of the gale, were now fleeing like frightened birds to
a place of safety. Down came the night, and with it a torrent of rain. Chapman, no mean authority in such matters, declared that in all his experience he had never witnessed such a deluge except in the Indian Ocean, or in the
monsoons of the China Sea. The rain did not simply fall;
it seemed to be impelled by some hidden power, and it
smote our decks spitefully as if disappointed in the endeavor
to do harm.

All night long the swish of the rain, the howling of the
gale and the thundering crash of the breakers kept up their
stormy chorus, while more than once the distant boom of a
signal gun came upon the wings of the hurricane bearing to
our ears the sad news of a ship in distress.

At earliest dawn, just when the first gray streaks began to
appear low down on the eastern horizon, the gale began to
abate and the wind to haul round to the southward and
westward. By seven o'clock, the wind being still blowing
from the same quarter and seemingly settled, we hove up
our mud-hooks, or rather anchors, made sail, and stood out

to sea with our starboard tacks aboard and the wind abeam.

By the time we had reached the easterly edge of the "Gulf Stream" everything was ship-shape, anchors stowed and spare spars securely lashed for a long passage, most of the chafing gear seized or laced on, and the crew were as jovial as if they had sailed many voyages together So that, with a tight ship, fair wind and plenty of sea-room, we looked forward to a pleasant run to the latitude of the "Trades," when we could sit on deck and let the wind blow us along."

But the rugged sea-gods of the North-Atlantic, fearing, perhaps, that we might become effeminate by our long sojourn amid the gentle breezes of the tropics, determined to present us with a memento at parting.

" Northeast, neither good for man or beast," says the old proverb, and so it proved this time, and " Old Boreas, blustering railer," seemed bent on surpassing his previous achievements.

Dark banks of clouds heralded his approach ; the sea rose and tumbled, foamed and roared at his beck, and we all, as humble subjects, made hot haste to bow to the storm-king.

In came the stun'sails, followed by the royals and flying-jib, then the to'gallant sails were clewed up and furled snug; after which all hands were called to "shorten sail," when we close reefed the top-sails, reefed the foresail and furled the spanker ; but the darkening sky of a leaden hue very forcibly suggested the prudence of a still further reduction of canvas, so the mainsail was hauled up and the jib hauled down and both furled snug, royal yards sent down ; then we took the fore and mizen top-sails off her, and fore-sail, and hove her to the wind on the larboard tack.

The hurricane now broke upon us with all its fury; at every plunge the stout old *Niantic* buried her nose under the seas and the dark waters hid everything forward of the

fore-rigging. This would never do; if we were not anxious to lose our masts, spring a leak, or start a butt, which
last misfortune was dreaded by us all of us on account of
our immense cargo of lead in pigs stowed in the lower hold,
causing the ship to rise very slowly to meet the seas.

At last the orders came: "Take in the main-topsail; haul
down the foretop-mast stay-sail; and in a few minutes the
men were aloft on the topsail yard holding on by their eyelids and fiercely struggling with the immense sail. At last
the topsail was furled in a fashion, the stay-sail was stowed,
and the *Niantic*, under bare poles, was stripped for the fray.

When a few hours before I had watched the noble ship as
she darted swiftly on her course, her long white decks gleaming in the sunlight, and her sails rising in bellying folds
tier over tier from rail to truck, the sight was magnificent.
Now, when, under a sky of inky blackness, the wind shriek-
ing dismally through the rigging, and the white seas cover-
ing her as she struggled wearily inward, her bare poles describing an arc of nearly sixty degrees as she rolled slug-
gishly with the dead weight in her hold, quivering throughout
her whole length under the tremendous shocks of the furious
seas, the spectacle was appalling in its sublimity.

There seemed to be a living, enraged spirit rushing about
the ship, and, as the poet says, dashed

> "—— As a wave that from the clouds impends,
> And swell'd with tempests on the ship descends;
> White are the decks with foam, the winds aloud
> Howl o'er the masts and sing through every shroud;
> Pale, trembling, tired, the sailors freeze with fears,
> And instant death on every wave appears."

While I stood lost in awestruck admiration of the scene I
was joined by Chapman, who had been earnestly conversing
with Joe Byers one of the oldest seamen of our watch.

"Well, Bill," said I, "we got the sail off her none too soon.
That job's done, anyhow; that's one comfort; we can't do any
more now except wait until it blows itself out."

"Don't be too sure of that, my lad; there's plenty more hard work to be done, and the sooner the better, for done it has to be, and it ought to have been done long ago unless the old man wants to jump the masts out of her. Just look at the way they're jumping. At that rate we'll have many a long spell at the pumps, if there's any ship left to pump. Ah! at last; will you?"

Chapman's surmise proved to be correct; all hands were set at work hoisting up the heavy pigs of lead and stowing them between decks. It was a fearful, dangerous and exhausting job at any time, but especially so in a living gale of wind, and the ship rolling like a log. All night long we were at it, and when we returned on deck we had the satisfaction of seeing, by the increased buoyancy with which she rose to meet the seas and her comparative steadiness, that our labor had not been in vain.

In the course of the forenoon the gale abated and we set close-reefed topsails, reefed foresail and fore-topmast staysail, wore ship and stood to the southward and eastward on our course in order to catch the northeast trade winds.

As the wind kept backing to the west'ard the weather became more moderate, and we set the mainsail, jib and spanker, then shaking two reefs out of fore and maintopsails, set to'gallant sails over them. Under this canvas we kept on for four days, at the expiration of which time we got into fine weather, and breathed a sigh of relief as we thought that, for a time at least, we had seen the last of Western Ocean weather.

We then made all sail, crossed royal yards, shook out all reefs, and set mizzen to'gallant sail, royals and flying jib, rigged out all starboard stun'sail booms, and set the sails with the lower stun'sail. The wind was west sou'west, and everything drawing.

Never shall I forget that memorable storm of the 19th of September, 1834. I have seen some heavy blows in all parts of the world, but for downright, hard, persistent blowing that equinoctial gale surpassed everything else.

We were then fast nearing the long wished-for region of the trade winds, the weather fine and the breeze favorable. The morning watch below was devoted by all hands to drying, mending and stowing away of our coarse, heavy clothing, and getting out jumpers and hip trousers of old sail-cloth or light duck, more suitable to the weather to be expected in the low latitudes. On deck the men were engaged in various light jobs, such as making spun-yarn, sinnet, or perched up aloft seizing on chafing-gear, shifting running rigging end for end restrapping blocks, staying masts and setting up standing rigging, scraping bright side when practicable, and ending with the arduous task of making an hour's job last through the entire watch. In this conscientious effort they uniformly succeeded, for the officers cared but little about the time spent in the work, provided that it were neatly done, and the men kept busy.

This is in reality the most pleasant part of a seaman's occupation; there is no fatigue, no danger; the hands alone are busy, and the eyes can wander around the horizon and search for some object to vary its sameness, while the fancy, shackled by no corporeal fetters, pierces beyond the distant point where the arching sky bends down to meet the sea, and revisits the home of childhood and the friends of youth. Alas! poor Jack! His hard fate severs him from both, and he bears his loss with quiet and unpretending resignation, yet many and many a time (when hove to in a gale off the Horn, or swinging at our anchors in some lonely harbor on the west coast of Africa, or watching the phosphorescent waves and sparkling skies of the Coral or the Banda Sea, "Where the blue hills of the tropic isles are laden with odors rare") does the irrepressible yearning for home and kindred find expres-

sion in the plaintive lines so often sung by these wanderers
over the trackless waters of the deep.

> " The home we loved near the bounding deep,
>   Where the hills in glory stood;
> And the moss-grown graves where our fathers sleep,
>   'Neath the shade of the waving wood,
> I remember yet, with a fond regret,
>   The hills and the flowering lea,
> And the greenwood shade, where the wild birds made
>   Their nests 'neath the old mountain tree.
>
> We are pilgrims now in a foreign land,
>   And the joys of youth are past,
> Kind friends are gone, but the old tree stands
>   Unharmed by the warring blast.
> The lark may sing in the clouds of spring
>   And the swan on the silvery sea;
> But we long for the shade where the wild birds made
>   Their nests 'neath the old mountain tree.''

One fine morning we were in about 10⁰ north latitude,
and the crew were leisurely employed in such work as I have
described, when an event occurred which served, for a time
at least, to vary the monotony of our voyage.

"Sail ho!" from aloft, where Jack Lenine was most ener-
getically idling his watch away on some fancy job at the fore-
to'gallant mast-head.

"Where away?" shouted the mate, Mr. Capie.

"Two points on our lee bow, sir," came the answer, " and
about ten miles off," added he.

Little attention was paid to the appearance of the strange
sail, until about twenty minutes later the mate sang out,
" Fore to'gallant mast head, there !"

" Aye, aye, sir !"

"Is that sail in sight, yet ?"

" Yes, sir; she seems to be making no headway."

"Can you make out her rig ?"

"She looks like a brig, sir, but she swings round so that I
can't rightly say what she's like."

"Keep your eye on her, there, Jack, and let's know as
soon as you raise her hull !"

" Aye, aye, sir."

By this time the attention of all on deck was drawn to the stranger, and various were the surmises regarding her character and condition.

"Some craft waterlogged and abandoned," ventured one.

"Perhaps they've run short of provisions, and are waiting for us to run down and supply them," said another.

"I tell you what it is, mates," said Tom Thorn, a veteran who had made many voyages to the West Coast of Africa, "palm-oiling," as he divined, "blackbirding" as we strongly suspected, "that there craft is in some trouble; its either coast fever or a mutiny, I'll be bound."

"On deck there!"

"Aye, aye!"

"She's a bright-sided brig, sir; her sails are all set, but the yards are swinging every which way as though the braces were all let go, and she was not under any control, or any one in command. Looks like as if she was in distress, but I can't make out any signal."

"Keep her away two points," said Captain Griswold, who had now come on deck. "Mr. Capie, call all hands and clear away to get ready to lower one of the quarter-boats."

We who were on deck laid aside our work, and, after all hands were called, we cast off the gripes of the lee quarter-boat, and got all in readiness for lowering.

The chief mate went aloft with his glass, and soon reported that no living creature appeared on deck. Some objects which he supposed to be bodies lay scattered here and there.

"Back the main-yard!" and, in a few minutes, the *Niantic* was bowing and curtseying gracefully a short distance to windward of the silent stranger.

As no answer came to our hail we lowered away, and, passing under her stern, read, "*Victoria*, Copenhagen."

Making fast to her main-chains, we jumped aboard, and gazed in mute astonishment and awe at the strange sight that met our eyes.

Stretched out at full length, with his face downwards and his hand clenched in agony, lay the form of a seaman.

Cautiously turning him over to ascertain if he still breathed, a sickening spectacle presented itself in the eyes starting from their sockets, the yellow face and the protruding tongue. He was of course stone-dead, and had been so for some time, for the body was partially dried up by the scorching rays of the sun beating down upon the unprotected deck.

On the fore-hatch we found another; a third victim had met the Destroyer's last blow on the to'gallant fo'castle.

Where were the rest? Had they saved their lives by flight, or were they, too, dead and rotting below?

The fetid atmosphere which pervaded the fo'castle told all too plainly the sad story which a hasty examination verified. In the cabin the captain and his companions lay dead in their berths.

All had, doubtless, perished from yellow-fever, and, not wishing to stay any longer where we were exposed to fruitless danger, we hastily examined the brig's papers, and found that she had sailed from Rio de Janeiro, Brazil, for Copenhagen with a cargo of coffee and hides.

Of course we could do nothing else than leave her as we found her. Any other line of action would have voided our insurance policy. A man of war or a whaler might have put a crew on board, and taken her into the nearest port, thereby gaining a snug little sum of salvage money, but for us this was impossible, and our crew were only too glad to leave to others a prize which was likely to cost so dear. So we pulled aboard with a will, and, hoisting up the boat, filled away and stood on our course, breathing more freely when the *Victoria* was hull down astern.

But, although out of sight, she was not out of mind. The old shell-backs of the fo'castle filled our waking hours with gruesome yarns, and our sleep with horrible dreams of suffering and death on ship-board.

We were now in the Horse latitudes, the delights of which had been fully appreciated by your humble servant when on board the *Paget*. Nor was any change for the better perceptible. Baffling winds; continuous rain, with drops almost as large as nuts; intense heat that made the pitch bubble out of the sides and the deck; plenty of discomfort; no stint of growling, grumbling, cursing, swearing, bracing and hauling, but scarcely a puff of wind in spite of most conscientious whistling for a breeze.

One afternoon, as the brassy glare of the fiery sun blazed upon the waveless sea, one of the men hauled up a bottle which had drifted alongside. "Rum, I hope; gin, I guess; tracts, by jingo!" muttered Bill Chapman, who, despite his previous good resolutions, would, I fear, have very eagerly welcomed a glass of grog to cheer his spirits.

It proved to be neither rum, nor gin, nor tracts, but papers of some sort written in Dutch, and unintelligible to us, so they were taken aft to Mr. Capie, and proved to be papers which the captain of the *Victoria* had thrown overboard. These sad memorials of a gallant crew narrated a long and desperate struggle for life aboard of the unfortunate brig.

The yellow-fever had been raging at Rio de Janeiro, and, despite every precaution, had been brought aboard the *Victoria*.

Scarcely were they out of sight of the coast of South America when two of the crew sickened and died, the contagion spread, and, at the time the captain confided his message to the deep, he and one of the seamen were the only ones alive. A list of the officers and crew, with the places from which they hailed and a prayer to God for mercy, closed this dreary document.

Here, then, perhaps in this very spot were we lay rolling and tumbling, had the poor fellows of the *Victoria* writhed in their death struggles without a friendly hand to moisten their fevered lips with a drop of water.

> " With noiseless tread death comes on man;
> In the midst of life's unfinished plan,
> With sudden hand it snatches him.
> Ready or not ready, there's no delay,
> Forth into the unknown he must away."

Of a verity the spectre of the fever-stricken brig seemed to hang like a nightmare about us, and we longed for a breeze to waft us out of an atmosphere which appeared tainted with pestilence and death.

"That reminds me," said the never-ending Tom Thorn, "of the time I was in the bark *Swallow*, bound from Ambris to Cienfuegos. The coast fever broke——"

"Damn and sink you and your blasted yarns," roared Chapman, "d'ye think we want to listen to such bl——dy stuff. I, for one, have had more than my allowance of it."

"Who the hades asked you to listen to it," retorted Thorn, and a quarrel seemed imminent, when a puff of air aloft and a slight ripple attracted the attention of all to the coming of the long prayed-for breeze.

Rounding in the starboard braces, and boarding the fore and main tacks, and trimming aft their sheets as well as the head and spanker sheets, we had the unspeakable relief to see that the wind was freshening and blowing steadily from the north'ard and east'ard.

Thorn's stories were forgotten. We bade a hearty adieu to the doldrums, and with a clean full went tearing along towards the line and the Cape of Good Hope. For three entire weeks the winds blew from the same quarter with but little variation, and we started neither tack nor sheet, brace or halliard, except to sway taut in the last dog-watch.

Now I began to experience some of the pleasures of a long voyage. The days passed delightfully in various little jobs around decks and aloft, or in assisting one of the able-seamen, generally Chapman, on some fine work in the rigging ; rattling, setting up, rope-making (for we had a winch aboard), and with capping the ends of the rigging.

Of course "chin-music" was supplied in abundance by the old salts, who always had a yarn to spin apropos to the occasion. A new hand, or one who had never been in the "doldrums" before, had a mouthful of stories for us in the fo'castle, and one of them may be worth repeating. Speaking of the girl he had left behind him on a former voyage, his mother had reported to him, on his return, how disconsolate she had been, when she was not indignant at his sudden departure. One day between her fits of scolding and crying she hoped he would have gales of wind—gales and gales of wind. My mother, who was a widow of an old sailor, and had made two or three voyages with her husband, said, "Tut, tut, my child, don't wish that, for all that they would do then, would be to put the ship under close-reefed main-top sail and heave to ; the sailors then would have nothing to do but to sit under the lee of the long-boat and spin yarns about you and me. No, no ! if you would punish him, wish for light and variable, baffling, disappointing whiffles of wind, with small rain, big ropes and small blocks, and only one stun'sail boom. Aha ! that'll work him up, and to your heart's content."

The waters were alive with albacores, bonetas, skip-jacks, dolphins, and flying-fish darting from crest to crest, now flashing through the air, even plunging into the waves to escape their finny or their feathered foes : a light placed in the weather fore-shrouds at night-time would bring scores of these beautiful little fish on our decks.

At other times would be seen the elegant little bark of the argonaut, or paper nautilus, so called from the delicate fragility of its sculptured shell, and its purity of tint, hoisting its membraneous sails to the breeze, and rowing itself along with double-banked oars or tentacles ; or, perhaps, another variety known as the "Portuguese man-of-war."

This is a soft nautilus, without shell, which looks as if constructed of the most transparent Bohemian glass, of a hue somewhat like an amethyst. These float by on the waves, and are to be seen of all dimensions down to the tiniest pink bubble.

> " Light as a flake of foam upon the wind,
> Keel upward from the deep emerged a shell,
> Shaped like the moon ere half her horn is filled,
> Fraught with young life, it righted as it rose,
> And moved at will along the yielding water,
> The native pilot of this little bark,
> Put out a tier of oars on either side,
> Spread to the wafted breeze a twofold sail,
> And mounted up and glided down the billow
> In happy freedom, pleased to feel the air,
> And wander in the luxury of light."

Now turn from the blue enameled ocean to the air, and observe the whole horizon teeming with bird-life. Conspicuous over all is the kingly albatross, soaring on his magnificent pinions, appearing at times as if suspended in the air. These, with Cape hens, molly hawks, Cape pigeons, etc., follow the good ship without cessation ; rapidly wheeling about, crossing and recrossing each other in giddy flight, hour by hour and day by day, possibly for even months together.

As far as can be seen they never rest on the waves. When met with they are often miles away from the nearest land. Yet dawn succeeds dawn, and there they are still hovering in our wake, eagerly looking out for anything in the shape of food that may be hove overboard. Such is their keenness of sight that nothing escapes their notice. Of all these winged attendants, none is so beautiful as the Cape pigeon, with its dappled black and white plumage. We caught several of these pretty birds by lengths of strong thread which we floated from the taffrail, and in one instance we hitched a piece of colored bunting to his pinion where it joins the body, and, letting him loose, had great interest in watching him morning after morning still in our company until we got out of the latitudes of such pretty attendants.

One day we caught a very large albatross, most irreverently and unpoetically dubbed "goney" by seamen.

A stout line and a chunk of pork fastened to a small block of wood as a float were sufficient to land one of these famous sea-birds on our decks, for having once seized the dainty morsel they will never let go until it and they are on deck together.

Once on deck they are unable to escape, for the even surface prevents them from using to advantage their immense wings. Our captive was about seven feet high, and his wings about eighteen feet from tip to tip.

There he stood a prisoner, but a very formidable one; none of us cared to expose ourselves to a blow of his wings, or a snap of his frightful hooked beak.

We had two dogs aboard, one a Newfoundlander of medium size, the other a black-and-tan, and they soon came nosing around the intruder. The larger dog, after taking stock of the enemy from a safe distance, was prudent enough to choose the flank and rear as his point of attack, and even then he displayed much less valor than discretion, evincing a rooted and instinctive dislike to any close acquaintance with wings or beak.

The old rogue seemed to be waiting until his younger and more imprudent ally had paid for his temerity by being impaled in his goneyship's beak, at which moment our canine friend expected to convert his feint into an assault, and seize his enemy by the neck.

A frantic howl of pain and terror, and the next moment Snap was dangling in the air, the loose skin of his back affording the albatross a secure hold, and preventing the infuriated bird from doing the dog more serious injury. Now was Nero's opportunity, but so appalling were the howls of Snap that his ally was thoroughly demoralized, and, with his tail between his legs, made hot haste to gain the cabin.

At last one of our men who had been on a whaler, and who caught and helped to eat many a goney, took the bird by the throat, and chopping the head off, released poor Snap, who tore aft with a hole in his skin as a memorial of his prowess.

Our ex-whalemen cleaned and polished up the beak and presented it to the captain ; the rough skin of the web-feet was converted into tobacco pouches ; the long feathers were distributed among the crew, the wings were stuffed and cleaned, the bones preserved as "curios," and next day our shipmate invited us to partake of an Irish-stew made out of the goney aforesaid.

In spite of the relish with which he swallowed down huge chunks of the meat, we did not take to it ; for it tasted to me much more fishy than porpoise ; so we left him and Bill Chapman to finish the mess between them.

Having now reached 40° south latitude, we gradually fell in with the prevailing westerly winds, and, squaring yards, stood away to the eastward, passing the longitude of the Cape of Good Hope, and entering the Indian Ocean.

The unusual cry, " Land ho !" at daybreak one morning, startled me out of a most comfortable nap.

" What land can it be ?" said I to my friend Chapman.

" There's nothing about here but St. Paul's and Amster· dam, he answered ; we're too far to the nor'ard to sight Desolation. All three of them are desolate enough for that matter, and are of no use except for castaways, and mighty little good to them."

These Islands, St. Paul's and Amsterdam, lie in about 37° 30' south and 78° E.

They are, as Chapman said, desolate rocks in the midst of the Indian Ocean, and of little benefit except to shipwrecked seamen, who, having reached their barren shores, may manage to survive until they attract the attention of some passing ship. St. Paul has a spring of water drilled out of

the rock on the lee or east side of the island, which was
done by the Dutch East India Company nearly two hundred
years ago, at a time when large bodies of troops were conveyed in their ships to their numerous and rich possessions
in the East.   With the humane intention of assisting any
unfortunates who might be on the islands, Captain Griswold
gave orders to stand to the southward of the island of St.
Paul so as to be able to round to under the lee, close in
shore, firing a short 12 lb. carronade from time to time, and
keeping a sharp look out.   This was done, but with no answer except the echo that reverberated amid the hollows of
the cliffs.

"What's her course now?" said I to Chapman, as he came
from the wheel.

"Nor'east by north for the Straits of Sunda and the
China Sea; but we shan't be able to make the passage
direct up the China Sea this voyage.   We shall have to
make the eastern passage, sighting Sandalwood and through
the Banda Sea away to the outside of Mindanao and the
Phillipine Islands.   To make this passage our course from
here is about nor'east by half east—curse the luck."

"Why can't we sail through the Straits, Bill?"

"Why can't we go through the Straits?   Why, because we
can't; that's why," said Bill in a very surly tone.

"But I don't see why we couldn't, for all that," persisted I.

"Why, confound it, boy, do you want a master of this or
any other ship to be blasted fool enough to tear his ship to
pieces trying to beat dead to wind'ard for well nigh unto
two thousand mile through the narrow sea, with a living gale
in his teeth the whole way?"

"But how do you know we should have head-winds all
the way?"

"How do I know, eh!   Well, I'll be blowed!   Did ye
ever hear of the 'monsoons?'"

"Yes, I may have heard tell of them, Bill, but you must remember that this is my first voyage to China, and you'll have to teach me a good many things, and not growl at me, unless you want me to ask Tom Thorn or Jack Lenine."

"Well, supposing I did growl! A good growl is better than a bad feed. It's enough to make a man growl, to think of having to go knocking about among a d—— lot of piratical islands four or five thousand miles out of your course."

"Well, it can't be helped."

"But, look here, George, you musn't mind me when I'm in the blues, and you needn't ask Tom Thorn or Jack Lenine nor anybody else for'ard for information as long as Bill Chapman's aboard. So you don't know about the monsoons, eh! Well, I'll tell you, if you can get a chart or a map of any sort."

"Now, then, here we are at St. Paul's and laying our course nor'east by north. If we have a good breeze, we ought to be up to the Straits of Sunda in about five weeks. After you pass through the Straits, Hong Kong, Macao, and the Bocca Tigris, that's the Canton river, you know, bears about north by east about two thousand miles off, and that's the course we'd steer, only for the d——— monsoons."

"You never knew about the monsoons, eh! Well, they blow down the China seas from nor'east to sou'west from October to April all through the winter and spring. Now we're in November; we wouldn't be near the Straits till December, and you see we should have the nor'east monsoons dead in our teeth for four months to come. No use in trying to beat against them, I tell you."

"In April, around they go and commence blowing from the sou'west and keep at it till October again. Talk about gales of winds! Talk about a heavy sea! Why some of those Western Ocean laborers on board of the *Columbus* and such similar craft, who blowed about hurricanes and cyclones,

don't know what a real blow is like.   They should be out in
April or October down abreast of Luzon, when, at the
change of the monsoon the typhoon comes down blowing fit
to make you bald-headed.   Them's the holy terrors, and no
mistake."

" Well, now then, sonny, we shan't go through the Straits,
that's settled.   The old man will make a landfall off the
sou'eastern end of the Island of Java and bear away to the
east'ard until he sights Sandalwood; then we'll get into the
Banda Sea and the Molucca Passage, and keep outside of
the Philippines to get the variable winds, and when we are
in the latitude of Formosa we shall have the wind free, even
if we do not catch the tail-end of the monsoon, and a few
days' sail will see us anchored in Hong Kong.   I wish we
were there.   Take your chart away, I'm tired of looking at
it.   Blow, good breeze."

My chum was heartily weary of the long voyage, and I
was extremely eager to put foot on shore again.

The wind continuing favorable we sighted the eastern extremity of Java in about five weeks and bore away to the
east'ard past the islands of Bally, Lombock and Sumbawa,
until we sighted Sandalwood in 9° 45' S., 120° E., when we
hauled to the nor'ard and passed through the Straits of
Sapy, between Sumbawa and Komodo.

We were now in the Macassar Sea, directly south of the
island of Celebes.

I may here state that the island known to sailors as Sandalwood is named in several charts Trendana or Trumba.   It
is in latitude 10° south and longitude 120° east, bearing
southeast from Sumbawa and south of the western part of
Flores.

Extreme vigilance was now more important than ever; innumerable islands were on every side of us; the seas were
narrow and dangerous, our charts not over reliable, the
winds variable and uncertain, violent squalls of frequent oc-

currence, and above all, the natives who swarmed on these
islands, and infested these seas, were treacherous, savage
and piratical, ever ready to rob and slay.

Well may it be said that these are the isles

"Where every prospect pleases,
And man alone is vile."

During the day we passed island after island, each surpassing in beauty the one that preceded it, the rich woods
resonant with the songs of birds, and the smooth white sand-
beaches forming a line of silver which stood out in bold relief between the forests and the sea.   As night fell, the stars
shone forth with dazzling brilliancy, and the stars of the
Southern Cross sparkled like diamonds set in the deep azure
of the firmament.   The moon shed her mild radiance over
the phosphorescent waters and lit up the deep recesses of the
forests on the shore.

One morning while threading our way through the count-
less islands of the Macassar Sea, the light wind died away
and we were entirely becalmed.   Instantly, as if by magic, a
line of dusky athletic forms gathered upon the beach and
stood watching us intently, gesticulating in the most frantic
manner.   At last, as if by a common impulse, they rushed
down to a small cove which ran inland a considerable distance, and in a few minutes we were dismayed at seeing a
whole fleet of proas filled with armed Malays pulling toward
us in the form of a crescent.

Alarmed beyond measure at the imminence of the danger
and our comparatively defenceless condition, we hastily mustered what arms we possessed, and made ready to repel
boarders, determined to sell our lives dearly.   What the
issue might have been I cannot tell, for, when the proas and
their villainous-looking crews were within five hundred yards
of us, a kindly Providence sent a refreshing breeze, and we
escaped most certain capture. and, doubtless, a horrible

death.   There are blood-curdling tales about the man-eating habits of those dusky devils.   Ah! ———

We next passed the Banda Sea, picking our way through the archipelago called the Spice Islands, and, with a spanking breeze from the south'ard left the Malaccas and found ourselves in the open ocean to the east'ard of the Phillippines.

In a few days more we bore away to the west'ard, and, sighting the bold Chinese coast, came to an anchor in Hong Kong roads, after a passage of 120 days from port to port.

Hong Kong is an island on the coast of China, and contained then only a fishing hamlet, with a joss-house in the centre of the habitations.   After remaining a few days at Hong Kong we received a "chop," or government permit, to proceed to Canton, or rather Whampoa, sixteen miles below, which is the anchorage for all foreign vessels, and which are not allowed to proceed any nearer to Canton.   Arriving at our anchorage (Whampoa) after a day's sail from Hong Kong, and mooring ship under the guidance of a native pilot, we were immediately surrounded by a regular shoal of sanpans, wash-boats, hoppo-boats, compradores and others, all eager for a chance of making the mighty dollar, an instinct as potent in the eastern as in the western mind.   I may here mention for the edification of those who are interested in "political economy" that the washerwoman in her sanpan will wash and mend the clothes for the seamen, irrespective of the time the ship may remain, for the sum of one dollar, charging proportionably more for the officers.   She will also fill the mattresses with fresh bamboo shavings, making a bed not to be excelled; also, when the ship leaves for home, giving to each one a "cumshaw" or present, generally a large pot of preserved ginger, all for the same charge. After meals they would come on board and collect the scraps that were left, on which they dined "sumptuously."

HONG KONG.

As soon as our ship was secured at her moorings we unbent sails, spread awnings fore and aft to protect us from
the rays of the tropical sun, and made all snug for our stay.
A boat's crew was then picked out, composed of the youngest hands, myself being one of the number, whose duty it was
to row the captain up to Canton nearly every day, except Sunday, and back, a pull of sixteen miles each way, a pretty good
task in that climate. We would leave the ship at four in the
morning and return late at night, escaping the heat of mid-
day. During the boat's stay at Canton she was given in
charge of a keeper from the "Factory," the captain giving
each of us fifty cents for rations, which amount was invested
in (do not turn away in disgust, my gentle reader) rat or
puppy, and eggs washed down with "samshu," a native
spirit distilled from "paddy," or unhulled rice, unrectified,
and much more apt to produce delirium tremens than "Jersey
lightning."

One day, while employed in the above duty, and meeting
with several boats' crews belonging to other American vessels, also on the same duty, with whom I indulged in various
potations of "samshu," I became so very drunk that upon
the return of the boat to the ship I was unable to use my
oar, but was conveyed on board, stowed for'ard under the
bow grating. When we came alongside the ship at night I
somehow clambered on board, and down 'tween decks,
where we had our hammocks slung, and where we lived. A
barrel of salt meat was lying on its bilge, and close beyond
it another on its head. I stumbled over the first, struck the
chime of the second, and cut a fearful gash between my
nose and eyebrow, the mark of which I bear to this day. I
fell over on the deck unconscious, and remained so all
night, lying in a pool of blood until morning. When all
hands were called I was still in the same position, and
the mate coming down to see what had become of me, and
seeing the state I was in, thought I was dead. I was carried

on deck and into the cabin, where stimulants were administered. After some time I was restored to consciousness, my
wound sewed up, and, in a few days was able to resume duty.

We had now a very responsible duty to perform, viz.: to
transport to Canton the treasure we had on board, consisting
of 150,000 Spanish pillar dollars. Our "long-boat" was got
ready for this purpose, and the most resolute of our crew
armed. On our passage up the river we had to run the
gauntlet of an assemblage of Chinese "canaille" who assailed
us with showers of stones, which they are very expert in
throwing. Our men did not dare to fire, for it was blood

CANTON BELLES.

for blood with the "Chinese laws" then, and may be so now
for aught I know. However, the delivery of the treasure to
the "American factory" was safely accomplished.

Our ship had now to be prepared for receiving homeward
cargo (after discharging our pigs of lead), which generally
from this port consists of tea, silk and cassia. In order to

protect such a cargo from destruction from rats, the ship must be thoroughly fumigated and the vermin suffocated by charcoal fires.

The manner of proceeding is to build a large charcoal fire on top of the ballast, under the main-hatchway, firmly sealing up every aperture to exclude air and to prevent any escape of "gas," the fo'castle, cabin, stern dead-lights, and in fact every opening fore and aft, being thoroughly secured. The crew and officers have to remove for the night and sleep on board of some other ship, leaving, however, an anchor watch on board, which is relieved every hour. This precaution has to be taken in case of fire, and to protect the ship from the thieving propensities of the Chinese, who, if they had the chance, would strip her of everything they could lay hands on, even to her copper sheathing. The next morning the hatches are taken off, and at that time three barrels of rats were collected and sold to a Chinaman.

At the time of which I write it was a common practice when in port, or in very fine weather at sea also, to scrape and burnish the ship's sides, but now it is obsolete and not practiced either in American, Dutch or Scandinavian ships. A sad accident occurred whilst performing this work which occasioned the loss of seven of our crew, and from whose sad fate your humble servant had the barest escape. The proverb, "Caution is the mother of safety," had been fatally neglected in this case, for the stage we used for the men to work on, and which was slung over the side, consisted of a ladder which had been broken in the middle and fished, a board being laid along on top to sit on when at work scraping. I had told the chief mate of the insecurity of it frequently, and whenever I had to work on it always practiced "self-preservation" by setting on one end where I would sit with the stage ropes between my legs. Whilst we were all busy at work I heard a sudden snapping and at once grasped the stage ropes and clambered on deck; looking astern I beheld my comrades plunged into the river where the tide was running not much less than eight miles an hour, with a strong under tow from which it was impossible, with the utmost effort, to rescue them. As for the crews of the sanpans and bum-boats by which we were surrounded, they made no attempt at rescue, for a Chinaman will not exert himself to save the life of a foreigner or a Chinese female.

This sad loss, as may be imagined, gave a melancholy tone to our ship's company during our stay in China and after our departure, and illustrates that not only in the tempest does "Jack" require the protection of the "traditional cherub" that sits up aloft.

It was customary for all the captains of the American ships in harbor to meet on each ship in rotation and dine together on Sunday. On the occasion of the festive meeting being held on board of the *Niantic* our steward, having prepared some extra nice pastry, of which he felt some professional pride, resigned it to the care of the cook to bake, but, to the mortification of the steward, he found it spoiled by being scorched. The steward accused the cook of having done so intentionally, and with malice aforethought. The steward naturally complained to the captain, who, ordering him aft, administered a scathing rebuke, accompanied with the threat of having him seized up in the main rigging and severely flogged should he repeat the offence. Now this cook was a sullen negro, a native of the island of Martinique, of very short stature, but immensely powerful, being what is called double-jointed. Beside this cook I was the only one on board who could speak French, and he accordingly made a confidant of me. He told me that the steward and he had been shipmates years previously in a piratical vessel commanded by the famous "Gibbs," who, with Wansley, was executed for piracy in New York harbor in 1831. He also told me that on leaving New York he had sworn to kill

CHINESE BAMBOO BRIDGE.

that mulatto "—— of a ——" before the voyage was over. This threat was carried out to the letter some thirteen months later when off the Madagascar coast, on our passage home.

To resume. At last our outward cargo began to arrive in "chops" (lighters). These were accompanied by the Chinese weigher in his stately barge, who came on board with his staff of teapot, cups, scale, and tea-table bearers, and who continually sipped tea, as strong as brandy, without sugar or milk. We continued taking in cargo for about three weeks at intervals until it was all stowed. The intervals of spare time were busily employed in racking off, purifying and refilling water-casks, repairing and setting up rigging, tarring down, mending sails, painting ship inside and out, yards, masts, mastheads, bowsprit and headgear, &c., and finally bending sails.

Hatches were now battened down, and the good ship *Niantic* was again ready to dare the dangers of the deep on her return homeward. Just at this juncture war was declared between Great Britain and the Chinese Empire. The forts of the "Bogue" or "Bocca Tigris" were armed, the river was blockaded with immense rafts, and we were practically held prisoners, being denied the privilege of proceeding to sea without a chop or permit from the Chinese government. Thus we had the mortification of laying war-bound for three months, ready for sea, and yet not daring to lift an anchor. We had, however, plenty of amusement in watching the military occupations of the Chinese soldiers, and the most comical effect was produced by the way the infantry managed their matchlocks, with which they were armed.

The front ranks bearing the matchlocks on their shoulders, the rear ranks would aim the piece and touch it off with a lighted punk; thus the front rank formed merely, as it were, a perambulating rest for the matchlocks. The forts were armed with cannon made of bamboo, hooped with iron hoops, and slung in chains overhead. These were swung to and fro when getting range, making the aim most uncertain. At last we procured the long-delayed permit, obtained a pilot, unmoored, made sail, and proceeded down the river between rafts of large timber, with scarcely room to squeeze through.

Arriving at Macao, a Portuguese colony, where the U. S. frigate *Columbus*, Commander Read, lay in the roads, she signalled us to heave to under her lee, when we were boarded by one of her double-banked boats bearing official dispatches for the secretary of the navy, and inquiring whether we could make room for half a dozen seamen whose term of service had expired and wished to return home (a providential God-send, for the government paid ten dollars for each man), and who, although that sum was paid, would also stand regular watch. After receiving eight men we filled away and stood on our course, entering the China Sea with a strong and favorable breeze.

After a fine passage of nine days down the China Sea, being favored by the nor'east monsoon, we anchored at Anjer, a point in the Straits of Sunda, which divides Sumatra from Java, where we traded for fruits, sugar (joggery), monkeys, sparrows, and various other articles, giving in return pieces of iron hoop, broken knife or razor blades, a few pins or needles, or any metallic thing whatever.

After about a day's stay we weighed anchor, made sail, and stood out of the straits into the Indian Ocean, which we entered with a splendid gale from the east'ard. In eighteen days we reached the longitude of the south point of Madagascar, where the quarrel before mentioned between our steward and cook culminated in the murder of the poor steward. It was my starboard-watch below for dinner, and on my going to the cook's galley to get the dinner kids for the watch I was taken aback by seeing the chief mate (Capie) standing with an uplifted axe over the cook, commanding him to drop the butcher's knife with which he was attacking the steward, who stood at the galley door defending himself with a saucepan. At the command of the mate, coupled with his fear of the axe, the cook desisted from the attack, but not before the steward had received two serious wounds, the hand and wrist having been laid open.

The cause of the quarrel was that the bread had been burned, and this had awakened the old feud. Captain

ANJER BEAUTY.

Griswold ordered them both aft, and, after a fair trial, condemned the cook to be seized up and flogged. But no sooner had sentence been pronounced than the cook rushed forward, and down into the fo'castle, opened the lids of some of the sea-chests, and frantically searched for a knife or some other deadly weapon. He was followed by the two mates, who struggled to get him on deck, but in vain, although both were powerful men (and if the cook had secured some weapon he would have killed any one who ventured into the fo'castle), and it was not until a four-fold tackle had been hooked to the fore top-sail sheets, and overhauled down into the fo'castle, and hooked on to him with a good selvage strap, which would fetch anything, that they got him on deck. He was immediately seized up in the rigging, and the mate laid on one dozen well directed blows with a heavy rope's end. On being cut down he went to his galley, deliberately took the butcher knife, stuck it between a small beam and the galley roof over-head, and awaited events. In a few minutes the steward came along, and, putting one foot inside the galley, asked the cook which was his saucepan. As quick as thought the cook jumped up, seized the knife, and plunged it into the steward, running the knife completely through him, so that the point came out at his back. The steward retreated or staggered, with both arms upraised perpendicularly, against the ship's side, when the cook sprang over the lashed spars after him, and again plunged the knife into his left armpit, the point coming out beside the left shoulder blade. All this transpired so quickly that none of the watch, who were busily engaged in getting a new jib ready for bending (it was blowing a gale at the time), had a chance to interfere for the steward's protection. The poor fellow lingered for about an hour and a half after the stabbing. When he attempted to speak the air would issue from his wounds. We committed his body to the deep with the prayers usual on such occasions.

The best notice of a burial at sea that I have seen was written by an actor named Henry J. Finn, who was lost on the steamer *Lexington*, burned on Long Island Sound, January 13, 1840, with a hundred others, and here is a copy from my note book.

BURIAL AT SEA.

Deep mists hung over the mariner's grave
  When the holy funeral rite was read,
And every breath on the dark blue wave
  Seemed hushed to hallow the friendless dead.

And heavily heaved on the gloomy sea
  The ship that sheltered that homeless one—
As though his funeral hour should be
  When the waves were still and the winds were gone.

And there he lay in his coarse, cold shroud,
  And strangers were 'round the coffinless ;
Not a kinsman was seen among that crowd,
  Not an eye to weep nor a lip to bless.

Not a sound from the church's passing bell
  Was echoed along the pathless deep
The hearts that were far away to tell
  Where the mariner lies in his eternal sleep.

Not a whisper then lingered upon the air,
  O'er his body one moment his messmates bent,
But the plunging sound of the dead was there,
  And the ocean now is his monument.

But many a sigh and many a tear
  Shall be breathed and shed in the hours to come,
When the widow and fatherless shall hear
  How he died—far, far from his once happy home.

As for the cook, he was immediately seized by the officers and watch on deck, and placed in durable irons, put in the sail room, and securely chained to the ship's side. I was deputed as his jailor and attendant. Every Sunday I used to take his hands out of the irons to allow him to wash. Thus he was kept until he was handed over to the authorities on our arrival in New York. After the murder he almost every day told me he was glad he had killed the mulatto. The cook's name was Jaques Charles, and his victim's Charles Edwards, a native of St. Johns, N. B. Edwards was a fine specimen of manly symmetry and strength.

The remainder of our passage home was accomplished without any more tragedies or mishaps.

In a few days we lost the Indian trades, and rounding the Cape of Good Hope we encountered very heavy weather, being compelled to lay to for nineteen days in a fierce gale from the west'ard, under a close-reefed main-topsail, foretop-mast-staysail, and sometimes a reefed fore-sail. However, having the current which sets to the west'ard under our lee, we were enabled gradually to make our course slowly. As the current was against the wind they managed between them to kick up a tremendous sea. We rounded the Cape about thirty days after the death of the steward, and making about 1,400 miles we struck the sou'east trades, when squaring yards and piling canvas upon our good ship, we considered ourselves fairly homeward bound. In ten days we sighted St. Helena, in five more Ascension, and after crossing the Equator in 20 west longitude lost the sou'east trades in about 6° north latitude.

After a week's baffling winds (which tried the temper of the captain, officers and crew), accompanied with torrents of rain such as one only sees in the tropics, we fell in with the nor'east trades which carried us nearly up to the Bermudas. Encountering very heavy weather, with several gales of wind in the vicinity of Cape Hatteras and the Gulf Stream, we finally took a pilot on board off the Delaware Capes, and in two more days came to an anchor in the East river, New York, after a passage of one hundred and ten days.

Here we were back again after an absence of over fifteen months from home, during which time we had encountered terrific weather soon after leaving port, narrowly escaped foundering at sea: in seeing a fever-stricken vessel, whose entire crew had fallen victims to the destroyer; losing seven men by drowning, and another a victim to revenge at the hand of a shipmate, while another was fettered to be delivered into the hands of justice. How little is thought when Jack embarks as to how and when he will return, or whether he will return at all. But perhaps it is better so, for if he thought too much very likely he wouldn't go to sea at all.

The first night of our arrival, the 16th of December, 1835, we witnessed, as we lay at anchor, the great fire in New York which laid waste so much property and ruined so many business men and insurance companies. It was a truly awful but grand sight, as the fire illuminated the whole harbor, and cast the reflections of the shipping in the dark waters, a sight never to be forgotten, and in fancy as I write I can recall it as though it had happened but yesterday. Twelve acres were said to have been burned over.

After the fire had subsided the chief mate went ashore and made affidavit concerning the murder, and officers were sent on board who took the cook ashore a prisoner, as well as taking the witnesses, I among them, in charge. We were taken to the United States Commissioners' Court, where the prisoner was committed for trial, and the witnesses held in default of bonds. As we would be paid for our time and live well with the jail warden at his table, we elected to be locked up in preference to giving bonds. After three months the cook was brought to trial, and was found guilty of murder in the second degree, and was sentenced to be imprisoned for five years at hard labor.

Nine years later I saw him in the capacity of cook on board the ship *Jessore* of Boston, which vessel was lying becalmed a few degrees to the west'ard of the sou'east point of the island of Java, bound to Sourabaya for rice. I was one of the boat's crew that boarded her. I was then in the clipper brig *Fagle*, built expressly for the opium contraband trade on the coast of China, regarding which I shall relate hereafter.

During my detention in the " City Prison," New York, as a witness, I, of course, made the acquaintance of several sailors who were detained for various reasons; some as witnesses for mutinies, others as witnesses of cruelties committed by officers on seamen, etc. But being a favored guest I was allowed to go and come as I pleased, having only to report every twenty-four hours. In the course of my rambles I visited one sailors' boarding-house and another, and would often return with a sail-bag filled with bottles of liquor packed in straw, and, placing it inside the railing outside the prison, one of the sailors in the prison, who were on the look-out for me, would send down a line through the bars, which I would make fast to the bag, and they would haul up the bag and take the bottles out. There were at that time about a dozen seamen in the jail, and these would get gloriously drunk. The officials could never discover how the liquor was obtained. One particular night, when they were well filled with liquor, they made a raid on the rooms occupied by the debtors, who were at that time imprisoned for debt, and taking or capturing cots, tables, chairs, etc. (private property of the debtors) by force, took them down into the corridor and made a large bonfire. There was a great uproar, as may be supposed. The fire-bells were rung, the prison officials were bewildered, and the "leather-heads" (as the city police or night watchmen were then called) assisted in quenching the fire and preserving order.

I had no hand in these proceedings, for I was not in the prison at the time, being out on parole, and as the officials could make no discovery as to how the liquor was obtained, the matter was allowed to die a natural death.

Chapter VI.

Once more upon the waters! yet once more!
And the waves bound beneath me as a steed
That knows his rider. Welcome to their roar!
Swift be their guidance, whereso'er it lead."

As I remarked toward the close of last chapter, how little
Jack thinks how and when he will return, so did I little think
when my money, both from my ship and from the government
as a witness in the murder case, being all spent, I shipped on
board the bark *Rapid*, Captain Ward, engaged in the Cuba
trade, that before I returned I should go upon what, in those
days, was facetiously termed a "blackbirding cruise." That
means a voyage in a slaver. Yet, so it was. But I am free
to say one such cruise was quite enough for me.

We got out to sea under canvas in charge of the pilot,
hove to off the light-ship, where he was discharged, and with
the wind nor'east proceeded on our voyage. The wind
freshened so much as night came on that we were compelled
to reduce sail until we were staggering along under double-
reefed topsails, and whole courses with jib and spanker, we
being on the larboard tack with the wind two points abaft
the beam.

This wind held on for several days and brought us into
the nor'east trade winds. After a fine passage of eight days
we came to anchor in the harbor of Havana. Having discharged our cargo of miscellaneous goods and "Yankee notions" we commenced receiving homeward cargo of box
sugar, which came alongside in lighters. With our cargo all
in and ready for sea it was customary for the crew to have a
holiday ashore just previous to sailing. They were allowed
to go by watches, one half the first day and the other the
next. When my turn came, and I was enjoying my leave in
usual sailor-like fashion, I met a Frenchman belonging to a

large ship also lying in the harbor, who was on the same job as myself, namely, that of enjoyment. He told me that he intended to desert from his ship, where he only received fifty francs a month, while he could get over six hundred in another business. I inquired in what line, and, pointing to a fine-looking clipper bark at anchor in the offing, he in-

LEAVING THE BARK RAPID.

formed me that she was waiting for a crew for the purpose of going to the African coast for a cargo of slaves. The wages were to be $120 a month and a slave apiece.

At my suggestion we walked down the mall, and soon saw a boat shove off from her and pull toward us. Two swarthy but well-dressed men stepped ashore, and the Frenchman addressing one of them in Spanish, which I understood, asked him if he wanted a crew. He replied that he required forty active, resolute men, who would not be scrupulous about the business in which they would be engaged. He readily informed us of the nature of the business, and said if we wished to join we should be paid $120 a month with a nigger drawn by lot.

I immediately agreed to join, and going on board the *Rapid* collected my clothing during my anchor watch, hauled up the small boat that was towing astern, and jumping into her, with my "dry goods," rapidly sculled off to the bark *Amistad*, and set foot on her deck just as the anchor watch had struck eight bells (4 A. M.)

After breakfast I was called to the cabin to sign articles, which stated that we were bound on a commercial voyage to the "west coast of Africa."

The next day we completed our quota of the crew, and were informed by the lieutenant (the title given to the second in command or chief mate on board Spanish or French vessels), that we should sail during the night to avail ourselves of the land breeze which sets off the land at that time. If any of us wished to go ashore we might do so, but we were to be sure and come on board at sun-down.

At the stated time, we were all ready, hove short, loosed sails, and waited for the land breeze, and as it sprung up and fanned our fevered and anxious brows, we hove up, made all sail, and, standing out of the harbor past the "Morro Castle" we entered the Carribean Sea, heading to the north-'ard under the influence of the trade-wind, with a clean full on the starboard tack, with all the sail we could carry. We showed such a pair of heels that would have puzzled any British cruiser that might have wanted to overhaul us— eleven knots an hour, within five points or less of the wind. I have seen her working to wind'ard at nine points on both tacks.

We stood on this tack, and having cleared the Straits of Florida, and reached 30° N. latitude, she was slewed round on the other tack and stood to the south'ard and east'ard, crossing the Gulf Stream, weathering the Bahamas and the

"BLACKBIRDS" UNDER COCOANUT TREES.

entire West India Islands, going clean, full, close-hauled, and on the larboard tack for twelve days, when the trade-winds, hauling more to the south'ard and east'ard, and being near the Brazilian coast, tacked ship and pointed her for the African coast, then distant about 3,000 miles, keeping a lookout at the mast-head night and day.

After a passage of twenty-five days we came to an anchor off " Ambriz," a Portuguese trading colony consisting merely of a collection of mud huts and " Ham Barracoons."

Here we lay at anchor, with slip ropes and buoys on our cables ready for slipping and standing out to sea on the first appearance of any British man-of-war who might wish to interfere with our "commercial enterprise." Sails all ready for setting without going aloft, being merely stopped with twine which could be broken from the deck, and, in fact, everything ready at a moment's notice to slip off and show any Britisher the way to walk.

We soon negotiated for about 1,100 " birds " (blackbirds) of whom two-thirds were stout adults, the remainder consisting of women and full-grown boys. These poor wretches had been taken prisoners of war in tribal battles, and were thus disposed of like so many cattle.

They were kept in barracoons ashore until such time as we were ready to take them aboard, when a party of our crew, supplied with manacles, landed, and driving the negroes to the beach, branded them between the shoulders with the name of the ship. Fifty at a time were huddled then into a large boat, or lighter, owned by the people on shore, and, being alongside, were hurried on deck, and finally below. The men were put in the main hold, the women in the cabin, and the boys in the fo'castle. Officers and crew lived on the homeward passage on deck.

After lying ten days at our anchorage off " Ambriz," which is at the mouth of a river of the same name, and having filled up with our cargo of live stock, with a supply of water and provisions on board, we hove up, made all sail, and stood out to sea with our living cargo of 1,150 " black-birds."

The wind being about S. S. W. we laid our course going

two points free, but were hardly out of sight of the coast when to us the exciting cry was heard "Sail, ho, on the weather bow." She was about two points forward of the beam, and was going free, and to all appearance was a British cruiser But she gave us no trouble, for, being no match

SLAVE-SHIP ARRANGED FOR LIVE CARGO.

for us in point of sailing, before the sun went down she was nowhere to be seen even from the to'gallant mast-head, and, while we rejoiced over our escape, doubtless our enemies were regretting their loss of prize·money, for

" Sweet is revenge, especially to women ;
Pillage to soldiers, prize-money to seamen."

After a swift passage of twenty days, we came to safe and

sound within a cables length of the shore of the Isle of Pines on the south coast of the Island of Cuba.

I must here state that during the passage the hatches were opened every morning and a detail of half a dozen negroes were released and made to clean up the filth, then supply the rest with food and water. The women were attended to in like manner by one or two of their number, also the boys, which latter were not manacled to bars as the men and women were. Every morning six or eight bodies were hove overboard like logs of wood, without either shroud or canvas.

After discharging our human cargo and cleaning up, and the crew getting a nigger apiece according to agreement, which we sold to the consignee, we got under way for Havana preparatory to another voyage to the African coast.

We arrived in the harbor of Havana in a week after leaving the Isle of Pines, having been delayed by light and contrary winds interspersed with calms off the southern and western coast.

The voyage for which I had signed being now completed, having lasted two and a half months, I received a little over six hundred dollars in doubloons, and we scattered in different directions, some two-thirds eventually returning to the slaver for another voyage to the African coast. But as I have said, this sort of "commercial enterprise" not being to my mind I, after spending a week ashore in Havana, shipped on board the brig *Ann McKim*, Captain Trask, bound to Baltimore, with a cargo of molasses and box sugars, which port we reached after a tedious passage of eight days.

Reaching Baltimore, I shipped in a two top-sail schooner called the *Isabella*, Captain Downs, for New York, with flour in barrels, where we arrived after a very pleasant passage of four days.

And now, having my pockets pretty well lined, a desire to revisit my native city and sip of the pleasures of "Home,

Sweet Home," came upon me, and I resolved to go to Montreal, spending a month very pleasantly, seeing old friends, "though I scrupulously avoided wealthy relatives," and visiting well-remembered scenes, for

" Dear is the schoolboy spot,
    We ne'er forget,
    Though there we are forgot."

BUMBOAT.

Chapter VII

" He that has sailed upon the dark blue sea,
  Has viewed at times, I ween, a full fair sight ;
When the land breeze is fair as breeze may be,
  The white sail set, the gallant frigate tight,
Masts, spires, and strand retiring to the sight,
  The glorious main, expanding o'er the bow,
The convoy spread like wild swans in their flight,
  The dullest sailor wearing bravely now,
So gaily curl the waves before each dashing prow."

Having had what I considered enough of home, I returned to New York and shipped on board the *Rome*, of
Salem, Captain Marshall, bound, as the articles read and
were signed, " to a port or ports in Asia, and back to a port
of discharge either in Europe or America." We sailed from
New York in the month of December, 1836, not knowing,
and caring less, where to in particular. One old experienced
seaman predicted, from the fact that we had great guns
under the ballast and were well provided with small arms,
pikes, cutlasses, and ammunition, that we were bound to
the west coast of Sumatra for pepper; these having formed
part of the outfit of the vessels in which he had before
sailed on such voyages, and being required for protection
against the piratical population with which that group of
islands is infested.

A heavy gale of wind from the nor'west drove us well on
our easterly course, but the good ship *Rome* was a dull sailor
and steered worse, being square both ends, and one of those
ships "built by the mile and sawed off in lengths to suit."

After we had reached 8° north, and had been through the
" Horse latitudes," we struck the nor'east trades, and,
standing close-hauled for a month on the port tack, we got
the prevailing westerly winds, doubled the Cape of Good
Hope, and sailed into the Indian Ocean.

After a passage of one hundred and eighty days, during

which we did not speak a single sail nor see anything except the sea and the firmament, with the usual number of birds, we at last arrived on the west coast of Sumatra, short of water and provisions. The first harbor we made was a land-locked bay that indented the coast called "Tampa Tuan." Arming a boat's crew of eight oars we pulled for the shore, the ship standing off and on, and not coming to an anchor.

On touching the shore, a young seaman and myself being bowsmen, jumped ashore to hold the boat, when, to our intense astonishment and alarm, we were immediately sur-

A GERITULAS.

rounded by about two or three thousand Malays, as naked as when they were born, but armed with "kreeses" (long knives,. My mate and I instinctively grasped our sheath knives, resolved to defend ourselves if attacked, but we were unmolested, as a "Geritulas" (Rajah's deputy or secretary) came down to the beach and permitted us to get what we wished for.

After procuring a supply of water, yams, buffalo beef, and fruits which we paid for, we stood out of "Tampa Tuan," and down the coast to the south'ard and east'ard.

Before coming to an anchor a large "proa" came alongside with a "Geritulas" on board who told our captain where we could fill up with pepper.

We had a partial cargo of unbleached cotton goods suitable to the native market which were intended to be bartered for such produce as the captain considered advantageous, and accordingly after reconnoitering the coast, we finally came to an anchor at a place called Tarabangan Rayah, but with our cable ready to slip in case of emergency.

We then threw our stone ballast overboard, got the guns up and mounted, cleaned the small arms, which were kept in the fo'castle, as the Malays invariably murder the officers first.

I will now describe the manner of weighing the pepper, which I am sure will convince any one of the vast superiority of the honest dealing of the so-called Christian over the heathen.

First, the fifty-six pound weights were taken ashore and tested, then brought aboard again, when the handles were secretly screwed out and the hollow weight filled up with small shot, so that our tested weight of fifty-six pounds became one of about ninety pounds. Then the Malays would lay five bags of pepper at a time on the scale to be weighed, consequently five empty bags would require to be placed with the weights, in the opposite scale. But the bags which we had substituted would weigh double or treble as much as those containing the pepper, by reason of their having been soaked in brine long before we arrived on the coast, besides having heavy pieces of canvas sewn inside of them as a lining.

*   *   *   *   *

An amusing and ludicrous trick used to be played by us on the natives, but only resorted to at such times when they swarmed in such numbers on our decks that we were in fear of some treachery or conspiracy affecting our safety, and wanted to clear them off. In such instances we let loose a live pig, of which we had several on board, to be turned into pork some time or other, and no sooner did our little squeaker make his appearance and begin to show his pleasure at being at liberty by running about than they, with consternation and alarm in their countenances, hurried off

shouting "Teda, Teda, Macan, Babu!" which, being inter-
preted, "No, no eat pig," plunged into the sea from the
ship's rail, as if a whole herd of swine with the devil in them
was after them.

Pigs are an abomination and pollution to those of the
Mahommedan faith, as the natives of Madagascar are.

When all was in readiness for taking in cargo, a shore
gang of four men was picked out to accompany the captain
and supercargo, Mr. Lunt, ashore, and to assist in the
weighing.

After weighing enough to make a large surf-boatfull,
the Malays would load the boat, some steadying it, whilst
others would man the oars. All being ready, they would
wait till three heavy rollers had expended themselves, and
then make a start through the heavy surf, which ran so
high that at times the bow would be at an angle of 50°,
or more ; the unpleasant effect of which was not diminished
by the close company of great numbers of ravenous sharks
eager for their prey, and which they were pretty sure of
should the surf-boat get broadside to the surf, which sometimes has happened.

When it came on to blow heavy while we were ashore,
so that we could not return on board, we had to remain
where we were, sleeping on mats, living on curried fowls
served on a leaf, and drinking cocoanut milk, while we
amused ourselves by chewing betelnut mixed with lime, I
suppose, to aid our digestion ; anyhow, it is the correct
thing in polite society, and a universal custom.

On one occasion, when we were thus land-locked, I made
the acquaintance of the Rajah's factotum or Geritulas—
prime minister, I suppose. He was an official, who, finding that I was versed in different languages, offered me a
position in the Rajah's service, promising to facilitate my
escape from the ship, and, as an extra inducement, to give
me four wives, besides slaves. But as Mormonism was not

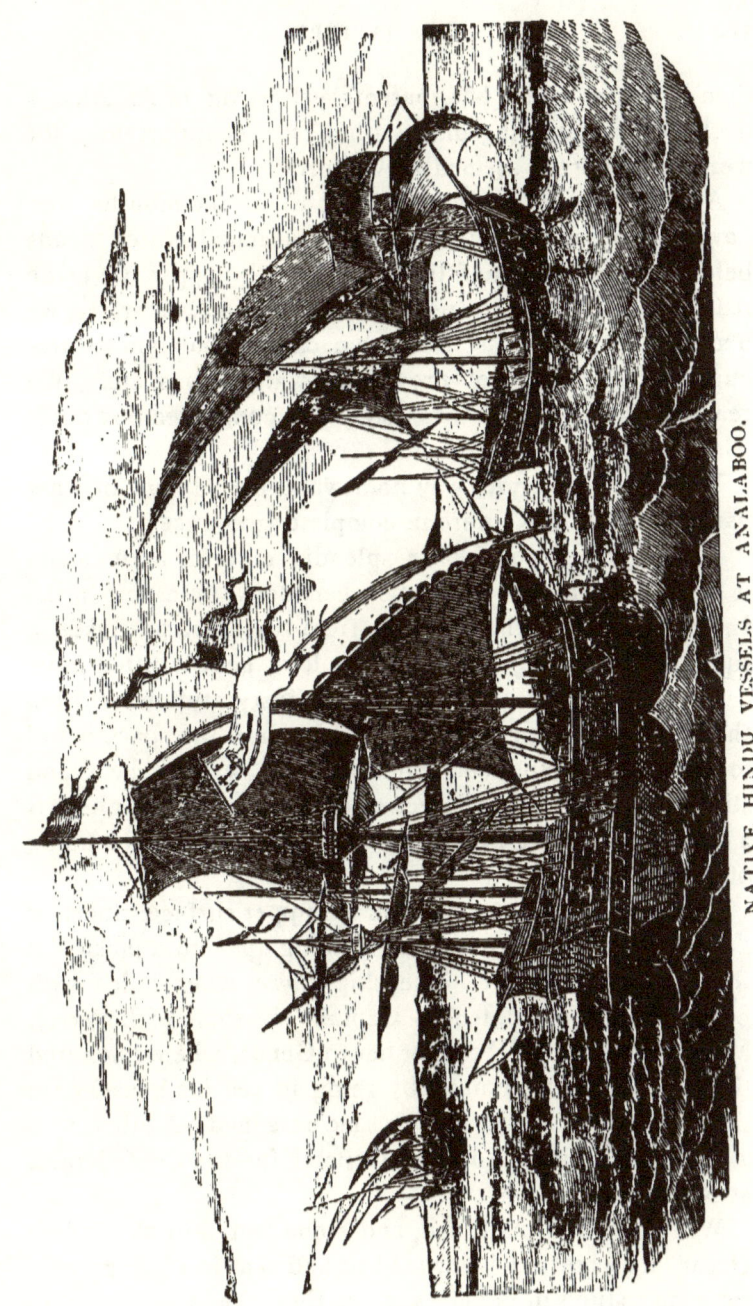

NATIVE HINDU VESSELS AT ANALABOO.

then in vogue, and I had parents yet living in America, I
declined his tempting offer, although the opportunity for
wealth and honors seemed very alluring.

At length, after a stay on the cost of six months, and
having disposed of our cargo of unbleached cotton goods
before mentioned, and filled the ship with pepper, we made
ready for the return voyage.   But before finally starting, we
had to sail up the coast to a town called Analaboo to procure a fresh upply of provisions, water, yams, etc.   We
reached that place in two days, and completed our outfit
without delay.

We finally got under way homeward bound, but for what
part of the world we were in complete ignorance.

I ought to tell you what a splendid cure for rheumatism
it is to stow away pepper between decks in a port in the
Indian Ocean.   The sufferer from rheumatism takes a
squilgee (an oblong board, with a long handle fitted in its
center), and shoves the dried and dusty stuff back from
the hatchway to the sides of the ship, until the space is full
to the deck.   No man can stand the terrible heat and
stifling dust more than fifteen minutes at a time, so there is
a chance for curing fifty rheumatic patients at each loading
of a ship.

The pepper becomes hard on the upper surface, almost as
a stone, and always requires breaking up with a pickax at
the port of delivery.   The ship *Rome*, when laden with
pepper, was commanded by Captain Marshall, of Beverley,
Massachusetts.   He brought her to Genoa, where I honored
the memory of Columbus by going to see his house.   On
that voyage we had a Mr. Cassiac as a mate, I think, who
afterwards became Adjutant-General for the Confederates
at Richmond, Virginia.

When we had made sail, and stood out into the Indian
Ocean, we were much alarmed to find that in rigging out a
top-mast stun'sail-boom, and setting the sail, the ship

showed a list of four or five streaks, thus showing her crank condition, owing to the nature of her cargo and the way it was stowed. The crew went aft in a body to the captain to express their fears that the ship in her present condition would never be able to weather the Cape of Good Hope.

Captain Marshall, who was a very fine man, and of a kind, fatherly disposition, endeavored to assuage their fears by explaining to them that from his experience in the pepper trade their fears were groundless, as the fine sand which at starting was all through the pepper, would, by the motion of the vessel, gradually find its way to the bottom of the vessel or hold, and would long before reaching the Cape make her sufficiently stiff.

However, to give them perfect confidence, he ordered the ship to be put dead before the wind, and as much pepper as could be got on deck in the wake of the watches, the anchors to be stowed as far below as possible, with the chain-cables, sent down to'gallant masts and yards, stun'-sail-booms, and to burn all useless old spars about decks. This was done at once, with the desired effect of soon rendering her fairly stiff.

We reached the Cape of Good Hope in a little short of two months, but here we encountered a succession of strong 'westerly gales, which compelled us to lay to under bare poles for nearly a month, slowly drifting around in the current which set westerly. This lasted until we fell in with the sou'east trade-winds, which were blowing very strong, and we headed for the famed Island of St. Helena, where we rounded to off Jamestown in forty-one days from the Cape, and come to an anchor, short of almost everything. The French squadron, charged with the duty of conveying the mortal remains of the Emperor Napoleon I (the Little Corporal) to France, was on the point of setting sail for France, and I had the satisfaction of viewing his embalmed features as they lay in state on the jetty under an awning.

One night, during our passage from the Cape, the good ship had a very narrow escape from going down stern first, or at any rate being dismasted. We were running before the wind under all the canvas we could spread, when the seizings of the tiller ropes having given way, they rendered round the barrel of the wheel, thus losing entire control over her steerage, which caused the ship to swing head to wind, and the yards being square, it was a sheer miracle that she did not founder, or else have everything brought by the board. However, by judicious and prompt seamanship and handling, hoisting the jibs and canting the head-yards in season, she was again got before the wind.

The captain shows his skill as a seaman and training as a manager of unruly and high-tempered men and officers, when in such a case the tempest howls and the crew murmurs in vain—the well handled ship outriding the danger, and the crew obeying orders promptly, securing the safety of all. Another incident of this part of our voyage from the Cape to St. Helena, is now fresh in mind. We were all engaged in sending aloft to'gallant mast and yards, when one evening it jammed in the trestle-trees or cap, or both, which gave rise to high words between the mate and the men, who were aloft receiving and rigging the mast, and on the completion of the job the quarrel was renewed on deck. At night the men seized the mate, who was a Frenchman, but a very smart seaman, and were about to throw, or rather heave, him overboard, when the captain, hearing the tumult, came forward and appeased the men. The mate loudly insisted that the men should be put in irons, but the captain would not consent, saying that he could get along without that kind of work, and so the matter ended.

We remained only two days at St. Helena, during which we received our supply of water, of which we had run quite out, laid in a fresh stock of vegetables, etc. But before leaving, the entire crew paid a visit to what was the tomb of the "Great Napoleon," who ended his chequered life of grandeur and ambition in this sea-girt prison.

On the passage between the "Cape" and "St. Helena" a curious circumstance occurred to my ship and bunkmate, Arthur Hider (call it spiritualism or what you will). I had gone below on my watch on deck, to light my pipe after steering my trick, and was in the act of applying the light, when Arthur (who was in the other watch, and consequently had turned in) gave a sudden start, with an alarmed and eager expression. I exclaimed, "What the devil's the matter?" He answered, "George, I have just this moment seen as plainly as I now see you standing before me, the apparition of my dear mother, bearing the appearance and habiliments of the dead." I thought him crazy or gone wrong. But years after, when I met him after a considerable separation, he told me that on his arrival in New York he learned of the death of his mother, and on comparing the date and time of her death with his memorandum of the above occurrence, which he had made in his log-book at the time, that allowing for longitude, etc., it had taken place exactly at the time he had been visited by, as he concluded in his mind, his "mother's spirit." I had often heard of such experiences, as told by shipmates, but paid no attention to them, considering them idle tales or dreams, but this was right before my eyes, and Arthur was a truthful man, and really believed that he saw the apparition, and the event seemed to prove it. Whatever it may have been, there seems little room for doubt of the fact. Who can account for it?

At St. Helena we took in fresh water, provisions of all sorts that were to be had, and none too soon, for many of the crew were suffering from a too generous diet of salt-horse, and not a few had rattling teeth in answer to the

demands of the sailor's old-time enemy the scurvy. Among
other supplies, there were a number of shoats which afforded
an immense amount of roaring fun to the sailors. Whenever the cook called for one the sailors in the watch were
very officious in getting one or more out of the long-boat,
and, of course, one always managed to slip through the
fingers of the fun-loving young Jack tars, and then the fun

PIG LOOSE ON DECK.

began. All over the deck, from stem to stern, the lively
animal was raced with ever so much effort at catching, but
very little intention of stopping the spree too soon.

   We received our orders to proceed to Genoa, in Italy,
and accordingly weighed and set sail for that port, distant
by rough reckoning about 6,000 miles. We carried the

sou'east trades with us as far as 6° north latitude, when, as is
generally the case between the sou'east and nor'east trades,
we got into a series of light baffling winds and heavy rains,
with terrific thunder and lightning, interspersed with torrid
heat, till we struck the nor'east trades, which we did after
our patience was nearly, but not quite, exhausted

Strange to say, on this occasion, when we got into the
nor'east trades, we were astonished to find the air full of
very fine sand, which fell on the rigging and decks. In these
latitudes we also saw shoals of flying-fish, which present an
ever varying picture, as they seemed to skim from crest to
crest of the waves. I may mention that they are very
palatable food, as well as very convenient and welcome,
when picked up on board and cooked fresh.

After leaving St. Helena, we passed close to the Island
of Ascension, and on the sixtieth day from the former
entered the Straits of Gibraltar, and passing cl se to the
rock and town of that name entered the Mediterranean.

The Rock of Gibraltar, as every one knows, is a vast
fortress in the possession of, and garrisoned by Great
Britain.   It stands like a huge sentinel guarding the
entrance to the Mediterranean Sea, and as the current sets
outward no vessels hostile to that power could well enter
without exposing themselves for a lengthened period to the
guns of that fortress, which is considered impregnable.
Steam has to a certain extent now modified these condi-
tions.   It has been frequently the scene of sanguinary contests between the various nations that have contended for
its possession, more particularly Spanish, French and English; and with Malta, and now, within the last few years, the
Island of Cyprus, forms a link of strongholds, provisioning
and military store depots, necessary for England to maintain
as long as she remains a first rate power, which some wise
heads predict will not be long.   But let us hope they are
mistaken.

GENOA.

In twelve days from entering the Mediterranean we came in sight of the port and town of Genoa, which we soon entered, and, rounding to inside the mole, dropped anchor, after a passage of seven months.

Having made our stern fast to an immense iron ring in the mole, and hove taut in our cable, we were thus moored head and stern. Then, as is always the case when ships arrive from a long voyage, and Jack is supposed either to have plenty of money in his pocket, or to have a sum more or less due him, whether in Christian or heathen countries, we were immediately waited upon by attentive visitors of all kinds, who come off in boats to pay their respects to his pocket—bum boats, tailor's pimps, and others of still more questionable repute, who importuned us to go ashore with them, and see the delights and beauties of Genoa, "the superb," whatever that may mean, and what could be had for money.

Having sprung our foremast off the Cape of Good Hope, we had to step a new one, but as one-half of the crew were dissipating ashore, and revelling as sailors generally do or did, and many who ought to know better, in the precarious pleasures of "women and wine," we had only half a crew at work, and so it took two weeks to get the new mast in and rigging set up.

At length we got orders to lift hatches and discharge cargo, which was stowed in bulk. On the top of the pepper a thick blue crust had formed as hard as if it had been frozen. It had to be broken through with spade and pick ax.

After the discharge of the cargo had been completed, I and three others formed the idea of going to Marseilles, in France, one of the most important sea-ports in the world. The captain reluctantly consented to give us our discharge, as he wished us to continue in the ship, which was going to Messina, Sicily, for fruit for New York, but I wanted to

see "La Belle France," and the others coincided with me.
They put themselves under my guidance, and after receiving a little over one hundred and fifty dollars apiece, we
determined to see a little life on shore, and rest for a while
from our labors.

After about ten days' jollification in Genoa, and, seeing
the sights of that city (among others the site on which the
house in which Columbus was said to have been born, but
which we learned has been replaced many years ago by a
more modern edifice), after reducing our purses by fifty
dollars each, hardly earned but easily spent, we procured
passports through the American consul, and took passage
by steamer to Marseilles.

Here was a novel position for a sailor who had never
before been aboard a sea-steamer, and then to be a passenger! Most assuredly every part and thing was critically
surveyed by each one of us, and the remarks passed would
no doubt have amused my readers of the present day, or
any of the engineers of the same time.

The harbor of Marseilles is quite artificial, being dug out
from the land, and docked, the ships laying head in and
packed like herrings.

On landing we took up quarters at a boarding-house,
kept by a French woman (or lady, modernized), who was
called English Mary, for what reason I know not.   She
averaged at least the year through five hundred boarders
at a time.   The business had been handed down from her
ancestors for many generations, and she was reported extremely wealthy, and was unquestionably smart.

Well! The memories of the past, how sweet sometimes!
May they, the sweet ones, I mean, last forever! or, as the
Turks say, a thousand and one years, while the sad ones
may go to Jericho, or any other hot or cold place out of
the way.   Well, this smart "English Mary" had a pretty
daughter named Julié, and she, bless her little heart, took

MARSEILLES.

a fancy to your humble servant, to which I certainly had
not the slightest objection.   I attributed her liking for me
to the knowledge which she attained that I was somewhat
of a linguist and an arithmetician—qualities in those days
not frequently possessed by those in my sphere.   However
that may be, we had a good time of it, till the time came
to say, "Good bye! sweetheart, good bye!"   No doubt my
chums had equal luck in some other quarter, for—

> " What lass but loves the sailor boy—
> We o'er the ocean roam, sirs;
> In every clime we find a port,
> In every port a home, sirs."

One day, as we were cruising among the quays and shipping, we chanced on a fine large French brig called the
Aigle, Captain Avril, for St. Thomas, West Indies, and
Guyama, Porto Rico, with an assorted cargo for a wealthy
French planter.   She had commenced loading, and, as we
were willing to ship in her, the captain took us to the
government office for the purpose of signing articles.
The wages were to be fifty francs a month.   My three
shipmates signed first, and when I signed, the captain
noticing that I hailed from Montreal, Canada, asked me
whether I could speak French.   On my answering in the
affirmative, he at once said to the official, "Put down ten
francs more, which I will pay out of my own pocket," and
from that time I had to act as spokesman or interpreter for
our entire party.

The following day we went to work setting up rigging
and bending sails, and while still on this job I remember
well, as I had soon good cause to, returning to the ship
after dinner half seas over, having imbibed more than my
share of a large bottle of wine containing about three pints,
called in France "*un litre*" (because it makes your head
lighter, I suppose), which was always placed at dinner
between every two persons, and, in a spirit of foolhardiness
and bravado, I jumped overboard from the brig's stern, and

was rescued from my perilous position by one of our number, Arthur Hider, plunging in after me, and swimming with me to a place of safety. I returned to work as soon as I got some dry clothing on.

As my knowledge of French had gained me promotion and extra pay, so it also nearly caused me some trouble by arousing the suspicions of a gensdarmé, who, hearing me speaking French and seeing me in the garb of a sailor, thought I might be a deserter from the French naval service, and was only assured such was not the case, but that I was a native of America, by the persuasion of the boatswain of the *Aigle*, in whose company I was enjoying myself at a "cabaret."

After a short time we were ready for sea, and having hauled out of the harbor basin and made sail we stood out to sea, immediately encountering very heavy weather.

Scarcely had we been to sea forty-eight hours when I became very sick, my body having the appearance of being attacked with both smallpox and measles at the same time. This was caused by my sudden immersion while heated and sweating in the water strongly impregnated with copper from the bottoms of so many vessels, when I jumped overboard at Marseilles.

And here I would draw attention to another virtue or qualification requisite and most often faithfully and even affectionately carried out by the real seaman (one of the good old sort), and that is in the quality of nurse and physician, not separately, but together. In my case on board the *Aigle* Captain Avril had me removed from my bunk in the fo'castle and placed in his berth, and at once became my physician and nurse till I had recovered.

Sailors, when sick, often become romantic and fanciful, at other times they have too much to do to think of such things; and I, as I lay thinking that I was about to "kick the bucket," upbraided myself with having invoked the just

BUM-BOAT.

vengeance of "Cupid" (the God of Love), in having neglected his admonitions when he brought me alongside my
pretty Julié, and taken her to have and to hold "for better
or for worse." The morning when we had our last breakfast
together she hung on to my neck and sobbed as if her little
heart would have broken. I had no thought of marrying
then, otherwise I might have had a good, snug berth for life. I
dare say she afterwards married some staid citizen of credit
if not of renown.

As we neared the Straits of Gibraltar and the broad Atlantic I rapidly improved in health, until I became conva-
lescent, and took my trick at the wheel, and able to stand
my watch, but not yet strong enough to go aloft.

Out in the Atlantic we shaped our course between the
Moorish coast and the Madeira Islands, through to the
west'ard of the Canary Islands, where we had almost inces-
sant rain, with continued thunder and lightning, until we
got to the south'ard and west'ard of the Cape de Verdés,
where we ran into the nor'east trade winds, squared yards,
set all light canvas and stun'sails that would draw, and went
booming before a strong breeze until we neared the West
Indies, sighting the Isle of Desiderada, and in another week
cast anchor in the harbor of St. Thomas, after a passage of
sixty-two days.

The day following our arrival was a Sunday, and the
boatswain came for'ard after we had washed decks and had
breakfast, and summoned us to work (customary on French
ships), but we Americans refused to turn to, but went aft
and told the captain that it was not customary to work on
Sundays in American ships while in harbor, but he, turning
and pointing to the French flag floating from the main peak,
told us that we had shipped and signed under that flag and
no other, and that on the morrow he would imprison us in the
Danish fort until the brig was ready to sail. The remainder
of the crew, consisting of ten Frenchmen, went to work.

During the passage out, and just after getting the trade winds, no look-out for'ard being considered necessary, we had an opportunity of providing ourselves with luxuries which had not been included in the agreement when we signed in France, and of which I am ashamed to say, I, as well as my three comrades, availed ourselves liberally. But what won't Jack do for good tack when at sea? Well, the fore-hatch had an opening, a scuttle, down in which the brig's stores were kept, and just abaft of this was the cargo consisting of the most delicious wines, brandies, sardines and other delicacies that France could supply. Every night down this opening Bill Waters, one of our number, would go and bring up a case of wine, brandy, or sardines, and, breaking open the case, heave it overboard and stow the contents in our chests, which would last till the following night.

One day while I was on the quarter-deck doing some fancy work, this Waters appeared on deck drunk and calling out "George, come and have a drink," was watched by the chief mate, who saw him go down the scuttle and bring up a case. The mate thereupon told me that he would not report him to the captain if the game was stopped at once. It was stopped for that day, but at night the cargo was again broached.

As before stated Captain Avril having threatened to lodge us in the Danish fort till the sailing of the *Aigle*, and we dreading lest he might carry his threat into execution, and perhaps eventually carry us back to France to serve a period in the galleys, as was then the French law with regard to disobedience of orders at sea, or in a foreign port, held a counsel of war, in which it was resolved to leave the brig peacefully if we could, forcibly if we must. In pursuance of effecting our escape by the first method it was considered expedient for one of us to see the American Consul, which I undertook to do; so I went below, dressed myself neatly, got into the bob-stays, and watched a negro youth pulling around us till I drew

CITY OF CHARLESTON, S. C.

his attention, when I held up a five franc piece, the meaning of which action on my part he readily understood, for he came and took me off, covered me with a sail, and pulled for the shore. I at once walked up to the American Consulate, but on inquiry was informed that the consul had gone the day before to St. Croix, a Danish island some forty miles distant. After loitering ashore till dusk I returned on board and was astounded to learn that all our chests and personal effects had been taken aft to the after store-room and locked up.

We had now no alternative but to use desperate measures, and soon made up our minds what course to pursue, and to carry it into effect that night.

The boatswain slept in a hammock on deck, with a loaded musket by his side, and there was a Frenchman as anchor-watch to be disposed of. After all were sound asleep except the man on watch, we sallied forth from the fo'castle, knocked down the watch into unconsciousness with a heaver, while simultaneously two tackled the boatswain, gagged and lashed him securely in his hammock, and the task of securing the companion-way was but the work of a few moments.

The officers being thus paralyzed by the suddenness of the attack, and taken perfectly by surprise, the rest of our plan was easily carried out, for we quickly hauled up the long-boat which was towing astern, with her lug-sail always in her, broke the fastenings that held our property, bundled chests and all into the boat, cast off and bid adieu to the *Aigle*, hoisted our sail, and with a fresh land breeze soon saw St. Thomas fading from view in the early morning. About ten in the forenoon we landed at St. Johns, the town and harbor of St. Croix, West Indies, where several brigs and schooners lay bound to different parts of the United States or the Spanish main.

While in the Island of St. Thomas, I was shown the

castle, now in ruins, where the "Blue Beard" of our childhood story-books is said to have killed so many wives, and
to have met the just punishment due such an atrocious
ruffian.   The fact that the same Mr. Blue Beard has a
castle assigned to him in many other countries is no draw-
back to the one in St. Thomas.

After landing at St. John's we parted company, all obtaining berths in different vessels.   I shipped in the hermaphrodite brig, *Daniel Webster*, bound to Charleston, S. C., and
after a fine passage, considering the time of the year, March,
arrived at the destined port in six days.

ST. THOMAS.

PARK, HAVANA, CUBA.

Chapter VIII.

I lost no time in getting a ship at Charleston, for, as I was taking my dunnage ashore from the *Daniel Webster*, a gentlemanly-looking man, pointing to a ship lying at anchor in the harbor, asked me if I did not wish to ship for Europe? The ship to which he drew my attention was bound for Hamburg, and wanted a few good men to complete her crew. He said, if I was willing to go, I would just suit. I agreed. "Then," said he, "come up to the house and get something to eat, and I will take you on board, and ship you." This man was, as I was told, Elias Moses, father of Franklin Moses, afterwards Governor of South Carolina. I found that I had engaged on board the ship *Inez*, of Newburyport, Captain Cook, a fine fellow, with a crew of ten excellent seamen before the mast.

We were not long in getting ready for sea. Starting on our voyage, we had hardly cleared the coast, when it came on to blow most terribly, alternating from nor'west to sou'west, and compelling us to scud under close-reefed main topsail and reefed foresail. We were loaded with a very buoyant cargo of rice and small cotton bales, and had the good ship *Inez* not been a capital steerer (we could handle her like a pilot boat) she could never have gone through such an ordeal and kept afloat. She was a small ship of 351 tons measurement, but staunch to the backbone (which means the keel). The captain sent the same food to the fo'castle that was served in the cabin, which was never known to occur on any other vessel that I ever heard of. His treatment of the crew was very kind and considerate, and won all hearts.

We had a very quick passage, making the "Chops" of the English Channel in twelve days, and were off Cuxhaven, at the mouth of the Elbe, on the sixteenth day, but it took us three days to work up to Hamburg, having to beat up (the wind being contrary, and blowing right down the river), which we could only do with a flood tide.

Arrived at Hamburg, we moored to the Dolphins (floating docks, like our New York ferry docks), about one hundred yards from the shore, and commenced discharging our cargo into lighters.

CANAL AT HAMBURG.

Every night the crew went ashore to enjoy themselves, for which there are numberless opportunities in Hamburg, or in that quarter of it set apart for the sailor community, and which was outside the walls and gates. In this quarter, beer houses and saloons, dance halls, etc., abounded, all of which had a complement of handsome and gay young damsels, whose duty or calling it was to contribute to the pleasures of their visitors as partners in the mazy waltz, that being the favorite dance, and by waiting on them at the tables, and elsewhere, thus relieving them of the burden of carrying superfluous cash. We also enjoyed the popular, though to some it would appear childish, amusement of the flying horses, or roundabouts. But to Jack ashore anything to laugh at is fun, and every one knows that a sailor on horseback, whether in the flesh or in wood, is a sight to cause laughter in any one, whether of his own calling or a landsman.

An incident occurred to me then which I never recall

CANAL AT HAMBURG.

without cursing the despotic laws of the Hanse towns of Germany, which are, or appear to be, brought to bear with particular severity against seamen of other nationalities than their own, especially if they are suspected of belonging to the Latin races. It was a lovely moonlight night, and I was ashore as usual on the Berg, as this part was called, enjoy· ing myself with a shipmate, and, feeling as happy as a king, or perhaps a good deal happier, when, all at once, I missed him from my side. We were in a dance-house in company with some damsels, and, not being able to see him anywhere, I rushed out of the door, and blew an ivory call in the shape of a hound, which had been given to me on board of the slaver, mentioned in a previous chapter. I had no sooner done so, when, as if an apparation had risen out of the earth, two gendarmes, with naked sabres glistening in the moonlight, stood, one on each side of me, arrested and marched me off to a police station, where I was charged with giving a false alarm. The officer at the desk, to whom the charge was made, asked me with what I had whistled. I told him with a call used on a slaver, and the

CANAL AT HAMBURG.

reason for my doing so was calling for a shipmate in whose company I was, and whom I had missed, that being the signal agreed upon should one wish to communicate with the other. He told me that those whistles were used by the local police, and the use of such by any other person was a violation of law, and ordered me to surrender it, which I refused to do. He then directed the gendarmes to take it from me by force, but he had reckoned without his host, for no sooner did they attempt to carry out the order than I knocked them both down, being very quick, and with muscles well tempered by " Father Neptune." But my pugilistic powers availed me nothing, for, summoning a crowd of gendarmes who were asleep at the other end of the station house, I was overcome by numbers, and locked up in a cell about six fe.t by four, on the floor of which, composed of flag-stones, I eventually fell asleep, and slept the sleep of the tired (if not of the just) till 6 A. M., when I was taken to the court-house, or senate, as they called it, and being placed in the janitor's apartments, I was told that, if I had six shillings on me (small pieces of money forty-eight to the dollar), I could have a bowl of coffee and a roll. Having the needful, I embraced the opportunity, and, after my night's lodgings on the cold ground, I can assure my readers it was very welcome.

The court opened at 9 A. M., and I was marched up into the presence of the judge, before whom I was arraigned. He began by telling me I was a Spaniard (a nation much disliked by Northern Germans), as I looked so swarthy. I told him I was not a Spaniard but a Canadian, but as he persisted, I told him in forcible English that he was a liar. I was then convicted, and fined five marks (fourteen shillings), a sum about equal to two and a half dollars. I was then asked where my captain was to be found, and on my replying at the Baum house, the two police accompanied me there, and saw the captain, who laughed and paid the fine, and gave me the rest of the day to recuperate my fallen spirits. I may mention that, on being paid off at the end of the voyage, this captain did not deduct the fine he had paid for me.

This was my first acquaintance with Germany, and it was not a cordial welcome. However, I managed to make a friend of a keeper of a small hotel near the ship, on one of the small islands, of which there are many in Hamburg. In looking about the city I saw the new Exchange, which had just been completed. There were nearly five thousand members, and I had the pleasure of overlooking them during a part of their business hours from the gallery, and listening to the roar of voices. My friend said they were buying and selling stocks, bonds and other securities, but to me it seemed all confusion, and but little less than a riot. The most severe task for me was climbing the tower of Saint Michael's church, which is four hundred and sixty feet high, and is ascended by six hundred steps. The river divides into many small streams, and they are full of boats, barges, and all sorts of ships from every nation, for Hamburg is one of the largest shipping ports in the world. I saw women hauling at the ropes of the canal boats, while their husbands sat smoking in the boat. Everyone smokes, and generally a pipe. The women are very much addicted to the habit of scrubbing doors, windows, floors, and everywhere you go they are out in force.

After discharging cargo the ship was cleaned, tarred down, painted, and put to rights all over, in readiness for six hundred emigrants and also a cargo. The men who put the cargo on board sang at their work, day and night, and in my ears those songs were very pleasant, waking echoes and memories that sent me far away to the shores of the St. Lawrence. Everybody sings in Germany, and music seems to be a very essential part of the nation's existence. I suppose it would not be out of the way for me to say that the Germans also indulge in beer. In fact, beer and song, and pipe and story-telling are important elements of the life of the good people of Faderland.

It was nearly two months before we got all our passengers aboard, bunks up, sails bent, water filled, and provisioned, and being all ready we dropped down the Elbe with a fair wind and bid adieu to Germany.

The passage to New York was made without anything of note happening in sixty days, during which we had nothing but light and baffling winds, and, after landing our six hundred emigrants, Captain Cook told the crew that if any of them wished to remain by the ship they could do so.

I and three others remained until the cargo was discharged, and the ship cleaned and put in good order, and then, hearing that as much as $100 was being paid for the run from Quebec to England, we concluded to steer for that port and try our luck.

Being informed that the bark *Ceres*, of Sligo, Ireland, was loading with staves for Quebec at the stave yard in the East river, we shipped in her for the passage, but we had not been aboard more than two or three days when one of my comrades, who were Irishmen, had an altercation with the mate, an Englishman. The Irishman, being a big, powerful fellow, just caught the mate up and hove him overboard. We fished him out, and while he was in the cabin changing his clothing, we hastily bundled our bags and hammocks into a boat lying alongside, and pulled down to Coenties slip, and got on board a barge belonging to a tow just starting out for Albany, where we arrived in two days and nights, and got a free passage to Whitehall in freight canal boat on the Champlain Canal.

Arriving at the latter place in a day and night, we endeavored to procure a free passage to St. Johns, at the northern extremity of Lake Champlain (and in Canada), but were unsuccessful.

After spending several days in Whitehall devising schemes by which we might proceed to St. Johns, we finally resolved to take the first boat that suited our purpose, and were not long in making a selection. We secured a small boat with a sail, mast, and four oars in her, but no rudder, which omission we supplied with an oar. During the day we laid in a stack of cheese and "soft tack," and some whisky, and when all in the town were in the arms of "Morpheus" we started down the Lake, beaching the boat at night in some

lonely cove hidden from passing vessels, and turning her
bottom up converted her into a lodging-house.

Not being in a hurry it just took us five days to reach St.
Johns, where we had the fortune to meet with a good-
natured Scotch farmer, who was going to Laprairie, opposite Montreal, and his team returning light, he kindly consented to take us free. We reached the River St. Lawrence
in the afternoon, and Montreal the same evening, where we
spent the night on board the steam ferry-boat, the captain
giving us permission to do so, having completed his last trip
for that day.

The next day we obtained a free passage in the steamer
John Bull, getting our grub the same as the deck hands, in
return for doing some splicing and other odd jobs of sailor-
ising.

The afternoon following our embarkation in the *John
Bull* we arrived in Quebec, and, taking up our quarters in
a sailor's boarding-house in Champlain street, under Cape
Diamond, we remained just two weeks, enjoying ourselves
by visiting the fortifications and all places of interest, varying the performance by drinking Jamaica rum, which could
then be had in its purity, and was considered a very whole-
some stimulant; at least, it did not disagree with us, perhaps
because we did not get overloaded.

ENTRANCE HALL TO A HOTEL IN CHARLESTON.

Chapter IX.

Having had my rollick ashore as detailed at the close of the last chapter, I again became a wanderer on the face of the deep, and shipped this time in the bark *Ganges*, Captain Bligh, of Port Glasgow, Scotland, bound for Liverpool with a cargo of square timber. She was a clumsy-rigged, ugly steering vessel, and the captain was as bad or worse, for the ship was only as she was made, whereas he made himself a driveling drunkard, not being once sober all the way to Liverpool. Had it not been for the mate, who was a Scotchman, a veritable giant in stature, named Scotland, of great physical strength, and who devoted himself untiringly to his duties, being an excellent seaman, we should have undoubtedly been all lost.

Just after sailing, the captain being maudlin drunk on the poop, one of the seamen, by name Mulhally, a big muscular Irishman, seized the captain, and holding him over the rail, said :

" By Jasus! for two pins I would just dhrop ye overboard ye drunken ould sot, and let a bucketful of salt wather into ye to dhrain out the sperrits."

Well, to return. We weighed, made sail, and with a pilot on board proceeded down the St. Lawrence. It was then the middle of November, and excessively cold. Ice was forming and the winds very boisterous. We got as far as the

sou'west extremity of the Island of Anticosta when the wind
came out from the nor'west a regular screecher, so that we
were compelled to reduce our canvas until we were under
close-reefed foresail and foretop-mast stay-sail. I suffered
severely from the cold, being without any flannel or warm
clothing of any kind, and when a sea swept the decks, or a
spray drenched the rigging, it would freeze instantly, so that
we who were sprinkled continually, were, so to speak, clothed
in ice. From this state of things we had hardly any relief,
night or day, for having no fo'castle, and consequently no
bunks, and but a few having hammocks, our only refuge was
below in our watch off, sleeping as best we could in spaces
formed by the sticks of timber, being of different lengths.

Fortunately we had fine weather after leaving the Gulf of
St. Lawrence.

Our captain never came on deck. But when we made the
Irish coast and had got near " Tuskar," we were confronted
by a heavy gale from the nor'east; our boats were swept
away, and had it not been for the incredible exertions and
excellent seamanship displayed by our chief officer, we should
most assuredly have been wrecked on the Irish coast and
within sight of the Wicklow mountains.

However, providentially, we reached Liverpool after a
passage of forty-eight days, and were paid off the next day,
glad to be clear of such a ship, and from such a captain, for
however a sailor may get drunk ashore he abhors drunkenness when on duty, especially in one placed in authority, and
to whom he has been taught to look up to and depend upon
in time of danger.

After two days in Liverpool I learned that an American
ship had put into Waterford in distress, and wanted a crew.
She was the *Galen*, of Bucksport, Maine, from Swansea,
Wales, with a cargo of railroad iron for New York. She
had got to the west'ard as far as the " Old Head of Kinsale,"
when she sprung a leak and attempted to put into Cork, but

missed, and got into the Tower Hook up to Waterford, where she discharged cargo, hove down, unsheathed, re-caulked, and recoppered.

When I heard of this ship, I communicated my desire to go to Waterford to my shipmate Mulhally, from the "Ganges," and he, being a native of Waterford, immediately said, "All right; if you go, Davis, I will accompany you, for, as my parents live in Waterford, I can at any rate assure you of a roof, and we won't want for grub." So we took passage in a small black-looking steamer called the *Gipsy Queen* for Waterford, paying seven shillings and sixpence (one dollar eighty cents) each for the passage, and, after a rough winter night's run to the "Salties" across St. George's Channel, made the Tower Hook and Duncannon Fort next forenoon. I remember the pleasant run we had up the river to Waterford, and the delightful sensation of looking at the bright green grass on the hills, although it was December. After a few days' vacation, we shipped on board the *Galen.*

When we went on board she was again receiving her cargo. After three weeks spent in that work she was ready for sea. We embarked over five hundred passengers, were towed down the river, outside the Tower Hook to the Irish Sea, and made sail for New York.

Mulhally, who, with the rest of the crew, excepting myself, had received two months' advance wages, had deserted before we sailed.

It was now blowing half a gale from the sou'east, and we were under doubled-reefed topsails, whole courses, jib and spanker, going two points free, or abeam. As we cleared the Irish coast, and entered the Atlantic, the gale increased, veering to the south and sou'west. The ship was rolling fearfully under close-reefed topsails, and reefed foresail, and foretopmast-staysail, close hauled in the wind, and barely laying our course.

We soon began to realize that we were leaking badly, and, still more horrible discovery, we found that, through bad stowage, the railroad iron had got loose, and some having got athwart had drilled holes in the ship's sides, which let in quantities of water at every lurch, while, at the same time, the loose iron was still boring other holes.

We had no other resource than to work incessantly at the pumps. The bowsprit had worked loose at the knight-heads, the gammoning getting loose, and at every pitch the water poured down into the fo'castle, the bitts having also worked loose. Thus we passed three weary and harassing weeks, continually at the pumps. Being then in the longitude of the Azores we wore ship, the wind still blowing a living gale from the west nor'west, and concluded to work to the south'ard, and make a southern passage, but at last realized that we were too far gone to last much longer, the leak having gained on us so considerably, and still gaining daily, we determined to take the first opportunity of the wind in any degree abating to abandon the ship, and take to the boats.

The five hundred passengers were in the meantime almost completely paralyzed with fear. Some of the men gave an occasional spell at the pumps, but we, of the crew, were so worked out that I had scarcely time to know (so to speak) that they were even aboard.

Fortunately, after we had stood to the south'ard on the starboard tack for about a week, we spoke the ship *Vespasian*, of Boston, bound from Batavia, Java, to Cowes, Isle of Wight, for orders, and whose captain agreed to lay by us until we should leave the ship, which we found had now eleven feet water in the hold. We turned to at once, and got our boats out, and began transferring our passengers to the *Vespasian*. The entire crew being thus employed, we had conveyed some four hundred of them to the other ship, and were returning for the remainder, when the *Galen* suddenly pitched by the bow, and went down, taking with her nearly one hundred human beings, including one of our crew who had been detailed to superintend their debarkation.

> " Then rose from sea to sky the wild farewell—
>   Then shrieked the timid, and stood still the brave—
> Then some leap'd overboard with dreadful yell,
>   As eager to anticipate their grave;
> And the sea yawn'd around her like a hell,
>   And down she suck'd with her the whirling wave,
> Like one who grapples with his enemy,
>   And strives to strangle him before he die.
>
> " And first one universal shriek there rushed,
>   Louder than the loud ocean, like a crash
> Of echoing thunder; and then all was hushed,
>   Save the wild wind and the remorseless dash
> Of billows; but at intervals there gush'd,
>   Accompanied with a convulsive splash,
> A solitary shriek, the bubbling cry,
>   Of some strong swimmer in his agony."

Never shall I forget that awful scene, when

> " Rose from sea to sky the wild farewell,"

not only from those thus hurled into the raging sea to find a watery grave, but also from the relatives and friends on board the *Vespasian*. It was a sight to appall the stoutest heart, and one the memory of which will endure as long as I have the power of remembrance.

When all was over, the *Vespasian* filled away and shaped a course for the Island of Fayal, one of the Azores, or Western Islands, a group of nine islands under the dominion of Portugal, distant one thousand miles from Lisbon, being the nearest point in Europe in the same parallel of latitude.

We arrived in the harbor of Fayal the following day, about one hundred and fifty miles from the spot where the *Galen* foundered. The crew and passengers were landed. Their necessities were seen to by the American consul, Mr. Dabney, who attended to both crew and passengers being housed and fed, except the captain and mates, who remained on board the *Vespasian* until she reached Cowes.

When we were at Fayal we saw U. S. Consul Dabney, father-in-law of Dr. Webster, who killed Dr. Parkman at

Boston. His grandson is consul now. It was there that the captain asked me to swear to a protest for insurance to be laid before the U. S. Consul, but I could not do so, because I had seen Captain Snow with a large augur in his hand coming out of the lower hold, and knew what happened afterwards must have been results of his boring. I also could see the big bulges in the ship's sides and bows made by the shifting railroad iron, which was loose, and at every lurch of the vessel plunged into the sides or bows, which of course could not last long. That was the *Galen*, of Bucksport, Maine.

While on the island waiting for a ship I boarded with a Portuguese family, who lived close to the edge of an ex- tinct volcano, and paid three dollars a month for board and washing. The husband's name was Antonio De Silva, and more inoffensive, industrious, kind-hearted people do not exist. They did as much for me as for a son or brother. Their customs were primitive, and one reminded me of the Scriptures where we read of grinding corn or grain between two stones, and that was the method used in the Azores. Their tools were very few, and such as boys make. I was told that the land belonged to a few, could not be bought by the people, who were little better than slaves, and that, poorly cultivated as it is, it being naturally a rich deep mold from volcanic rock, the crops are abundant and sure. The rains are plenty, but sometimes fall in floods, doing great damage.

Shortly after landing the consul summoned the crew to the consulate, and informed us that we were allowed as ship- wrecked seamen, by the United States government, a sum of twenty-six cents per day for subsistence, and I with one or two other old whalemen, being conversant with the Portuguese tongue, engaged board with a peasant living in the interior of the island, close to the edge of the crater of an extinct volcano, for three dollars a month, thus saving over five dollars a month out of my allowance for pocket money, which was pretty well, considering that I could keep jolly drunk for ten cents a day, and that on real pure and good Pico wine, so called from the name of the island on which it was produced, and on which is a famous volcano. It was no doctored stuff that will make you mad, and neither jolly nor drunk.

When I took up my quarters with Antonio De Silva, the peasant, I was covered with vermin; but these were soon got rid of by baking my clothes till they were all exterminated, and washing myself. De Silva also instructed me that for the benefit of my health I ought to wash my feet in warm water every night before turning in (a custom universal in these islands), also eat an orange the first thing in the morning, never later. These islanders are stout and hardy, sickness comparatively unknown, and they live to a great age. No doctors; but whether this is the cause or effect of the general healthiness I will not pretend to say, but leave to the decision of my readers. I generally walked down barefoot to the port in the day, and passed the time as pleasantly as I could, yarning with one and the other whom chance threw in my way.

The manners of the people of the Azores are exceedingly primitive. They wear sandals on their feet, and instead of ploughing merely make holes in the ground with a sharp stick, and grind their grain between two stones, the upper having a hole in the middle for a hopper. A cow yoked to a beam turns the upper stone around. They also have oxen to tread out the corn or grain as mentioned in Scripture. They have other primitive customs which were very amusing.

While on the island, each seaman and passenger was cautioned by some of the natives who had been in whalers, and thus not so bigoted as the others, to wear crucifixes fastened round their necks as a protection against some of the islanders, who were so fanatical against all not of the Romish

PICO.

church that they would not hesitate to murder any one not
having that symbol on their person. In fact, two of the
original crew not shipped in Ireland, and not being thus
protected, were found assassinated in the interior of the
island, and no clew was found as to the perpetrators of the
crime, for there are no officers of justice, and only about a
company of soldiers for the whole group of islands, except
at St. Michaels, where there are a few more, but all bare-
footed, and wearing anything but a regular uniform, so warm
is the climate.

After we had been a few days in Fayal, two large brigs
came to in the harbor partially laden for Boston, and all the
passengers of the *Galen* as well as the crew, excepting four
and myself, were embarked for America. Four months
elapsed before another vessel bound for America presented
herself. By this time I felt so much at home that I almost
considered myself a Portuguese, and did not care to leave
and say adieu to the good people I had become acquainted
with, nor to leave the comfortable quarters, including the
cakes and wine. But good times as well as bad must have
end, and after a stay of six months on the island, I and the
four remaining crew of the defunct *Galen* were directed by
the consul to go on board the brig *Sarah and Abigail*, bound
for Boston.

The *Sarah and Abigail* had been on an unsuccessful whaling voyage among the islands of the North Atlantic, and came
to Fayal to fill up with oranges and wine on her return to New
England. We of the crew of the *Galen* were shipped as *United
States protected seamen*, the government paying ten dollars
apiece for us. The first night out all hands were mustered
on deck to choose watches, and we were mustered also, but
we told Captain Doane bluntly that we were passengers and
would not stand watch ; upon which he said, "Very well, if
you refuse to stand watch you shall have nothing to eat."
Well, the threat fell harmless upon us, for the vessel being

SENTINEL.

loaded mostly with wine and oranges it seemed to us that with a seaman's instinct for foraging under ordinary circumstances, it would only reflect discredit on our abilities if we allowed ourselves to starve. Accordingly, with the silent acquiescence of the crew for'ard, we carefully took out a board of the bulkhead separating the fo'castle from the hold, so that with the ruby wine and the fruit, to which we helped ourselves liberally, on the principle that "the gods help those who help themselves," and what the crew gave us in the way of solids we "fared sumptuously every day."

We encountered continuous westerly winds almost the entire passage, sou'west alternating to nor'west. Thus we continued hammering at it for over a month, when one night off the eastern edge of George's Banks, with an ugly chopping sea, the wind blowing pretty strong from nor'west, and close-hauled on the starboard tack, and under whole topsails and courses with jib and mainsail, owing to indifferent seamanship, or neglect, or both, in consequence of the topsail yards being too sharply braced in such a laborsome sea, the mast heads were twisted, and brought down everything above the top on deck and over the sides. We were in a pretty pickle. Of course, as a matter of good fellowship, in distress, we passengers, or consul's men, such as we are frequently called, turned to with a will to lend a hand in clearing away the wreck, and to rig jury masts.

This dangerous work had scarcely been accomplished, when another catastrophy befell us, by which we lost a seaman overboard.

It was blowing heavy at the time, with a terrible sea on, as we were hove to under a storm fore and aft mainsail, when the mate sent one of the crew, a Dane, to stop the head of the jib, which was furled, the gasket having worked loose. Suddenly a terrific sea struck the boom and carried it away in a moment, and as the cry "Man overboard" rang out, we beheld our shipmate drowning before our eyes, without the power to do aught to save him.   Never did I witness such an appalling spectacle, and the appealing look, and the despairing cry he gave as we hove to, drifting to leeward, while he appeared to drift to wind'ard.

The cry "Man overboard" is always an appalling one, but, in the hurry and activity induced by the efforts to save, the feeling is to a degree mollified; but to have to stand and see a shipmate thus perishing, as it were, within hail, knowing that it is madness or impossible to attempt his rescue, produces a feeling which it is not in my power to put into words.

After a dreary passage of forty-five days, we had the supreme felicity of once more treading "America's free soil," and were not long availing ourselves of the chance of leaving the dominions of Captain Doane on board of the brig *Sarah and Abigail.*

Not feeling at home in Boston, I resolved to make tracks for New York, and, learning I could go to Providence, R. I., by rail, and thence by steamer to New York, I resolved to pursue that route of travel.

This was my first experience as a passenger on board of a railroad, and it may interest some of my readers to know that at this period, 1840, the passenger cars were open both on top and sides, while the seats were without cushions, merely boards placed across.   The rate of speed was also not to be compared with that now attained.   The new sensation was exhilarating, and I enjoyed that ride.

I arrived in New York with what a sailor mortally hates when ashore ; in fact, I know of no landsman but what has an equal aversion to it, namely: empty pockets.   I had but twenty-five cents left on my arrival, and I thought of the cook of the *Sarah and Abigail*, with no amiable feelings, when I recollected that he had not paid me for a pair of new Blucher shoes which I had sold him for three dollars. However, if I were to come across him now, I do not think I would sue him, for I suppose my claim would be barred by the "statute of limitation." There is no such statute to bar one's memory. That's one good thing.

J. W. PETTIGREW.

(See page 307.)

BOSTON, MASS.

Chapter X.

" Still must I on ; for I am as a weed,
Flung from the rock, on ocean's foam to sail
Where'er the surge may sweep, the tempest's breath prevail."

After idling a week or so at a sailor's boarding-house in James street, I shipped aboard the ship *Oneida*, Captain Funk, one of the Havre line of packet-ships, or "liners," as they were then called, plying between New York and Havre, which latter port we arrived at after a rather tempestuous passage of twenty-two days, nothing of note occurring, except that the mate was not sober during the whole passage. Being cousin to the captain his weakness was overlooked. I may also mention casually that each watch was allowed half a gallon of fine brandy every day for dinner, and in harbor boarded ashore, and lived like lords, all at the ship's expense.

In a few days we commenced discharging cargo, and it was astonishing to witness the French dock laborers take a bale of cotton, weighing from five hundred to six hundred pounds resting on their hands behind their backs, and trot away with it up a stage (at an angle of thirty degrees) reaching from the ship into the warehouse.

When discharged, we began loading a cargo of miscellaneous goods, and embarked about eight hundred passengers. We hauled out of the Napoleon dock, made sail, and stood away on our course for New York, making the passage in thirty-two days, during which we had a succession of light and baffling breezes, and splendid weather, interspersed with calms.

Arriving again in New York, I went back to my old boarding-house in James street, where I made the acquaintance of a seaman, a native of the Azores, who told me that he belonged to the U. S. revenue cutter *Ewing*, on the New York station, and, as his term of service would expire on the first of June, then at hand, I could, if I would lay by for a few days, ship in his place. This I did, and was shipped accordingly.

I liked the service well, was attentive to my duties, and rose in the estimation of the officers, having a station assigned me as captain of the fore-top. The life was extremely pleasant in summer, plenty of boating and going ashore, and when crusing off the coast and becalmed passed the time fishing, hauling the seine, clamming and and oystering. Our duty was to visit the harbors on the station, board coasters especially, to examine their papers, and see that the regulation, requiring the name of the vessel and the hailing port be painted on her in letters at least four inches long, had been complied with.

Visits of gentlemen and ladies to the revenue cutter occurred almost daily in fair weather. As we were lying off shore one day a party of ladies appeared on the dock, and one of them waved a white handkerchief as a signal. Orders were given to man the captain's gig, and in a short time they were on board the *Ewing*. After looking over the decks, inspecting the officer's quarters, they gathered around one of the lieutenants, and plied him with many questions, by way of eliciting information or sea lore. I can only find space for stowing away one item, relating to the means of distinguishing a vessel by the number of masts she carries. The spokesman, or lady speaking, looking away to seaward, cried out as if in admiration of a fine schooner:

"See, what a beautiful ship in full sail!"

The lieutenant said, "Excuse me, madam, that is a schooner. A ship has three masts, all square rigged."

"Is there any rule by which one may know the kind of ship one may see?"

"Yes. A sloop has one mast, a schooner two masts, a bark has three masts, one not square rigged, and a ship has three masts, square rigged.

"Ah, I see. How lovely! I have seen a steamer with four masts; what would you call that?"

"According to the style of rig. Usually the foremast is square rigged, and the others schooner rigged."

SLOOP.

"Thank you. Then the vessel we see coming into port is a schooner, for it has two masts."

"No, that is a brig, but she is what is called a jackass brig. She has one mast square rigged and the other is schooner rigged, with topsail."

Just then another lady attempted to impress her friend's memory by repeating the rule, "Sloop two masts, schooner one mast——"

"Excuse me madam; sloop one mast, schooner and brig two masts, bark three masts, one schooner rigged, and ship three masts, square rigged."

First lady: "Oh, see that beautiful sloop coming from the east."

"That is a cat-boat. The mast is set very close to her bows."

"Yes, dear," said number two, "cat-boat one mast, sloop two———"

"Sloop one mast," the officer interrupted politely, "schooner two, brig two, bark and ship three."

"Well, it was always a mystery to me, and I am glad to have a clear explanation for once. It must be pleasant sailing in this brig."

"This is a topsail schooner. She carries an immense squaresail forward, with stun'sails both sides, and with the wind dead astern is a very fast sailer."

"Oh, I'm so much obliged. My uncle is a sailor; owns that schooner lying at the dock."

"That is a hermaphrodite brig, madam. Foremast square rigged, and the mainmast schooner rigged."

"We never shall be expert, as I see. There are so many different vessels, it must take a lifetime to be able to distinguish them at a glance. I suppose I ought to repeat the rule until it is learned by heart. Brig; no, bark one mast———"

"Sloop and cat-boat one mast," said the officer, patiently, "schooner and brig two masts, bark and ship three masts. Then the barkentine has the foremast square rigged, and the other two schooner rigged."

"Oh, see, there is a barkentine sailing by in the distance!"

"No, madam, that is a ship with a jigger-mast."

"We are ever so much obliged to you, I am sure, and now we can tell our friends something sure about nautical affairs. I wonder what uncle will say when he hears me— sloop three masts, schooner one———"

"Madam, excuse me, sloop one mast———"

"Yes, so it is, sloop one, brig two, schooner three, ship four. We must go now. I hope we have not exhausted your patience. I'm sure you are very kind. I shall remember this lesson as long as I live. Sloop one, cat-boat two, brig three, schooner four, ship—— No, a ship can't have five masts. I shall have to give it up."

We had duties also when on the New York station, which extended from Block Island to the Capes of Delaware. Once, when in New York harbor, we were signalled from the barge office that we must overhaul an English ship then leaving port. All sail was set in a jiffy, and the ship was rounded to by a shot across her bows off Montauk Point. Her officers were ordered into the cabin, and her men were put in irons, and the vessel was brought back by a crew from the *Ewing*. The offense, we found out on our return, consisted in landing a load of passengers on Staten Island, and sailing at once without paying port dues, or showing any regard for Uncle Sam and his patient servants in the Custom House.

During the time I was attached to the *Ewing* I had the narrowest possible escape from assassination, and what grieved me most was that the assassin's hand was that of a messmate whom I had looked upon as a friend. Though born in Albany, N. Y., yet his sisters had worked for my father when I was a child, at fur-sewing. His name was Bill Austin, and he had been coxswain of the first cutter. Not being competent, nor steady, I was appointed in his stead, and this was my offense, or his provocation.

On the occasion in question, we were lying at our moorings in Buttermilk channel, New York harbor, when, at nightfall, I was despatched with the cutter and crew to bring off the liberty men—a certain number of our crew allowed ashore daily when in harbor. Bill Austin had been ashore this day, and came into the boat with the others, but scarcely had I given the usual orders, "Up oars, shove off, let fall, give way," when Austin jumped aft to the stern sheets and endeavored to take the "yoke ropes" from me, exclaiming, "I will steer this boat." I of course resisted, and forced him into the bottom of the boat, where I had him so secure as not to give further trouble on our way aboard. The rules of the service gave me while away from the ship on duty, and in command of the boat, as much actual authority as has the captain on board.

When we came alongside, I did not report him, as I should have done, but having hoisted the boat up, and "piped down hammocks," I filled my pipe, and went on deck to have a smoke. I stood smoking, and resting my elbow on the after part of the pipe-rail around the foremast, the bright moonlight gleaming over my shoulder, when my friend Austin came up the hatchway, and, when within about six or eight feet, drew his sheath-knife, and, with a rush, raised his arm, and would have plunged the knife into my heart; but, being aided by the glitter of the knife, I, as quick as thought, caught his descending arm, and, tripping him up with my foot, brought him down. The noise of the struggle brought the executive officer on deck, and Austin was put in irons for the night. The next morning I interceded with the first lieutenant for his release and liberation from custody, as I had no animosity against him, and could readily forgive him. To this request the officer at first demurred, but, considering that I had won general esteem, he at last granted it, and Austin was released, but, feeling mortified and humiliated, he deserted a few days after. He was a fine seaman, but of an ungovernable temper, and drank very freely. Many a good seaman has swallowed his honor and self-respect in strong drink.

I continued in the service three years. It was on board the *Ewing* that I first commenced saving my earnings, and became the owner of a bank-book.

One day while coming through Hell Gate, on our return from a cruise, it having fallen a dead calm, and the boats ahead towing the *Ewing* to keep steerage way on her, and the management of the boats requiring caution with narrow watching, and giving orders, such as pull starboard, easy larboard, and vice versa, the lieutenant commanding looked over the bows, and, calling to me, began finding fault, to which I retorted, as I was in charge of the boat as coxswain. On coming to an anchor, with sails furled, yards squared, I at once demanded my discharge. This the first lieutenant attempted to persuade me to forego. I persisted, and finally procured my discharge on the 1st June, 1843. Before leaving the *Ewing*, I packed my friend Arthur's clothes with mine in order to facilate his desertion, as his term had not expired, and, as we had made up our minds to go to the Lakes together, having been so long shipmates, first in the *Rome*, then in the *Aigle*, where he saved my life, and lastly in the revenue cutter. I now drew my savings from the bank, giving my chum Arthur half of the entire sum, amounting to one hundred and fifty dollars. While aboard the *Ewing*, some months previous, I had a conversation with one of the officers who had been stationed on the Lakes, and had advised me strongly to seek the Lakes as a fine place for a young seaman to get money. I resolved to make for those regions, and procured a free passage to Albany on a barge, and thence to Buffalo on an Erie canal freight boat, where I arrived in eleven days after leaving New York.

Looking about us for a few days in Buffalo I shipped in the brig *Preble*, Captain Rickards, for Chicago and intermediate ports, with an assorted cargo of all kinds, which we had to discharge into our largest boat and land on the beach, as at all of the places there were no docks.

In three weeks we arrived at the mouth of the Chicago river spite of all drawbacks, and my readers would scarcely believe that at that time, only forty-four years ago, the present immense city, and centre of a stupendous trade contained scarcely three thousand inhabitants, only one bridge spanning the river, and only one tavern or rum shop.

At the time we laid there the only other vessel besides ourselves was a small steamboat. The houses were merely small frame and log houses, and on coming to the end of a street one looked out on the vast and open prairie.

After a stay of two weeks in Chicago, during which we discharged the remaining freight and filled up with grain, we set out on our return, and, making sail, we shaped our course for Buffalo, arriving at that port after a passage of twelve days.

The sailing on these lakes is excessively hazardous on account of the sudden and violent changes of the wind, and the fact that blow as it will a lee shore is always present, and the harbors of refuge very few and far between.

While at Buffalo I became acquainted with the father of a young man who had been a shipmate with me on his first voyage in the ship *Niantic* to China in 1834–1835. He was employed as passenger agent on one of the railroads which were then being constructed to the then far west, and had his homestead in Oswego, to which town he gave me a pass.

His son, my old shipmate, was away on a voyage to the west coast of South America and California, in command of a staunch clipper armed brig called the *Maletadel*, and was engaged in an illicit trade, that of smuggling specie and bullion out of Mexico, a heavy export duty being levied by the government on such exports. Of course, this specie was in payment for imported goods, and this smuggling was connived at by the merchants and others on whom the burden of this onerous tax fell.

My old shipmate, then, Captain H. W. Johnson, was expected home shortly, and he returned in a few weeks and was heartily glad to see me. They (the family) wanted me

ERIE, ON LAKE ERIE.

to stay with them through the winter; but as I was uneasy ashore with nothing to do, and it was now only the middle of August, I proposed making another voyage before the winter set in.

I will here narrate an incident which may amuse some of my readers as being illustrative of the awkwardness of a sailor on horseback.

I was asked to fetch the letters from the post office three miles distant, and for that purpose was provided with a horse saddled and bridled. Thus mounted I proceeded on my errand, but had not gone far when I got off at a brook for a drink, and in getting on again, not noticing that the reins had got over his head, I reached over to get hold of them, when he threw me over his head on the ground, and started on a run for home, but some farmers caught him and I made the journey home with him in tow, that is, leading the horse by the bridle.

To return, I accordingly shipped as mate of the schooner *Delaware*, Captain Bill Morgan, bound for Cleveland, and, after a few days' sail to the head of Lake Ontario, entered the Welland Canal.

This canal was not yet finished, and the laborers engaged on the work lived in miserable huts along the banks. They were no better than a lot of desperate outlaws, and would come aboard vessels bound through and take what they pleased; at the same time it would have been hazardous to one's life to have remonstrated with them.

At last, to our infinite satisfaction, we cleared the canal and steered for Cleveland. We were overtaken by a terrific gale, which forced us to bear up for a harbor, and fortunately succeeded in bringing up under the lee of Long Point, on the Canadian shore, where we laid a few days windbound. The time was economically spent in cutting wood for our use.

At last the wind becoming favorable we soon made sail, and bore away for our port of destination, and arrived in three days. Having discharged a quantity of freight we received a full cargo of grain for Oswego.

Once more under sail we bore away with a fair wind for Port Colborne, the westerly entrance to the Welland Canal, again to run the gauntlet of the outlaw hordes, and having got through without any serious trouble we entered Lake Ontario, and with the wind blowing almost a gale from the west'ard, but fair, made Oswego, and succeeded with some difficulty in getting safely in, as it requires considerable experience and skill in navigating a vessel into this harbor in heavy weather.

This last voyage sickened me of lake navigation, being always on a lee shore, and continually handling cargo, and I longed for the dominions of Father Neptune.

"The sea! The sea! The open sea!
The bold, the brave, the ever free."

The crews of the vessels sailing on these Lakes were mostly composed of the native inhabitants who were farmers or backwoodsmen in the winter, which they passed felling timber or chopping firewood, and becoming sailors (?) in the summer. When sailing in a square-rigged vessel, which requires men to go aloft to reef or furl, if it came on to blow hard suddenly, rather than go aloft, they would let it thresh and blow to pieces, and then pay for it *pro rata*. That's what it costs to be a half-and-half sailor.

CABIN—CANAL BOAT.

—————

Chapter XI

" O'er the glad waters of the dark-blue sea,
Our thoughts as boundless, and our souls as free ;
Far as the breeze can bear, the billows foam,
Survey our empire and behold our home."

On my return to Oswego I found my old shipmate of the *Niantic* still at home, but making preparations for going to New York, and I made up my mind to accompany him, and we started in a few days after my arrival. Again in New York we fetched up together at Pearsall's, near Fulton market, where we rested for about a week.

The clipper brig *Eagle* had just been launched and was being fitted out for China in the opium trade. I signed articles for a voyage in her under Captain Ichabod Sherman. She was indeed a thorough beau ideal of an American clipper. Strongly manned, armed, heavily sparred; her main yard extending nearly across the pier as she lay alongside; she carried an extraordinary spread of canvas, amounting to 40,000 square yards.

Her owners had to give a bond before she could obtain a clearing, in the sum of thirty thousand dollars to the United States Government, as security for the good behavior of the brig, viz.: that she should not engage in any illegal undertaking against the peace and dignity of the United States.

Once to sea we had many opportunities of testing the sailing qualities of our beau ideal; for when we made a sail hull down ahead in the morning, we would overhaul her by noon, and before sunset she would be invisible from the deck or lost to sight entirely.

We shaped a course to the south'ard and east'ard, in order to meet the nor'east trades, which we did after the

usual succession of variable and baffling winds, with heavy
rains, in about 6° north latitude.

And here we were again in the region of the flying fish,
dolphins, albicore and boneta, when we got out lances
and harpoons to have some sport; for pretty as the dolphin
looks playing and leaping around the bows, yet the excitement of getting out on the bark's ropes and hurling the harpoon and lance into their vitals and killing one occasionally,
thus showing one's skill, is as good as can be enjoyed by any
professor of the "gentle art" ashore. Besides, which a dolphin properly cooked is a change which any one would enjoy
after living on "salt horse" for any length of time.

In twenty-five days after leaving New York, we passed
through the Horse latitudes, the region of the trades, and
meeting the westerly winds, stood towards the east, in order
to double the Cape of Good Hope.

Our course was about the same as that of the *Niantic*, ten
years before, in which I made the eastern passage to China
through the innumerable islands, passages, straits and inland seas comprising the Eastern Archipelago. We finally
arrived at Macao, a Portuguese colony, after a swift and
pleasant passage of sixty-four days.

Macao was first colonized by the Portuguese about the
middle of the sixteenth century, and is situated on a small
peninsula, near the mouth of the Canton river. It gradually
expanded in size, and attained greater importance, and, at
the time of which I write, was a place of call for orders,
and also captains of ships having their wives with them
would leave them there, because foreign women are denied
entrance into the Celestial Empire. Chinese women are
admitted to this country, but with considerable opposition.

Here we discharged our cargo of ginseng root, and then
proceeded to Hong Kong.

Since I was there last in the *Niantic*, Hong Kong had
been ceded to Britain by treaty made after the close of the

CHINESE BARBER SHOP.

first opium war, namely: in 1842, and had improved most rapidly, for where, as when on my first voyage, the place consisted of a few miserable Chinese dwellings, the new town, which had sprung up since the possession of the island by the British, contained many fine buildings. The principal part of the town was built on a hill. Lord Saltown was governor of the island.

At Hong Kong, we loaded with a cargo of opium for the ports on the nor'east coast and Shanghai. This coast was then imperfectly known, and we had to keep the lead constantly going; but, in spite of all our caution, we got ashore at the entrance of the East China, or "Yellow Sea," and in four hours the *Eagle* was "high and dry on her bilge," so that we could walk right round her, the tide in this part having a rise and fall of seventy feet. However, at high water of the next tide she floated, and we proceeded on our voyage.

We supplied opium at Ningpo, Chusan, Amoy, Woosung, and various small ports, and finally arrived at Shanghai.

The opium, instead of being put ashore, was delivered into receiving ships moored in the roads off the ports, and rode there dismantled, and roofed over. At the change of the monsoon, and the inevitable typhoons setting in, these receiving ships were removed to a harbor of safety.

The Chinese opium smugglers, when they required a supply of opium would run up alongside, and, quickly putting a bag of Spanish pillar dollars in one scale, it would be balanced by opium in the other, the price being weight for weight, and when they had obtained as much as they required would be off to dispose of their cargo. Sometimes they would be pursued by Chinese government revenue boats, and, if overtaken, a bloody and determined resistance was inevitable, for, if captured, the smugglers were certain of death by strangulation, or being pressed to death between two planks or bamboos, and of course they preferred death

CHINESE LOTTERY OFFICE.

in fight. Thus, figuratively speaking, "fighting with a halter round their necks."

Shanghai is advantageously situated on the River Woosung, near the Yang-tse-Kiang. The tide flows rapidly at about the rate of eight or ten miles an hour. The great advantage of Shanghai as a port is its easy communication by water with the interior provinces, and the populous cities on the Yang-tse-Kiang, and the Imperial Canal.

At this port we discharged the remainder of the opium we had on board, and received an immense amount of treasure in bars of (lycee) silver and specie for Hong Kong, to which port we returned after an absence of three weeks, and discharged the treasure into a British man-of-war about sailing for England.

In a few days the ship *Old England*, of and from Liverpool, arrived in the harbor, and our brig was chartered to carry her cargo, consisting of baled goods, up the coast to Amoy. While receiving the cargo one day, at dinner time, an altercation took place between one of the seamen and the mate of the English ship, the mate, seizing a hand-spike, with one blow struck the seaman dead. The mate was taken ashore in manacles by a man-of-war boat, and I suppose held for trial.

Arriving at Amoy, and discharging the cargo taken from the *Old England*, we returned to Hong Kong, where we passed five weeks painting, refitting ship, and setting up; also rattling, tarring down, and otherwise making her "ship shape" and "Bristol fashion." Captain Sherman had been instructed on leaving home, that should he be offered a round sum for the *Eagle* to let her slide, but, having not had an offer suitable to his views, we now prepared ourselves for the approaching change of the "monsoons," and consequent setting in of the typhoons, which blow with terrific fury, and with such force that a West India hurricane is a gentle zephyr in comparison.

With this purpose in view, we weighed anchor, and, under easy sail, stood into the "Typa," a land-locked harbor (within sight of Macao), wherein shipping are thoroughly protected from the immense power of the furious typhoons— (from the Chinese "ty," strong or powerful, and "phoong," wind).

We had been lying in this "refuge" but a short time when Captain Graves, of the ship *Navigator*, of Salem, Mass., being short-handed through desertion, applied to our captain for volunteers to recruit his ship's company.

I and three others, tiring of our inactivity, volunteered, and shipped in her for Sydney, New South Wales, thence to Manilla, and back to Whampoa.

The monsoons having changed, and the dangerous typhoons having now expended their force, we weighed, and stood out of the "Typa" for Hong Kong, and were speedily chartered and laid alongside of a large Liverpool ship, the *Minden.*

The *Minden* had arrived at Hong Kong with a full cargo of British goods, part of which was consigned to parties in China, and part to Sydney, New South Wales, but her captain, having obtained a charter at Hong Kong to load with new crop teas, etc., for England, concluded it would pay better to engage another vessel to carry that part of his cargo marked for Sydney, and thus leave him free to load for England.

The passage to Sydney occupied thirty-two days, passing through the China Sea to the east'ard of Borneo, and to the west'ard of Philippines, through the Sooloo Sea, and west of Papua or New Guinea, through the Torres Straits, and lastly into the beautiful harbor of Sidney. Here we discharged our freight of British goods of all kinds, and, taking in sufficient ballast to keep the ship on her legs, weighed, and made sail for Manilla.

While in Sydney the usual liberty was allowed the crew to go ashore for a day, just previous to sailing, and some of them coming on board very drunk and riotous refused to obey orders, and could not be controlled. The captain went ashore and procured a guard of soldiers, who came on board, and removed the ringleaders on shore and flogged them, which was an arbitrary act, and a stretch of authority on the part of the captain, as well as of the British officer in command of the military.

We were bound to Manilla for a cargo of rice for China (the crop in that country had partly failed that year), and arrived in Manilla after a passage of twenty-two days.

Being provided with Spanish pillar dollars to pay for the rice, we had to transport the specie ashore in the long boat at great risks from the attacks of the " Ladrones," or pirates, with which these islands were then infested. We, however, delivered the dollars safely, received our cargo of rice in bags, and made ready for sea; then weighed anchor, and bore away for China, distant one thousand two hundred miles. Arrived in Whampoa reach, the seaport of Canton, we moored ship after a passage of twelve days, unbent sails, after drying them, sent down royal-yards, lashing them to the swifters, and then commenced discharging the rice into chops (native lighters).

We had been at work a couple of days discharging the rice, when the old trouble between the officers and crew broke out again. One of the latter, who had been flogged at Sydney, was talking in a loud tone of voice while at work, when the mate ordered him to shut up, or he would serve him the same as at Sydney, to which the man retorted that he would not shut up, as he could and would work and talk as well.

The mate at length, assisted by the second mate and captain, sought to lay hands on the seaman, who defended himself, in which he was ably seconded by the entire crew,

SUNSET.

who quit work, resolved that they should receive good treatment as men, or claim the protection of the U. S. frigate *Brandywine*, which lay moored off the "Bocca Tigris," or "Bogue Forts," a few miles below our anchorage at Whampoa. The captain and mates, awed by the resolute attitude of the crew, retreated into the cabin and submitted. I instantly wrote a letter to Commodore Parker in command of the frigate *Brandywine*, flagship of the American Asiatic squadron, submitting our grievances, and reciting the tyrannical and cruel conduct of the captain and officers of the *Navigator*, and invited an investigation, with the object of putting a stop to further acts of oppression.

This letter I had conveyed by a native boat called a "fast boat," for which service and answer I paid about three dollars. The reply was enclosed in a piece of bamboo instead of an envelope, to the effect that my communication would be attended to next day.

The following day the first lieutenant of the frigate came on board, instituted an inquiry, and concluded his investigations by announcing that all who wished their discharge and leave the ship could do so. I with others—in all, two-thirds of the crew—availed ourselves of the opportunity, had our discharges made out, and, with orders on the Compradone at Whampoa for our pay, went ashore in a sanpan.

Immediately on receiving our pay I engaged as seaman in the Boston-built pilot schooner *Gazelle*, Captain Doane, the other portion of the discharged *Navigator's* crew separating and shipping in different vessels.

The *Gazelle*, though a small craft of ninety tons measurement, carried a crew of eighty men, was well armed, and painted sea-green, so as not to be so conspicuous at a distance, and carried such a crowd of canvas that when under all sail, with a beam wind or close-hauled with a stiff breeze, she would lay over, and the captain would carry sail until the water would almost reach the main hatch combings,

and her long, tapering yellow pine masts would bend until
they formed an angle of twenty degrees, especially when any
suspicious piratical-looking junk or lorchas hove in sight. She
was employed in carrying treasure from the opium receiving
ships to Whampoa, for shipment to Canton, or more generally
to England or Calcutta, and sometimes Bombay. The large
crew and armament, in connection with her admirable sailing qualities, were necessary to protect her from the attacks

GAZELLE.

of the hordes of Ladrone pirates who swarmed in these
waters. I have often assisted in loading her with millions in
" Lycee silver," in pigs like lead or iron packed in strong
boxes, like those used for the purpose of packing and shipping tin. One night, on our second trip to Canton or
Whampoa, loaded with treasure to the planksheer almost,
and while riding at anchor in Cumsingmoon passage in a
dead calm with a strong ebb against us, the *Gazelle* was
attacked by a number of these pirates, about one hundred
and fifty of them having stealthily jumped overboard from

junks anchored further up stream, and, dividing into two lines, so as to come alongside on both sides simultaneously, drifted silently down on us with the swiftly-running tide, seemingly as much at their ease in the water as on the land, and, heaving fire-balls and stink-pots on our decks, attempted to board us. We had our boarding nettings triced up, but they being bold, daring fellows, about fifty or more suc-

CHINESE JUNK.

ceeded in getting a footing on our decks, only to be repelled after a desperate struggle. We drove them back into the water, that is, those who were not killed or so wounded that they were unable to escape. On our side, though we had but one, a Venetian, killed, yet many were more or less seriously wounded. I was fortunate enough to escape with some flesh wounds, which, though not dangerous, were sufficiently severe to leave scars and marks which will last me as mementoes of the fray as long as I live.

I sailed in the *Gazelle* until the change of the "monsoon," which took place about the middle of October, 1844, when I

REPELLING ATTACK OF PIRATES.

left her, she being at that time at anchor lying off Hong Kong.

I was now getting home-sick, and wished to get back to the realms of civilization, but before a chance presented itself of shipping in a homeward bounder I sailed for a couple of months in a lorcha, a Portuguese-built sort of junk, built for swift sailing, flying the colors of Portugal, manned chiefly by Portuguese, and hailing from Macao. She was engaged in carrying passengers and light freight between Hong Kong, Canton, Macao, Whampoa, Lintin and other small places, whose names I cannot recall to memory.

At last I shipped in the ship *John G. Coster*, lying moored in Whampoa reach, Captain Benson, bound for New York, with a very valuable cargo of the costliest shawls, silks, teas, &c., and fancy articles.

One night, just before sailing, on being called to stand my anchor watch, and had just got on deck, I was taken aback by perceiving down the booby hatch the reflection of a light, and going down to the 'tween decks to ascertain the cause, was surprised at seeing the man whom I had relieved, who was an English seaman named Murray, a desperate and determined character, in the act of overhauling some small cases containing some very valuable goods. One of them he had open, which contained magnificent crape shawls of great value. I demanded an explanation, when he, in reply, and to strengthen his argument, placed a heavy navy pistol at my head, and gave me my choice of either becoming an accomplice and sharer of the spoils, or of having my brains scattered. I, under the circumstances, and remembering that, in some cases, "discretion is the better part of valor," elected the former proposition, and got as my share three beautiful shawls out of a case containing seven, and one dozen silk handkerchiefs out of a case of five dozen. Remembering also that in many cases "silence is golden," I concluded to follow that wise maxim, and said nothing to any one about the matter, but stowed my plunder in my mattrass in my hammock well protected from the sea air, until I arrived in New York. This seaman, Murray, was about to exchange the following day for an American seaman on board a Liverpool ship bound for that port, and on the point of sailing, so he wished to feather his nest, and thought the present was his best opportunity.

Having completed our lading we were soon ready for sea,
when we unmoored, and, with a native pilot, made sail
and worked down the river, and finally to sea, with the
nor'east monsoon astern of us. We packed every stitch of
canvas on her that would draw, and in twelve days came to
at Anjer, in the Straits of Sunda, and furled sails. We remained there about a week, filling water from the shore and

PROCESSION—ANJER.

stocking the ship with fine poultry. Captain Benson, com-
bining business with pleasure, took a trip to Batavia, the
crew meanwhile trading for "joggery" (native sugar, not unlike maple), Java sparrows and monkeys, as a little speculation, in barter for sundry odds and ends in the way of cast-off
clothing, broken knifes and razor-blades. I procured a large
number of Java sparrows and a few monkeys, some of which

were white-faced. Most of them, particularly the white-faced ones, died; and about half of the sparrows, from the cold, in doubling the Cape of Good Hope.

When the captain returned, we weighed anchor, made sail, and, standing through the straits, soon were on the

MONKEY MERCHANT.

broad bosom of the mighty Indian Ocean, staggering along at a lively gait under a press of sail, with a favorable gale from the east'ard, which carried us nearly up to the Cape of Good Hope, making the passage from Anjer in twenty-eight days. There we encountered heavy westerly winds for two weeks, lying to most of the time, till, with the aid of the westerly current, we at last doubled the Cape, after that the sou'east trades sent us a kiting once more with every stitch of canvas set.) Topmast, to'gallant, and royal stun'-sails both sides, and fore, main, and mizen standing, sky-sails, with a flying mainmoon-sail, with lower stun'sails, which we carried up to 15° north latitude, when, taking the nor'east trades, hauled in the larboard stun'sails, bracing up the yards by the larboard braces, with the wind abeam, carried the nor'east trades up to 28° north latitude, where, losing the trade winds, we fell in with variable but light winds. The latter part of the passage took as much time to accomplish as the passage from the Cape to where we lost the trades.

At last we made Fire Island and the light-ship, received a pilot and tug, made fast in the afternoon at the foot of Wall street, alongside the wharf, after a passage of one hundred and ten days from Whampoa.

When in the sou'east trades it is customary for ships, especially Indiamen, to furbish up, so as to make a good show in coming into port, and gratify the owners.

The whole crew were thus employed in painting inside and out, aloft, the spars, masts, mastheads and blocks, stun'-sail boom ends, bowsprit and jibboom ends, sprit-sail yards, and everything requiring painting. I had completed the task of painting the spars on the foremast, with everything attached, and had come on deck, when the chief mate, notic-ing that the men who had been painting the spars, etc., attached to bowsprit had neglected to paint the dolphin striker or martingale, said to me, as I was going along with my paint-pot in hand, " Oh! Davis, just step out and paint the dolphin striker!" I said, "No, let those who were painting out there complete their work. I have had a big job to-day, and have done it well. Is it not well done? Then, I do not see why I should finish what others have neglected to do." "Do you refuse duty?" demanded the mate.

I made no reply, but walked aft where Captain Benson was standing. I laid down my paint-pot in a secure spot. I said, "Captain Benson, I appeal to you as the fountain head of this ship. I have been hard at work all day, and have done the part assigned to me carefully and well, and now Mr. Reed has ordered me to complete the work which others have been so careless or lazy as to neglect." Captain Benson merely said, "Davis, go and have your supper!" So the matter ended.

Captain Benson was a very large and very powerful man, a native of Connecticut, and weighed about two hundred and eighty pounds. He stood six feet two inches, and, when on a previous voyage to China (in command of the ship *Roman*, of New York), via west coast of America and the Sandwich Islands, had kept well to the nor'ard to obtain the strong easterly winds, which at certain seasons prevail in these high latitudes. Approaching the Asiatic Coast and the Japanese Islands, he endeavored to run into a Japanese harbor in order to obtain supplies, as he had run short. The *Roman* was hove to at the entrance of the harbor, the boat lowered and manned, with the captain in her, when two Japanese government boats, each with an official in her, came from the shore, and forbid the captain to proceed any further in shore. His boat then ran in between the two Japanese, who closed on him, when he raised an official in each hand out of the stern-sheets, and kept them under water till they were drowned like rats, then pulled aboard the *Roman*, and filled away on his course. This was related to me by an eye-witness, and, judging from the huge muscular development of Captain Benson, I could well believe in the truth of the story.

I had no difficulty in landing my silks from the ship, the custom's authorities not being so strict in those days;

and shortly afterward, with the silk shawls under my arm, entering a dry-good's store in Pearl street, near Maiden lane, was offered three dollars for each shawl, at which I closed the sale, and disposed of the balance of my cargo at my leisure at good prices all round. I had also about one hundred and fifty Java sparrows, and a few ordinary

ANJER BEAUTY.

monkeys, with a white one or two, if I recollect aright, all of which I sold at good prices, so that, with my pay, I found myself the sole owner of about fifteen hundred dollars—quite a millionaire in my imagination.

And now, what could I do better then visit my native city, Montreal, and disport myself as an independent gentleman living on his means?

I was astounded at, I may say, the advanced state of civilization my fellow-townsmen had attained during my absence, as compared with their mode of life when I first went to sea. For, whereas, at that time the ground floors of the houses of the working classes were bare, and without wooden floors, and scantily covered with furniture of rude and ancient construction, now, when I visited it, almost every house boasted a piano, and floors covered with Brussels or more costly carpets, and liberally supplied with books, such as the works of Victor Hugo, Dumas, and other French authors.

I passed two months at Montreal enjoying myself, visiting neighboring villages, etc., till at last, tired of having nothing to do, I returned to New York and sought another ship.

CHINESE EATING HOUSE.

Chapter XII.

I now shipped as second mate of the brig *Walter R. Jones, Jr.*, Captain Moses Nickerson, of Cape Cod, bound for Norfolk, Va., to load with corn for an eastern port. We had an entire crew of negroes, who were first rate seamen. On the fourth morning out from New York, and during my watch, we made Cape Henry, one of the Chesapeake capes, when the captain, coming on deck, and looking round and perceiving some of the crew "caulking" (nautical, sleeping), said to me, "Mr. Davis, if you catch any of these black sons of b——s sleeping on their watch, take a handspike and knock their brains out." I instantly replied, "Captain Nickerson, I did not ship on board this vessel in the capacity of a butcher, but as an officer." That ended the matter, and the captain took no further notice.

When we arrived alongside the wharf at Norfolk, officers boarded the brig and took our negro crew to jail, where they remained until we were loaded and ready to sail, when they were brought on board again. The owners or charterers, as agreed, having to pay for their board while in jail, and their wages going on all the same, though the ship was deprived of their services in the meantime.

Receiving our colored crew, who had been enjoying a holiday in the "calaboose," we hauled out from the wharf-slip, made sail, and, standing down toward the Capes of the Chesapeake, shaped a course for Naragansett bay and

Dighton, R. I., where we arrived after a passage of seven days
(stopping at Fall River some hours to do some business),
and prepared to discharge the corn into lighters as we lay
out in the stream.

We were nearly unloaded, when Captain Nickerson and I
had an altercation about the extreme parsimony with which
the brig had been fitted out for the voyage. No spare rigging, no spun yarn, no marlin, and not a decent marlin-spike

SLOOP.

on board, and, as words ran high, I announced my determination to leave the brig there and then. In this I was
joined by the first mate, a Mr. Brown, of South Yarmouth,
Cape Cod, and, procuring a whale-boat with a lug-sail from
an acquaintance, made the passage to his home on the Cape,

through a passage or some sort of straits back of Newport, in a day and part of a night, with a nice breeze from the west'ard most of the time at sea.

Mate Brown gave me a sailor's welcome to his home, which I availed myself of, and remained some days, when a brig in distress and dismasted, bound for Boston, put into Hyannes, and I was engaged to assist in refitting and to get her ship-shape for sea service, as also to assist in navigating her round to Boston, which was all accomplished in three weeks.

On being paid by the underwriters for my services, I took the train for New York, via New London by boat.

As I got on the wharf at New London to go on board the boat for New York, I was met and recognized at once by the first lieutenant of the U. S. R. M. schooner *Ewing*, a Mr. Chaddock, then on that station, and who had been second lieutenant of the *Ewing* in 1842, on the New York station, and who was since lost, with nearly all on board, in the *Brother Jonathan*, at the mouth of Columbia river bar in 1866. He told me that as the *Ewing* was about relieving vessels in distress on the coast now, she needed some good seamen, and would like a dozen like myself. Of course I am fond of flattery; still I shipped in her, as I had an affection for the ship, and immediately joined and signed articles on the 1st December, 1845, for one year.

We cruised on the coast that noted severe winter until the latter part of March, 1846, relieving vessels in distress, for which purpose we had an extra complement of men on board, also large quantities of provisions and water in order to relieve their hunger when required, and protecting the revenue at the same time.

On one occasion, while thus cruising off the coast, we sighted a large bark apparently abandoned, with all sails blown away. On boarding and overhauling her, we discovered that her decks and bulwarks had been clean swept of crew and every movable; long-boat, galley, deck-houses, spars, and all had shared a common fate, which supposition proved afterwards to be correct, for no one ever appeared in New York, or was picked up belonging to the ill-fated bark. We took her in tow, with a couple of men on board to steer her, and brought her into New London. Each man afterwards received about one hundred and fifty dollars salvage money. But before leaving this subject, I must narrate that the boat's crew that boarded her the first time, and of which I was coxswain, having found a half pipe of

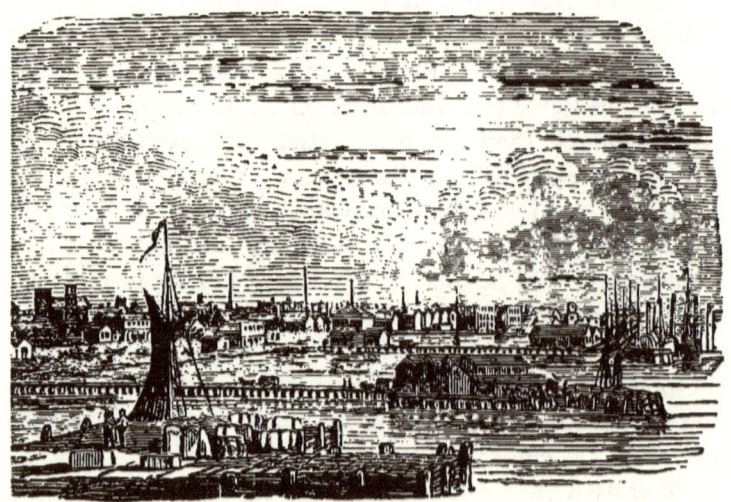

NEW LONDON, CT.

splendid gin on board, broached it, and got drunk, myself included. For this offense, when on duty, after we had the derelict bark safe at anchor in New London, Captain Moore was about to put me in irons, and had actually ordered the executive officer, Mr. Chaddock, to do so, or rather to have it done, as I, being coxswain, and in charge of the boat and crew, was responsible for their good conduct, but, as I was

told afterwards by the wardroom steward, the first lieutenant interposed in my behalf, on the ground that I was
enthusiastic in the performance of my duties, was obedient,
and had sailed with him years before, and had never before
known me to violate the rules of the service in any particular,
and moreover was an excellent seamen. Captain Moore, in
consideration of these representations, consented to over-
look the offense, and I was saved the degradation. That
came very near proving a very expensive "drunk."

One morning, when lying at anchor in New London, I,
being cook of our mess for the week, had prepared a mess of
what seamen term "lobscouse," and is a favorite dish. When
breakfast was announced by the boatswain's pipe or call, all
hands, as is customary, repaired to their respective messes,
except a quarter gunner, Bob Richards, who had lingered on
deck, and when he came to get his breakfast, he, sitting down
on the locker addressing me, said, "Davis, where's my lobscouse." I replied, "That it had all been eaten." He retorted with, "You son of a b—h, why didn't you keep some
for me?"

Fighting being prohibited by the rules of the service, I
had to forego my inclination of pitching into him there and
then, but saying, "Bob! I'll make you sorry for saying that
word to me." About two months after I prevailed on the
boatswain to include me in the same watch of liberty men
ashore that Richards belonged to, but I was fearful that
Richards would decline to go ashore if he knew I formed
one of the same liberty men. So, as it was dark when
we went ashore, I stowed myself under the bow grating
and thus escaped his observation. As soon as he had leaped
on to the wharf I immediately followed, and, going up to
him told him I intended to have it out with him for what he
had called me on the above-narrated occasion.

Richards was a much larger and heavier man than myself,
and many of the crew knowing what was to be the finale of

our quarrel had made bets pretty freely on the result, the odds being against me. However, I did my best and I whipped him till he was taken away, and he was laid up for about a week.

New London was a sort of sailor's paradise where everyone felt at ease, had full liberty to spin all his ancient yarns, now called chestnuts by landsmen, and to patiently listen to contests in which one Jack Tar tried to outsail all the others on the sea of gab and froth. From hundreds of sea-tales heard there I can only give space to one in which Luther Barker, born in New London, and shipped in early years on a whaler, was the victim of a captain's whim. He had a fond father, who showed his affection for his son by swinging him by the heels and cracking his skull against a stone wall. The doctor trephined his skull, and, it was said, inserted a silver plate to keep the cold air off his brain, which, in spite of all such caution, often became overheated, and Luther would make himself more or less troublesome to his associates. On one of his whaling voyages the captain confined him in a sort of hen-coop, built for the purpose, for four months, while the ship was sailing from the South Pacific to New London, full of whale oil. Every day, and several times a day, the captain would take food to him, usually scraps from the table, and call "chick, chick, chick; kip, kip, kip." As soon as he got ashore, Barker brought a suit for damages and recovered $2,000. When the money was paid in court Barker hauled the money over the table and called, "chick, chick, chick; kip, kip, kip," as the captain had done to him in the hen-coop. The captain's name has slipped my memory, which is a misfortune, for I would delight in immortalizing the brute.

I was told that a sailor from New Bedford was towed astern in a cask for a month or two, by a very humane captain of the bark *Peri*, of that port. I say humane, because he might have kept the cask astern for three or four months,

or the entire return voyage. Of course, a jury gave a verdict for damages, but how could a small sum of money com-
pensate a man for a month's bouncing on the waves astern
of a plunging ship in an iron-bound cask ? "Man's inhumanity to man" is verified, or was, by many a brutal captain
or mate in my day

In March, 1846, war impending between the United States
and Mexico, the *Ewing* received orders to recruit her crew
to a war standard, for which purpose our first lieutenant
went to New York and soon filled up the number from the
recruiting offices and sailor boarding-houses, and then we,
all hands except the commissioned officers, had a week on
shore at nights, where we made a regular old-fashioned time
of it, with fife and drum, hurrah and song, with banners
bearing strange devices, and our spirits, which were already
patriotically high, raised a little higher by a copious infusion
of the spirit of John Barleycorn, esquire, a friend of the
commissary. That was a free and glorious time, and our
expectations ran high. Some of the older ones anticipated
golden harvests, others, younger, thirsted for victims of their
courage and prowess among the blanked Mexicans. And
these feelings were heightened, as we marched up and down
the streets of that little town in the land of wooden nutmegs,
by the girls who waved their handkerchiefs from the windows, or threw bouquets of flowers to us, and shouted themselves hoarse as we marched to and fro in the moonlight.
Some of the streets were illuminated with all sorts of lights
in the windows and bonfires in the streets, and decorated
with flags everywhere. If we had not got away as we did in
a week or so we should have been of very little use as against
Mexicans or even smugglers.

We got ready for sea, and sailed under sealed orders on
the 4th April for the Gulf of Mexico. This sailing on a war
footing was a new experience to the crew of the *Ewing*, and,
like the war horse, we "sniffed the battle from afar," and

pictured ourselves returning with honor and glory and a good swag of prize money.

But even then there was an undercurrent of feeling and sentiment that came to the surface now and then when there was no war spirit loose. The younger men would gather in

HURRAH BOYS! ORDERS FOR MEXICO.

groups of four or five, under an awning, or in the fo'castle, or even about the guns or coils of rope, and talk or sing songs.

We arrived off the passes of the Mississippi on the 2d

MOUTH OF THE MISSISSIPPI

of May, where we received orders which directed us to cruise in search of Mexican merchant vessels, and co-operate with the navy in maintaining a blockade of the enemy's ports.

We captured several coasting craft creeping along shore between Vera Cruz and the Rio Grande, and which, with a prize crew aboard, were sent up to New Orleans for adjudication.

During one of these cruises we encountered a very heavy norther, in which we sprung our foremast, and were on the point of heaving our armament overboard, but a council of officers decided against it. However, we were obliged to return to New Orleans and step a new foremast.

While performing this operation a most melancholy accident befell us—more sad, inasmuch as it happened through the incompetence or gross negligence of the bo'son, who had the superintendence, and which might otherwise have been avoided. The heel lashing of the port or larboard sheer leg had not been properly secured from tripping, and as we set taut on the new spar, which was in the water on the starboard side, the whole business (as it is now termed) came crashing down, carrying away bulwarks, and killing two men on the spot where they stood, on the spar which they had been lashing,

During the norther that sprung our foremast, as just narrated, I had occasion to go out to the lee foreyard-arm, not being able to go into the head, and was about fifteen feet outboard, and in the act of adjusting my clothing, when the lee-lift parted, but I just saved myself by catching the foot-rope as I was in the act of falling, thus narrowly escaping certain death.

When I was waiting my turn to ask for letters at the window of the post office in New Orleans some one tapped me on the shoulder; it was a Captain Logan, from Vermont, but who was brought up in Montreal, where he and I went to school together. He asked me to go with him as

SOTO LA MARINA.

mate in the *Isaac Allerton*, but I had other plans and could
not accept.   He afterwards retired with a competence,
bought a farm near Skaneateles, New York, a beautiful
spot overlooking the lake.   Many of his neighbors are
Quakers, and he is half inclined that way now.

A boat's crew, of which I was a component part, fully
armed, one day had a very narrow escape from falling into
the hand's of the enemy. We had gone ashore on a foraging expedition at a place called Soto la Marina, on the
Mexican coast, and had already met with some success,
when we espied a body of Mexican lancers coming down
on us at full charge. A scamper for the boat ensued, as it
was *sauve qui peut*, and we fortunately got away in time, for,
though the soldiers sent some shots after us from their
carbines, we escaped without casualty.

Another little episode occurred while cruising.   An
armed boat's crew in charge of a gulf pilot had landed on
Padre Island for the purpose of shooting "buffalo" to
supply the *Ewing* with beef. The beach of this island was
covered with wreckage of ships laden with army stores,
which had been cast away. A cask of whisky having
been found intact, we quickly knocked in the head with
the butts of our muskets, and partook of the contents pretty
freely, but not sufficient to lose our heads, with the exception of one named Jack Lang. He got so drunk that he
forgot his musket, and when we returned to the *Ewing* a
great commotion was made about it. Lang was brought on
the quarter-deck to answer for his conduct, but he in-
geniously pleaded that it was sunstroke that was answer-
able for it all.   Therefore he got off, and the sun was
blamed.   The derelict musket was afterwards found by a
boat's crew sent ashore to look for it.

While lying off Vera Cruz composing part of the U. S.
Gulf squadron, of which the sloop of war *St. Mary* was
one, we were eye witnesses to one of those executions,

which, although they seem to be most cruel and against the laws of nature, yet are deemed necessary to insure that perfect discipline so essential when before the enemy. The man who thus suffered the extreme penalty of the "articles of war" was named Jackson. He was coxswain of one of the boats, and one of the best, if not the best, seaman aboard. He had been suddenly called away on his special duty as coxswain, and, at the moment of being called, had hastily thrown a pair of shoes he had in his hand under one of the gun-slides. The first lieutenant, on duty as officer of the deck, in the course of his rounds seeing the shoes, ordered them to be hove overboard. On the return of Jackson he sought for his shoes, and, not finding them, asked some of his messmates what had become of them, and being informed that the officer of the deck had ordered them to be hove overboard, he instantly went aft, and, addressing the deck officer, demanded if he had given orders for his shoes to be pitched overboard, and on the first lieutenant answering in the affirmative, Jackson, without another word, knocked him down. Within an hour Jackson was tried by court-martial, pronounced guilty, sentenced, and hanged at the foreyard-arm.

I have heard that a society exists in the United States, with branches in New York and the principal cities, whose bye-laws provide for the arrest, trial and execution of criminals who have evaded the laws of the State "within the hour." It is said that with a membership of many thousands scattered throughout the States, and belonging to many professions and trades, and during ten or twelve years the "Mystic Shrine," as it is called, has not had a single case to try. Prevention is better than cure.

Before closing my reminiscences of the *Ewing* in the Gulf of Mexico, I will relate how, after leaving the Balize at the nor'east pass, bound up to the head of the passes, and then down to and through the nor'west pass to the

VILLAGE OF BALIZE.

Gulf, we lost two seamen overboard from the jibboom, while at work bending a new jib; had just finished, and the sail being too suddenly hoisted, flapped them both overboard. Nothing more was seen of them except their caps and some blood, their bodies having undoubtedly been immediately seized by alligators.

We were also so unfortunate as to lose two more young seamen overboard while cruising in the Gulf at night. We were under easy canvas, with a very moderate breeze, when a school of porpoises came darting and plunging towards us, intending to cross our bows. Then two seamen each seized a harpoon, and stood on the "back-ropes" near the "dolphin striker." One of them having launched his harpoon successfully, it stuck into a porpoise, and, as is the wont of porpoises when wounded, it doubled back, and the shaft of the harpoon having got between the two men they were both tripped overboard

I reckon that a few extracts from the log about the different captains who commanded the *Ewing* while I was in her will be interesting, because they were a varied lot. One was Captain Gay Moore. If it was fortunate to have a red head then he was one of the most fortunate the navy was ever honored with, for his head was very fiery, inside as well as outside. It was stuffed with tyrannical notions. One of our watch said in making him they had used a spoiled devil. His courage was what might be expected from such a negative man, as an incident in the voyage to the Mexican coast will exhibit. One hazy morning, off the Tortugas, we were standing off one of the keys, only a short sail from Key West, when the lookout at the masthead called out sail, ho! and the usual answer and inquiries brought Captain Moore on deck looking very pale in spots, and acting nervously, and when he caught full sight of the hull of a man-of-war, ordered the decks cleared for action, guns shotted, matches lighted, magazines opened, and every man at his station, and then he went at once below and just hid in his state-room. The first lieutenant hailed the vessel, and the response was "*The Bainbridge,* United States brig of war." Then our brave captain, finding it was not a Mexican, came out into daylight once more.

On the coast of Mexico, a few days before the attack on Vera Cruz, in a sudden blow, a norther, he became alarmed and ordered the guns thrown overboard. One of the old salts growled to himself : It would be luckiest for Uncle Sam just now if Captain Moore should accidentally blow overboard and leave the guns to fight the Mexicans with. The guns were not thrown over, for the sailing-master persuaded the captain that the norther would be over in a day or two—and it was.

The next, Captain Rudolph, from Charleston, was drowned at Charleston station. He was a slave owner, and as that was the style then he had his ebony table waiters dressed in uniform, with plenty of big brass buttons, and we fared well in the fo'castle in his day, for he was a generous-hearted man as well as a good officer.

A curious old fellow was Captain Ottinger, who was said to be a Jew. One very amusing trait of language kept us sailors always in good humor, and that was, Let go ank*war*, and in the same pompous tone, "In sail," meaning shorten sail. He indulged in many other queer orders.

Captain Martin was what is called a martinet. He was always buzzing about like a bee, noisy everywhere, but giving very little trouble about ship, for he respected his mates and other officers, and they returned it with interest; so all went well.

I remember Captain Faunce, who came from Plymouth Rock, Mass., and he now lives in Jersey City. He established the first life-saving stations, was a good seaman, and always a gentleman on board or on shore. On my last ship-

ment in the *Ewing* he was in command, and made me
bo'son.   The first captain of the *Ewing* was Captain Bicker,
but I never saw him.   He commanded before my first shipment, but the sailors who sailed under him said he was an
all-over good captain.

And now to take up my log again—

On the 1st of December, 1846, my term of service having

BALIZE PILOT.

expired, I claimed my discharge, as one of the pilots of the
association at the Balize.   A former shipmate in the *John
G. Coster* from China, when he was second mate, had
induced me to join the pilots' association with a view of
becoming a pilot.   My duties at first consisted in my being
one of the boat's crew engaged in putting pilots on board
outward-bound ships, and afterward was promoted as boat-
keeper of a pilot house, a schooner performing the same

duties to inward-bounders. For this I received $25 a month and found.

I remained in the service of the association for about six months, and then quit, as I could not reconcile myself to their constant dissipation—drunk day and night, and continually gambling. These very bad vices result in a great measure from a neglect of early education. In men who have a liking for reading and study, drinking and gambling have little or no attraction. Men must have some amusement, and cards are handy, easily carried about quickly learned, and, when one is inclined that way, readily adapted to gain money by many skillful tricks which deceive the eye and mislead the green opponent. It is not safe to trust any habitual gambler at cards. I soon made my way to New Orleans. One of the laborious occupations on the levee at that city is rolling the cotton bales up the stage and into the hold of the vessel, where they are pressed into place by great screws, so as to fill every foot of space 'tween decks and hold. By employing several negroes and working myself very early and late, I was able to earn very good wages. But such work was soon monotonous, and lacking in the charm that belonged to life on board ship. The stevedore's lot is not to be envied in that city. I learned that an expedition was organized and equipped at New York and New Orleans having for its object the reduction of Vera Cruz and the Fortress of St. Juan de Ulloa.

My old shipmate, Arthur Hider, of the *Rome*, *Aigle*, *Ewing*, Lakes, and house of detention, N. Y., when I was a witness in the murder case on board the *Niantic*, had just arrived from a voyage, and had already shipped in the *North Carolina*, of Bath, Captain Drummond, with a regiment of regulars on board and a cargo of fresh water in cypress barrels. I therefore determined to ship in her.

We sailed with orders to rendezvouz at the Lobos Islands, in the Gulf, north of Vera Cruz, some one hundred and

LEVEE, NEW ORLEANS.

fifty miles, where was assembled a large fleet of ships and steamers of war, transports with troops, water, and surf-boats for landing troops, &c.

We arrived at the Lobos Islands two days after leaving the S. W. pass. I had nearly forgotten to state that we lost a man overboard while lying at anchor in the river. While towing down the Mississippi, in my anchor watch, with a boy with me, with a marlin-spike I forced the store door open, rolled a barrel of apples, some hams, and a small firkin of butter, with other things, into the fo'castle.

We had not lain at the Lobos Islands longer than a day or so when the ships composing the expedition were assembled, weighed and made sail to the south'ard, finally coming to under Sacrificios Anton Lizardo, Vera Cruz. The next morning was one of extreme activity and excitement, for as soon as day broke the whole fleet was alive with preparations for landing troops, field artillery, and munitions of war, and it was a grand sight to see boat load after boat load of troops following each other to the shore. Nineteen thousand men were then landed on the sandy beach near the city, and were set to entrenching themselves and erecting batteries. The siege of Vera Cruz, San Juan de Ulloa, was commenced.

Before leaving New Orleans I invested about five dollars in a keg of whisky containing ten gallons, and, on the night previous to the debarkation of the troops, it having been diluted to make forty gallons, I sold it at the rate of a dollar a glass, realizing the handsome sum of two thousand dollars. I have often thought that if all liquor dealers fix up their stock in that way there is no wonder why so many of them are rich. It is all profit to the seller—all loss to the drinker, except a little sop for his fancy now and then, and a superstition that somehow it is good for him.

After the surrender of Vera Cruz and San Juan de Ulloa, about ten days after it was invested and bombarded and our charter expired, we returned to New Orleans and were paid off.

While being paid, and my turn had arrived to go into the cabin for that purpose, Captain Drummond addressed me thus:

"Davis, do you expect to be paid off or to be sent to Baton Rouge, the Louisiana State prison?"

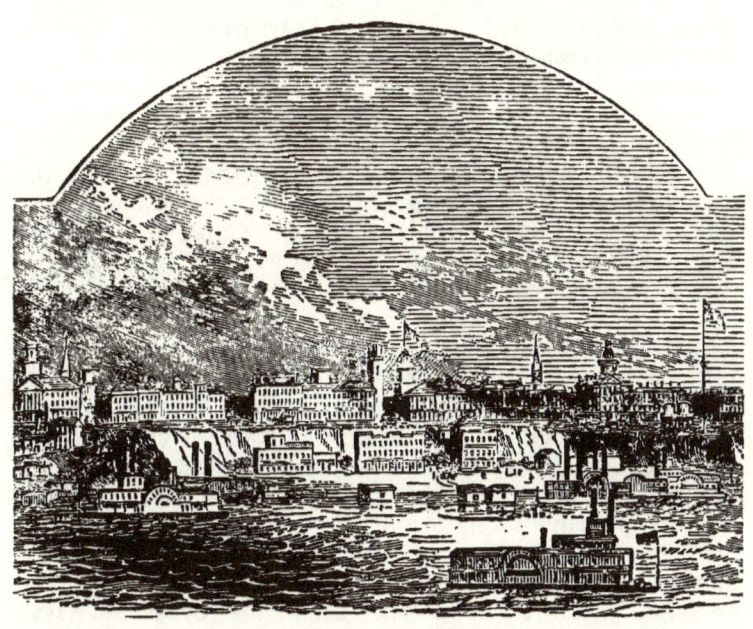

BATON ROUGE, LA.

I asked him to explain, when he said:

"You broke open the store-room on deck, and did so ana so (enumerating what I had appropriated) coming down the river."

"Yes, ι openea a room containing ship's stores, and marked so, but have not touched the captain's private stores."

My answer settled the matter. The logic of facts was enough for him.

It was with regret that I read this notice of the death of that good man and sailor, who, although he tried to send me to Baton Rouge so he could pocket my pay, yet I owe him no grudge and am glad of the opportunity of reprinting so much in his praise, for he deserved well of us all.

"Captain Robert R. Drummond, the last of a line of veteran sea captains, and one of the best known sailing masters in this port, died suddenly of heart disease on Monday night, at his residence in Brooklyn. He was born in Phippsburg, Me., in 1825, and when he was but fifteen years old he went to sea with his uncle, Captain William Drummond, in the *Rappahannock*, the largest ship afloat in those days. He had been a sailor ever since, having been all over the world on voyages, but for over thirty years he confined himself to the trade between New York and Cuba. For twenty-one years he sailed in one vessel, the *R. W. Griffiths*, between those points. Twice he met with serious danger in her, the first time having to throw overboard a cargo of boilers and valuable machinery intended for a large establishment in Cuba. Two years ago he lost his vessel by striking on a rock off the Bahamas, and his crew took refuge on a barren island for two days, when a vessel came by and rescued them. During the rebellion, when his vessel ran a double risk between the English privateers and Southern cruisers he came safely through by sailing under the English flag. Captain Drummond's long experience and his reputation for coolness and bravery made him very highly esteemed by owners of vessels. In all his voyages he never lost a life.'

A little adventure that took place after the capture of Vera Cruz will give some idea of what was going on generally, as I suppose all over that city, while everything was topsy-turvy. Some of my shipmates suggested that we go into the town and see what was going on. I had my whisky money to care for, and hesitated, when a soldier came along and said that he and another were intent on looting a church. He had heard of great riches being stored in the cathedral

of Vera Cruz, and had determined to have his share as soon
as he could get it. We joined him and his comrade and
made a party of four. On getting near the church we were
charmed with its antique and rather odd style, or no style of
architecture, and stood for some time a little way off gazing
up at the front. This was an error in practice, for it collected a crowd of curious people, who suspected the building was to be blown up. We went round to the rear and
broke open a small door, entered, and fastened it on the inside to keep out intruders. That term did not belong to us,
but any one interfering with us would have been intruders
We soon loaded up with as much as each could carry, with
vestments, altar-cloths, rugs, candlesticks of gilt over brass,
chalice, and a number of other things which we supposed
could be converted into money somewhere. We did not get
much for the articles. Every one we showed them to knew
they had been stolen, or captured, which is about the same
thing, and only offered about a quarter of their value. But
the excitement and the supposed danger of the enterprise,
and the feeling, when it was all over, that we had done some
small part of the punishing of the Mexican enemy was better
pay than money, at least for me. It never came into my
head that we were committing a robbery, and as to the sacri-
lege, that was not thought of by any of us.

I took my half-dollars, "whisky money," to the exchange office and exchanged them for gold, and then
shipped on board the ship *Louisiana*, Captain Hunt, one of
the regular packets between New York and New Orleans.

. In twenty-two days, with a very rough passage, we made
fast to the wharf foot of Maiden lane, East river, and were
paid off the next morning. Soon after I took my passage
in a steamer for New London, for the purpose of obtaining
what personal property I had left at the time we were
ordered to the "battle ground" in the Gulf, and to draw
some money I had deposited in the "Whaling Bank." I

then returned to New York, and shipped in the ship *Union*, Captain Hoyt, for New Orleans. She was also a regular packet plying between those two ports, and we made the passage in seventeen days without anything of note occurring.

I had been informed that money was to be made trading down the banks, coast as it is called, of the river with the negroes on the plantations, exchanging whisky, tobacco,

CHICKEN THIEF.

etc., for chickens, eggs, and money when it could be got. I concluded to try my luck in this trading speculation. I started with a cash capital ("all paid up," modernized), of eight hundred dollars, and purchased a sloop-rigged craft of four tons, decked with a nice cabin. The craft engaged in this "commercial enterprise" are styled "chicken thieves." I bought this "merchantman" for four hun-

CUSTOM HOUSE, NEW ORLEANS.

dred dollars, laid in a stock of good whisky, hams, cigars, crackers, and other articles too numerous to mention, and started down the coast, or the river, trading with the slaves. This business had to be conducted after nightfall (for the reason that the slaves were at work during the day, and the overseers on the *qui vive*), when my customers waded out to the boat with their produce on their heads.

After disposing of my cargo, I proceeded to Barrataria; at the same time I disposed of my poultry and eggs to the shipping aground on the sou'west bar, and to the pilots, and also to the tow-boats. Arriving at Barrataria bay I reloaded my craft with oysters nearly a foot long, called "Raccoon oysters," and sold them in New Orleans readily at the rate of one dollar a barrel. The time from Barrataria to New Orleans occupied generally about two days and part of two nights, the distance being about one hundred and twenty miles.

I continued at this business about three months, when one night, as I was lying at anchor off a place called the "English Turn," a little below New Orleans, trading with the slaves, two overseers, discovering what business I was engaged in, came down to the levee, and fired at me with their shot guns, but without taking effect. I thought then I would quit this nefarious business after this voyage, and, after receiving their fire, hauled up my anchor immediately, and, dropping out of reach, made sail down the river, stopping at various plantations. When I had disposed of all my cargo, I took in a load of oysters at Barrataria and sailed up to New Orleans.

During my voyage back to New Orleans I was lying at anchor one night at some little distance above the head of the passes, when I felt my little craft careen over. I jumped out of my berth, and, looking through a small hole in my cabin door, beheld an enormous alligator with his short forelegs on the deck, his snout stretched across sniffing and smelling to see what there was for supper. I had a pair of large horse-pistols always loaded at hand, and, aiming through the aforesaid hole for his eye, sent a ball crashing into his brain. The way he sculled for the shore, crying like a child, was a caution. They always make for the shore when wounded and never die in the water.

Arriving at New Orleans, I disposed of my schooner for one hundred and seven-five dollars, and, disgusted with the business which left me a loser of about four hundred dollars, I shipped on board of the hermaphrodite brig *Long Island*, bound for New York, making the passage in fourteen days.

But as I was fond of New Orleans and its inhabitants, and at home with the French and Spanish creoles, with whose patois I was conversant, I determined to make another voyage, and accordingly shipped in a small vessel called the *Auburn*, Captain Durfee, also a regular packet between New Orleans and New York. Arrived at New Orleans, we discharged and loaded in less than a week, and returned to New York, making the full voyage out and home in less than seven weeks.

I again shipped for New Orleans, this time as second mate of the ship *Arkansas*, Captain Hilliard. He was the sole survivor, if I remember right, of the steamer *Lexington*, burnt on Long Island sound in 1838, and who saved himself by swimming on a cotton bale, on which he endured the fearful exposure of a winter's day and night.

Besides her cargo, the *Arkansas* had a large number of both cabin and steerage passengers, among the latter of whom I was a general favorite, and in consequence never short of a drink; indeed, so profuse were they in their offerings, that on several occasions I was somewhat the worse for my potations, which, being noticed by the first officer, he at last reproved me. This so worked upon my feelings that I determined to leave the ship, and as soon as we struck the dock at New Orleans, I jumped ashore and left, *sans ceremonie.*

I have often listened to the names of the different dishes in a restaurant, and mentally contrasted them with the terms used on shipboard, and now propose to give a few of the sailor's names for the food that is supplied to them.

Webster's Dictionary defines lobscouse as a hash of meat and various vegetables: an olio. An olio is a mixture, a medley. Mr. Webster was a very learned man, but he did not quite correctly describe lobscouse, which, being a marine mystery, may have been beyond his limit of investigation. A sub-genus prevails in jails and lockups, but it is not worth mention here. The true lobscouse is compounded of salt horse and spuds, or yams, stewed and hashed. Onions or other vegetables are traditionally included, but practically omitted. When scouse is made without either meat or potatoes (salt horse or spuds) it is called dandy-funk.

And as to Webster, which is a great name in American history, I may be permitted to repeat a doleful eulogy that was recited by an old shipmate from Marblehead, near Boston. He said, "It is a matter of great wonder that Webster, who was always so busy in public affairs, could find time to write such an immense dictionary, and a thousand pities that he should have been hanged for killing such an old skin-flint as that Dr. Parkman was." Anyhow, the remark showed the kind heart of the old sailor, and I doubt he ever found out there were three of that name, the statesman, the lexicographer, and the unfortunate doctor, who, in a fit of desperation struck his tormentor a heavier blow than he intended and was sentenced to be hanged. There was so much said and written about his having been spirited away and another body substituted at the execution, that it was never determined if he was hanged or not.

There are other terms in common use in the cabin and

cook's galley. Flour, water, salt, and fat from cooked beef is called duff. Griddle cakes are flapjacks; biscuits are sea-cake. They are kept in a bread-barge, a small box, say two feet long by fifteen inches in breadth and depth, with a hole near one end of a side large enough to admit a hand and take out one. When the sailor in the fo'castle asks for a sea-cake one or two biscuits are taken out of the barge and pitched at him, and he catches wi'h his hands or his nose, as the case may be. When the barge is empty some one calls out to the youngest of the watch, "There's a southerly wind in the bread barge," and the barge is taken to the cook's galley and stowed afresh. Potatoes are spuds, rice is swampseed, beans are tornadoes, snappers or band of music, and bean soup is snapper soup. Bread crumbs and other broken victuals from the cabin table are manavelins Beef is generally salt-horse, at least in my day what appeared in the fo'castle, had earned its dignity after several long voyages at sea. Pork was grunter, and mutton, when we had any, was simply mutton. Fish are moonstruck. Codfish and potatoes were twice-laid, and the sailors had to spit out such bones as they'd rather not swallow. The codfish was kept in two chests, one on each side of the mizzen top, and samples were brought down when wanted by the steward. Pot-pie is sea-pie, molasses leather-strap or black-strap. We never saw any sugar in the fo'castle, that dainty being entirely confined to the land of knives and forks, the cabin. The cook is always called doctor. When eight bells are struck the youngest in the watch goes to the cook's galley and gets a kid of salt horse and a kid of swampseed or snapper-soup, and a tin pot of black-strop, with the bread barge, which together form the sumptuous repast of Jack before the mast. In fine weather the sailors eat on deck, and literally the deck is their table, and they furnish their own tin plate, spoon, sheath-knife, and coffee-pot. In a man-of-war sheath-knives are prohibited. When a cow, pigs, sheep, chickens, and other live-stock were carried the sailor who took care of them was called " Jimmy Ducks." No milk, chickens, or other fine grub ever appeared in the fo'castle unless surreptitiously. Occasionally some member of the watch on deck in the night would try his hooks on the duds (milk the cow), by way of proving that he had not forgotten his farm lessons ashore, but as chickens can be counted at least after they are hatched, and there were no weasels or skunks to charge the theft to, and the rats never came on deck, so from a sort of necessity the coop was not disturbed against orders. Necessity of various kinds on shore as well as on board assists very much in promoting honesty and virtue, although too much will usually work a contrary result.

I shipped on board of a large schooner bound to the Rio Grande with stores for the quartermaster's department of the army. We arrived at Bagdad in due course, and hearing that very high wages for deck hands on board the government steamers were being offered, I resolved to desert the schooner.

Always bearing in mind (as my readers may remember I mentioned in an early part of the book) " that caution is the mother of safety," I made fast a rope about one foot from the deck, and, stretching it across just for'ard of the cabin door, made it taut on the other side, so that any one coming out in the dark in a hurry, would be sure to trip over it; having taken this precaution in case the noise I might make in dropping overboard should bring the officers on deck, when they would undoubtedly have made a target of me. I secured a piece of plank to my breast and a bag of clothes on my back, and then, letting myself as quietly as I could overboard, swam ashore to an adobe hut occupied by an old Mexican who kept me concealed till next morning. At day-break I engaged on the steamer *Col. Cross*, lying alongside the wharf, and was directed by the engineer to con-

ceal myself in the engine-room on deck, from which safe retreat I had the satisfaction of viewing the captain and mate
of the schooner from which I had deserted, making a fruitless search for me, each having a loaded pistol.

The steamer *Col. Cross* was employed running up to
Camargo with recruits and munitions of war and stores.

We had made two trips to Camargo and back, when one
night, lying at Bagdad, and a norther blowing, the steamer's
carpenter, a German, came to me and proposed that I should
join him in making a haul of a large sum of money which he
said the mate kept in a chest in his state-room on the boiler
deck.   This mate was an inveterate gambler, and the scheme
was to the effect that when he went ashore to play monte,
his room should be broken open and the money taken. The
carpenter offered to supply me with the necessary tools and
a large spike to open the door, for the mate always took the
knob out of the door when going ashore.   I offered some
excuse, and the carpenter said he would do the job himself,
but I must not blow on him.   So in the night when the
mate had gone ashore, he pried open the door, opened the
trunks and ransacked everywhere, but found no money. The
carpenter was greatly disappointed, and said some one else
must have been ahead of him and carried off the treasure. The
next morning, while we were washing decks, the mate, infuriated at having found his state-room and trunk broken into,
and his things rummaged promiscuously, rushed round the
decks like a madman with a cocked pistol in his hand, and
swore if he only knew who had been in his room he would
blow his brains out.   That night I left the boat, unknown to a
single soul, for I felt convinced that the carpenter would reveal the secret, and then my skin would not be worth a cent
to me, because I had not warned the mate against the mischief. I walked through a wild and desolate country, covered
with chapparel, to Point Isabel, where I got a chance to
work my passage to New Orleans in a small schooner, and I

considered myself fortunate to arrive without any holes in
my carcass, after a passage of six days.

Considering that I had had enough for a time of romanc-

FLORIDA FRUITS.

ing in the sunny South I shipped in the brig *Jasper*, Captain
Moran, for New York, with molasses in barrels, and sugar,
and back to New Orleans.   We made the entire voyage
in a little less than two months.   Nothing material occurred

on this voyage, neither did I get into any more scrapes. Although a little personal excitement is very good in its way, yet it does not do to be always in hot water, and I imagine that I had experienced my full share of that.

On our return to the "Crescent City" I next shipped mate of the brig *Texas*, Captain Golden, for Tampico, on the Gulf coast of Mexico, with small bales of cotton for carriage on pack mules.

We had very fine weather till we came to off Tampico bar, with a slip on our cable. We had not finished furling sails when we were struck in a moment by a terrific "norther," and had to slip our cable in a hurry and scud before its fury under bare poles, until we could get an aftersail on to her, and heave her to the wind. We rode the larboard tack for nearly a week. During this time I suffered the torments of the damned in consequence of an awful felon on the middle finger of my right hand, and had to write up my log with my left, as well as I could, and when the crew were engaged making and shortening sail I had to take the wheel, being able to steer with my left hand only. After having been blown some one hundred and eighty miles to the east'ard, and from the Gulf coast the "norther" moderated, and by degrees shifted to a pleasant easterly breeze, when we made all sail, which soon enabled us to make Tampico bar again, and luckily picked up our mud-hook. We procured the services of a very small tug-boat, and were towed up a narrow passage to Tampico. The banks of this passage were thickly wooded with banana and plantain trees, which grew down to the water's edge, and, leaning over to the centre, intermingled their branches, forming a complete arch which greatly impeded our progress, so that we had to send men aloft to cut our way through.

We discharged our cargo into the lighters, and then returned in ballast to New Orleans, making the passage in nine days, the round voyage occupying two months.

NEW ORLEANS—CRESCENT CITY.

I was compelled to enter the Charity Hospital as a patient, the felon on my finger had become so painful and serious that medical treatment was necessary. During the first night in hospital so many of the patients died around me that I was scared, and suddenly took French leave in the early morning. I betook myself to a friend's house, a stevedore by the name of Philips, with whom I resided until the felon got entirely well. Then Mr. Philips gave me a job rolling cotton on the levee and on the stage into the ship. I worked at this for about two months, sometimes earning as much as ten dollars a day, always two working together, and frequently rolling two hundred bales of cotton at a bit (twelve and a half cents) a bale.

Contracting habits of whisky drinking, which beginning to tell on my constitution, I determined to go to sea again as a means of reform, and accordingly shipped before the mast in the ship *Louisa*, Captain Emerson, for New York, making the passage in fourteen days.

In the 'tween decks of the *Louisa* were a large number of trunks, valises and traveling bags, and all kinds of personal effects which had belonged to the victims of the yellow fever, and the epidemic was then prevailng in New Orleans. The crew broke open and ransacked the trunks, etc., and appropriated what valuables they could lay their hands on and stow away in a small compass. By this many of them became the unlawful possessors of very valuable jewelry and precious stones, besides some good second-hand clothing and other articles, and all ran the risk of a visit from "yellow jack."

While writing about the hospital in New Orleans, I cannot refrain from mentioning the home provided for disabled seamen called the "Sailors' Snug Harbor," on Staten Island, New York. An aged, decrepid and worn out sailor is received, if the applicant has served five years under the flag of the United States, either in the navy or merchant service,

and if he has no contagious disease, and if he will further
agree to adopt total abstinence from alcohol, and obey the
rules of the institution as to dress, habits, and other social
matters.   I have visited it many times, and have among its
inmates several old-time shipmates.   As you pass into the
carriage gate you will likely see in its keeper Lieutenant
Stull, an old seaman, seventy-nine years old, whose father

SAILORS' SNUG HARBOR—1850.

was once wealthy, owning a plantation and many slaves on
the ground where the battle of Antietam was fought, but
who was stripped clean to the bone before he died.   Lieutenant Stull was and is a fine specimen of a man in stature
and countenance, and his fittings within are equal to the
external rigging.

Captain De Peyster, who commanded the *Columbus* when I made the acquaintance of those sea-dogs Cornish and Huntington, was the second governor of the Sailors' Snug Harbor. In those days the governor handled all the money required to run the institution. He committed suicide, as is supposed, although I cannot believe it, in 1866. One of my mates in the *Gazelle* was an inmate until he died in

SAILORS' SNUG HARBOR—1887.

1885. Isaac Dixon, now there, was with me in the revenue cutter *Ewing*. He was a native of Durham, in England, and of Quaker parents.

Many faces that were familiar a few years since have disappeared, and now, although I know many who are there, it is from frequent visits to the place, which is a paradise in its way. One absent one deserves mention for the bit of

romance in his log.   John Potter was a native of Dantzic,
Germany, and was quartermaster on the *Ewing* when I
sailed in her.   He left the revenue service, and went as
quartermaster in coastwise steamers running to southern
ports until his health failed, when he turned up one day and
I invited him to make my house his home, and we messed
together again for four years, this time on dry land.   He
died in the Sailors' Snug Harbor, and left a will in my
favor.   He told me that after being away from home fifty
years he returned to Dantzic, and found that his sister had
died while he was on board in the stream just before landing.   No other member of his family was alive.

   The library and reading room is a haven of rest and
recreation, where those inclined may revisit those ports
which they have frequented in actual life, and live over
again in imagination their earlier years.   In the halls below,
or in rooms set apart, any one of them may be busy making
hammocks, small baskets, and other things which can be
sold for money.

TEMPLE BAR, LONDON.

Chapter XIII.

" *   *   *   O, I have suffered
With those that I saw suffer ; a brave vessel,
Which had no doubt some noble creature in her,
Dash'd all to pieces. O, the cry did knock
Against my very heart ! Poor souls ! they perished.
Had I been any God of power, I would
Have sunk the sea within the earth, or e'er
It should the good ship so have swallowed, and
The fraughting souls within her."

Shipping a second time in the *Auburn* under the command of Captain Hoyt, we had a fair passage to New Orleans; discharged cargo, and received a return cargo of sugar, molasses, and some cotton 'tween decks; cast off, and were towed down with many other vessels by the *Mary Ringsland* (tow-boat) outside the sou'west pass and to sea. We had a succession of fair but boisterous winds generally, and until we reached the vicinity of Cape Hatteras were congratulating ourselves on a speedy arrival in New York, but "man proposes and God disposes."

On the 19th March, 1847, at daybreak, we were to the nor'ard of the Capes of the Delaware, running parallel with the Jersey coast, with the wind at west nor'west, when suddenly the wind died away and came round to east nor'-east, increasing every moment until we were nearly up to Barnegat, by which time we were under close-reefed topsails, reefed foresail and fore-topmast staysail.   On the starboard tack, the gale still increasing in force, and carrying on a press of sail in the vain effort to claw off, with the lee sail almost under water, we were forced to take the fore and mizzen topsails off the ship.   Then the wind hauled to the south'ard and east'ward, about sou'east, with a fresh hand on the bellows, and suddenly, with a deafening roar, away went our maintop-sail clean out of the bolt-ropes. We were embayed, and, in spite of the most strenuous efforts to

set the mizzen-top sail, no sooner was it clear of the gaskets
and the lee clue partly sheeted home, than it gave a slat and
flew into ribbons.   Every resource of seamanship was exhausted, and we were finally driven on the outer bar off
Barnegat.   The immense seas made a clean sweep over
our decks, one more heavy than another sweeping our
captain with nineteen passengers into a watery grave, while
we were helpless to save them from their fate.

" For the Angel of Death spread his wings on the blast."

We managed to launch the largest boat next to the long-
boat, into which the second mate, six of the crew and myself succeeded in getting a stout line, for the purpose of
carrying it ashore to haul a hawser by it to the land, and
make it fast to something, to safe life by making a boatswain's chair, but the boat in going through the breakers
was unfortunately capsized in the surf, and all perished
except the second mate and myself.   When the boat got
broadside to, and I saw that she must go over, I remembered, from my experienced with the surf-boats on the coast
of Sumatra, that the only chance of getting clear was by
jumping from the higher gunwale of the boat as she was
going bottom up, thus to avoid being covered, and consequently suffocated and drowned.   The second mate followed my example, and shared my luck.   Thus, out of
forty-four souls that left New Orleans in the *Auburn*, only
the second mate and myself were saved.

> " Then breathless, with my digging nails I clung
> Fast to the sand, lest the returning wave,
> From whose reluctant roar my life I wrung,
> Should suck me back to her insatiate grave :
> With just enough of life to feel its pain,
> And deem that it was saved, perhaps in vain.
> With slow and staggering effort I arose,
> But sunk again upon my bleeding knee
> And quivering hand : and then I looked for those
> Who long had been my mates upon the sea ;
> But none of them appeared to share my woes,
> Save one."

I was cast unconscious on the strand, and when I recovered consciousness found that my belt containing three

hundred dollars in gold was gone, and a gold watch also.
These had probably been taken off me by the land pirates,
or wreckers, who, at that time, were very numerous on the
coast. The *Auburn* became of course a complete wreck.

I reached New York, after a fashion, somehow, "a battered hulk" with only what I stood in, but fortunately I still
had some money in the savings' bank, and soon refitted
myself with clothing.

I found that my old favorite the revenue schooner *Ewing*
had returned from the seat of war, and was stationed at New
York for the protection of the revenue, and, like many a
truant lover, I returned to my old love and shipped in her
for the third time.

I was going across Hamilton ferry to Brooklyn for the
purpose of signalling the *Ewing* when I met Captain Martin, her captain, on the ferry-boat, the same officer with
whom I had words in 1843. I asked him if he was short of
men. He immediately said, "Go aboard of the *Ewing* at
once."

I had not been attached to her more than a week when
the boatswain, who happened to be Bill Austin, the man
who had endeavored to stab me six years previously, when
I first belonged to the *Ewing*, absented himself beyond his
leave on a drunken spree, and I was promoted as boatswain
in his place.

Being a trifle higher in station than a seaman, I conceived
the idea that "it is cheaper to keep a cow than to be always
buying milk," and resolved to marry or, nautice—"get
spliced in a long splice." As it has always been with me,
to think is to act, I took unto me a wife for better or
worse, and together we are now finishing life's cruise in
company.

I could fill up a big log book with the many jokes and
gibes that were flung at me when my shipmates found out
that I was going for a voyage on the sea of matrimony, but

as many of them were such side-splitting tales, with a big
nut to them, I should utterly fail if I tried to repeat them.
Then everyone knows that a good joke, like champagne, is
best when it is first popped off.   However, there was one
worth repeating that was spun as a sort of warning to me
and by one of my messmates, and he was not particular as to
how many others should hear it.   This is how he reeled it off:

Ben Barney and I were on a cruise uptown in a Madison
avenue 'bus, and we struck a regular hurricane.   Ben, wishing to show how very polite he could be, offered to pass up
the fare of a lady who sat near the door, and, without
looking at the money, dropped it into the locker—the cash
box. The lady fairly screamed at Ben, " I gave you a quarter,
sir ;" and she withered him with an acid smile and a fiery
glance through her gold-bowed glasses.   Ben jumped up to
look in the cash box just in time to see the quarter slide into
the hold through the scuttle.   He fairly blushed scarlet and
crimson, and stammered out that he thought the money was
all right, and was not much used to the ways of the 'busses,
and hoped the driver would make it right.   So he hammered
on the roof and asked the driver for twenty cents in change.
The driver chaffed him by saying that he was not a millionaire, and could not afford to give him twenty cents for
nothing, and he did not see how he could be expected to
get down into the box and heave out the quarter.   If the
passenger wanted the change she should go to the office and
get it.

Ben was angry at the driver, and said, " Blast your eyes,
if you are so mean as that I'll pay for my mistake," and he
poked about in his pockets for change.

While he was busy searching in one pocket or another,
the lady looked a picture of injured innocence, and piped
to another lady passenger, in a bitter tone of voice, " Do
you think, really, that the old fellow who took my quarter is
in any way connected with the company ?"

Ben heard the remark, as all the others did, and he answered in great confusion, "Me, lady, bless you, I don't belong on land. I'll pay back your money. But I can't find a cent."

He looked at me, but I shook my head as much as to say I have no cash, and he finally pulled out a memorandum book, saying :

"Lady, please give me your name and address, and as soon as I return to my ship I will lay in a fresh supply of cash and return your twenty cents this very evening."

"Oh, never mind," she said, in a mincing way, "it teaches me a lesson. Hereafter I will pay my fare myself."

"Oh, I'll bring the change, lady; you can be sure of that. I just happen to be at the end of my purse Been out all the morning, and made a number of calls. What's the name, please?" He laid his memorandum book on his knee and held his pencil ready to write, but she said :

"Yes, I dare say you *intend* to ; but never mind ; let it go. It's all right. I've learned a lesson. I'll pay my own fare hereafter."

She repeated the words several times, looking at the other passengers, and seemed to delight in giving a varied emphasis each time. I wondered if she had not been a school-ma'am some time or other. She settled down in the seat with an air of resignation, as much as to say she knew she was swindled, but was resigned. Ben asked again in a pleading way for her name, and seeing that some of the ladies seemed to feel for the old sailor, she snapped it out, but with a streamer at the end, that she had learned a lesson.

When Ben had written her name and address he took courage and said, "I'm ready to make all amends, and you shall have your money, but I have also learned a lesson. While I am not saying what it is so much, I've got it all the same."

Just then a very pretty young woman, whose eyes sparkled with suppressed mirth under her dark bangs, spoke to Ben, and said:

"I'll tell you, sir, what to do. We'll collect the fares that come into the coach until the twenty cents is made up, and that will save you further trouble."

Ben took off his hat to the young women, and said, "Many thanks, miss. I'm a thousand times obliged to you for the suggestion."

At that instant a well-dressed woman climbed in, and as she was taking out her money the young woman explained to her what had happened with the quarter, and the lady replied, "Oh certainly," and five cents went into the hands of the lady with spectacles and an acid smile. It was but a minute or two before enough money had been taken, and the twenty cents was safe in the purse of the much injured woman. Then she got out without a word or a look even to any one.

As soon as she was beyond ear-shot, Ben said, after drawing a long breath, "That wor a stress of weather. I didn't go to do it, but I'd got her money to her this very night. I didn't tell her the lesson I learned, but I hope she'll remember the one she learned."

There was a laugh among those who had seen the thing from the start. Then the young woman who helped Ben out of the difficulty rose to go out, and as she passed she smiled a good-bye to him, and he took off his hat, and said, "Thank you, miss. Merry Christmas to you, miss." Then, after seeing her on the sidewalk, he said, looking over to me, "What a difference there is atwixt women. Wonderful, ain't it?"

In October, 1848, the *Ewing* was transferred from the revenue to the naval service, in order that she might proceed to the coast of California for the purpose of surveying and establishing lights, custom houses, and many other governmental duties.

Captain Bartlett was commissioned to command the *Ewing*, and he offered me extra pay, which he would give from his private purse, if I would remain in her. He wished me to remain in her with him, as I, having sailed so many years in the *Ewing*, understood how she should be handled in all weathers. I had, however, been married but a few months, and did not relish the idea of parting with my better-half so soon, and going away and leave her for such a long and perilous voyage around Cape Horn to the cost of California. I therefore declined his offer, although, at the same time, I was loth to let her sail without me, for I had passed many a jovial hour aboard of her, and knew her so well, that she seemed almost like an old friend.

I had almost forgotten to relate that, when on board the *Ewing* in 1842, and lying in New York harbor, the British frigate *Warspite* arrived with Lord Ashburton, to negotiate the extradition treaty between the United States and the British possessions in North America and the West Indies; and, indeed, in the whole world, I think. Well, while the *Warspite* was lying moored in the North river off the Battery, a large party of North river boatmen (it was supposed) whitewashed the *Warspite* all round. As may be supposed, his lordship was immensely enraged at what he considered a great outrage and insult, but although he offered the large reward of $25,000 out of his private purse, the perpetrators were never discovered. The indignity lately imposed on a British man-of-war in New York harbor by "Captain" Paul Boyton, the renowned swimmer in rubber water-tight clothes, was also the cause of a commotion among the English officers on board. But practical jokes are jokes, and ought not to be considered criminal. The whitewash and Boyton's dummy torpedo are "a pair of

'em." Another circumstance worthy of passing note in connection with the time of my belonging to the *Ewing* in
1842 is recalled.

One morning early at daybreak, and in my anchor watch
on board of the *Ewing*, the U. S. brig-of-war *Somers*
arrived, and came to in the East river off the foot of Wall
street. She had come into port just after the execution of
three on board of her, viz.: the bo'son's mate, a seaman, and
a midshipman (the last named being a son of Secretary of
the Navy Upshur), who had conspired together to murder
the officers, take possession of the vessel, and cruise in the
tracks of the packet ships plying between Europe and
America, make them their prey, and, following the maxim
that "dead men tell no tales," put all to death by making
them walk the plank. The plot was discovered by one of
the conspirators accidentally dropping the written and signed
agreement out of his pocket while at work, which was picked
up by one of the commissioned officers.

In the same year of the historical Yankee trick of white-
washing the British frigate *Warspite*, the United States
Government authorized Colonel Colt, of revolver fame, to
experiment with an explosive to be fired by electricity, and
assigned an old hulk of a storeship, just returned from Wilkes'
exploring expedition, for that purpose, and she was moored
between Castle Garden and Bedloe's Island, where the
Bartholdi statue of liberty now stands. I was one of the
boat's crew detailed to carry the apparatus to and fix it upon
the side of the hulk. It was about the size and shape of a
half barrel, and may have weighed one hundred and fifty
pounds. We fixed it to the side of the vessel with screws,
and returned to the deck of the *Ewing* in time to see
Colonel Colt operate his apparatus. He stood on the starboard side of the trunk, and I was opposite him on the port
side, when he took a wire in each hand, and, looking toward the
hulk, said, "Now, gentlemen, notice the result," and at that

moment he touched the ends of the wires together; at the same instant the old hulk seemed to rise up high in the air and carry a vast sea of spray and water with her. She was torn into fragments.

In the autumn following, a boat's crew was ordered to go up the East river on a tour of observation in the second cutter, of which I was coxswain. The *Ewing* lay in the Buttermilk channel, and the suspected schooners that were reported as having no names painted on the stern, as the law directs, were said to be near the south end of Blackwell's Island. The flood tide was running up the river at a race-horse speed, and the wind was dead ahead, which made a terribly choppy sea. We were cruising about as ordered when the cutter was thrown upon a spile near the end of the dock, and a large hole was stove in her bottom under the bow. Seeing her filling rapidly, I ordered the crew to take off their monkey-jackets, and, rolling them into a big wad, stopped the leak so well that one man could bail out the little water that came in, and we pulled back to the *Ewing* half frozen, for it was bitter cold and we were very wet.

As I was reading the proof of this passage I noticed in the *Guardian*, of Manchester, N. H., that Mr. James W. Pettigrew had received a pension for services in the Mexican war. He was a shipmate with me in the *Ewing*, and was on board when she sailed from New London, Connecticut, in 1846, for the seat of war in the Gulf. He was made bo'son, and was a very able seaman, a good genial companion and hearty messmate. Another shipmate on the *Ewing* was John G. Brushwood, a native of Virginia, who was promoted to first lieutenant while we were off Vera Cruz. He was an unjust man in many respects, and had once been kicked out of the service for cheating the men beneath him of their salary. He used to receive the money due the men from Washington, and, when he paid them, kept part of their earnings for himself. Through powerful influence he again entered the naval service, and was promoted as above stated. At the commencement of the civil war he was stationed at New Orleans and was in command of a steam cutter. At the first sign of hostilities he hauled down the stars and stripes and delivered the vessel over to the Confederate authorities. For this act of perfidy he received an appointment as captain in the rebel forces. I suppose he thought, as did General Robert E. Lee, that his native State was first entitled to his allegiance before the United States.

To return from my digression. The revenue cutter *Forward* was ordered from the Delaware station to relieve us, and remained on the New York station the whole of that winter, '48-'49. She was an extra fast sailer, and very wet. In May, '49, we were relieved by the cutter *Gallatin*, and the *Forward* returned to her old station.

The *Gallatin* was one of the old style revenue cutters, and entirely unfit for the duties required of her. Therefore a new vessel was ordered to the New York station, and we were ordered with the *Gallatin* to Wilmington, Delaware, and delivered to the collector of customs. The non-commissioned officers and crew were dismissed the service and paid off, the majority returning to New York.

The crews of the revenue cutters were composed of men of all nationalities, but the officers were nearly always American born citizens, who had large experience in the coasting trade. Every duty on board the revenue cutters was performed as nearly as possible in man-of-war style, and the officers were subject to nearly the same regulations as in the United States Navy.

On my dismissal from the revenue service at Wilmington I returned to my home in Brooklyn, N. Y., for, being now a married man, I had something better to look forward to than sailors' boarding houses. Still, my tastes were not yet softened down sufficiently to reconcile myself to a life ashore, or to be one of those "landsmen who lie down

NEW YORK, FROM BROOKLYN.

below." I accordingly cast about for another ship, and was soon engaged as seaman on board of a steamer bound for Cuba, which was lying and fitting out at one of the docks in Jersey City. I, with the rest of the crew, consisting of nine seamen, were engaged in getting her ready for sea, and had been so employed for two weeks, when lighters came alongside with her cargo of heavy goods in large cases, which I immediately divined to consist of arms and munitions of war. Although every precaution was resorted to in order to allay any suspicion regarding the nature of the projected voyage, yet the United States authorities must have got some information, for, after we were fully loaded and ready for sea, and pilot engaged, the steamer was seized by the U. S. Marshal. She was doubtless engaged as a part of the Lopez expedition organized for the invasion of Cuba, and so our voyage was nipped in the bud and came to naught.

One of the resorts of the crews of outfitting vessels on the east side was an old Dutch tavern in Peck Slip, where all sorts of liquid or other refreshments were served for cash, and a good deal of that commodity was handed over its bar not a little of which once belonged in my pocket.

In looking about for another ship I finally shipped in the *Matilda*, Captain Land, bound on a trading voyage to the coast and Gulf of California, and to call at Mazatlan, San Diego, Santa Barbara, Monterey and other minor ports, wherever we could make a good swap, exchanging American goods and Yankee notions for hides, copper, lead, &c.

On my birthday, the 17th June, 1849, I sailed on this my first voyage round Cape Horn, with a full complement of crew and plenty of stores on board, spars and water-casks securely lashed, with a pilot on board, tug alongside, fasts singled, orders received, and top-sails mast-headed; at the word, we let go, and with the first of the ebb-tide, and a gentle nor'wester, and the jib set as she swung head down

OLD DUTCH TAVERN, PECK SLIP, NEW YORK.

stream, we passed Fort Columbus on Governor's Island, pointed for the "Narrows," and then for the broad Atlantic.

Crossing the bar, and reaching the light-ship, the tug was let go, and the pilot left us. We made all sail, including all stun'sails alow and aloft both sides, wind about as dead aft as you could get it, stowed and double-lashed anchors, after securing the boats and every movable about decks which had not been secured by the riggers alongside of the wharf. By this time we were out of sight of land, and approaching the westerly edge of the Gulf stream. The weather then began to look squally, and the wind to veer to the nor'ard, so we hauled in all stun'sails, rigged in the booms and unrove the gear. The easterly horizon assumed a leaden hue, the wind finally settled in the nor'east and began to pipe. Then we furled royals and sent down the yards, hauled down the flying-jib and stowed it. The wind increasing in force, we took in to'gallant sails. Watch now close-reefed the mizen-top-sail, brailed the spanker up and secured the foot of the sail. At midnight the gale began to moderate with rain, and veered more to the south'ard. At daybreak we shook out the reefs in the mizen-top-sail and set the spanker. At seven bells set to'gallant sails, and all hands on deck ; at eight bells tacked ship, wind sou'west, ship going two points free on the starboard tack, we sent up royal yards and set the sails, with the flying jib, rigged out the starboard top-mast, and to'gallant stun'sail booms fore and main, and set the sails. The reader will see that in such threatening weather, and changing winds, there was heavy work for Jack aloft.

As we neared the tropics, the regions of the trade winds, the weather grew more balmy and settled. The crew discarded their woolens and substituted such as they had of jumpers and hip-trousers made of some old sail or of old canvas appropriated from a former ship. Thus appareled in rigs suitable to tropical weather, we were then approach-

ing the abode of the never-failing, but ever-to-be-found, Doldrums or Horse Latitudes.

The fine westerly breezes at length became unsteady and
fickle, so we hauled in all stun'sails, rigged the booms in,
unrove the gear, and when we had gone through the Horse
latitudes with the usual exasperating experiences, at last
struck the faithful nor'east trade winds in about 8° south
latitude, bracing the yards with all sail set on the port tack,
about one point free. In fourteen days we had sailed
through the nor'east trades, and were brought up all a
standing by a fierce sou'west gale of wind off the Falklands.
We had the day before sent down royal yards and stun'sail
booms, and stretched life-lines along the decks, and were
now under close-reefed fore main-topsails, and reefed foresail, main-sail and mizzen top-sail, with spanker and jibs
furled, with the fore top-mast stay-sail on her. On the starboard tack, the third day after we had been introduced to
the sou'wester aforesaid, the wind lulled and commenced to
veer to the south'ard. We wore ship, and had hardly cleared
the decks and coiled up the running rigging on the belaying
pins when it commenced to blow in earnest. The wind
finally settled in the sou'east with terrific force, driving hail,
snow and sleet. We were then running with the wind
abeam one or two points free, and at a screeching gait, but
with the decks covered with snow and sleet. We were scudding along at this rate very fast, and leaving the region
where rude Boreas holds undisputed sway and comes roaring up from the Antarctic pole like a lion searching for its
prey, or rather like one thousand frosty, hungry lions.
When off Cape Horn the Southern Cross is nearly overhead.

This constellation is composed of four stars in the form
of a cross, and is said to be the brightest in the southern
heavens. It may be said to assume to navigators in the
southern hemisphere the same relation as the Polar or north
star does in the northern.

We doubled the Horn in about 57° south latitude without experiencing anything but the usual varying and tempestuous

ROUNDING CAPE HORN.

weather, with hail storms, and encountering an iceberg here and there. The hail storms off the Horn are unlike those in lower latitudes, for the hail does not merely fall, but seems to be driven into one like so many nails. One night, when aloft reefing, my hands were so cut by the hail that they bled just as if they had been scored across their backs with a knife, and all aloft at the time were served so impartially, except two youngsters who were on their maiden voyage, and had gone aloft with mittens on. But the danger of losing hold on the ropes is so much greater with mittens on that I always preferred to work bare-handed.

In about seven days from the Horn we made the port of Valparaiso, which opens to the nor'ard, but is inclosed by high hills on all other sides. We ran in and anchored in five fathoms, a cable length from the shore. There is no dock, and cargo had to be unloaded on launches that are moored to the shore, from which the goods are toted by men. There is an inner harbor called Fisherman's Bay in which goods can be landed in any weather, for it is protected on all sides. On one side of this inner port there is a castle, and on the other Fort St. Antonio. When we were there unloading and loading cargo for four days we found very little to attract us ashore. No theatre, or other place of amusement; a little guitar and fandango business, but that soon became stale ; no news room, nor even newspapers at the hotels, and very little to draw one out for a walk where the sidewalks are in the middle or all over the streets, and there is no public square or promenade where people can see each other if they can't converse. My Spanish was understood by everybody I spoke to, but there was very little inducement to talk. We were glad to get away from Valparaiso. As we sailed out early in the morning the gray barren hills around the city, without one residence to break the monotony, seemed to say, "We intend to resist all efforts at cultivation as long as possible," and the almost daily earthquakes seemed devised by some enemy of the human race to perpetuate the sterility. The great range of the Andes, or Cordilleras, rise 13,000 feet like a wall on the east, or rather like a vast cloud, with sharp cones of volcanoes at frequent intervals, one of which, the Akonkagua, lifts its smoky head nearly 24,000 feet.   It is difficult, in the early morning, and for some hours after sunrise, to make out the mountains distinct from the clouds.

These were my impressions, but a shipmate says that a residence in Chili for some time would entirely change my opinion.   He says the southern part of the country is the best, and abounds in plants and flowers, various, rich and beautiful, with many kinds seldom seen elsewhere, and nearly all European fruits, besides many native species.   The shade and ornamental trees are of many and handsome varieties.   The forests have many very hard woods, which are useful for furniture, and even so firm as to take the place of iron in wagons and other things in constant use.   The country is almost free from snakes and venomous reptiles and insects, the skunk almost alone supplying their absence.   I did not hear that St. Patrick had ever visited that region, but, if one might conclude from the church-going habits of the people, the religion he professed prevails among all classes.   However much it may effect the presence of reptiles in fields, it does not entirely banish them from the heads of the people, whose delirium tremens was of the genuine type.   This shipmate was as good as a cyclopædia or a dictionary to all in the fo'castle.   He was a graduate of Columbia College, New York, and had studied law.   His father, Samuel Myers, was a merchant, and gave his son a good start in life, but Sam, Junior, preferred roaming over the deep, deep sea to litigating on shore, and so he did duty for us who had been less fortunate in book-learning.   He said he sailed from one port to another until he made the one he wished to study next, and then he got discharged or deserted, and stayed as long as he liked, or until his money was gone, when he shipped again.   A dozen years of such a roving life had stored his

mind with rich treasures from many countries, and he would
be a valuable man in many places.   When we landed at
Callao he received a letter from home with the news that a

THE SHELL-VENDER.

rich aunt had left him a snug fortune, $50,000 or more, and
he answered the letter, sending his reply by the British
steamer then in port, at an expense of $1.25 an ounce or less,

to New York. He started back by the Panama route and I have not heard from him since.

We next dropped anchor at Callao, which is the port of Lima, capital of Peru. It is built on a tongue of land, and the harbor is protected by the barren island of San Lorenzo on the west. The houses are nearly all of mud walls with flat roofs, but there are strong forts. The old town of Callao was destroyed by an earthquake about a century before my visit, and they point out its ruins under the water not far from the site of the modern town. Having leave to go on shore on a Sunday, I found the way to church, where I saw a good many handsome young women scattered all over the floor at their prayers, telling their beads or ogling the strangers, and I was one of that class, as they could easily see. A young man, who saw that I was interested more inspecting the veils of the ladies than in saying prayers or listening to the priest, came close to me and said I could kneel down near any one of the ladies I might take a fancy to, and she would not be offended if I spoke to her. Callao is a lively city, but there is little business enterprise as compared with any Yankee port of the same size. It must have grown much since I was there, but I have no doubt that Jack Tar would find his church-going just as profitable as mine was. Customs change very slowly in all Catholic countries, and more slowly where they speak Spanish. The kind of human animals that hang around and live on Jack's wages in the various ports of the world belong to one order, although the family, genus and species may differ, as the naturalist says, no matter what their language may be, it always means one thing and no other—skin the sailor as soon and as clean as you can, for if we don't some other one will, and the chances are we'll never see him again.

When a ship stays in port long enough, and leave can be had, it is the custom to take a run up to Lima, the capital of the country, which is only seven miles away. So three of us from the fo'castle went to see the sights. We feasted on the way on some native fruits, of which the only name I can recall is cheremoya, which is three or four inches thick, and delicious. It is the prime fruit of Peru, and the only country in which it grows to maturity.

The city of Lima is well worth a visit, but I must not attempt to describe it, for that is not in my log. I saw some of the lions, for instance, the mountain near called San Christoval, where you may see the famous bird, the condor, sailing high and still as if he was a leaf floating on the sea of air. But as our time was limited we could not make the ascent, although I was very desirous of seeing that noble bird in his native haunts. We did visit the cathedral and inspected the great silver altar, which was very showy, and reminded me of the church we looted in Vera Cruz. The long walk on shore had tired my shipmate, Sam Mack, and he thought it would by a good thing to splice the main brace with a stiff drink of spirits with a dash of quinine. On inquiry we found that drug sold at $12 an ounce, and we were told that we might hunt half the hotels and drug-stores of Lima before we found any. They were waiting for a supply from New York or London.

We climbed to the top of one of the pyramids built by the Incas of ancient Peru, before Pizarro's time, and saw the places where it is believed they offered human sacrifices to their feathered gods.

One of the learned ways of levying tributes on visitors at Lima is to sell, if possible, the skull of the famous adventurer Pizarro. Just how many different and distinct skulls that embodiment of avarice and inhumanity had it would be interesting to scientists to know, and difficult to ascertain, for they are scattered over the civilized world, adorning many private and public museums.

Another trait prevails at Lima which shows the native kindness of the hearts of the people who thrive on the traveler's wants, necessities and desire for luxuries. This is the invariable habit of the guides and hosts, of catering to the visitor's curiosity in seeing the sights, and when the traveler's time is limited and there is little left for visiting various desirable objects about town, a number of photographs are shown, and which generally, if not always, include the smiling faces of very charming young ladies, whose society would be most welcome under some circumstances. Even the photographs of local beauties is a pleasing variety and a desirable addition to the pleasures of a trip to Lima.

I have been told that a similar custom prevails in many cities and seaports of Italy, and I can believe it is true, for the Italians are warm friends of the sailor. However it may be in Italy, the trait is prevalent in every seaport on the Pacific coast at which we touched in pursuit of commerce and information.

My reader must surely have often heard it said that the Spanish was a very musical tongue, and I am a willing witness to that fact, and also that when spoken in Lima by my cicerone, in pronouncing the names of the beautiful young ladies whose images in actual " pictures of silver" he showed me, seemed more charming than ever. Many times since I have repeated such of those names as I could remember, as a sort of ˙charm against home sickness. One more musical than another was Senora Donata Lozano, the last pronounced Lothano, *th* as in than. I hope the name was fictitious, for I have had a picture engraved here that reminds me of her very truly. But then her grandchildren will not recognize it. I have never been able to account for the fascination of those Spanish names. Was it the climate? My recollection is that the climate was sublime, heavenly. It might have been the new and strange scenes and accessories. They were curious enough, but not likely to upset one whose

SENORA DONATO LOZANO.

eyes had done duty in many ports on every quarter of the world. Perhaps after all it was because those names were said to represent young and lovely women. Yes, I am persuaded that is the secret. Ah! how many a young sailor, less cautious than I was, has been wrecked on such shoals and quicksands.

Our return to Callao was by starlight, for the *Matilda* was to sail the next day, and I had no intention of staying ashore, where there was so little attraction either in climate, productions, or people. The appearance of the mountains in the starlight was so peculiar and cloudlike, and so immense, seeming to fill half of the eastern heavens, that I never until then felt the utter lack of the power of expression. I was struck dumb, as they say, because I had no language adequate to express the sublimity of the scene. They are vastly more impressive at such a time and in such light than in the day time.

In contrast with the serenity of nature ashore the human nature afloat was very vivid. Every person on board seems determined to exhibit his worst side and uses the roughest language to emphasize the exhibition. The captain damns the mate, the first mate damns the second mate, the second mate passes the unsavory compliments along and distributes them to the sailors; the sailors add a seasoning of their own, and pass them to the cook, and do not neglect each other. Anything in the way of kindness or common courtesy is too precious to waste at sea, or it may be such commodities spoil when exposed to sea air.

The best that Callao had to give us was a good supply of sweet potatoes. Thinking that the officers might, as is the custom, keep them all to themselves, the fo'castle made up a purse and bought a lot on their own account. When the potatoes came aboard the mate saw that some bags were marked and others had white rags tied to them, and was furious when he learned what the men had done. But the captain sustained the men, and we had many a good feast from Callao's potatoes.

Not long after leaving Callao, and when we were opposite the town of Coxamarca, we were treated to several water-spouts, and they gave rise to many different opinions among the sailors as to what caused them, and whether the water rose from the sea or fell from the clouds. Having been very near to one some years before in the Atlantic, I offered the opinion that the water fell, and was the accumulated rain of many clouds swept and rolled into one by the swift circular wind or cyclone, and poured down as a torrent.

One of our crew had been in Ecuador, and spent some weeks at this Coxamarca. His report was that it is a beau-tiful place for a residence. The people are skillful in the mechanic arts, though, like all Spaniards, they make more swords and knives, guns and pistols, than plows, harrows, hoes, &c., yet the list of articles for peaceful use is quite long.

The great interest in the place for me was the traditions kept alive there of the inhumanity of Pizarro, shown to the Inca Atahualpa, who was first unmercifully talked to by a heartless priest and then murdered by the brutal soldier.

We passed Lambayeque, the Lobos Islands, Payta, Cafe Blanco, and the Gulf of Guyaquil, where the great volcano Chimborazo was in full view, and the next day we crossed the equator. No other landing was made until we reached the coast of California. We touched from port to port along the coast during two months or more, trading off our merchandise and Yankee notions for native products, hides chiefly. The city of Mazatlan, in Mexico, at the entrance to the Gulf of California, kept us busy three days, and we could have disposed of the half of our cargo, only the cap-tain thought we should be able to make better terms for native produce in California, and so we sailed away for Santa Barbara. There was no port in Lower California,

which was said to be a mountainous, rocky, sandy, unpro-
ductive, uninviting region.   Only a few spots have any soil,
and for seven hundred miles there was no town worth landing at.   Our first port, after Mazatlan, was San Diego, or a
bay of the same name, and from there we sailed with a fair
wind inside the islands of St. Clement and St. Catalina into
the bay of San Pedro, the port of Los Angeles.   This bay
and harbor might well have been named the New Piræus, for
it is very much like the port of Athens, in Greece, as far as
nature has made it, and whether houses, castles, walls and
other works will ever be added is of course an open question.

Sailing thence, inside the Santa Barbara islands, we made
that port in fine weather.

At the time of Richard Henry Dana's visit, in 1838, when
he was "before the mast," and his vessel stopped here to
gather hides to be shipped back to Boston, Santa Barbara
was a small Spanish village almost entirely unknown to
Americans.   In the centre of the town stood a heavy-walled
presidio or fort, and about it were gathered a score or more
flat-roofed adobe cottages with white-painted walls.   But
with all its primitiveness Santa Barbara made a strong impression on Dana, and one of the most delightful portions
of his book is that in which he describes it.

The town exerted the same influence upon the young
sailor that it does now upon all who visit it.   Travelers who
are familiar with all the attractive towns in the world are
never chary in giving unlimited praise to Santa Barbara.
Dana says he never tired watching the waves roll in upon
the yellow sanded shore of the bay, or seeing the ever-chang-
ing hues that crept over the mountain sides.   And a visitor
of to-day says the same.   The town has grown since 1838,
and has become modernized and fashionable, but it has
never lost its charm.   It is not a beautiful village in itself,
strictly speaking.   It is the exception, rather than the rule,
for the houses to be pretty, and the main street of the place

that extends through the centre of the town from the wharf back toward the old Santa Barbara Mission is far from being an attractive thoroughfare. Not only is it narrow, and at this season of the year dusty, but the shops that line it are, for the most part, rudely built and exceedingly plain, with only the charm of wide porticos, beneath which one finds an agreeable shade. Running parallel with the main street are other ways; and these are even dustier still, and are faced with cottages which, with rare exceptions, are exceedingly unattractive. And as for the life of Santa Barbara, it has none. There is not a manufacturing establishment in town; the theatre, as a plain, almost ugly, hall is called, is rarely opened; the shop fronts with their dust and unmolested windows speak of the dulness of trade; the nearest railway is now, 1886, eighty miles away.

If one came to Santa Barbara hoping or expecting to make a living here he would be woefully disappointed. There seems to be no opening of any description. A few energetic men, obliged to settle here because of a lack of good health, have been tempted to erect an ice machine in order to supply a long-felt want. But even their enthusiasm has cooled before the apathy with which the idea has been received by the people, who, with rare exception, have professed their inclination to get along without ice. And when one finds he cannot make money and find employment by making ice he subsides, and accepts the fate which seems bent on relegating all, the rich and the poor, the sick and the well, to an idleness that is in keeping with the proverbial quiet of the town. A few here own ranches out in the country, and make money out of their properties. Of the others, there are those who keep small shops and those who buy of the dealers. Nice, with which Santa Barbara has been compared, is like it in this respect at least, that every one you meet appears to have nothing to do but to enjoy life. But never, since it was founded, was Nice as quiet as

Santa Barbara, and if one were to search the world over would there ever be found the exact counterpart of this lazy, listless village, tucked in here at the base of high blue mountains, with its feet bathed by the waters of the blue Pacific. Not original in itself, its surroundings are of great variety and almost indescribable beauty, and nature seems to have selected the valley which Santa Barbara occupies as the particular region upon which to bestow its most priceless gifts

La Purissima, a little cluster of adobe huts, which in time may have been displaced by the better buildings of a city, for the site was a good one, being at the mouth of a fine creek, was then a good trading place for us, where we did a brisk business for a day. We also touched at Monterey, Santa Cruz, and then to San Francisco, which was formerly called Yerba Buena, where we filled our water casks, replenished our stock of onions and other vegetables, and a quantity of beef.

We were eighty-four days from San Francisco to Hong Kong, and the time was filled up in the usual way on board merchantmen. I have neglected to notice a young man in our watch who hailed from Yarmouth, Maine. He had been well educated in the seminary of his uncle, Woods, who left there to become president of the Pennsylvania University, at Pittsburg. He was a very well mannered young chap, and was quite a favorite among us. His superior knowledge of books and ways on shore made him an oracle in such matters, and we often referred to him when there was a difference of opinion, or question of fact, and frequently for facts also. He told us many amusing stories of land life, among which was this, concerning a visiting uncle of his, who was asked to do an errand for his mother in Portland, which is ten miles or so away, but in those days was reached by water in a row or sail boat, or on land with a horse and wagon. So a shopping errand was a service not

easily appreciated by those who can go around the corner
for any and everything the heart can wish for.

This is the log in his words as near as memory serves:

"My mother got my uncle Charles into an awful lot of

UNCLE CHARLES FACING FATE.

trouble by giving him a commission to do a little shopping
for her on a hot August day in 1847. We kept a yacht of
about thirty tons anchored at the Long Point, near our
house, and uncle wished to take a sail in her up to the city

that day, hence the errand. There was a long list of names of things to be bought, among which were a pair of garters. Mother's had been lost a day or two, and she was every few minutes, as she went about the house, stooping over, her foot lifted on a chair, and pulling up a stocking, which of course would soon slip down into uncomfortable wrinkles again. I sailed the yacht down for him, and passed near Diamond Cove, which was a great resort for picnics and other pleasure parties, and when we tied up at the wharf I went on errands of my own, leaving him to his wits.

"Uncle knew Portland. That was bad for him that day. He belonged in Sebago, a few miles up the country, and was a widower with a comfortable farm and good bank account. It was the duty therefore of every young unmarried women to set a cap for him, and as for the old maids it was their business to keep close watch over him lest he throw himself away on some young, giddy, disgustingly pretty girl, when they all knew he needed a middle-aged woman to take charge of his fine home. He felt that all feminine eyes were on him, and he knew that his male friends were on the *qui vive*, or close watch, for a good chance for a joke on him. But as he was in for it, and as the errands was for his brother's wife, who had an uncommonly handsome unmarried sister, he did not dare to shrink from duty.

"He got all the other articles, pins, needles, nutmegs, and whatnot—a big basketful—and left the garters for the last. He told me his experience in finding them when we were sailing home, just about sundown.

"'Gosh, dern it,' said uncle, ''f I'd a known aforehand jest wat kind of garters to get, they wouldn't ha' worked me up so. I never suspected the' wuz fifty or a hundred kinds of them gal-fixins. Tarnation things cost a heap o' trouble, an' an allfired lot o' durned foolishness among a hull lot o' bald-headed old sinners, who'd a blame sight better bin thinkin' of ther speretooal condition.'

"Uncle was pious, and considered practical joking very sinful, and jokes of any kind the invention of the Evil One. So his Satanic Majesty must have smelt very hot and sulphurous that day, for every one he met, while he was carrying that basket, broke out on him in one way or another, but all with an allusion to his probable marriage. Some commended him, others jibed, and some cried it was a burnin' shame for him to be huntin' a woman when his wife had hardly grown cold in her grave. I was in a hardware store when uncle went by with his basket about full, looking quite like a country peddler of notions, when one of his neighbors spied him and run to the door. 'My sakes alive,' says he, 'if that ain't old man Wood, my next neighbor but one, a tuggin' a big basketful of yarn, thread, needles, little packages in soft paper, 'n the Lord knows what.'

"This was 'Squire Watson, who was as full of eyes as the fabled Argus of the ancient Greeks, and who made good use of them all, as his neighbors knew full well. And he went on talking to the storekeeper, Jim Hamlin, a regular gossip and chatterer. 'Wull, I do declare, if old Wood don't seem as if he was going to take to himself another helpmeet. The old rooster! Who'd suspect him at it so soon? Must be some city gal this time, sure. Them things wuz never cak'lated for country use, for he hain't no one 'round his house to use 'em. Lives kind of a bachelor life now. Children all married off, 'ceptin' Jane Maria, 'n she'll be jined to Deacon Puffer's scapegrace of a son about corn shuckin' time.'

"Just then Mr. Hamlin broke in with, 'Hain't he stayin' up at Yarmouth with his brother Henry?'

"'Yes, that's so; 'n I reckon he's arter Henry's wife's sister, who's awful pretty, or mebbe one of the young ladies in his brother William's seminary. Charley Wood has the tin and the fixin's, fine house and farm, and good horses and wagons,

an' jest about all a rational woman can ask for; but his wife—
let's see. How long's she been dead?'

"'Nigh on to three years, ain't it, Charley; you ought to
know,' he said, talking to me.

"Three years last May," I answered.

"'Wall, I swum,' said the 'Squire, 'how time duz fly. He
won't raise the snakes 'ef he duz seek consolation at this late
day. Bin a leetle dilatory I should say. A man at his time
o' life hain't any too many years in prospect that he kin
afford to throw 'em away in long courtships.'

"'Jimminetti, no,' said Mr. Hamlin. 'You wern't so
darned slow; hey, 'Squire?'

"'Wall, no. But you see in my case there wuz young
children to look arter, 'n I needed some one to take a pus'nal
interest in my affairs about the humstead.'

"'Sartainly, that's so,' said Deacon Puffer, who came in at
that time, and seeing the drift of the conversation joined in.
'It was my case, too, when I married Widow Sanford, fur I
had five children and she had three. Both of us wuz
anxious 'bout the little ones.'

"'But it's Charley Woods of Sebago we're talkin' of,' said
Hamlin.

"'Goodness gracious! Man alive,' said Deacon Puffer.
'You don't say; he ain't married yet. He's bin gone from
hum nigh on to three weeks, 'n everybody took it fur granted
that he'd bring hum a bran' new wife.'

"'So he may; he's stayin' at his brother Hank's, at Yarmouth.'

"'Oh, I see; only a step to his other brother's, who
keeps about a hundred young ladies in a seminary. Yes,
yes, that's it, sure enough. But what on airth kin he
want o' one o' them?'

"'Ain't sure that he want's a young wife,' said the
'Squire.

"'So I should say. He's as old and gray as a rat. But then, it is the rule for such old fellows to make fools of themselves. There's no law agin' such doin's; hey, 'Squire, is they?'

"'Nun, 'cept gin'ral opinion. But practice goes agin opinion for success, any day.'

"'Is it a success for an old man to marry a girl young enough to be his granddaughter?'

"'I should venture the remark, "No sirree." I should.'
"But Hamlin broke in, saying:

"''Tis astonishing what tarnation fools old widowers will make of themselves, anyhow.'

"'Don't know about that. There's Crane, the stone mason, married his fourth wife a few years ago. She was tremendous pretty, an' he wuz four times ez old ez she; but they've lived like two kittens in a nest. He trots around, an' she orders him 'bout like ez zif he wuz a boy. An' sure enough he did look an' act ten years younger, she fixed him up so neat to go to meetin'.'

"I was at the door, and in the act of taking leave of 'Squire Watson, when uncle Charley came in, and, after speaking to or shaking hands with several in the store, turned to me and said:

"'Charley, I wish you would kindly fetch this basket o' things to the boat. I hain't found them—some o' the things—yet, an' I'll go and meet you at the yacht, say in a quarter of an hour.'

"'Squire Watson opened fire first.

"'Wall, Woods, but we've caught you at it this time. Hey, old chap. Who is she?'

"'At what? There ain't any she in the case as I know on.'

"'What's them things in the basket for, ef 'taint for a woman?'

"'They're for a woman, that's true; but she's Charley's mother. Some shoppin' for her. Been stayin' there for a few days.'

"'Near the seminary, conveniently, I say?' said Deacon Puffer.

"'Only a few rods off. Right in sight. Been there afore. Go often.'

"'So would I in your case, Charley. Good place to console widowers with new, young and handsome wives. Some o' them gals is oncommon purty.'

"'Wall, that's so; but I hain't got no eye on any of them.'

"'But its fixed on some one, o' course. Now who is it? Out with it an' I'll treat,' said Mr. Hamlin.

"'Give us her name,' said 'Squire Watson.

"'O, let up on a feller, won't yer?' said uncle. 'I tell yer tha' ain't no woman in the case, at all at all. An' that's Gospel truth. The basket o' things are fur my brother's wife, an' I've a pair of garters to git yit, an' I must be off.'

"'Yes, yes, I see. It's all right, Charley,' said Hamlin, 'the basket of things are for Mrs. Hank Wood, an' the garters are fur her that will be Mrs. Charles Wood.'

"Well, uncle and I had to run away and look for the garters, which we found, and to make sure bought three pairs, of different patterns. I told mother of the talk in the store, and she thought it was taking too much liberty to joke on such a serious topic, and aunt Amy said she respected any one in distress too much to poke fun at their misfortune.'

"That caught uncle, and he gave her a significant look which she caught, and blushed scarlet.

"'Of course they were married?'

"Oh, yes, after a little time, and they live at the homestead overlooking Sebago Pond, with Kearsarge mountain on one side and Ascutney on the other, in full sight. A beautiful home, and I hope to see it soon after this voyage ends."

Joe Benson spoke out and said :

"Shipmates, have you ever heard of Port Byron on the Erie canal ? Well, up aloft there I was introduced to this life, in the house owned by my father, which stood near the flouring mills on the Four Mile creek. We used to run away from school and go in swimming in that creek, and sometimes go down a mile or so to the Seneca river, and once we wandered as far as to Montezuma, where night and a rain overtook us, and we got passage home on a raft of timber, arriving about midnight, to find half of the village out hunting for our bodies in the creek. Most of the boys who were my playmates then have finished their life's voyages, and only here and there one remains, so far as I know. One is known as Byron M. Pickett, a sculptor in New York City. His father was a barber, and played the violin at dances. He was very proficient in telling such tales as the ' Arkansas Traveler,' and accompanying himself on his fiddle. He could keep a company in a roar of laughter for an indefinite time with that, or any one of many similar tunes and songs which were always at his tongue s end.

"Mr. William Howland owned an island in the river near, of several miles in extent. I remember his great house in the middle of the island, on a slight rise of ground, surrounded by magnificent forest trees, with wild grape vines trailing from tree to tree, and broad lawns, beautiful meadows bordered by the river, fringed with elms, and gardens, orchards, and all that money, fine rich soil, and favoring climate can produce. As boys, we sampled his orchard and melons, but I always felt guilty, because he would never refuse when asked for a taste of fruit, or anything else that grew on the farm. He invited us to come and hold coon hunts as often as we liked, and we were always sure to get one or more coons at his place. It was he that indirectly set my fancy at work about the sea. He employed an old sailor on the place to look after the fences and other light work, and one summer, having some fine imported stock, he hired me to help the old tar. Many an hour he reeled off his log to me in a corner of the fence, or under the shadow of an oak or a basswood, until I was full of a desire to see the ocean.

" I had graduated from the village school, read every book of travels by sea or land, and devoured over and over again the "Lives of the Early Navigators," "The Buccaneers," and of course " The Pirates of Barrataria," beside " Captain Kidd." I believed I could find the very spot where his main treasure was buried, and longed for a chance to try. So I ran away from home, and have only seen it once in twenty long years. The place was so changed, the people dead, moved away to the west, or roving as I was, that there was no longer any charm for me, since my mother was no more below the skies. Father had gone west with my brother and sister, and I turned my face toward the sea again, and here I am. I may anchor ashore some day, if some fair maid will take me for what I am, but if not I shall find a berth in the Sailors' Snug Harbor, or it may be in Davy Jones' locker."

All hands were friends of Joe Benson, and rather looked up to him for his superior education and quiet, gentlemanly manners. He never swore or used any violent language, and he was never known to quarrel with any one. He afterwards became mate in an Indiaman, and the last I saw of him was on her deck as they were heaving up anchor for the return voyage to New York.

We took a Malay on board at San Francisco who was anxious to return to his native country, and could do so readily from Hong Kong. He could speak a little English, and Jim Dayton, one of our watch, knew a few words of Malayan, so the two got along very well together.

I never liked the Malays. Their faces are against them. If there is any truth in the theory of evolution of the white man from the apes, it must be true that our line skipped the Malay in its progress upward. I incline to the theory of Agassiz that mankind were created in separate and distinct groups, each in its appropriate part of the world, and each adapted to its surroundings The Malays are very numerous in the east. They are everywhere as workmen, sailors and mechanics. The reddish-brown of their faces and bodies is a deeper and redder tint than that of any American Indian. We might call them copper-colored. The hair is black as jet, coarse, and the beard thin, and generally pulled out by the roots in youth and all the time. They are fond of roving about from island to island, port to port. Cowardly, treacherous and vindictive, they will nurse a smothered resentment and diabolic design under the most profuse show of good will and affection until a chance presents itself, and then pounce on the victim like the tiger in its native jungle. They are not by any means civilized, nor can they be. They ate the first missionaries sent among them with the Christian religion, at a grand public banquet. They are natural-born pirates, a disposition which they inherit from a long line of piratical ancestors. Though separated from each other by thousands of miles, this people, wherever found on the islands of the Indian Ocean, or on the continent of Asia, have very similar language, features, manners, habits and form of body, which shows their identity at a glance. I was never really afraid of any live man, but that Malay gave me more uneasiness than any other mortal ever did before or since.

Pope says :

"The proper study of mankind is man."

And another poet, whose lines are quoted here, but whose name I never knew, says :

"The work of man is man to study well
Where'er he move, or where the races dwell,
On barren shores, or in the tropic belt,
Or where alternate heat and cold is felt."

We had a philosopher on board, but he was not in my watch. He held forth in the fo'castle, on deck, aloft, wherever he could find a listening ear, on the various theories as to the creation of man, and inclined to accept that in which it is taught that the great races were created at different times in this order: Negro, Malay, American Indian, and Caucasian, forming a progressive series, in which intellect and the moral faculties are developed in the order indicated.

WHAMPOANS.

We had a good field for such studies in the east, and we compared notes in the fo'castle very minutely, if not critically

At Hong Kong we discharged part of our cargo, and once more weighed, and stood out into the China Sea, bound up to Shanghai, some six hundred miles up the eastern coast, near the mouth of the Yang-tse-Kiang river. We had a wearisome and tedious passage up, and were obliged to beat nearly the whole way, with an occasional slant, which took us three weeks to accomplish. Arriving at Shanghai, we discharged the remainder of our cargo, and, with only ballast enough to stiffen her, bade adieu to that port. Steering down the coast we reached Hong Kong in three days, coming to an anchor to wait for a chop or permit in order to go up to Whampoa. Obtaining the permit after a week's delay, we proceeded up in charge of a Chinese pilot, and arrived next day.

While ashore at Hong Kong, after getting clear of the *Navigator*, and before shipping in the *Gazelle*, I went almost every morning to see Chinamen flogged. I was horrified, but also was fascinated, by the brutal work. The victims were tied by the feet to the lower arms of a St. Andrew's cross, and their arms and hands fastened to the upper arms, when two lascars, one of them left-handed, applied the lash or rattan to the back from the shoulders to the waist. A wink from the officer who directed the service (civil?) would give the lascars the sweet privilege of cutting off a strip of skin, which can be easily done with the rattan. The kind-hearted operators close the scene by sprinkling strong brine over the wounds to increase the effect.

I wonder if the whipping-post in Delaware has any of the horrors of the Chinese cross.

A ludicrous sight was one Chinaman driving another about the streets, as children do at home with us, and lashing him severely as punishment for some crime or other.

> " Treat every man as he deserves,
> Who shall 'scape whipping ?—None ! "

I was then on my old ground again, and considering myself an authority on matters appertaining to China and Chinese, like some of the late English writers on America and the Americans, who know about as much of the latter as I did of the former, undertook to be a chaperone to my shipmates. The success of my service as chaperone may as well be omitted.

Then we got the ship ready for a cargo of teas and silks, in the same manner as narrated in former pages, viz.: by smoking the rats out of her, or rather suffocating them with the fumes of charcoal. As is usual, we were employed setting up standing rigging, rattling down and tarring, mending sails, and painting ship inside and out. All this occupied two weeks, when our homeward cargo began to

CHINAMAN FLOGGED.

arrive alongside in "chops" (Chinese lighters), accompanied by our old tea-shipping friend, the Chinese weigher and his paraphernalia. In another three weeks we were filled up, hatches battened, sails bent, water racked off, purified and filtered, with everything ready for sea once more.

With the pilot on board, and the ship unmoored, we proceeded down the river towards Macao, and, with a favorable monsoon, discharged the pilot, and steered for the Straits of Sunda, between the islands of Sumatra and Java.

We had a fine passage, fair wind and favorable weather, and in ten days came to an anchor in the straits off Anjer Point, and, as in former voyages, traded old knives, razorblades, pins, needles, and other trifling articles for monkeys, Java sparrows, and other curios; also for "joggery," a native sugar. I looked to see if I could trace any of the relations of the monkeys I had taken away with me in the *Niantic* and *J. G. Coster*, but their faces were all so much alike that I could not distinguish any individuality, and therefore gave up the research, but perhaps Darwin, if he had been there, would have been more successful. To my eye, a monkey is a monkey—or, if he don't die on my hands, a certain number of dollars. I have no respect for the theory of man's descent from monkeys, or from anthropoid apes, and very little, if any, for those who advocate such absurdities, although I am inclined to agree with Col. Bob Ingersoll, who said he would sooner believe he had descended from an ape than from some men he knew of.

Remaining at Anger two days, during which we had replenished with yams, sweet potatoes, and native fruits for the ship's company, we weighed and made sail. With a steady breeze through the Straits of Sunda, next morning at break of day the distant outline of the Javanese coast was all but lost to view, and we were now fairly in the Indian Ocean homeward bound for New York, favored with the general sou'east winds that prevail in these latitudes. We carried this breeze up to the longitude of Madagascar without any interruption of note for eighteen days, when the winds became more variable, and began to veer to the east'ard, then to the nor'ard, and finally to the west'ard, which obliged up to lie close hauled on a wind. As the breeze now began to blow big guns, we began to shorten sail, and before next morning we were hove to under storm canvas, namely—a tarpaulin in the weather-mizzen rigging, and on the starboard tack. We remained on this tack

and under this sail for nine days, when at last, the wind
suddenly veering to the sou'west, we set the close-reefed
main-topsail and fore-topmast staysail, and wore ship very
handsomely, as there was a tremendous sea running. We
had hardly got her on the other tack, when the wind took
another start, and veered to the sou'east. We then set the
fore-topsail close reefed, and reefed fore-sail. That evening,
in the last dog-watch, we put the close-reefed mizzen-topsail

CHINESE JUG.

on her, and shook out the reef in the foresail, and jogged
along all night in comfort under that canvas. Then it became apparent that the sou'east trades had us in hand.
Next morning at seven bells, after the watch below had
their breakfast, all hands were turned to making sail. Reefs
were shaken out fore and aft, and the muslin was piled on
to her, whole topsails and courses, to'gallant sails, royals
and flying jib, then stun'sails. Then came the order,
"Haul up the weather clew of the mainsail, and rig out the

FAIR STORY TELLER.

starboard stun'sail-booms, and you boys lay aloft, rig out the fore and main royal and to'gallant stun'sail-booms, and reeve the gear," shouted by Mr. Thomas, our chief mate. "Royal yards, there! stand by to receive and cross the skysail yards; lay aloft on the mizzen there, you monkey, and cross the mizzen skysail yards," said the second mate to the smallest boy on board. After the stun'sails had been set, the skysails were then sheeted home and set. On the passage home, we were employed (all that could handle a palm and needle) in repairing and middlestitching every sail in the sailroom, and even stun'sails, including the sails on the yards which were inbent, one at a time, so they could be middlestitched.

We crossed the equator in 36° west longitude in thirty days from the Cape, sighted the Highland lights in twenty-five days more, were towed up the bay and alongside the wharf, foot of Dover street, October 14, after a passage from Whampoa of one hundred and five days. This was a particularly uneventful voyage for me. Everything went and worked smoothly. There were no quarrels, disputes, nor any thing in particular to disturb the general routine of ship life, and I was glad of it, for I had seen quite enough of tragedies at sea.

I now fully realized the benefit of having a home to come to after a long sea voyage, and determined to take advantage of it by having a good rest for a few weeks and enjoying myself in my own way. During my stay at home I came to the conclusion that by making long voyages and embarking in small ventures out and home on my own account, I could make more money than in making short ones, I therefore determined to continue in the line of action I had elected as long as I followed the sea for a livelihood.

In pursuance of this resolve I next shipped for a voyage to China and back to New York in the clipper ship *Sea Witch*, Captain Benjamin. It was bitter cold, being the

ARABIAN DANCING GIRL.

middle of December, but in twenty-four hours, with a favorable and stiff breeze, we reached the southeasterly edge of the Gulf Stream, where the temperature was almost tropical. After we got clear of the Gulf Stream we clapped all the kites on her, and we had a rapid and pleasant run of twenty days to the eastern board of the broad Atlantic, and shortly fell in with the delectable Horse latitudes, experiencing the usual succession of calms, rains, thunder and lightning, and, in the intervals, broiling heat, with catspaws of wind from every point of the compass, necessitating a continual bracing of the yards night and day. We were thus tortured for twelve days, after which we struck the regular northeast trade-wind, and, bracing up on the port or larboard tack, with the wind a point free, stretched away at a merry rate to the regions of the South Atlantic, where the winds are variable but generally from the west'ard. We thus sailed through these northeast trades until in twenty-four days we reached the 50° parallel of south latitude, and met with the prevailing westerly winds, when, squaring our yards in due season, doubled the Cape of Good Hope and entered the Indian Ocean. The northeast monsoon was then blowing down the China Sea, and it was imperative that we should take the eastern passage through the innumerable islands of the eastern archipelago, and accordingly laid our course for the southeastern point of the island of Java. Then sighting Sandalwood, an island lying south of Java, began threading our way through the maze of islands and narrow passages of those regions, passing outside or to the east'ard of the Philippines, entered the Chinese Sea, and bore away for Hong Kong with a leading wind. After a most fortunate passage of ninety-eight days, came to an anchor in Hong Kong roads without carrying away a rope-yarn or meeting any Malay pirates. I suppose that steam has thinned out those pirates, for the European nations who have possessions in the East have war steamers plying for the protection of their com-

STREET SCENE IN WHAMPOA.

merce in those seas.   A steamer is a terror to a piratical
sailor.

In a few days we received a chop, or Chinese government permit, to go up the river to Whampoa with a native
pilot.   We hove up, made sail, and arrived at Whampoa,
where we moored ship, and learned that we would have to
wait until the last of June, or the beginning of July, in order
to load with the new crop of teas, which would not be
ready before that time.   It was then only April, and the lay
of three months gave us plenty of time to overhaul rigging,
rattle down, tar, paint inside and out, repair sails, and
renovate any and everything inboard and outboard, from
truck to keelson.

At last, in the latter part of June, the first chop arrived
alongside, and the lading was begun.   But it progressed
very slowly, on account of the chops arriving alongside
only at intervals, and it was the middle of July before we
were full.   At last, being "chock a block," ship was unmoored and sail made on her ready for sea, and, with a pilot
on board, worked down the river to Macao.   But, as the
sou'west monsoon was then blowing up the China Sea, we
could not sail directly for the Straits of Sunda, but were of
necessity compelled to make a circuit by nearly the same
route as if bound to China from New York when the northeast monsoon is blowing down the China Sea.   After
meandering through the innumerable straits and passages
of that labyrinth of islands, we emerged into the Indian
Ocean, near the Island of Timor Laut, after a passage which
occupied us eighteen days.   Then we were fairly in the
Indian Ocean and homeward bound, with the prevailing
sou'east winds which almost invariably blow from the same
point in those latitudes.

The fo'castle is a veritable exchange of seaman's yarns,
and frequently the scene of wordy contests for the champion-
ship in telling the biggest whopper.   It is not to be supposed

CAPT. JOHN STIVERS AND MATE

for a moment that an old salt will intentionally tell a lie, or even stretch the truth. He knows better, because he is aware that experienced ears are around, and older or more experienced hands are ready to catch him at it if he should try it. So when old Captain John Stivers yarned about the foundering of a ship that he sailed in we listened intently, feeling that something good was in store for us. And there was, sure enough. Well, Captain John paid out in this style:

"Once on a homeward passage from Liverpool to New York the ship sprung a leak in a gale, and the cargo being railroad iron all hands were put to the pumps, passengers volunteering through fear and anxiety. In spite of all, the water gained every hour, and the captain decided to take to the boats; so they were floated, provisioned, watered, and crew and passengers crowded in, filling them all to the utmost, the storm still raging, and seas mountains high. When all was ready, the word was given to shove off, the vessel suddenly sank, swamping every boat and drowning every soul of the passengers and crew."

We listened, breathless, to the thrilling tale—until some one inquired, "Who reported the disaster?" when Captain John saw that he had missed a link in his chain cable, and so was afloat. We never let up on him. He now lives ashore, as I do, only he keeps a grocery at Stonington, and I—well, my son-in-law now has my store.

As we neared the equator, we stripped one mast at a time, overhauling the eyes of the rigging, the lifts, foot-ropes, and brace pendants of the yards, likewise the rigging appertaining to the bowsprit; then rattling, tarring down, painting all spars alow and aloft, and the ship inside and out. Many of us had been in China before, and it may be supposed that we compared notes in the fo'castle very carefully, and as the Chinese importation, immigration, or invasion question is uppermost now and then, it may be worth the space if I give my opinion on that peculiar variety of *genus homo.* If their historians tell us correctly, they have worn similar dresses, and kept to the same customs and habits, laws and religion for thousands of years. Centuries would be tiresome enough to us. They very seldom change anything, not even an undergarment. They may take off a part of their costume for washing, but it appears in its place again very soon. They also are so alike each other that it is impossible for a stranger visiting the country for the first time to pick out one from another, or to identify one if he has been on board a while and returns to land, and attempts to come aboard again in an hour or so.

They have only one royal road to rank and fortune, which is by learning. The whole nation is a competitive class, striving for promotion to some public office or employment. In short, they are a civil service nation gone to seed. The system is said to be complete, and without objection, since only the most capable men ever get office at all. The salaries of public officers are very low, not enough to pay their expenses in some cases, for instance that of revenue collectors, who are said to extort money as a necessity for their own needs. On my third visit to China I had learned to pick out the nine different kinds of mandarin, one from another, by their dress and attendants. We found the Chinese industrious, peaceable, mild in disposition, docile, and having a profound respect for the aged. Such good qualities of course have their opposites, and they are insincere, liars on principle, and every man suspects every other. Gambling is nearly universal. A common sign in the windows of shops is, " There is no cheating here," while " Look out for your purses," meaning beware of pickpockets, is seen in all places.

The fact is, their government is too fatherly, meddling with every act from the cradle to the grave. Custom is very onerous, even to the little matter of regulating the size of visiting card you may or must give on making or return-

ORIENTAL BEAUTIES.

ing a call, so they vary from an inch or two to a yard square. But your extremely polite visitor may rob you then, or any time a chance may occur.

The Chinese eat everything without exception that is palatable, and some things that we hold in disgust: as rats, mice, etc., though I confess a rat stew is good if you do not know beforehand what it is. Their favorite spirit is made from rice, and they do not make wine from grapes. Tea is the universal drink, and they are very fastidious in their taste. Drunkenness is common enough, and opium is said to be used by great numbers, but as it is a secret vice I did not see any of it.

There are many countries which one may visit to advantage without the least desire to remain as a resident, and China is one. You can buy silk goods, such as a handsome shawl or handkerchief at a low price, and, if inclined, a thousand little objects for ornaments carved in ivory, or made of metal, which will pay you from fifty to five hundred per cent. on their cost if sold in New York or London. But it is no place for a white man to tie up to. No good anchorage. Too many people. Swarms of people, like flies at home. Human life is very cheap, and unless you are in some exalted station, public or private, you are a mere speck of dust.

Turning these and other topics over filled up the long days of the voyage, and time passed rapidly as the ship glided through the waves on the homeward stretch.

We had by this time nearly reached the latitude of the Bermudas, when the northeast trades deserted us in latitude 23° north and longitude 33° west. Thence we had a succession of variable winds all round the compass until we struck sounding to the west'ard of the Gulf stream. We made the Highland's light the same night, and received a pilot, and next morning, with a beautiful day, sailed up to New York (without a tug and with the wind at west sou'-

west), with three standing skysails, and a main moonsail, and came to, dropping our mud-hook under foot close in to the wharf, after a not bad passage of ninety-eight days from Macao—a passage not to be ashamed of even for a clipper, considering the lengthened route, in consequence of the sou'west monsoon necessitating four thousand miles extra to be traversed.

The winter was now approaching, and I, having made in investments on my own account more than double my wages, considered myself entitled to a spell ashore, after which I would undertake another voyage to the Antipodes or East Indies, and, if successful in my investments, seek on my return more congenial employment ashore.

BURLING SLIP, NEW YORK.

Chapter XIV

" Farewell ! a word that must be, and hath been
A sound which makes us linger ; yet farewell !
Ye who have traced the ' Wanderer' to the scene
Which is his last, if in your memories dwell
A thought which once was his; if on ye swell
A single recollection, not in vain
He wore his sandal shoon and scallop shell ;
Farewell ! with *him* alone may rest the pain,
If such there were—with *you*, the moral of his strain."

In pursuance of my determination to make another long voyage, I cast about for a ship for either India or China and met Captain Cressy in New York one day, whom I had known in Whampoa thirty years previously as mate of the ship *Horatio* of Boston, on board of which ship we, the crew of the *Niantic*, on my first voyage to China, passed the night while our ship was being smoked to clear out the rats.

He recognized me at once by circumstances happening on that memorable voyage of the *Niantic*, and telling me how he was about to sail in a week or ten days, and was bound on a long voyage round the Horn to the west coast of South America, Gulf of California, and California, and then to the other side of the Pacific via Honolulu.

I accordingly shipped with Captain Cressy in the *Flying Cloud*. The *Flying Cloud* was laden with a miscellaneous assortment of freight of all kinds for the California market, more particularly household goods, as the gold State was fast filling up with people. With a clear, frosty nor'wester, and a pilot on board, we cast off from the wharf foot of Wall street, New York, and, without a tug, we made sail on her. Her head fell off before the influence of the head sails, then her after yards were soon covered with her broad and snow-white canvas, with which our noble clipper soon reached the outer bar, where the pilot left, and we proceeded

under all sail. The ground tackle gear was first secured
and cables unbent, spare spars and boats lashed. After we
reached the western edge of the Gulf it came on to blow a
regular screecher, so that we had all we could do to keep
the sail on that we had set. In twelve days we ran into the
soul-vexing Doldrums. After the usual bracing and counter-
bracing night and day, accompanied by torrents of rain and
intense heat and thunder and lightning for nine days, the
northeast tradewind came to our unspeakable relief, when
on the larboard tack we braced up with the wind free,
bounded like a courser toward Cape Horn, which exhilarating vicinity we reached in nineteen days.

On this voyage the fo'castle was made more than usually
interesting by the presence among us of two or three old
salts who had seen unfrequented parts of the world, and
whose tongues were loosened now and then for our pleasure
and profit. As we were working our way slowly through
the Straits of Magellan against a sou'west wind, I remembered the severe hail and sleet storm we had on board the
Matilda on a former voyage round the Horn, and spoke of
it to Sam Mack, who had made three passages through the
Straits. He said the absence of hail and snow was remarkable, for the weather in that region was almost constantly
boisterous. But the weather is not the worst thing to face
in these latitudes, he went on to say for the Patagonian Indians are the most barbarous fiends in human shape on the
face of the earth. I was in the English bark *Kent* which
went to pieces among the rocks at the west end of the
Strait, and those of the crew who were not drowned escaped
with the captain, second mate, and steward, only to suffer a
thousand tortures of fatigue, hunger, fever, wounds, and
being dragged about the country by the cruel savages.
When we landed among the rocks there was no sign of inhabitants, and Captain Frazer said he hoped we should
escape their unwelcome attentions, but we were not destined

for such good luck. As soon as we had made a fire the devils saw it and hurried to see what it meant. Nearly every one was mounted on a horse, and carried a long spear. Some had beside the spear a lasso, to both ends of which there was tied a stone of about a pound weight. They were partly covered with skins, and had long black hair, falling to their waists. Their lungs were in good order, for they screeched and yelled, apparently delighted to find game, for such an idea as doing a kindness to a shipwrecked sailor never entered their brutal heads. The mate had saved his pistol and had a few rounds of ammunition, and proposed to the captain to kill as many of the devils as he could, and it might be scare away the rest. The captain argued that to kill a few would only draw a swarm about us, and enrage the whole, like a nest of hornets. Just then, as the mate and captain were discussing, a savage aimed a spear at Captain Frazer, who saw the movement in time to spring one side, and at the next instant the mate blazed away and there was one dead native. The others were frightened and ran away a short distance, but soon crept back to where their dead companion lay, and carried him away. They disappeared among the rocks, and we built up our fires anew, and began to dry our clothes, which were soaked in half frozen water. The steward had saved some biscuit and cooked meat in a bag. There were eleven of us, all told, but one poor fellow had broken his left arm by a fall after we got ashore, so there were only ten able-bodied. The ship or bark was only a short distance from shore, and we hoped when the storm abated we might be able to get something useful from her, or at least pick up fragments that might float ashore. While we were talking over these matters and trying to make the best of our situation, one of our men who had gone aside for a moment astronomizing, as he said, by way of forecasting the weather, returned in haste, and whispered to the mate that the natives were closing in on us in great numbers. So the mate took his pistol and crawled on all fours a little way from the fire toward the approaching Indians, and very soon settled accounts with another one. This time they did not carry off the dead or wounded, but ran away to stay. They evidently did not like the smell of powder. We kept watch and watch the rest of that night, and were not disturbed again by the natives. About daylight I crept out from our circle and looked about for something in the way of game for breakfast. I knew that the guanaco was to be found all along the Pacific coast, and hoped to see at least one, if not a herd, and was not disappointed. Less than half a mile from our fire there was a runway where those animals went down to drink, for they will drink water that is at least half sea-water. Creeping cautiously upward towards the highland I found a sandy plain with clumps of bushes and short tufts of grass scattered about, and not far away a herd of six or eight guanacos feeding, and headed toward the water. I ran back and soon had the mate and his pistol safely moored behind a rock near the edge of the plain, while I crept toward the herd, bent on playing a trick that I had heard of as sure to trap the silly beast. When a hundred feet or more away from the mate's hiding place, I lay on my back in a clump of grass and shook my trotters in the air, when the guanacos came trooping up curious to see what it was in the grass. The mate picked off the leader, and as the habit of those animals is when their leader is killed, they wandered round and round until five of them had been secured for food, and their hides to serve for beds. Hearing the firing the whole crew and the captain came out and helped carry in the game.

Well, to cut a long story short, we stayed there until the storm blew itself out, the sea calmed a little, and managed to pick up some of our provisions, cargo, spars, and whatnot from the wreck, with which we made ourselves quite comfortable. Among other things, we got a sea-chest with two more pistols, revolvers, and a lot of ammunition; so we felt now more safe than ever so far as the natives were concerned. The captain's anxiety was for a lookout for passing vessels, and means of hoisting a signal, both of which we managed after a fashion. Just as we had got comfortably settled down, built a little shelter of stones, fragments from the wreck, and parts of sails, we were attacked again by a troop of natives on horses. They came early one morning while we were scattered, some getting fresh water, others collecting grass and weeds for fuel, and so we were divided. But the mate's pistol did good service, and brought down two of the rascals and wounded others before we were overpowered. But what could we do against fifty or more savages, who were brave enough to face a pistol? I was seized and bound to a horse, and

LUXURY ASHORE.

so was the mate, as I supposed from his cries of agony, for I could not see him, and we hurried off among the rocks along the shore. I expected they would take us across the plain to some camp of theirs, but I was mistaken. Their camp was near the water, and about five miles from ours. The ride seemed to be five hundred, for I was hung across a bony horse like a bag, and tied by raw hide cords under his belly by the wrists and ankles. In that position every jolt the horse made seemed to threaten to cut me in two at the waist.

I can't tell you all we saw and suffered in the ten days we were at that native camp, but some things will surprise you; they have two of the vices of civilized life—drunkenness and gambling. The Indians had seen the wreck, and, among other things, had got one cask of rum. That served to keep every one, women and all, in a glorious condition, and we hoped to be able to escape by means of this habit, but were not successful at first. After five days two more of our company were brought in, the steward and a sailor. They brought us news of the rest. Poor Jim Banks had died from fever caused by his broken arm and exposure, but the others were doing well.

They have native liquor, which is the fermented juice of some seeds called garoba, or of a fruit called pikanino. Both these are used when they cannot get better alcoholic liquors.

The women do all the work at the camp. Bring fuel, water, cook, dress skins for clothing, weave a coarse cloth of grasses, or hemp, and are never at rest except when asleep.

The steward feigned sick, and so cheated the women who had charge of him that they unbound him, and gave him copious drinks of tea made of the leaves of a bush that grows among the rocks near the edge of the sandy plain. After three days of possum play the steward crept off in the night, and went back to our camp, where he proposed a rescue which was successfully carried out, and we were once more all together, and after that kept better guard. We were rescued by the good ship *Almira*, Captain Beech, bound from Liverpool to Valparaiso, whose mate had seen our signal and the smoke of our camp fire. We made port at Valparaiso in seven days, and there got passage back to England. Mack thought he should be able to point out the location of his residence in Patagonia, but the *Flying Cloud* kept a good distance off shore to avoid the rocks, which were as thickly clustered as paving-stones in Liverpool, and, too, the weather was hazy, when it did not snow or blow. We breathed a little freer when the Straits were left behind us, and the ship headed away for Valparaiso, where we arrived in eight days from the Horn, and lying to at anchor for three days did a lively business trading off household goods for provisions and cash, or hides. The various landings made from there to San Francisco were but a repetition in many particulars of my former voyage in the *Matilda*, only that the trade of the *Flying Cloud* was much more prosperous in every way, so that by the time we made the California coast more than half of the cargo was disposed of.

We took on several passengers at each port, bound for the gold diggings of California, and the chief topic of conversation all day and all night was the prospect of amassing wealth at the mines. No other topic could hold any one more than a moment or two, when the absorbing gold fever would assert its power and come uppermost again. At the Isthmus of Panama we received a number of passengers and some mail and newspapers from New York. Those who had letters would disappear for a short time, but would in nearly every case reappear with the letter open, and, finding friends, or acquaintances, read parts of the letter aloud to eager listeners.

It was a good study to scan the features of the various persons who were on their way to the golden land. All wore the eager look of expectation, but behind that were all sorts of faces—old, young, hard visages and smooth young faces. Some there were who evidently were bound on a trip of pure adventure, merely for the enjoyment of the excitement incident to a wild life among the placers and in the gulches. Others were more serious and earnest,

PANAMA

and seemed to feel that the risk was great, but could be overcome by resolution and courage. Still another class, who seemed driven onward to face the well known hardships and dangers for the sake of the hoped for treasure, which was needed at home to relieve some heavy debt, or as provision for declining years. Well, all hands, cook and pilot, at last blessed their eyes with a glimpse of the land of gold when we dropped anchor inside the Golden Gate.

We arrived at San Francisco in 1849, in October, just a few days before the State constitution was adopted, and when, it is said, there were a hundred thousand people in and about San Francisco, made up of persons from every nation and language on the globe. The men who went to California in '49 have been since called " The Argonauts," and they certainly did go on a long and perilous journey in search of a golden fleece or treasure, only in this case the expedition sailed west, while the ancient Greeks, under Captain Jason, sailed east. Some got treasure, and others were fleeced, so there can be no objection to giving them the name. Their story has been told many times, and well, and I could add very little to the books already printed, but still it may be interesting to know how much it cost us sailors to resist the temptation to desert and rush to the mines. We were told that nearly three thousand sailors had deserted in the year just past (1849), and that a rich harvest was sure for those who had nerve and endurance. I had both, but reflected that my desires had always been moderate, and there was no reason why I should change my plans and run into dangers and exposure that were unknown, but were certainly very great, and so I held on to the ship, and so did nearly all of the other sailors. The discussions were lively, and occupied us every moment while in the fo'castle, or at work, or it may be said all the time, for our very dreams run to mining, and were colored by the tales of adventures and successes that we heard.

GOLDEN GATE, SAN FRANCISCO—1849.

Our captain and officers were very uneasy, and seemed in a feverish haste about everything going on, I suppose expecting something like a wholesale desertion of the crew, and when Sam Mack left us for the mines they called us aft for consultation, and they talked very rationally considering the danger they thought they were in, for, as I have written before, the question had been settled before by the men, but the officers did not know that. They were greatly puzzled at our quiet manners and silence, for very few words were spoken by any of us, except by an old salt, Dave King, of Nantucket, who said, "Captain, we sailors have heard much of this new city, and the goings on there, and have seen nothing, and, for one, I would like leave of absence for half a day to take a turn on shore, and I've do doubt many of my shipmates would join me in a cruise."

The captain and mates stepped aside and conferred together a few minutes, when they returned to us and said: "I will give you leave to go on shore watch and watch until all have had leave." When that was spoken every man of the crew sent up a hearty cheer for our generous captain and his able mates.

When my turn came I made straight for the city, and looked about for a square meal. Provisions were at a higher price than in New York, but wages were many times higher, and so my dinner was costly. The restaurant, or hotel, was under a tent of cotton cloth, with boards only on one side. There were hundreds of such houses scattered about, with very little attempt at regularity. As for goods, they were piled in heaps on the ground in the open air, only the most valuable, or expensive, or perishable being in tents. It was said that very little was lost by theft. Thieving was too risky, for Judge Lynch had also come to California to stay awhile, and his stay meant business, as they say out there. The judge had many deputies, one of whom was sometimes

VIEW IN SAN FRANCISCO BAY, CAL.—MT. DIABOLO IN THE DISTANCE.

active when there was cheating at cards, but not to any great advantage to the community, for many a man was scooped out who had worked hard in the mines. Gambling and whisky were the great confederates for mischief to thoughtless men then, as they are now, just the same.

I went to the post office in San Francisco, thinking there might be a letter for me, as every one else did, and, after waiting in the line for nearly two hours, found I was not honored. Many a man turned away from the office without letters with a very sad face, and some walked up and down as if they had lost their wits. Others would go out on the sand hills and watch for incoming vessels, hoping to have a letter with each arrival.

In spite of all our good intentions, the desire for gold was too great, and we suffered the same depletion of our ranks, many having left the ship, leaving only two men and myself, and for this reason the *Flying Cloud* had to remain riding at anchor in the bay for upwards of two months before she could muster a crew. When at last we did get one, or rather a make-shift for one, old father Neptune would have been struck with astonishment and laughed to have seen such a motley gathering. Our new crew consisted of returning miners, who had been moderately successful in digging gold, and as we were bound to China they had conceived the idea that by making a detour by the way of the Celestial Empire, they might invest their treasure advantageously in the fabrics of the East, and thus augment their wealth.

They were a rough-looking crowd, swarthy as Arabs; rendered so through constant exposure to the elements, and most independent in their bearing and manner, so much so that the utmost caution and forbearance on the part of the old crew, and more especially the officers, had to be exercised in order to make matters work smoothly, and at the same time maintain that discipline and obedience to orders so necessary to the safety of a ship at sea.

WHERE CAPT. COOK DIED.

We were laden with a selected cargo suitable for the Chinese market, as well as some for the Sandwich Islands.

We had, on finishing our lading, hauled off from the wharf, and dropped anchor in the bay a cable's length from shore, for the double purpose of bending sails, etc., and doing such work as was required preparatory to weighing anchor and receiving our new crew, and thus removing them from shore influences and the effects of whisky drinking. In a few days they became more docile and tractable.

HINDOO COW AND CALF.

With the crew aboard who had come alongside and leaped on deck, presenting a grotesque appearance, some with a brace of revolvers thrust in their belt, some with a revolver and a huge bowie knife or two, others with a stiletto in the back of their shirt in a sheath inside, and some with trousers tucked in their boots disclosing bowie knives and revolvers in their boot legs, and all with a determined, "devil-may-care" look in the eye.

Our two days of sight-seeing (half a day for me) came to

JIM BARNEY REGALING THE FO'C'ASTLE.

an end, and with it the order to heave up anchor, and away we went across the wide Pacific. We were favored with both wind and weather, for it was neither hot nor cold, but just good for sailing, and for days together, and once for a week, we hardly made or shortened sail, or stirred tack sheet, or braces and halliards. Then we put the ship to rights, cleaned up everything, and had plenty of time for yarns, and there was the usual variety. One man in my watch had sailed to China three voyages for tea, and we had early in this voyage in the *Flying Cloud* made acquaintance and exchanged our experiences. He sailed out of Providence, Rhode Island, when tea was imported there almost to the exclusion of other ports in this country. India wharf is well known there now, but is no longer frequented by the tea trade.

He said that he and his brother had saved up a little money, and decided to go into the country and buy a farm. So they went up into Cayuga county, in York State, and bought a hundred acres of cleared land, and nearly as much of wood lot; also tools of all sorts, such as was recommended to them by the dealers, and some horses and other live-stock, of course including chickens, pigs, and all that. They went to work. His brother Ben married a daughter of a neighbor, and joined the church (hard-shell Baptist), but he, Jim, remained single. They made money, and also lots of fun for their neighbors, for their ways about the farm, and particularly in their management of horses, were shaped more or less, certainly more, by their experience on shipboard, and their language never lost its nautical style. Jim said he often went to church meetings just to hear his brother tell his experience in religion, and to watch the effect of his language on the others of the congregation. After a few years he longed for the excitement of the seafaring life, and concluded to try a voyage or two, and this, on the *Flying Cloud*, was his second, at the end

of which he was going up to the farm again. His description
of the life of a farmer was interesting to nearly all of us, for
nearly all in the fo'castle at that time had lived in cities and
knew very little about the country, except that it was a place
for growing cattle, hogs, chickens, corn and such things, and,
of course, grass and cordwood. Jim opened on us a flood
of light in such matters, and kept us willing listeners for
hours at a time. He said they had a school library well
stocked with books, and good ones, travels, biographies of
great men, adventures by sea and land, and hosts of others,
which were kept in a grist mill by a Mr. Kramer, a nice sort
of a man who knew how to take toll, and also how to make
a quiet little speech at church meetings. He was a blue
Presbyterian. That little town of Brutus was divided
among the Lord's shepherds as they choose the sailors for
the watches on board ship. First came the Baptists, who
took first choice, and proposed to charter the Ship of Zion
altogether in their own interest; next the Presbyte-
rians, who were very rigid and particular as to whom they
would admit to their launch, a sort of first-cabin set,
with peculiar ideas as to the chart that the Great Captain sailed by, meaning that they understood the route to
Jordan and beyond was fixed, laid down, and could not
be altered. After them came the Methodists, who were
a little more generous in their notions about theological
navigation, and held that the chart would always admit
of sailing one or two points free. They had the largest,
the most social and the loudest crew of all, whose weekly
evening meetings for swapping yarns and general chin
music, were always full of young folks who enjoyed the
spirit of the place, and many of whom naturally fell in
with the way of salvation as traveled there. The Methodists also had what they called a camp meeting in the
woods, over in the town of Cato, a mile or two from the
village in which the church was, and at that gathering

CHINESE RAT SELLER.

every one who could used to attend, as to a sort of extended picnic, kept up for a week or more. At such
times there were large additions to the flock, for excitement
ran high tide, and wind and weather favored. Last of all
the Universalists had a share, which seemed to be odds and
ends, culls, rejected samples, hard-to-suits, free-thinkers,
and all sorts of people who would not be suited with the
rules of the various sailing crafts at the other churches.
They claimed to have a chart which allowed them to sail
anywhere and everywhere, with a sure expectation of coming
to port in good order and right side up   Their meetings
were not so largely attended as any of the others, but to
judge from the conduct of those who stayed away from
church, and others who attended a little while and then back-
slid, the Universalists must have secretly included more
than half of the people of the town.

After a while—a few years—the Presbyterian church
building burned, and they sold the site to the Roman Cath-
olics, who built an edifice which is now doing its navigation on an entirely different chart from all the others, taking
sailing orders only from the head master at Rome. They
make few converts or recruits for their crew from the people,
and take as much care as possible to prevent losing those
who come to them from Ireland and Germany. The discipline on their craft is very much superior to that on the
others, and as for sailing to the chart and by the compass
they can hold their way with any of them, for the captain in
charge, that is the priest, always has the power to alter the
chart to suit each particular seaman or passenger, and if
any one loses his reckoning a new clean log-book is supplied
and he is encouraged to begin anew with his entries.

Then there was another entirely different craft, captain
and crew, who sailed under sealed orders, in a ship insured
against breakers and all other dangers, with a charter made
for the voyage, and guaranteed to be complete and efficient

by a Captain William Miller, a Second Adventist. They set several days for starting on their voyage, but always found sufficient reasons for delaying their departure. This failure to even begin the voyage was a great disappointment to many who had sold their farms, or given them away, in expectation of the trip.

Finally he described another crew of Gospel sailors who were very active, energetic and successful in gaining friends and recruits, drawing off many from the other ships, by desertion, openly or secretly. These last were called Spiritualists, not because of their use of spirits, but from the fact that they said the spirits used them to talk to friends and shipmates left behind when they went to Davy Jones' Locker. They used a new language which was composed of knocks, raps and guesses, and a company of them together would remind a sailor of a crew in a fo'castle with the mate and his watch dancing overhead and rattling things round rather lively on deck, instead of coming to the hatchway and calling as a regular officer would do. Howsoever, they got a good many passengers and a good crew, and are sailing without any chart at all, and apparently making as much if not more headway than any other craft.

There were quite a number of smaller craft, such as smacks and doreys, cruising about, some with one or two at the oars, and others with a single one sculling away as if all the world depended on his getting somewhere. These carried various names at their top, such as Free-Will Baptists, Seventh Day Baptists, Wesleyan Methodists, Campbellites, and many others whose names are dimmed on memory's log. Jim said that he did not like the shipping articles of any of those officers, and, therefore, could never make up his mind to ship aboard of any one of Zion's fleet. He hoped he was sailing under a good captain, his conscience, which he endeavored to keep always in shipshape, and had no doubt when his hull was laid up as unseaworthy that he

BOABAB TREE.

would meet with a good reception in the port to which all who tried their best to obey orders would bring up at last.

Jim and I have sailed in very much the same sort of ship, and under similar orders so far, whatever we may do hereafter.

The two thousand eight hundred miles from the Golden Gate to Honolulu, Sandwich Islands, were made in fourteen days without having once furled sails. Our captain traded for a day or two exchanging goods for native fruits and cash. Here I first tasted bread fruit, and liked it very much. It would be a great improvement on some of the stuff sold in our city bakeries for bread. In one respect at least bread fruit is safer to eat, for it is not loaded with marble-dust in the disguise of baking powder. We were told by a young man from Boston, who was living at Honolulu, that missionaries had been established in the island about thirty years, and that changing from savage to civilized manners and customs was very fatal to the natives. More than half the population of the island had vanished already. I heard wonderful stories of a great volcano to be seen in operation in the interior, but had not time enough to visit it. I have since read accounts of eruptions on a grand scale on Mauna Loa and Kilauea, and regret the more my inability to see them at the time of my visit to the islands.

From Honolulu we steered for China, and as the sou'west monsoon was in season and blowing up the China Sea, we, in approaching the Asiatic coast and China, were obliged to make a land fall somewhere to the south'ard of the Philippine Islands, and thence hauling to the north'ard and west'ard get a weather-gauge in the China Sea, and making a leading wind out of the sou'west monsoon, but making a detour of nearly two thousand two hundred miles out of our course. We came to Hong Kong roads after a passage of sixty-three days from San Francisco, with light but favorable winds.

At Hong Kong, as is usual and necessary I suppose, we

GATHERING SUGAR CANE.—SANDWICH ISLANDS.

remained nearly a week waiting for a permit for a pilot and a chop to proceed up to Whampoa. We beguiled our time watch and watch in going ashore and "doing the Chinese."

On one occasion, when ashore, I was edified by the sight of seeing ten Chinamen being flogged by right and left-handed lascars with wiry rattans, giving the blows alternately, cutting into the flesh at every stroke in a horrible manner,

CHINESE AMUSEMENT.

the blood actually making a pool at their feet. They were fastened to a triangle eight feet high, the hands made fast to the upper horns and feet to the lower ones. In due time we hove up (as we had received our permits from the Chinese authorities), and, with a native pilot, arrived at Whampoa the same night, and moored ship. Next morning we unbent sails, discharged what cargo we had left in the hold, for there was little left after leaving so much at the Sandwich Islands.

When discharged, we went through the usual processes of smoking and refitting, so fully described in former pages.

Nine weeks we rode at our moorings at Whampoa, during which we discharged, refitted, smoked, and loaded, and when fully prepared for sea the crew were given a day's liberty to go up to Canton.

It must be admitted that the Chinese have a fine sense of humor, as appears from the caricature engraved here, named "Chinese Amusement." We see an English (or a French) soldier in a cage, and two Mongolians inspecting him as we look at monkeys or rare birds. They may be supposed to say something like this:

"I say, Lee, if my eye-glass does not deceive me, that is a rare bird. Notice his red coat, and fine feathers generally."

"Ah, yes, it is true, it is a rare specimen, but see how sad and melancholy he looks, and, by the way, he does not sing. Poor fellow!"

"It has always been a wonder to me how these outside barbarians contrive to exist. They must be a miserable lot: all artificial, eyes, teeth, hair, legs, hands, everything artificial. Bah! let's go home and burn joss paper as a protection against evil demons."

We were well paid for our day's tramp ashore in Canton, where there is much life and great activity. The next day the pilot came on board early; ship was unmoored with a will, for we were homeward bound, and, the wind being favorable that same night, we were breasting the billows of the China seas, heading for the Straits of Sunda and Anjer Point, where we dropped anchor and furled sails.

We remained off Anjer two days, bartering in the usual style for monkeys, birds, and other curiosities. The ship recruited with yams, fruits, joggery, and sweet potatoes, poultry, eggs, etc. When we had gotten through with our shopping, orders were issued from the quarter-deck to

ENGLISH FACTORIES, CANTON—SINCE DESTROYED.

weigh and make sail, and in a few hours were standing out of the straits towards the mighty Indian Ocean under a pyramid of canvas, and with a fresh easterly gale after us. Clear of the land, we, with her head at sou'west by west,

WELCOME TO CANTON.

went a kiting toward the Cape of Good Hope at a lively gait. We carried this favorable wind, passing to the south'ard of Mauritius, the Isle de France, Reunion, and Isle Bourbon, thence to the Cape, where we were suddenly brought up by a succession of heavy westerly gales, which, after blowing themselves tired, soon merged into the sou'-east trades, which we carried up to 12° north latitude and 50° west longitude. The sou'east wind then merged into the northeast tradewinds, until, in the month of March, we approached Cape Hatteras. As we neared that much dreaded promontory, the mackerel "scales and bears' tails that make lofty ships carry low sails," filled the sky, and we kept well to the east'ard to get an offing. All that night we steered to the north'ard and east'ard under snug canvas. Next morning the wind begun to pipe from the east'ard and to increase in force, until, at twelve, it had increased to a living gale, accompanied with a corresponding reduction of canvas on our part, until just before dark, we wore and stood to the south'ard on the port tack under close-reefed topsail, reefed foresail, and fore-topmast staysail, distant from Sandy Hook by dead reckoning eighty

INTERIOR OF CASTLE GARDEN, 1851

miles, and bearing nor'west by west. We stood to the
south'ard until 12 M., when the wind commenced to veer to
the southeast, then we wore ship, and stood to the north'ard,
and made sail, shaking two reefs out of the topsails, reef out
of foresail, and kept on to the north'ard and east'ard until
4 A. M., when we gave her the jib and mainsail at daybreak, spoke a pilot-boat, hove to and received a pilot.
Soon after, weather moderating, took a tug, clewed and
furled all our canvas, by 2 o'clock P. M. were put alongside
the wharf in the East river, and soon had her hard and
fast.

We were paid off two days after, and, as I had determined
before leaving on this my last voyage that it should be the
last, I sought and soon obtained employment as a rigger in
the U. S. Navy Yard at Brooklyn, N. Y., where I remained
one year and six months.

Soon after I got to work in the Navy Yard my brother
became somewhat enthusiastic about the singing of Jenny
Lind, the Swedish nightingale. He did not invest a forune
in a first ticket as was done by Ossian E. Dodge, a humorist
of the old school, but took two back seats, and gave me one
of them. The music must have been divine, for that was
the universal verdict, and excepting a few right jolly
choruses in the fo'castle, which I could name, it was the
best vocal music I ever heard. The interior of Castle
Garden, where she sang in 1851, has changed very much,
and music of a very different kind is heard there now. A
chorus of voices from all the oppressed people of Europe,
not quite tuned to our free airs, and somewhat inclined to
the discord of anarchy, but generally good strong tones
that will soon swell out Uncle Sam's lungs, so when he
speaks there will be respectful listeners on both sides the
big waters.

And now, dear readers, who have accompanied me in my
nautical career from the time that, full of enthusiasm and

VIEW OF CASTLE GARDEN AND BATTERY FROM THE BAY.

proud of being able to explain the difference between a ship and any other craft, I stowed away aboard of the *General Hewitt*, and with fear and trembling was brought as a stowaway before the dreaded tribunal of the captain and others, but which ended in my being installed (to me at that time) in an enviable position of part and portion of her crew, up to the present when an old seasoned salt I am discharged from the *Flying Cloud*, married, and engaged in a shore-going occupation, but yet connected with what has been "my home on the ocean wave," I will say farewell! Years have elapsed between the time I ceased to follow the sea for a livelihood and my writing this my autobiography. Many and great have been the changes in terms as well as methods of navigation, and these mechanical changes are, I suppose, improvements. Men—that is to say, seamen—have changed as well as manners, but the sea remains the same, and I have felt while writing almost as if my youth had returned once more.

When I determined to leave the domain of "Father Neptune" and take up my quarters on *terra firma*, I took to myself a mate, as I have said before, made her my first mate, and have sailed in the same craft with her ever since, and if it will not be displeasing to my readers I propose to write up a few items of our log. In accord with the custom of society I suppose it will be in order to introduce her to you, my reader, and here she is—look at her. My first and only mate, my sheet anchor, my ballast, and in every way useful to me as pilot and sailing master. I am excitable, quick as a flash; she is quiet, slow to anger, and very deliberate in all she says and does. When I storm and rage, like the ocean torn with the winds on a lee shore, she is quiet and firm as a rock, with a face as smiling as the rose-tinted clouds in the morning sunlight, and as worthy of respect, and you know a sailor in a ship on a lee shore has the most profound respect for the solid rocks thereof.

If I was sometimes fortunate at sea, I have been more so on land. But I must not say too much lest I be suspected of spooning, and that would be unpardonable in an old salt like me. However, it is her due, and if it is not the correct thing to refer to her directly, it may be in better form to say as much indirectly. She has given me two copies of herself, daughters, who stowed all her good qualities without mixing any of my crudeness. One of them sailed away over the unknown sea a few years since, but the other remains, and is the sunshine of my declining years. Her little George (seven) is my middy, and I hope will continue my name long after my old hulk has gone to pieces. Her little girl (eleven years) left us suddenly, almost without warning, this summer, and went up aloft, where we can at present only know her in our silent moments. One can do no more than wonder at the mystery of life, and vainly ask why is it that I am spared by time when such young life is ended? All we can say is, with the poet Wordsworth :

" Thus Nature spake—the
   work was done—
How soon my Lucy's race
   was run !
She died, and left to me
This home, this calm and
   quiet scene,
The memory of what has
   been,
And never more will be."

There is one more whom I must not forget. He was brought to me by my surviving daughter, and will remain, I

MY FIRST MATE.

fondly hope or ner sake, to be her protector when I am
called to do duty elsewhere. He is one of Nature's noble-
men. Strong in body and mind, quiet, conscious of his
power, and kind-hearted as ever was formed. Sometimes
my old sailor notions lead me to criticise his, as it seems to
me, boyish ways, as I have in the matter of dancing at balls
and parties, when he calmly listens to what I say, or shout,
as it may be, for in a storm a sailor must shout to be heard,
and he answers not. He is wiser in his day than I in mine,
and I am glad of it. But I must not tire you by imposing
more of my private affairs on your kind indulgence.

I have spoken of myself as a "Sea Wanderer," and correctly so, for I am of a family of wanderers. Only this last
spring I received a letter from Australia, dated Victoria,
April 8, and written at the Woolshed gold-diggings by my
brother Alfred, in which he says: "Brother Henry is in
Derby, Western Australia, from which place he wrote me,
January 22d last. The mail is carried there once a month.
Truly he is on the utmost confines of civilization, among
bushmen, and even there, eighty miles from a post office," as
he writes.

The old proverb says, "A rolling stone gathers no moss,"
and we three brothers have been rolling stones. But then
we did not want any moss. We live in the present moment,
this world, and our motto is, "One world at a time." Live
while you may live is an old Roman saying which animated
the great Cæsar's legions. And yet it cannot truthfully be
said that I have no moss. My early education was limited
by my going to sea at the very time I might have gone to
college, and when the store of knowledge left us by the
ancient Greeks and Romans had been but dimly seen by me
in the distance, as something to be gained and enjoyed in
after years. I fondly expected that a seaman would have
many hours of leisure in which I could read and complete
what had been merely begun in the schools of Montreal. I

IN PORT.

knew a little of Julius Cæsar as the conqueror of ancient France (Gaul), and of the Rhine Germans, and of the poets of the Augustan age at Rome. Of the Greek authors much less is possible to the young student, and I had barely gone through the grammar and first reader. But I had tasted the sweets of the fountain of knowledge, and had a thirst for more, and that thirst, or desire, to know more about the world of men and things around us has been a monitor and help in many a time of trial and temptation.

The great enemy of every sailor is " King Alcohol," however he may operate, whether as whisky, rum, gin, brandy, or the finely sweetened and perfumed liquors and cordials; his work is deceitful, alluring, disappointing, and, if persisted in, always brings disaster, if not premature death. No man can bear up under more than a moderate amount of the poison. I say poison, for I do not believe it is in any way a food. It has often wrought great mischief for me, in loss of time, impaired health, loss of respect of superiors, and of many sums of money, spent for liquor, or stolen from me when my reason was stupified, and I was at the mercy (?) of the first rascal who happened to spy me and my condition. As I am not a temperance advocate, but simply a biographer, I suppose it would be out of place to say more on this head. This I do know, many a fine young seaman among my shipmates has been drowned in alcohol whom the ocean storms had spared. So it must be confessed that I found very little leisure on board for reading or study of any kind, except to ruminate on the day's doings, or to estimate the character of my shipmates or officers from time to time. Since leaving the sea my studies, so far as reading may go, have been continued. I try to keep up in everything relating to the sea, and, in so doing, read nearly every book that appears on that subject One recently published has given me much entertainment, and also a vast amount of instruction in nautical matters. I never knew before how easy it is to spoil a born nobleman by a position before the mast, nor did I ever dream that it was possible to navigate vessels against the rules formed from experience, and in spite of the charts and the elements. I learned also how a young seaman may sometimes unwittingly stumble into the acquaintance and good graces of Her Majesty's high functionaries, and also be one of a small band of heroic adventurers who may rescue a lost and forlorn damsel from under the very eyelids of the awful Turk, and find in her a long lost playmate of early childhood. Many other lessons I learned, of which, in courtesy to a fellow-seaman, I hesitate to speak, except to acknowledge my indebtedness for new and peculiar information. Had the book appeared a little sooner it would have given me a hint for the management of my story, when, instead of simply telling of my errors, the blame for them might have been laid on some other shoulders, while my successes could have been credited to myself alone. But it is now too late to mend such matters, for my story is written, and must be submitted as it is. I have been employed in all parts of a vessel, from the fo'castle to the cabin, but must say that I have found more true manliness, courage, and humanity in the fo'castle than in the cabin. The cabin has in too many cases had a demoralizing effect on those who were suddenly elevated to rank and power, and allowed the weeds of pride, arrogance, contempt of inferiors, if not also an indifference to suffering and the value of life to the seaman, to grow instead of the more beautiful plants of brotherly love, love of humanity, and considerate kindness to fellow man.

There is no place better fitted for bringing out a man's true character than the cabin. At sea the captain and officers are kings and princes, and owe no man allegiance, and are seldom brought to account for any conduct however atrocious short of actual murder. Far away from the restraints of society ashore the inner self expands into a noble, manlike Depeyster, or develops into a monster, such as was Cornish or Huntington.

These words of the poet Cowper apply to the sea as well as to the land :

> " I would not enter on my list of friends
> (Though graced with polished manners and fine sense,
> Yet wanting sensibility) the man
> Who needlessly sets foot upon a worm.
> An inadvertent step may crush a snail
> That crawls at evening in the public path;
> But he that has humanity, forewarn'd
> Will tread aside, and let the reptile live."

A little of the missionary work that is so generously offered to Jack in bethels in many ports might safely be diverted from the inmates of the fo'castle to the occupants of the cabin, where the teachings derived from the life and words of the Great Teacher and the apostles might be better understood on account of early training in books and later association with well-bred people ashore, where the officers usually reside in the best hotels. This little biography may help in some small degree to call attention to seamen, for whom even now much more is said and done than when I was before the mast, and yet much more remains to be done.

My home port is in sight, and I have only to run into harbor, round to and end the voyage. If my reader has followed me so far it will probably appear that I have written frankly, without reserve or bitterness. I have some friends whom I prize as my own self, and many acquaintances who greet me, bluff and salty as I suppose it should be said, with a hearty good will and outstretched hand; these all know me at first hand. The greater community can only know me through the lines of my book, where I have intended to leave myself between the lines without concealment or gloss. Happy and contented in my surroundings I live at peace with all, and with the poet I can say:

"So life glides smoothly and by stealth away
More golden than that age of fabled gold
Renowned in ancient song; not vex'd with care
Or stain'd with guilt, benificent, approved
Of God and man, and peaceful in its end.
So glide my life away! and so, at last,
My share of duties decently fulfill'd,
May some disease, not tardy to perform
Its destined office, yet with gentle stroke,
Dismiss me weary to a safe retreat."

Nature while dealing impartially with me has dealt gently. My eye still perceives the rising spars on the distant horizon at sea; I hear and delight in music and the prattle of little children, and the pleasures of the table remain and good digestion waits on a keen appetite.

However much I should enjoy writing about my affairs on land, I feel that they have no place here, and that

" My task is done—my song hath ceased—my theme
Hath died into an echo; it is fit
The spell should break of this protracted dream.
The torch shall be extinguished which hath lit
My midnight lamp—and what is writ is writ.
Would it were worthier! but I am not now
That which I have been—and my visions flit
Less palpably before me—and the glow
Which in my spirit dwelt is fluttering, faint, and low."

DROP ANCHOR.

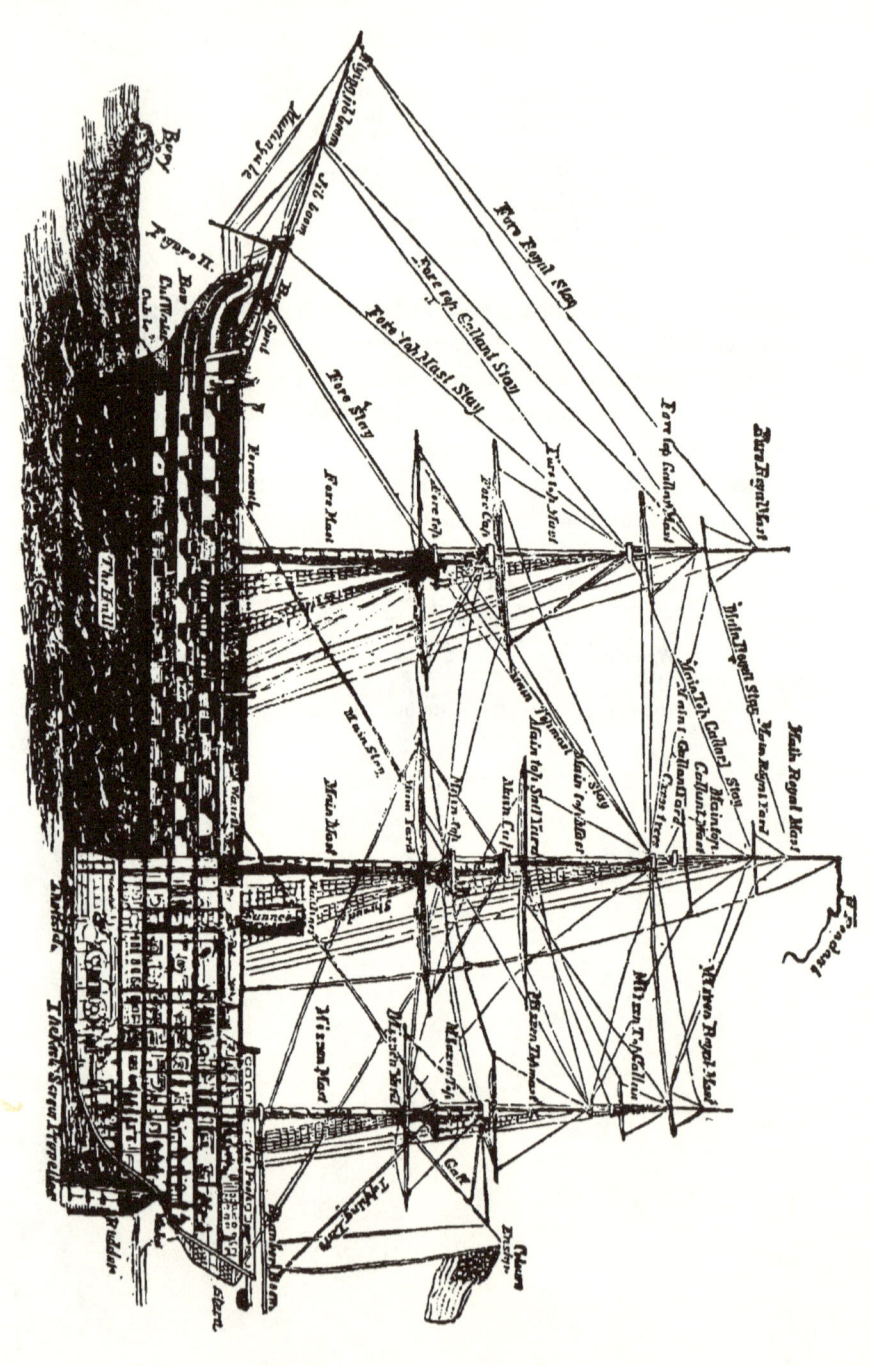

1. Flying jib.
2. Jib.
3. Foretop-mast-stay sail.
4. Fore sail.
5. Foretop sail.
6. Foretop-gallant sail.
7. Fore-royal.
8. Fore sky sail.
9. Royal studding sail.
10. Foretop-gallant studding sail.
11. Foretop-mast studding sail.
12. Main sail.
13. Maintop sail.

14. Maintop-gallant sail.
15. Main-royal.
16. Main sky sail.
17. Main-royal studding sail.
18. Maintop-gallant studding sail.
19. Maintop-mast studding sail.
20. Crossjack.
21. Crossjack-top sail.
22. Crossjack-top-gallant sail.
23. Crossjack-royal.
24. Crossjack sky sail.
25. Spanker.

A MEXICAN.

Chapter XV

" It is with narrow-souled people as with narrow-necked bottles—the less they have in them the more noise they make in pouring it out."—*Pope.*

After reading a captain's book on the same topic as mine, recently published, and enjoying many a hearty laugh at and over it and him, I feel moved as if by a familiar breeze to sail into him. But on second thought I only owe him for a little exquisite pleasure which is genuine, and cannot complain of the want of seamanship noticeable in the little volume for that is not genuine, and of course I don't owe him for that. I only said Oh! when I read the funny and stupid passages and so paid my debt to the captain. Not all, however, for I shall eternally owe him for a suggestion as to story telling, which is the occasion for this supplementary chapter, a sort of fifteenth amendment. If my readers wish to be prepared beforehand as to the character of the stories I tell, it will be well to read the editor's book drawer in Harper's for August, where the Supreme Mugwump expresses in very considerate language his want of confidence in the captain's story telling integrity. In my nautical experience many incidents happened that were so unusual, or so outrageous that I hesitated to even mention them, but as I said before, the captain has given me the lead, and we all must take off our cap to him, and I will now record one or two stories which, although they may seem tough, yet I will vouch for their truth and accuracy, for my memory is good and my courage still equal to any emergency.

In the old time before the war there was racing on the lower Mississippi between high pressure boats, both small and large. At such times the excitement ran high, and from the captain to the commonest roustabout negro all were alive to the fun. Horse racing was very tame and flat compared with the matching of two steamers. Rivals, such as boats from St. Louis and Memphis, or from any other city along the river had the habit of racing whenever they fell in company going down or up the river. As soon as one came up with the other, at a wood landing, or at some city levee, they would whistle a defiant challenge, and when the lines were cast off they would swing out into the stream amid the cheers of the crowd on shore and the hurrahs and yells of all on board.

Then the fun began. Wood was crowded under the boilers, and as anxiety increased, or the other boat gained a little, or perhaps was actually disappearing around the next bend ahead, the mate would suggest to the captain that may be a few hams or a barrel of pork would raise the head of steam, and in they would go. Of course the owner of the pork might be on board, and if he was he would be consulted, but the usual result was, "All right, captain, keep up steam if it takes the whole d—— cargo."

But in a prolonged race even the hams and pork might give out, when it became a very serious matter. A consultation was had around the barrel of whiskey which was sure to be on tap on deck, and was freely distributed without money or price. "I say, captain," the mate opens with, "we are running short of fuel The wood is just about out, the hams and pork gone long ago, and there is only one resort left. What do you say?" The captain nods to the mate and says, "Aye, aye, sir, it is a trying time. Col. Cotton, what do you say to the situation? Hear the infernal wretches over there on the other boat cheering and hurrahing as if to split their throats. They are only half a length ahead anyhow. If we only had a little more fuel now of a lively kind we would give them a stern chase. Hey, colonel, what's your opinion."

"Captain, if a couple of niggers will help you out don't hesitate on my account."

Of course modesty and humanity compels me to draw a
vail over the incident here.   I never did delight in cruelty,
nor in the race of life would I crush even a worm intentionally.   If the worm crawls under my foot of his own accord
—then its all day with the worm.   And if a couple of boxers
choose to stand up and pound each other to a jelly, why
should I not see the fun, if I pay for my ticket and cheer the
winner of the "friendly contest?"   So if a gentlemanly captain chooses to make a laughing stock of himself why should
I not enjoy the fun?

In the racing on the Mississippi sometimes a steamer blew
up.   Such an incident did not cause a very great commotion.   Very little was said about it in the newspapers.   It
was an item of news, and among the owners the occasion of
the remark, "There goes another boat; I say, Jim, there is
very little news in the paper this morning."

THE CAT IN GLOVES WILL CATCH NO MICE.

Speaking of gentlemanly captains, or sailing masters, those who dress in the fashion of land lubbers wear a gold watch and stunning watch chain, with a number of hangers to it, kid gloves and it may be patent leather boots or shoes, they have their uses and their places. One such was on the *Mohawk* as sailing master, and in a trying moment, not being a tried seaman hoisted a jib and foresail when her nose was held down by the anchor and the inevitable result was a capsize, and Commodore Garner and his friends were drowned like puppies.

A rough old seaman in a red shirt might have—would have been sure to have avoided the disaster by making after sail until the anchor was broke out.

While we were lying at Whampoa, in the upper reach, with other American vessels (the lower reach being assigned to English and other vessels), an incident happened which, if it did not actually begin, very much hastened the beginning of the first opium war between China and England. It is the custom for Chinese sanpans to hang arou d foreign vessels and after nightfall to smuggle various articles on board and on shore, snapping their fingers at the revenue officers both ways. One of these almost nightly happenings resulted in a fatal accident and caused a great commotion. A sanpan was moored under the bows of an East Indiaman and sending up kegs and jugs of sam-shu, the native unrectified liquor, when a careless sailor dropped a jug on the head of a Chinaman and killed him.

The government took notice of the matter and demanded a sacrifice of a life for a life, which of course was refused.

Soon after that, say within a week, two British seamen, having gone ashore, on a day's leave from the *Alliance*, were seized by a mob of Whampoans who beat them with bamboos until they were lifeless and literally pounded to a mass. It would be impossible to describe the excitement among British seamen, and also through sympathy among

the Americans, over this outrage. If any considerable number of either of them could have got ashore about that time
there would have been "bloody revenges." But officers
were very cautious, and no serious affair happened then.
Not long afterward, however, excitement ran wild among the
Chinese over the opium quarrel. The trade had been inter-
dicted by Commissioner Lin in November of the year before, and about the last of February, 1835, the Chinese
burnt over 20,000 packages of opium at Canton. One of the
scenes that were very entertaining to foreigners in Canton,
was the punishment inflicted on the poor wretches who were
detected in smuggling opium. The victims were placed one
by one between thick planks of camphor wood, and by an
arrangement of cords in many pairs, which were twisted by
sticks, the offending smuggler was squeezed flat as a pan-
cake. It might be well for Mayor Hewitt to consider if this
would not be a certain and sure punishment for the opium
joint disease, or crime, whichever the Board of Aldermen of
New York may declare it to be. It would always prevent a
repetition of the offense. Offenders of a lower degree were
treated to a species of tight cravat, which was equally as
effective as the camphor wood corset. The man was stood
with his back to a stout post about eight feet high, small
cords bound his hands and feet to the post, when a strong
cord was put around his neck and the post and twisted by a
stick behind. A pair of strong men heaving on the stick
very soon severed the head and reduced the number of
smugglers by one.

In the river Choo-Kiang, about a mile below the city of
Canton (which the natives call Sang Ching, provincial city),
lies an island of about an acre and a half, lifted originally a
few feet above the water, and later by a generous contribu-
tion of the "High and Mighty States General of Holland"
raised much higher to the eye by a fine military wall. The
whole story is this: The Dutch coveted possession of Can-

ton and tried by a clever ruse to get a foothold on the little
island. They got a grant of the island on condition of building a hospital, and set to work really to make a strong fort.
When the walls were complete they shipped from Holland
the guns, ammunition, etc., in large casks, which were light-
ered at Whampoa into sanpans, and run up to the island,
where they were hoisted over the walls by means of huge
derricks and tackles. This was a cleverly contrived scheme
and would have succeeded but for one little accident, as
will presently appear.

The Chinese government is managed on scientific princi-
ples, and that means observe all things but trust nobody. So
a government inspector was detailed to keep watch of the
Dutch and see that nothing which the treaty, or permit, did
not specify should be landed. The Dutch had been taken
by a Hollander this time, in the shape of a dishonest or un-
faithful cooper, for one of the heads of a cask fell out and
the inspector saw a gun where he was led to suppose there
should be hospital stores. "Hi yah!" exclaimed the as'on-
ished mandarin, "how can sickee man yam gun?" (How
can a sick man eat guns?) Sure enough. And the inspector
reported but the guns did not. No report was ever heard
from them although they went off. They were ordered off,
and the order was being carried out when I was on my first
trip to Canton. As we pulled up stream fi teen miles from
Whampoa, just before reaching the island, one of the boat's
crew explained and we saw the evacuation going on. So to
this day that island is known as the Dutch Folly.

The camphor wood corset would be a great addition to
the tortures inflicted in our prisons, almshouses and insane
asylums. The whipping post in Delaware might be improved
by the Chinese tight cravat attachment (not patented), which
would vary the monotony of the public exhibition and draw
larger crowds. The thieves and pickpockets of both sexes
would cheerfully contribute to the cost of making the addi-

tion, for it would immensely increase their incomes, or in other words, it would raise the wind. To consider the humanity in the case is not essential, for very few connected with the prisons, almshouses, sheriff's office, or the lunatic asylums would known anything about what is meant by humanity. This is a practical age, and the duffers who occupy, without filling, the offices in those institutions should be sent to school for instruction in what constitutes human nature and a proper regard for it.

In Charleston, S. C., I was handsomely treated. My duff was abundant, my grog unlimited, my sleeping quarters fine, and all paid for by the generous father of Governor Moses, whom I have mentioned before. I was also permitted to go about the city as I liked, and among other places sailed into the entrance-hall and reading room of the City Hotel, where my friend Moses took me to dine. There was much loud talking about the Seminole war among the fire-eating Southerners, and I picked up items of adventure enough there and then which, if they could have been realized into the service of Uncle Sam, would have exterminated the entire Indian race from the continent. I knew that British sailors could brag and boast of their ability to eat alive any number of American sailors when enjoying the comforting assurance of space surroundings, but the stories told by white men fighting Indians beat all records. The ancient Greeks were the braggarts of the world in their day, but as a modest Canadian I must say that the climate of the United States develops a peculiar species of the family of yarn-spinners that will some day be classified by a professor of natural history as a new genus of mankind, in which we will find Eli Perkins, Bill Nye, Col. Tom Ochiltree and Captain Suddenly Superior named as brilliant specimens. And as a sub-genus he will head the list by a yarner imported from service in the British navy and domesticated in the United States. The label on the new sub-genus will be C. S. S., which will indicate (like the well advertised specific S. S. S.) that it is a sure and sudden specific for melancholia, affecting the risibilities very much as a spark stirs up gunpowder.

This is a young country when we measure it by important men's lives. I had a call to-day from a man who was born two years before the new government of the United States was organized. He was hale and hearty, and offered his service in curing several ills which afflict my friends. I very seldom suffer anything but hunger. But his remedy for rheumatism suggests one that I recommended to Sir John A. Macdonald, who is appointed to succeed Lord Lansdowne as Premier of the Dominion of Canada. Here is his letter:

EARNSCLIFF, OTTAWA,
15th June, 1886.

DEAR SIR:

You will think me very ungrateful for not acknowledging ere this your kind letter of the 24th March, last, offering me a remedy for sciatica.

At the time I was suffering a good deal but have recovered under your treatment, which has completely relieved me. In consequence of my illness I have allowed my correspondence to get very much in arrears, which is my excuse for not replying to you before.

With many thanks for your thoughtfulness in writing me on the subject, believe me,　　　　　　Yours faithfully,

(Signed)　JOHN A. MACDONALD.

To GEORGE DAVIS, Esq.,
　　Paterson, N. Jersey.

And now in closing, after having proved my ability to relieve if not cure a very distressing malady, I modestly offer my services to Captain Suddenly Superior to mitigate if not entirely assuage what may yet prove, like a boomerang, a very distressing case of chin-music, complicated with *cacoethes scribendi* and the delight of seeing his name in print.

I am happy to be able to bear witness to the truth of my previous assertion, that after searching a vessel from the forecastle to the cabin the best seamen are almost invariably found before the mast. I began my sailorizing in the cabin of the *General Hewitt*, but I finished it an able seaman in the fo'castle.

GLOSSARY OF SEA TERMS

AND

NAMES OF THE PARTS OF A SHIP AND THE RIGGING.

A.

ABAFT, AFT.—Part near the stern. To carry anything aft is to take it toward the stern. The mast rakes aft, that is, slants toward the stern. How cheer ye fore and aft? That is, how is the ship's company.

ALOFT, ABOVE —In the upper parts of the rigging.

ALOOF.—At a distance. Keep aloof; that is, keep at a distance.

AMAIN.—Done suddenly by a number of men.

ANCHOR.—The combination of iron hook and bar of wood used to hold a ship, to which it is made fast by a cable.

APEEK.—The yards topped up like an X.

ATHWART.—Across.

AVAST.—Stop. Avast heaving (anchor); that is, don't heave any more.

AWNING.—Canvas, or wood boards, spread high over the decks as a shelter from sun, rain, and wind. The awning is spread or furled.

B.

BALE.—To bale a boat is to throw water out of her.

BALLAST.—Any heavy things used to load the ship to keep her steady in the water. Gravel is called shingle ballast. To trim the ballast, is to spread it about even, or in proper places. The ballast shoots when it shifts or slides out of place to one side or the other of the hold, to prevent which boards are lashed to the midships stanchions.

BARGE.—Small boat, used with twelve oars or a lesser number.

BATTEN.—To nail battens of thin boards over the tarpaulins on the hatches in bad weather, to prevent their being blown or washed off.

BEARING.—Point of compass from one place to another. A place may bear on the beam, abaft the beam, on the bow, head, stern, etc., when seen in a direction over or beyond those points.

BEARINGS of a ship, is the line on the hull at the surface of the water. To bear to, is to sail into a harbor. Bear round up, is to sail right before the wind. To bring your guns to bear is to point them at some object.

BEARING-UP, or bearing away, is changing the course of a ship, so as to run before the wind after she had sailed sometime with a side wind, or close-hauled

BELAY, is to make fast any running rope. Belay the main brace, is to make it fast.

BENEAPED.—A ship is said to be beneaped when she has not water enough to go over a bar.

BEND.—To tie to, to fasten ; as bend the sails, meaning apply them to the yards and fasten them. Unbend the sails, is to cast them off the yards. The ship's sails unbent, means that no sails are set. Bend the cable, or make it fast to the anchor

BERTH.—A place usually to rest in. Sailor's or officer's berth, where he eats or sleeps. The ship's berth is where she is moored. To berth a ship's company, is to allot them their places to mess (eat) in. To berth the hammocks, is to assign their places in which to hang.

BIGHT of a rope, is any part between the two ends. It is also a narrow inlet from the sea.

BILGE, is to break, as said of a ship's planks. Bilge water, is water that has leaked into the hold.

BINNACLE.—A box to protect the compass on deck.

BITTS.—Large timbers in the bow to which the cables are fastened when the ship is at anchor. After bitts, smaller timbers on the quarter-deck for belaying the running rigging.

BLOCK.—Wheels in a frame of wood or iron. through which cords or ropes travel.

BONNET of a sail, is an additional piece of canvas put to a sail to make it hold more wind. Lace on the bonnet, is to fasten it to the sail. Shake off the bonnet, is to take it off.

BOARD, is to go on a ship. Board and board, is when two ships touch each other. To make a board, is to make a stretch on any tack when a ship is working (sailing) on a wind. To board it up, is to turn to windward. The ship has made a stern-board when it has fallen astern, or lost way against a wind.

BOLT-ROPE.—The rope which goes round a sail, to which the canvas is sewed.

BOWLINES.—Lines made fast to the leaches of the sails to haul them forward when on a wind, which being hauled taut enables the ship to come nearer the wind.

BOWSPRIT.—Piece of timber standing out at the bow of a ship.

BRACES.—Ropes by which the yards are turned to form the sails to the wind.

BROACH-TO, is when a ship on a sudden lays her broadside to the sea, which is a dangerous position in bad weather.

BREAK-BULK.—To open the hold and take goods out.

BULK-HEAD.—A partition.

BUNTLINES.—Lines that come down from above the yard forward of the sail to the foot, by which the bunt or belly of the sail is hauled up outwards.

BUOY.—A float to mark the position of rocks, shoals, sand-bars, anchors, etc. Many kinds. Cone-buoy: nun-buoy, tapering from a large middle to a point either way; cable-buoy, empty cask to buoy up a cable in a rocky anchorage; life-buoy, used to support persons who have fallen in the water until a boat can be supplied. To stream the buoy, is to let it fall by the ship's side into water before letting the anchor go.

BUOY-ROPE.—The rope which fastens the buoy to an anchor.

C.

CALL.—A silver pipe used by the boatswain and his mates, when on duty, to call the men.

CAPSIZE.—Overturn, overset. To turn over a coil of rope.

CAPSTAN.—The windlass by which the anchor is weighed, sails or shrouds set up, and any other heavy work in hauling is done.

CAREENING.—To turn a ship over on one side, so as to get at the other side to repair or clean her.

CATHEADS.—Timbers on ship's bows, with sheaves in them by which the anchor is purchased from the hawse, and to which it is secured.

CATFALL.—Rope used to hoist the anchor to the cathead. Fish-tackle.

CAULKING.—Filling the ship's seams with oakum and pitch.

CHACE.—A pursuit. To chase another vessel.

CHAINS.—A place projecting from the sides of a ship, where the shrouds are fastened, to give them a greater angle and power to steady the mast.

CHAIN-PLATES.—Plates of iron to hold the dead-eyes under the chains.

CLEW.—To haul up the sails by the clewlines.

CLEWLINES.—Ropes through quarter-blocks underneath a yard to haul up the clews (corners) of the sails.

COBBING.—Slapping.

COME NO NEAR.—Is said by the man at the cun when the ship is on a wind and is coming too near the wind.

COXSWAIN.—He who steers a boat.

CRANK.—The ship is crank when she has not enough cargo or ballast to sail without oversetting

CROWFOOT, is a number of small lines spread from the fore parts of the tops through a piece of wood, hauled taut on the stays, to prevent the foot of the topsails catching on the top rim. They are also used to suspend awnings.

CUN.—To direct the ship, or tell the man at the wheel the course.

D.

DEADEYES.—Blocks of wood, bound with a rope or iron band, through which the lanyards or shrouds are reeved.

DEADWATER.—The eddy water at the stern.

DEADWIND.—Wind ahead against the ship.

DOG-VANE.—Small vane of cork and feathers near the wheel, to show the wind's course.

DOG-WATCH.—Watch from 4 to 6 and from 6 to 8, evening.

DOUSE.—To haul down, or strike, or lower a sail.

DOWN-HAUL.—The rope by which any sail is hauled down.

DRIVE.—The ship drives when the wind causes her to drag the anchor.

DRIVER.—A large sail set on the mizzen-mast in light winds.

E.

ELBOW IN THE HAWSE.—When the tide has sent the ship around the anchors and crossed the cables, it is said to have crossed; when three such crossings occur it is called a round turn.

END FOR END —When a rope runs out a block and is unreeved, and also when a cable runs out, or slips, it is gone end for end.

ENSIGN.—The flag at the stern, or spanker gaff end.

ENTERING-PORT.—A large port-hole in man-of-war.

F.

FACK, OR FAKE.—One circle of a rope or cable, when coiled.

FALL-OFF.—To fall to leeward or astern.

FID.—A square bar of wood or iron with shoulders above end, used to support the weight of the topmast at the head of a lower mast.

FID.— Marline spike (iron) for splicing ropes by separating the strands. It is round, an inch or more thick, eight or ten inches long, tapering to a point.

FISH.—A large piece of wood or iron applied to a mast to strengthen it.

FISH-HOOK.—Brings the fluke to the rail.

FISH TACKLE.—The tackle for moving the anchor to and from the cat-head.

FORECASTLE (Fo'cast'l).—Upper deck in the fore part of the ship; also the cabin under it where the sailors live.

FORWARD.—The fore part of a ship.

FOREREACH.—To shoot ahead, or pass another vessel.

FRESHEN THE BALLAST.—To divide or separate it.

FURL THE SAIL.—Wrap it close and bind it to the yard.

G.

GAGE.—The number of feet of water the ship draws or floats in.

GAMMON THE BOWSPRIT.—Secure it by a strong rope around it and into the cutwater.

GASKET.—A flat, plaited cord fastened to the sail yard of a ship, used to tie the sail to the yard when furled.

GIRT.—The ship is girt with her cables when too tight moored (too short cables).

GIRT-LINE.—Small line used to haul a heavy rope up aloft.

GRAPPLING-IRON.—An iron with four or more prongs or hooks.

GREAVE.—To burn the filth from a ship's bottom.

GRIPE OF A SHIP.—The thin part under counter to which the stern-post joins.

GRIPES.—The ship gripes when she turns her head too much to the wind, or carries too much weather helm.

GROUND-TACKLE.—Cables, anchors, grapnels, hawsers, etc., anything used to secure the vessel at anchor.

GROUND-TIER.—The lowest tier of casks in the ship's hold.

GRUMMET.—Oar-locks for large boats, made of coiled rope, used for fenders.

GUNNEL (gunwale).—The upper band of timber that finishes the hull.

GUN-ROOM.—Room for the small arms and the gunner on a war-ship.

H.

HAIL.—To speak to, or call to another ship.

HALYARDS.—The ropes by which the sails are hoisted.

HARD-A-WEATHER.—Put the tiller to windward.

HAUL.—Pull.

HAWSER—A cable.

HAWSE-HOLES.—Holes in the bows for the cables. Fresher-hawse, means to pay or veer out more cable. To clap a service in the hawse, is to bush it to prevent chafing by the cable. Across hawse, is to be athwart another ship's head, or bows.

HEAVE OF THE SEA.—The power of the swell of the sea to drive a ship out of or on her course, which must be reckoned in sailing.

HEAVE HANDSOMELY.—Gently or leisurely.

HEAVE HEARTY.—Heave strong and quick.

HEAVE THE CAPSTAN.—That is, turn it around with the bars.

HEEL.—Incline. Heels to port; that is, rolls over to left side. The after part of the keel.

HELM.—The tiller and the wheel used to steer a vessel.

HELM'S-A-LEE.—Tiller turned to leeward.

HITCH.—To make fast.

HOIST.—To haul, sway, or lift up.

HOLD.—Space between the lower deck and bottom of a ship.

HULK.—Hull, without masts or rigging.

HULL.—The body of the ship. To lay a hull, is to lay to with a small sail in a gale.

HULL-DOWN.—When a ship is so far off that the masts only are seen.

J.

JEERS.—The ropes by which the lower yards are suspended.

JEER-BLOCKS.—Blocks through which the jeers are rove.

JOLLY-BOAT.—Small boat. Yawl.

JIB.—Foremost sail of a ship. Triangular, extended from the jibboom to the fore-topmast head.

JIBBOOM.—A spar extending forward from the bowsprit. The flying-jibboom extends beyond the jibboom.

JIBE.—To shift the mainsail of a schooner or sloop. Jibe the boom over.

JUNK.—Old rope, or cordage, used for making spunyarn, sinnet, points, gaskets, mats, etc., and when picked into shreds makes oakum.

K.

KEEL.—The strongest timber in a ship, extending from stem to stern at the bottom, supporting the whole frame.

KEEL-HAUL.—Formerly practiced in the Dutch navy, by hauling a person down one side of a ship, under the keel and up the other side, as a punishment for certain offenses.

KNIPPERS.—A large plaited rope used to bind the cable and messenger together. Foretopman puts them on, and the maintopman takes them off.

L.

LABORS.—The ship labors, when it rolls and pitches much in a gale.

LANDFALL.—The discovery of land.

LAND-LOCKED.—Surrounded on all sides by land. A bay or harbor where the sea cannot be seen, being hidden by hills.

LANCH-HO.—High enough. Stop. Avast.

LANYARDS.—Small ropes at the ends of shrouds by which they are hove taut.

LARBOARD.—Left, as you face the bow. Larboard side is now called port.

LASH.—To bind.

LEE SHORE.—The shore against which a wind blows.

LEEWARD.—With the wind.

LIFTS.—Ropes from mast-heads to the ends of the yards, by which the yards are steadied.

LIST.—Incline. List to port, that is, to larboard.

LOG, LOG-LINE.—By which the ship's progress is measured.

LUFF.—To turn the ship's head towards the wind; to sail nearer the wind.

LUFF-A-LEE.—Throw the ship's head into the wind. A ship springs her luff when she yields to the helm by sailing nearer the wind.

LUFF TACKLE.—A large tackle not located, but movable to any place.

M.

MAST.—A large round timber standing on end on the keel of a vessel, and rising high in proportion to the size of the ship, on which the yards and sails are suspended. When there are more than one they are named main-mast, mizzen-mast, fore-mast, top-mast, etc. Masts are now made of iron tubes.

MEND THE SERVICE.—Put on more ropes, etc., to prevent chafe.

MESSENGER.—A small cable used to assist in lifting the anchor.

MOOR.—To secure the ship with two anchors.

MOORINGS.—Anchors, cables, chains and bridles, by which a ship is confined in a harbor; also called ground tackle.

MUSTER.—To assemble.

MOUSE.—A knob formed on a rope by spun yarn. To mouse a hook, is to fasten a small line across the part to prevent unhooking.

N.

NARROWS.—A narrow strait of water between two seas or lakes, or a bay and sea.

NEAP-TIDES.—Tides in the first and last quarters of the moon. Lower than the tides at the full moon.

NOTHING OFF.—Do not turn or go from the wind. A direction to the wheelman.

NUN-BUOY.—Buoy used in the British navy, large in the middle, tapering to a point both ways.

O.

OAKUM.—The substance of old hemp ropes and cables, untwisted and pulled into loose fibres; used for caulking ship's seams, stopping leaks, etc. That from untarred ropes is called white oakum.

OFFING.—To seaward from the land.   Deep water some distance from
    shore.   The ship stands for the offing when going towards the sea.

ON BOARD.—In the ship.   On deck.

ORLOP.—Deck on which cables are stored.

OVERBOARD.—Out of the ship into the sea.

OVERHAUL.—To examine, disentangle and clear away rope or any other
    thing or stuff in the way of board.   A ship overhauls another when
    she gains on the other in sailing, or comes up with her.

P.

PARBUCKLE.—A purchase formed of a single or double rope around any
    heavy body, one end being fastened and the other hauled.

PARCEL.—To put a lot of canvas around a rope before the rope or wire
    service is put on.

PARCELING is long, narrow slips of canvas daubed with tar and bound
    about a rope like a bandage before it is sewed.   Also, to raise a
    mouse on cords, ropes, stays, etc.

PARCEL A SEAM.—To place narrow slips of canvas over it before it is
    payed.

PAY THE SEAMS.—Pour out hot pitch or tar on the caulked seam.

PAY OUT THE CABLE.—Shove it out at the hawse holes.   To cover any
    body to preserve it against water or weather.   Cover it with a mix-
    ture of tallow, sulphur, resin, etc.   To bream.   To pay a mast,
    besmear it with tar, resin, varnish, etc.   To pay off the crew, pay
    their wages due.

PAY OFF.—To fall to leeward, as the head of a ship.

PEEK.—To ride a stay-peek, is when the cable and the shore-stay form a
    a line.   To ride a short peek, is when the cable is so much in as to
    destroy the line formed by the stay-peek.   To ride with the yards
    apeek, is to have them topped up by contrary lifts like an X.

POINTS.—A number of plaited ropes made fast to the sails for the pur-
    pose of reefing.   They taper both ways from the middle.

POINT.—To point a rope, is to taper it by taking out strands at the end.
    To point a sail, is to fix points of cords through the eyelet-holes of
    the reefs.   To point the yards, is to brace them up so the wind will
    strike them obliquely.

POINT-BLANK.—Direct, center shot.

POOP.—The after-part of a ship, from the stern to the mizzen-mast.

POOPING.—Shock of a heavy sea on the stern or quarter of a ship.   One
    ship running her stem against another's stern.

PORT.—Harbor, haven; any cove, inlet, bay, mouth of a river; any natural or artificial refuge, as a dock inside a breakwater, etc.

PORTS.—Holes in the sides of a ship for entering or leaving, or for firing cannon through.

PORT OF ENTRY.—Port with a custom-house.

PUDDING AND DOLPHIN—Large and small pads made of ropes, and put around the masts under the lower rigging.

Q.

QUARTER OF A SHIP.—That part of the side near the stern.

QUARTER-GALLERY.—A balcony on the quarter of a ship.

QUARTER-RAILING.—Narrow planks, from the top of the stern to the gangway, serving as a fence to the quarter-deck.

QUARTER-DECK.—Extends from the stern to the mainmast. On some vessels it is raised a little above the main deck, and does not extend to the mainmast.

QUARTER-BILL.—A list of the stations where officers and crew are to stand in action, or battle.

QUARTER-CLOTHS.—Long strips of painted canvas extended on the outside of the quarter-netting from the gallery to the gangway.

QUARTER-MASTER.—Officer who attends to the helm, binnacle, signals, etc.

QUARTER-WIND.—Wind blowing in abaft the main shrouds.

R.

RATLIN, RATLINE.—Small tarred lines crossing the shrouds, forming a ladder on which the sailors go aloft.

REACH OF A RIVER.—Shore of a river between two points in a direct line.

REEVE.—To pass the end of a rope through any hole in a block, thimble, cleat, ring bolt, cringle, etc. To unreeve, is to take it out.

RIDE AT ANCHOR.—A ship held by the anchor against wind and tide To ride athwart, is to be with the side to the tide. To ride hawse fallen, is when water breaks into the hawse hole in a rough sea.

ROAD.—The sea near the land where ships may safely anchor, though not entirely sheltered. Roadstead.

ROUNDING SERVICE.—Small ropes, or pieces of old ropes, put in between the layers of a cable before it is sewed.

ROUND TO.—To turn the head of a ship toward the wind.

ROUND UP.—To haul up the slack of a rope, or of a tackle.

ROUND-HOUSE —The master's berth; a cabin in the after part of the quarter-deck, with the poop for roof, called the coach.

Rother, Rudder.—By which the ship is steered ; a broad plank hung
on hinges to the stern-post, and turned by the tiller.

Rother-nails.—Nails with very full, wide heads, for fastening the
rudder irons of ships.

Rullock.—Niche in a boat's side in which the oars are used.   Rowlock.

Rowse in the Cable.—Haul in the cable; make it tight.

Run.—A ship's day's run.   A voyage.   An agreement among sailors to
work a passage from one port to another.   Also, the aftmost part of
a ship's bottom

Running-rigging.—Such rigging or ropes as passes through blocks,
etc., as distinguished from standing-rigging.   Old standing-rigging
makes very poor running-rigging—that is, a captain don't like to go
before the mast as a sailor.

S.

Sands, or Sends.—When the ship's stern sinks low in the trough of a
rough sea.

Scud.—Loose, vapory clouds, driven by swift wind.   To go right before
the wind.   Scudding under bare poles—that is, all sails furled.
This is also called spooning.

Seize.—To fasten two ropes together with a cord.   Seizing is doing such
work, and also the name of the cords used.

Serve.—To wind something about a rope to prevent it from chafing or
fretting.   Service is the name of the thing wound about the rope.

Settle —To lower.   Settle the topsail halyards—that is, lower them.

Sheer.—The long curve of the ship's sides, or deck.   To shear about, is
to decline or deviate from the proper course, as when not steered
steadily.   To break sheer, is to swing round and risk fouling the
anchor.

Sheers.—Two or more timbers fastened at their tops, and used to raise
heavy things, as masts.

Sheer-hulk,—An old ship cut down to the lower deck, and used in
repairing other ships, and provided with sheers, derricks, etc.

Sound.—To measure or try the depth of water, by a line with a heavy
weight at the end.   When tallow or some other sticky substance is
put on the weight, called arming, small things, earth, gravel, shells,
etc , are brought up from the bottom.   These indicate the distance
from shore, or the safety as to anchorage.   A sound is also a deep
bay, or inland sea, as Long Island Sound.

Sounding-rod.—Iron, or other rod or pole, used to sound the depth of
water in the hold of a vessel.

SHANK PAINTER.—A short rope and chain which holds up the shank and flukes of the anchor against the ship's side, as the stopper fastens the ring and stock to the cat-head.

SINNETT.—A small rope plaited from rope yarns.

SOUNDINGS.—Any part of the sea, or ocean, where an ordinary sounding-line will reach bottom

SPEAR OF THE PUMP.—The handle of a hand-pump.

SPILLING LINES.—Ropes to prevent the sails from blowing away in rough weather.

SPRING.—To break, as to break a mast or yard, is to split or spring it.

SPRING-STAYS.—The stays are large ropes from the mast-head forward, and fastened near the stem, to prevent them from springing backward when the ship is sending deep. The spring-stay is a smaller rope placed higher. The fore-stay, from the foremast head toward the bowsprit end; the main-stay extends to the ship's stem; the mizzen-stay, to a collar on the main-mast, etc. See the engraving.

SPRING TIDES.—At the new and full moon; they are higher than the neap tides at the quarters.

SPUR SHOES.—Large pieces of timber abaft the pump well.

STAY.—Going about or changing the course of a ship, with a shifting of the sails. To be in stays, is to lie with the head to the wind, and the sails so arranged as to check her progress. To miss stays is to fail in going about.

STOPPERS.—Short pieces of rope used to make something fast, as an anchor or cable, and also for preventing the running-rigging from coming up while the crew are belaying it.

STEM.—The piece of timber that unites the two sides of the ship at the fore-end. The lower end is scarfed to the keel, and the bowsprit rests on its upper end. From stem to stern, the entire length. The ship stems the tide, that is, makes progress against the tide.

STRETCH OUT.—Said to sailors in a boat to urge them to pull the oars strong.

STEADY.—Said to the wheelman; meaning, keep the ship on the same course.

STARBOARD.—Right-hand side of the ship.

STEEVE.—Turning up at an angle. The bowsprit steeves too much when it rises too high, or is too upright.

SUED.—A ship on shore that loses water is said to be sued. (Sewered?)

SWAB.—A large mop of rope-yarn for cleaning deck or cabin.

SWAY AWAY.—Hoist.

T.

TACK.—A rope used to confine the lower corners of the courses and stay-sails when the wind crosses the ship obliquely; also a rope used to pull the lower corner of a studding-sail to the boom; also the part of a sail to which the tack is usually fastened; and also the course of a ship in regard to the position of her sails, as the starboard tack or port tack. To hold tack, is to last or hold out. The tack of a flag, is a line spliced into the eye at the bottom of the tabling for securing the flag to the halliards. To tack, is to change the course of the ship by shifting the tacks and position of the sails from one side to another. Tack means to go about. Tack is also food. Hard tack is very dry biscuit

TACKLING.—Furniture of the masts and yards of a ship, as cordage, sails, etc.

TAFFRAIL. –The upper part of a ship's stern; flat, like a table, on the top, and sometimes ornamented with carved work.

TAMPIONS (Tomkins).—Wooden stopper of a cannon's mouth.

TAUT.—Tight, tort.

TELL-TALE.—A pointer which shows on the poop-deck the position of the tiller.

TIDE-GATE.—Where the tide runs strong or swiftly.

TIDE-IT-UP.—To go with the tide against the wind. Tide, to go with the stream.

TIER.—A row; a tier of guns, of casks, of ships, etc. The tiers of a cable are the ranges of fakes or windings of the cable laid one within another when coiled.

TIMBER.—A rib or curving piece of wood branching outward from the keel and rising to the top of the ship's side.

TARPAULIN.—Cloth or canvas covered with tar or waterproof composition.

TOP.—A platform around the head of a mast; it extends the shrouds by which they better support the mast.

TOP BLOCK.—A block hung to an eye-bolt in the cap, used in swaying and lowering the topmast.

TOP CHAIN.—A chain to sling the yards in.

TOP CLOTH.—A piece of cloth to cover hammocks.

TOPGALLANT.—Next above the topsail.

TOPMAST.—Second mast. The third is top-gallant-mast.

TOPSAIL.—Sail on the topmast.

TOP TACKLE.—A large tackle hooked to the lower end of the topmast top-rope and to the deck.

TOUCH.—The broadest part of a plank worked top and butt, or the middle of a blank worked anchor-stock fashion; also, the angles of the stern timbers at the counters.

TOW.—To drag, as a boat or ship, through water by a rope. Several boats or a ship make a tow.

TRACK.—To tow; to draw a vessel by a line from the shore.

TRADES.—The tradewinds. Winds in the torrid zone and beyond that region, which blow from the same quarter throughout the year, except when changed by local causes for a short time. Their general direction is from N.E. to S.W. north of the equator, and from S.E. to N.W. south of the equator.

TRAIL-BOARDS.—The carved work between the cheeks of the head, at the heel of the figurehead.

TRAVERSE —To go backwards and forwards.

TRUCK —A small wheel. A small wooden cap at a masthead, or of a flagstaff.

TRUSS.--A rope used to keep the center of a yard to the mast.

TWICE-LAID.—Codfish and potatoes.

U.

UNBEND.—To cast off a sail from a yard.

UNDER WAY.—A ship sailing is under way.

UNFURL.—Cast loose the gasket of the sail.

UVROW.—The piece of wood by which the legs of the crow-foot are extended.

V.

VANE.—A small flag at the masthead to note the course of the wind.

VEER.—Let out, as veer away the cable, veer or wear the ship—that is, put her about with her head to leeward, the contrary way to tacking.

VEER.—To shift. The wind veers—that is, changes, shifts.

VIOL —A large rope used in weighing anchor, and other heavy work. Also written voyol.

W.

WAKE.—Track of a ship in the water. To be in the wake of a vessel is to follow close behind in a line with her keel.

WALES.—Strong timbers all around a ship above the water-line.

WARP.—A hawser, or small cable. To warp a ship, is to draw her against the wind by anchors carried out and hawsers hove in.

WATER-LINE.—The line of water at the surface around a ship afloat.

WEIGH.—To haul up, as an anchor.

WINGS.—Parts of the hold and orlop deck nearest the sides.

WING-AND-WING.—A two-masted schooner sails wing-and-wing when the foreboom is to port and the mainboom to starboard, or *vice versa.*

WIND.—In the wind's eye, toward the point from which the wind blows. Between wind and water, means the part of a ship at or just below the water-line. Windbound, prevented from sailing by a contrary wind.

WORK TO WINDWARD.—To beat against a wind.

WORK DOUBLE TIDES.—To do two or three day's work in one.

Y.

YAW.—To steer wild, or out of a course.

YAWL.—Small boat with two or more oars.

www.ingramcontent.com/pod-product-compliance
Lightning Source LLC
Chambersburg PA
CBHW021324110726
47900CB00005B/1341